C000144401

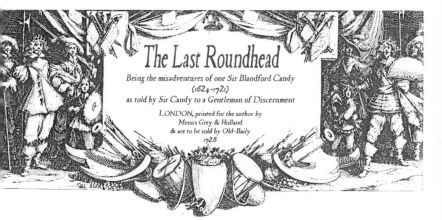

The Last Roundhead

Being the misadventures of one *Sir Blandford Candy*
(1624–1721)
as told by *Sir Candy to a Gentleman of Discernment*

LONDON, printed for the author by
Messrs Grey & Holland
& are to be sold by Old-Baily
1728

The
Last
Roundhead

The
Last
Roundhead

Collected, Curated & Corrected

BY

MR JEMAHL EVANS

Copyright © 2015 by Jemahl Evans

Jemahl Evans asserts his moral right to be identified as the author of this book.

All rights reserved. This book or any portion thereof may not be reproduced or used in any manner whatsoever without the express written permission of the publisher except for the use of brief quotations in a book review.

All characters appearing in this work are fictitious. Any resemblance to real persons, living or dead, is purely coincidental.

Paperback ISBN 978-1-909374-64-5

Epub 978-1-909374-65-2

Kindle 978-1-909374-92-8

Cover art by B.Lloyd

Typesetting by handebooks.co.uk

Caerus Press
An Imprint of Holland House Books

Holland House
47 Greenham Road
Newbury
Berkshire
RG14 7HY
United Kingdom

caeruspress.wordpress.com

For Mum (Sorry about the rude words)

Explanatory Note.

The Wynne Candy Archive is a collection of letters, journals, and memoirs belonging to the late Major General, Sir Clive Wynne-Candy VC, DSO, KBE (1880 - 1963), relating to a Wiltshire branch of the Candy family. Major General Wynne-Candy rose to prominence in the 1930's, when he was lampooned as Colonel Blimp in the British press by the cartoonist David Low, and then in film by Powell and Pressburger. His extensive archive was bequeathed to the library of Christ College, Brecon, after his unfortunate demise, mistakenly attending a Rolling Stones performance, in Twickenham in 1963.

The archive remained forgotten in storage at the school until a recent refurbishment. Some of the manuscripts suffered extensive water damage during the London Blitz; however, documents from the 17th century have been restored, and are now publicly available for the first time. Volume One, details the early life of Sir Blandford Candy (1624 — 1721) written in his own words. Blandford was present during many of the most significant historical events of the Seventeenth Century, with a career stretching from the Civil War and Restoration, to the Rye House Plot, and Glorious Revolution. As editor, I have merely standardised the spelling and grammar, and provided historical footnotes where appropriate.

Jemahl Evans, Tycroes 2015.

Cross Deep, Twickenham, 1719.

A squire he had whose name was Ralph,
That in th' adventure went his half,
Though writers, for more stately tone,
Do call him Ralpho, 'tis all one.
(Samuel Butler, *Hudibras,*
A Satire on Roundheads and Puritans.)

Damn the man. Damn the noise of building, and damn the scaffolding spoiling my river view. I am ninety-five years old; this damn noise will be the death of me. If I could drag my corpse over to that monstrosity, I would blow Mr Pope's foul face off.

Instead, I sit here waiting for God. I am a relic of forgotten times, with my faded coat and thieving servants. They laugh at me now; they think me deaf or my brain addled. A pox on them! What do they know?

What does that choleric little arse-worm Pope know of me? Calling me Ralpho — bastard! Damnable poets, the world would be a better place if we strung them all up. Samuel Butler turned me into a joke. Bunyan was a hypocrite, Waller a weasel, and D'Avenant nought but a syphilitic swindler. Now that hunchbacked goblin is my neighbour.

Limp-wristed wordsmiths! They snigger and snipe like naughty little schoolboys, but what do they really know of me?

I creak like an old tree in the wind. The greatest pleasure in life comes on the rare occasion I manage to piss easily. My hands are claws, their joints flamed livid red, agony in the winter. When I look in the glass, I scarce recognise the face that peers back at me. Sunken eyes, dark and heavy lidded with age, deep creases cutting through the leather skin. My hair, once golden, is now reduced to a few white wisps on a bald mottled pate. Where did my youth go?

My father gave me the name Blandford, after the town

where he owned a tannery. An insalubrious beginning, as I am sure you agree, but take not my candour for bitterness: my father was not the cause of my failings; my sins are my own.

I was a soldier and a spy, a murderer and a thief. In my time, I met kings and princes, even the Lord Protector. Yet now I sit drenched in my own mess, with only an idiot nephew left to read my words.

At least my eyes are still good enough to write.

They have heaped opprobrium upon me for half a century and more. Scorned my sacrifices, mocked my dreams, and named me traitor.

Now they say I am the last of them alive. They say I am the last Roundhead.

1. The London Road, August 1642.

God's pampered people, whom, debauched with ease,
No King could govern, nor no God could please;
Gods they had tried of every shape and size,
That godsmiths could produce, or priests devise.
(John Dryden, *Absalom and Achitopel.*)

The Summer of forty-two was golden; full of glorious light that shone on the last days of England's innocence. I spent it strumping my eldest brother's betrothed. That should tell you something of my character. Why did I do it? She was beautiful and stupid.

I had not planned on anyone finding out — I am not dungwitted — but made no account of women and their gossiping tongues. Of course, it all ended badly. My eldest sister discovered my peccadilloes, and godly hypocrite that she was, decided to save my soul. I found myself on the London Road, carrying letters for her, before I could offer a word of protest.

So, fool that I was, I rode my horse (a blue roan called Apple) east, cursed my sister, and wondered what the capital would hold for me. The first day was uneventful (travellers avoided each other; another sign that England was falling into catastrophe) so I spent it dreaming of London; I was Dick Whittington out to make his fortune. 'Twas past Newbury on the second day, as I wondered whether to look for an inn, that a harsh voice shook me from my reverie.

'King or Parliament?'

I had ridden straight into an ambush. A cart blocked the road, and men armed with muskets lined the thick hedgerow. There were others emerging behind me. I looked down at the ruffian pointing a pistol at me. Dressed like the others in a new buff coat, his lank black hair tied back, and mouth fixed in a malicious smirk.

'King or Parliament?' he said again. Smirky, as I dubbed him, seemed to be in charge.

'Ah, well, that is a very good question, is it not?' I said. And the wrong answer will get me killed, I thought.

'Do you mock us, boy?' One of the others grabbed my horse's bridle.

'No, sir.'

'So answer the poxy question!' said Smirky.

There were about ten of them, with dirty unwashed faces under ill-fitting pot helmets. Some were wearing an orange sash over their coats — the Earl of Essex' colours.

'I bear letters to Parliament,' I said, trying to sound confident, and hoping to God that they were Roundheads.

'Letters from who?' said Smirky. There was a hint of Irish in his accent.

'From my family to my uncle — Sir Samuel Luke.'

'Never heard of him,' said another, pointing his carbine at me.

'He is a Member of Parliament, and a friend of Pym, and Hampden,' I said, casting names like grenadoes in order to impress. I looked at their uncomprehending faces. That had not worked. 'He is rich,' I said, finally.

'You are coming with us, boy,' said Smirky.

'Am I under arrest?'

'What think you?' I thought he was a swine but I said nothing.

They took my letters, and searched my saddlebags, but they found not the purse tucked into my boot.

I was a Roundhead. There was little real decision in the matter, with only my uncle as a contact and he a rebel. Everybody in England was choosing a side. Most acted on high ideals, of duty and prerogative, or puritan crusade.

Some of us acted on mundane factors, like a murderous brother, and a devious manipulative shrew of a sister.

By nightfall, I was under guard near Reading, then taken

to an inn. Two bodies swung from an oak tree opposite. 'Tis an ugly death; the bowels loosen in the last throws of life, and if your neck snaps not in the drop — you choke. These two had choked by the look of them, bulging eyes and bruised features, swollen tongues lolling as they twisted in the breeze. They were not yet putrid in the summer heat, so not long dead. That was not encouraging.

'Traitors,' said Smirky, as he led me to the door.

Traitors? I wondered. Are not we all?

That was the first time I met John Hurry, in a shithole of an inn near Reading. It was just a one-storey shack with stinking hide windows. The room was light and big, but a stale smell lingered in the air, and the floor was covered in filthy straw. Three or four broken down tables and stools were occupied by some of Hurry's men, and a couple of hounds sprawled underneath. There, surrounded in squalor, he held court.

Of middling age and stout, his long brown hair and beard shot through with white, and an old scar ran down one cheek. Dressed like the others in a thick buff coat and orange sash. He glowered at me as I entered, black eyes dark like coals. My letters to Uncle Samuel lay, still sealed, on the table in front of him, along with the debris of a meal. A veteran of the continental wars who, like so many others, had returned to England at the prospect of home-grown spoils.

'And just who the fek are you, boy?' He growled at me in a thick Scots accent, his foul breath hitting me like a wall. 'Pask says he caught you skulking near Newbury.' He gestured to Smirky. 'You could be a Royalist spy.'

'Candy,' I said, recoiling from the stink. 'Blandford Candy. I take letters to my uncle in London,'

'You claim your uncle is Sir Samuel Luke?' He grinned, rotting teeth black from tobacco.

'Yes, sir.'

'Mayhap 'tis best I hang you, and then I need count you

no more a problem. Which you are now,' he said deliberately, and there was the evidence outside to tell it was no bluff.

'I am sure my uncle will see you well rewarded for seeing me safe to him,' I said. That caught his interest; I saw the flicker of greed cross his face.

'You are lucky, boy, I know of your uncle.' God's teeth, his breath stank like Satan's arsehole; it was hard to stop from gagging.

'Indeed, sir? Would you help me to reach him please?' I said. 'My letters are of import.'

'Are they indeed?' Again he grinned; he must have known about his fetid breath. 'Then, I must see what I can do for you, boy. As long as you make sure I am well rewarded. Your uncle is a rich man, let us hope he is generous,' he paused. 'For your sake.'

I could scarcely imagine my godly, puritan uncle had any association with one as coarse as John Hurry, but 'misery acquaints a man with strange bedfellows.'* The reality was I had no idea of my Uncle Samuel's disposition, other than my father's boorish characterisations over supper. I just hoped his pockets were deep.

Hurry swigged from a stoneware jug. 'Ah, you look like a good little boy, with your pretty blonde locks just like a maiden's. We could sell them for a fair price,' he said to his audience. I would not have put it past him either, the patronising Scots bastard.

He offered me a drink from the jug, with the same false smile drawn on his face. 'We can get you to him tomorrow, tonight we drink.'

I should have been more wary, I should have said no, but he had stung my vanity calling me 'boy' so often. I took the proffered jug and drank.

Gad, it was a bitter brew, the roughest whisky I have ever tasted, but there I was trying to prove I was no callow youth,

---

*   *The Tempest*, Act II Scene II

so I drank again deeply. The result? Within an hour, I was 'rageous drunk, telling Hurry of all my woes, of my letters to Uncle Samuel, my hateful brothers, one vicious uncaring sister and another too stupid to keep her mouth shut. I added my neglectful father like froth on syllabub. All vomited in a self-pitying drunken ramble.

Soldiers are rarely sympathetic beings, and the whole group of them found my trials hilarious. At first, there were a few snorts, but before long, they were rolling with laughter. Hurry, the turd breathed huffler,* wiping tears from his eyes in derision.

Drunkenly offended, I tried to make my trials worse than Job's. The more I whined, the more they laughed, and the more whisky I drank. I remember flashes of conversation, laughter, and Hurry's face leering over me with his god-awful breath. We made a toast to Parliament, and then to the King. For everyone was persuaded that the other side were the traitors. At one point, unsteadily going for a piss, I stepped outside, falling over to my knees in the mud and midden.[1]

The next day was a half-drunken ride down the Great West Road to London. I spent most of it puking over my saddle. By mid afternoon we were near Brentford, and Hurry turned us off the road, down a lane towards the River Thames. With troops billeted all over the villages around London, from Acton to Hounslow, space was at a premium, but Hurry assured his men of a good bed thanks to "Sugar Candy". Truly, an old pun, but the murderous scoundrel chortled at his originality.

We reached a great white building on the river with monastic kitchens and stables built off to the side. Gleaming

---

*   Cocksucker

jewel-like in the summer sun, with faux battlements and crenellated rooftop. Rows of large plate windows gazed out upon expensively manicured gardens and orchards heavy with fruit. There was a strong guard this time, all dressed in red and black, but again Hurry's pass and an animated conversation with the soldiers at the gates, saw the two of us through up to the main building.

I was taken off to a room whilst Hurry, after some words with a footman in black and red livery, went off with him. The room was opulently furnished with polished marble floors and delicate Spanish furniture, and I was uncomfortably aware of my state of dress. In three days, I had been reduced to vagabondage.

My discomfort became even more acute when a young man, finely dressed though in sombre colours, approached me. He was feminine in his beauty, with thick brown hair curling around his shoulders, dark eyelashes and an open smile.

'You are Sir Samuels's nephew?' He asked in a delightfully rich voice. Such genteel manners, as if we were at Court and me some visiting Ambassador.

'Yes, indeed.' I jumped to my feet.

'I am asked to bid you wait awhile, sir. Your uncle is with His Lordship at the moment, but will see you presently. Have you need of refreshment?'

I looked and stank like bum-squirts, but he was too polite to say.

'Perhaps water and a cloth to make myself more presentable?' I asked.

He smiled again and spoke quickly to a footman, then turned back. 'My name is Blake, sir. I am His Lordship's secretary.' He held out his hand, I took it and shook. Shaking hands was the new fashion; doffing hats was considered too subservient in such times. I was glad of that; my hair was filthy.

'I am Candy, I mean Blandford,' I stuttered out. 'Everyone calls me Blandford.'

'Well met, Blandford, ah good,' as the footman quickly returned with a pitcher of water, a cloth, basin, and cake of perfumed soap.

I cleaned my hands and face and considered trying to wipe down at least some of the stains from my shirt, but once wine, whisky, and vomit have made a home they do not leave with ease, so I gave up. I tied back my greasy hair, and rubbed a hand over my chin. I had no razor, but my fair colouring meant my whiskers were barely noticeable.

Blake watched in silence as I cleaned myself, smiling as I finished. 'Somewhat better, Blandford,' he said. 'Your face is clean at least.'

I looked at him suspiciously, waiting for the laughter, but his face was friendly and without guile.

'Where are we?' I asked, finally curious. 'Captain Hurry neglected to mention.'

'You are at Syon House, the residence of His Lordship the Earl of Northumberland. Sir Samuel has business with him, and they asked me to look to your needs.' He gestured to a chessboard. 'Do you play?'

'Ah, yes, although I am not very good.'

We pulled out the board with its matching pieces, and sat down to play. The board alone would have cost more than most men could earn in a year: of ivory and jet, and inlaid with gold. This is how the nobility live, I thought to myself, sitting back as Blake set up the pieces. It was quickly apparent that I was outmatched. Whilst we played, he asked me about my home and family. His questions were innocent enough, and I answered with ease, starting to relax.

After about an hour, a different red liveried servant entered, and addressing Blake said, 'His Lordship is ready now, Mr Blake.'

'Ah, excellent. Blandford, if you would care to follow

Richard, he will take you to your uncle, and His Lordship. I will be along presently.'

Nervously I rose and followed the footman, down corridors and steps, to a set of ornate double doors, which the footman flung open to announce:

'Mr Candy, Milord.'

I took off my hat — Earls expect subservience, best to give it — and I stepped into the room, darkened despite the sun outside. Heavy curtains blocked out the day, and only a couple of oil lamps let out a gloomy light. There were three people in the middle of the room: two men, standing, who turned to look at me — one rather short — and a richly dressed woman seated. A couple of other figures stood in the shadows, watching; dressed in red and black like the footmen, but armed with swords.

'Is it him?' said the woman.

She was stunning; no wench, nor bawd, nor common trull. A doeling's brown eyes, and chestnut ringlets curling around her big bubbies. Two pearls, the size of quail's eggs, dropped from her ears. I would have thought her some rich man's plaything, yet she spoke with a queen's authority. Who is she? I wondered.

'Yes, he looks enough like my sister, that I would know him in a room of strangers. Though it would make her weep to see a child of hers in such a state,' said the short man.

I blinked as my eyes became accustomed to the gloom. The man who had spoken was lean and grey haired, with what can only be described as a beak of a nose. He was dressed in a fine black doublet with high white collar.

'Uncle Samuel?'

He really was tiny but perfectly formed. I wondered if he knew my father called him a dwarf.[2] Blake came into the room behind me, closing the doors, making it even darker.

'What is your opinion, Mr Blake?' said the taller man; he was richly dressed in a blue satin suit and a thick lace falling band. That must be the Earl. So, who was the woman?

'He is young, and naive, Milord, but I sense no deceit in him,' said Blake. 'I think his story rings true.'

I had thought Blake a fop, whilst he interrogated me over the chessboard. At least he did not tell what a piss-poor player I was, but "naive" wounded me. Vanity again, I have always been vain.

The two guards visibly relaxed at Blake's words, his opinion clearly carried weight.

'Well, well, well, Blandford, you have caused us some trouble. I am your Uncle Samuel,' the tiny man identified himself. 'I have not laid eyes on you since you were nought but a babe, yet here you are, carrying important letters for me. Providence is the Lord's bounty, but it would only be wise to question such a gift.'

'Your pardon, sir?' I said, my favoured reply when called to account.

'You see, Blandford,' he continued, 'the letters you carried from your sister Elizabeth contained, shall we say, some sensitive information. Captain Hurry, whilst a good officer, would not be the best custodian of it.' He clenched his hands together as if in prayer, and looked at me mournfully.

Captain Hurry would sell it to the highest bidder, quicker than a bishop could bugger a choirboy, I thought to myself.

'What we need to know is, did he read the documents?' said the woman.

'I think not, Milady,' I replied facing her. 'At least they were sealed when he questioned me, but I am not certain, he could have read them later.' I had been blind drunk. Hurry could have danced naked in front of me, reciting the letters in iambic pentameter, and I would not have noticed.

'So he could have read them, Samuel,' said the Earl.

'I think we must proceed as if he has, Milord,' said Uncle Samuel. They did not look happy with that revelation.

What has my sister got me into? I thought to myself.

Elizabeth and I are going to have a little conversation about this when I get home — if I get home. I stood there silent. I had no real inklings as to their intentions or plans. It all seemed to go much deeper than simple family missives.

'Blandford, my boy, will you wait without again? We have some matters to discuss, and then I will see what I can do for you.' Aha, things were looking up.

'Well met, Blandford,' said Blake bowing. 'I hope we have time to play again.'

I smiled. 'I hope to improve, sir,' I said, shaking his hand. I followed the footman back to the waiting room.

I sat on my own for about an hour, until my uncle finally appeared. He beckoned me to follow him outside, where we turned our horses towards London, the fading sunlight on our backs. I was nervous, keen to make a good impression, so kept quiet.

A lesson there: if you know not what to say, say nothing. It gives men a thoughtful and considered aspect, and women, a mysterious and alluring one.

Even saying that, my first visit to the capital had my head near swivelling on an axis at all the different sights. Uncle Samuel's London home was near Baynard's Castle, alongside the Thames. A grand old four-storied building, full of staff, and fair dripping with wealth and ornamentation. My uncle was a rich man indeed. Grooms rushed to take our horses and stable them, and I followed Uncle Samuel into the house. It was fine, not like my father's clumsy extravagance. Father was rich, but my Candy grandfather had been a tanner. This house spoke of old money, lands, and wealth. I had thought my mother's family nothing more than Buckinghamshire farmers. Now I saw how she had married beneath herself.

Uncle Samuel led me to his study, with panelled walls, and

upholstered chairs, and a wall-full of books. He sat in a chair, his feet only just touching the floor.

'Finally,' he said, struggling as he pulled off a boot. 'Well do not just stand there, lad. Give me a hand.'

I jumped to help him. Boots off, he rubbed his feet and glanced up at me. 'Sit, sit,' he gestured to a chair, then took out Elizabeth's letter and looked at me rather sternly.

'Your sister writes that you are a drunkard and a gambler?'

Bitch! 'After last evening spent with Hurry, Uncle, I am not sure I would ever wish to drink again.'

'And that you have a glib tongue,' his eyebrows rose.

Twice bitch, had she kept no secrets?

There was no real answer to that I could think of without sounding, well, "glib" so I stayed silent. I did not wish my uncle to know the real reason I was running away, and prayed silently that Elizabeth had written nought else. I also swore to myself to read her letters in future before delivering them.

Uncle Samuel sat back and looked at me, over the spectacles perched on his beaky nose.

'She asks that I find you a position. So, Nephew, what position do you think would suit?'

'I am really not sure, Uncle.' It is true: apart from vague dreams, of wealth and renown, I had no idea.

'Then let us look at what your choices are,' he smiled at me. 'I can offer you a commission with me in the army; a chance to win your spurs?'

That did not sound attractive.

'Or I can see you with funds to the New World, to seek your fortune?'

Puritan colonies, no thank you.

'I can even see you safely back home to Hilperton, if that is what you would prefer?'

Hilperton be damned!

'It is your choice, Blandford,' he paused. 'So, what are you going to do now?'

Sir,

I have received your assurances regarding the plate and supplies you had previously promised. Happily, I am able to come to Hilperton in person, so you need have no concern for the security of such.

I also note that the deeds promised in familial agreement have not yet been transferred. I must confess I am dismayed. How am I to support my new family without the requisite funds, whilst also doing my duty to the King?

My Lord, the Marquess of Hertford, has given me leave to marry, and I will make good speed in returning. I despatch this letter only to give warning of such, for I travel in person in its wake.

Of the rebels we have seen little since we swept them from the field at Marshalls Elm. Lowborn knaves and thieves cannot stand against gentlemen. It is said they gather to march against us in Sherborne, and in preparation for such, the castle defences are strengthened. With God's will, we shall not be dismayed.

I have received word from James in Oxford that he is to join with the King in Nottingham, and will be unable to return to Wiltshire with so little time. The London Road is riven with bandits and thieves who waylay all that travel.

I confess I am perplexed by Blandford's absence, although his character is such, that the base act of treason would not surprise me. Should he stand with the rebels then word will surely pass to us. I have sent the same to James in Oxford.

I have the sad duty to inform you that Mr Marten was killed near Wells four days since. He fell from his horse and was severe bruised to his chest. He did not speak again before passing into the arms of the Lord.

I earnestly ask you to convey my sincerest regards to my sisters Elizabeth and Anne. I will bring ribbons for their hair on my return, which should please little Anne.

I remain your most humble and obedient son.

Henry Candy,
Sherborne, Dorset. August 10th 1642.

2. Watling Street, September 1642.

We'll break the windows which the whore of Babylon hath painted,
And when the popish saints are down, then Barrow shall be sainted;
There's neither cross nor crucifix, shall stand for men to see,
Rome's trash and trumpery shall go down, and hey, then, up go we.

(Traditional, *Hey then up go we.*)

I joined the army. Cornet Blandford Candy, of Luke's Troop, in Lord Fielding's Regiment of Horse. It sounds grand, does it not. I had taken a commission in my uncle's troop to fight the King.

Well really, what did you think I was going to do? Go crawling back home? Sail to the New World and battle savages? I would rather have plopped my whirligigs* on a hot skillet.

With only one day in the capital before joining the regiment, my uncle gave me some coin, and told me where to get fitted with a buff coat and boots, pistols and sword; the outfitters were making an outrageous profit on all the young bloods riding to war.

I bought myself a new hat to go with my boots and coat. It cost me seventeen shillings; made of thick red felt, with a black band, and wide brimmed in the cavalier style. I adorned it with a black ostrich feather, and thought myself very fine indeed.

'You look the perfect gentlemen, sir,' said the shopkeeper.

I looked in the broken glass he held, tilting my new hat to the side and agreed.

There was still some coin in my purse and time to waste, so after arranging for the rest to be delivered to Uncle Samuel's, I decided to go to the theatre. It cost thruppenny for the afternoon performance. I almost balked, but the King's Men were on stage; the best acting troupe in England. It must

---

*   Testicles.

have been their last performance in London before Penington closed the theatres. I remember little of the play; I remember it was awful.

I took my place on a bench in the pit. The old building is gone now, but it was a great monkish refectory, with stout walls and high vaulted roof, lit by beeswax candles along the galleries, with chandeliers hanging over the actors speaking onstage.

'I am not ignorant he is designed a bridegroom to the fair Isabella, and it were saucy injustice to distract a blessing now hovering o'er two kingdoms.'[1]

It was cool inside away from the sunlight, and the words carried easily down to me in the pit. When full, the theatre could have held a few hundred people, but that afternoon there were only three or four like me in the poor seats, and some richer patrons sat above in the oak built galleries. Even the actors looked bored as they performed; 'twas fit only for the Fumbler's Hall, and not worth the entrance fee.

'I was not born to the trade; I had a soul above my fortune, and a toy I took, to lose what was beneath my birth and titles, or purchase an estate fit to sustain them.'

'Twas drivel! A sorry tale much in mode at the time: a woman, dressed as a boy, in love with a man, who was in love with someone else. The man playing the woman's part lacked any passion for the role. He had not bothered even to shave for the performance. He was brought to life finally when, as I thought, one of the troupe jumped onto the stage from the side gallery, swinging a cudgel: then the player darted around the stage, still trying to deliver his lines as the rogue kept up the chase.

'With reverence to your blood, as 'tis the king's, with all my age, my wounds upon me, and that innocence, the prince's word hath new created in me. I do not fear...'

At first I thought it was a part of the act; a comic interlude to break the dullness of the verse — but the look on the actor's face, and shouting from backstage, told me this was unexpected. Then we were bathed in daylight as the first floor shutters were opened, and a group of booted apprentices burst into the pit.

We were forced from our seats with the threat of a beating, but there was no riot. With less than twenty in the audience and the actors forced off the stage, the performance was over. I trooped outside, to where there was a large crowd screaming and shouting, threatening to burn down the theatre, that it was blasphemous, frivolous, and immoral; some white-sashed guardsman stood around gleefully watching.

A giant of a man, with big bushy beard, buff coat and soldier's boots, burst out laughing when I walked out of the theatre into the jostling crowd.

'Look, William. One of the boy actors that plays women,' he shouted, pointing at me. 'He has a titty on his noodle.' He reached over with his great ham-hand, and plucked the hat off my head.

'Give me back my hat, you rogue,' I shouted reaching for it, but he held it high beyond my grasp.

'No need for anger, pretty. I only want to have a look.' He stuck my new hat on his head. 'What think you, William? Could I play the woman?'

'Give me back my hat I say,' I demanded. 'Uncouth scoundrel!'

His friend William was shorter, more wiry, dressed in a buff coat as well, but shabby and stained, with mismatched riding boots and a dirty wool bonnet. He looked more my father's gamekeeper than a soldier. He was laughing at me as well.

'Give him back the hat, Zeal,' said William to the giant.

'You gentlemen are a disgrace. If you are the quality of men fighting for Parliament, the King will be laughing in his cups,' I said. 'I pity your officer having such scoundrels and ragamuffins under his command.' I snatched my hat back from the brute and turned on my heels.

'Now you see here, pretty.' A ham-hand grabbed my shoulder, spinning me around. 'I was only having a bit of fun, no need to get your stockings in a twist.' They were still laughing at me, as he spun me around some more.

'Stop calling me pretty, damn-your-eyes,' I said. I actually stamped my foot in anger, but that simply made them laugh at me all the more.

I stormed off in a huff; my youthful vanity pricked as always. I stopped in a tavern and took a small ale to calm myself.

The shadows were lengthening and lamps lit by the time I returned to Uncle Samuel's house. My uncle wished to see me in his study as soon as I arrived. He had visitors with him, a middle-aged man, and dark haired boy of my own age, both dressed for war.

'Ah, here is my nephew,' said Uncle Samuel as I entered. 'Blandford, this is my Lieutenant, Mr Russell, and his son,'

I doffed and bowed, but Russell grabbed my hand, shaking it enthusiastically.

'Welcome, Mr Candy. You have joined with the Lord's Host,' he said with a smile, then gestured to the serious looking young man standing next to him. 'This is my son Peter; he will share your rank in the troop.'

I got out a greeting as Peter took my hand and pumped it like his father. You can always trust a man with a firm handshake. When someone shakes your hand like a noddie mecock,* you know he is a two-faced bastard. My uncle spoke again.

'Blandford, perhaps you and Peter should become acquainted.' He nodded to Lieutenant Russell. 'We have some matters to discuss and then you will depart for the regiment.'

Peter led me outside to the courtyard, Apple was saddled and waiting for me with my purchases. Waiting with him

---

*   Effeminate weakling.

were two soldiers from the regiment and a cart of supplies. Both chosen men, so Peter told me.

I strode out, looking for the troopers who would be under my command, determined to make an officerly impression. When I saw them my heart sank; it was the two soldiers from the theatre. The oversized brute saw me first, then nudged his shabby friend who turned. They both grinned widely.

'Hullo, Pretty,' said the giant.

Throughout England the drums beat out muster in village, town, and district. On a map it looks clear-cut: The North, Wales and Cornwall were for the King; London, the South East, and the West Country declared for Parliament, whilst the midlands were a muddle.

On the ground it was a bitter affair of confused loyalties, of broken friendships and families. I wasted no sleep on it myself — my brothers were not worth the worry — but there were many who spent anguished nights in decision. Our idiot King finally unfurled his standard at the end of August. The rag fell down the next day.

Bad omens; the fool should have given up there and then.

We had a fortnight, Apple and I, accustoming him to the noise of warfare and me to the blade. We had to be quick learners. I had a better seat than most in the troop; I had hunted and ridden since childhood. They were in the main farm boys and tapsters. I was also a good marksman, but had never used a sword before, and needed help to stop from cutting off my own ears.

We left London at the start of September as two regiments, one of Foot, and one of Horse, with carts, animals, and supplies. Our cavalry were all well kitted out: pistols and sword, buff coats, and boots and armoured corselets. Most wore pot helmets, but I kept to my hat. I had paid for it, and I wanted to show it off. The red-coated infantry marched in companies all singing as they went along.[5] It was a fair split between pikes and muskets. More muskets would be better — the drill books said two muskets to each pike — but pikemen were cheaper to raise.

The weather was still good, and with morale high, and psalms sung by the men, it felt more a pilgrimage than an army on the march.

Peter and his father both were tall, devout Presbyterians. I complain of the godly and their hypocrisy, but the Russells were no zealots. Theirs was a quiet devotion, and after spending time in their company, they almost had me believing in the New Israel. Our cause was for a remaking of England even then. For the Russells it was always a religious war, a bishops' war, a war on popery. Later, there would be interminable discussion on faith and grace and free will, of bishops and divines, and bitter division. In the beginning there was only hope for the future.[*]

Lieutenant Russell had been a mercenary in Germany — like John Hurry — but the difference could not have been more profound. Well spoken and mannered, even when addressing the coarsest trooper, calm under fire and good humoured. Peter was made in the image of his father in both temperament and looks, with the same dark hair, cut short in roundhead fashion, and laughing blue eyes. Both were good swordsmen and they took time to instruct me. After a month of sharing a tent, I was already closer to Peter than I had ever been with my two brothers, and I respected his father more than my own. My own being a miserable old drunk.[6]

'What is he like?' I asked Peter.

'This poxy thing is damned uncomfortable.' As senior Cornet, Peter carried our troop standard. A red square of silk, a foot in width, with the Latin motto, "*SALUS PATRIAE*

---

[*]   See Appendix for different religious groups.

24

SUPREMA LEX"* emblazoned in gold. 'Who?' he asked, looking over.

'Essex, the Lord General?'

He laughed, footing the standard on his stirrup. 'An impotent cuckold by all accounts,' then in a lower voice, as his father looked around and glared at the two of us. 'His first wife was a great beauty, but divorced him because his cock would not stir, whilst the second openly presented him with a bastard.'

'So he likes buggering boys?' I questioned, keeping my voice down.

'No, I think 'tis a case of a willing mind, but a weak body,' Peter said.

'Let us hope he is better suited to the job of general than lover then,' I said. Essex' reputation did not inspire me with confidence.

'What matters it? He is the most important man we have; he has experience fighting for the Dutch, and so commands the army. Anyway, have you not heard? God is on our side,' he pointed to the words on the banner.

I was not sure if he was being sarcastic. The phrase was on everyone's lips, but as far as I could tell, God seemed to be on the Cavalier side as well — at least so they claimed. It is one of the stock phrases trotted out by our rulers when they want to send young men to a bloody death. The lies told during civil war can make your head spin.

The two of us plodded along in silence as I pondered the Earl of Essex' command. Putting the man with the biggest title in charge is a damn fool way to run an army.[7]

'Father says Hurry has been made a Colonel of Horse; he has his own regiment.' Peter mentioned it in as if passing, but watched slyly to see my reaction.

'You are jesting? The man is a monster,' I protested.

The breakdown of order had been heaven to roughs like

---

*   The nation's salvation is our highest duty.

John Hurry, who threatened and bullied innocents for profit. All done, of course, in the name of Parliament. By good fortune, our paths had not crossed since my arrival; I had told Peter of my encounter with him. His troop was billeted near the heath in Hounslow, where rumours of theft and murder hung around him and his smirk-faced bastard of a Lieutenant, Niall Pask.

'Men like Hurry enjoy the pain and torture of others, and revel in the power a carbine and sword gives them.' Uncle Samuel had told me. Now the Lord General had made him a colonel, and given him a regiment? Damn I hated the bastard. My opinion of Essex sank even lower.

'Experienced soldier, said the Earl.' Peter was stirring the pot; he knew my opinion of Hurry.

'Huh,' I snorted. 'He's a mercenary brigand, not a soldier.'

Peter giggled, 'So says young Caesar,' leaning over to punch me, almost falling as the standard unbalanced him.

My horse skipped out of his reach at a flick of the reins. 'Too slow,' I taunted him.

'It was your hat; I was dazzled by its wonder.'

'Prick,' I retorted in mock annoyance.

'No, truly, how could any maiden resist you with such a beautiful bonnet?'

'Pish, I had better luck than you with the strumpet in the White Hart.' I had tumbled her the night before we left, and I knew it rankled with him.[8]

'Fatter purse, more like,' he threw it back.

'Fatter cock, she said.' I was chuckling now, as were some of the men behind.

'She says that to everyone, she said it to Everard last week, and his is the size and colour of a maggot,' Peter pointed out loudly, drawing a burst of laughter from the rest of the squadron.

William Everard was our scrawny little troop scout, the shabby dissenter who ruined my afternoon at the theatre. His giant brute of a friend was called Zeal of the Lord Miller, and was, despite his appearance and name, a good man.

'Will you two show some dignity for your rank?' This from Peter's father. 'Children,' he said, rolling his eyes.

The weather broke on the third day, and dampened the mood as we inched closer to Northampton. The road became a muddy scar worn through the landscape, sucking at our horses' hooves, turning our smart column into a wet trudge. The signs of war were everywhere; smashed windows, and empty homes deserted in a rush. All along the route, the discarded debris from troops that had already marched this way littered our path. We found batons everywhere, about a foot or so long. Everard brought some to show Lieutenant Russell, whilst we paused to rest.

'Dildos?' I asked. I was young with only one thing on my mind.

'Pikemen lightening their load,' said Russell, cuffing me. 'Take off a foot from the base of your pike, and it is easier to carry. A fool's trade; in battle the enemy will outreach you, so you bargain your life for an easier walk. *The Lord abhors dishonest scales, but accurate weights are his delight*,[*] he said, then smiled at the two of us. 'I am not sure King Solomon had lazy pikemen in mind though.'

'Come on, lads,' he shouted, chiding the column back into movement.

The next day was a Saturday, and with only half a day's walk, we were within reach of Northampton and rest. By now, our numbers had swelled to near four regiments, plus a few pieces of ordnance. The preacher — Obadiah Sedgewick — gave the troops a fiery sermon to raise their spirits before we set off.

Sedgewick had chosen profanity as the subject of his sermon. I stood at the back listening, and watching our troopers, who sat with rapt attention to every word of his

---

[*]   Proverbs (11:1)

speech. He stood there like a teacher lecturing the class and they were enthralled, hundreds squatting on the floor around him.

Starting soft and slow, so you could barely hear his Wiltshire accent, haranguing and cajoling by turns, selling them God as he built to a shaking climax, like a Barbary slaver selling whores.

'Above all, my brothers, do not swear, not by heaven, or by earth, or by anything else. Let your yes be yes, and your no, no, and you will not be condemned.' The preacher thundered as he came to a close.[9]

Peter leaned over and whispered in my ear, 'Well, you are damned then.'

We were late arriving at Northampton; troop encampments surrounded the town. Much of the army was already there, which meant shit billets full of soldiers and rumours. Truly the two go hand in hand. Some said the King was marching on us, some said he had gone to France, no one knew, not even the Lord General. Essex himself arrived the same day as us, with Uncle Samuel in his entourage, but the mood of the army was not good. Discipline was weak, and there had been desertions and fighting between units.

The day after our arrival, the Earl of Essex called the army out in full array. Ten thousand men on display, as pikes, muskets, and horse paraded before the town, with their trumpets blowing and drums beating. We had been polishing armour all night in preparation and fair glowed as we paraded past. Essex, a podgy figure with a charlie-beard, dressed in a suit of scarlet and gold, rode around inspecting the regiments. Half the town had come out to see the display.

Pikes, with their metal breastplates and helmets, all

marked with an orange sash. Brightly dressed cavalry and dragoons* rode by, their cornets and ensigns fluttering in a slight breeze. The whores and wives that follow every army loved it, lewdly calling out to their men as they paraded past.

Afterwards, most of the men were going to the sermon. Sedgewick assailing them with more tirades of brimstone and hellfire. Peter and I, tired of sermons, went into Northampton to explore.

We crossed the river, went in through the stone gatehouse and headed to the centre of the town. The main square was dominated by All Hallows church then; an old Norman building with a tall spire. Gone now, in the fire of seventy-five. They rebuilt it of course, all Roman columns and painted domes — I preferred the old building. They did the same with St Paul's after sixty-six — and people say the Stuart kings were no papists.

The town was in chaos. Whilst our own unit was piously attending service, other men had been much less devout. There was no discipline. We passed one weeping townsman, whose house and shop-front had been ransacked by soldiers accusing him of popery.

'My cheese, they took my cheese,' he whined at us.

Another, dressed as a merchant but with torn coat and ripped pockets, sat head-in-hands in the gutter, robbed and broken.

Next-door, boxes and linen flew out of an upstairs window, barely missing us, and a woman's shrieks of anger came from inside the house. No need to investigate; it was easy to discern the cause. Everywhere there were drunken soldiers, pissing, vomiting, and fighting.

We were no army; we were a plague.

'Every smashed window is another soldier for the King. The Earl must control this,' muttered Peter grimly.

'Food, ale,' I pointed at a sign just off the square. 'There is

---

*   Mounted infantry.

a tavern, come on.' I pulled him along with me.

I knew it was a mistake as soon as we entered. Dark and gloomy, flagstones covered in muck, and low ceilings with smoke-blackened beams, but with the enticing smell of stew in the pot. It was full of soldiers, raucous and drunk. We sat at a table next to the wall. I smiled at the maid, ordered food and ale for us both, fumbling in my purse for some coin. Peter, with his back to the wall, grew ever grimmer as he looked around.

'Oh cheer up, you look as if you were in Gomorrah itself,' I said, trying to lighten his mood.

It did not work, never did with Peter. He could be a right miserable bastard when he decided he saw injustice.

The maid brought back our ale, pretty, red hair and good teeth, not old enough to have been broken by the drudgery of her toil. She gave me a saucy smile, and wandered off to get our food. I gulped at the ale, eyeing her pretty arse as she swayed back to the bar.

'Ach, that is good,' I said, wiping my lips on my sleeve. 'My throat was as dry as a nun's twat.'

'Can you never be serious?' Peter asked. 'So many of these men have no discipline, what are they going to be like in battle?' He paused and supped his drink. 'Father is worried, I can tell you, as is Captain Luke, and this...' he gestured to the room. 'Drunkenness and the pillaging of our own people? I would not be surprised to see half the town join the King.'

There was a loud shriek, and I turned in my chair. The maid, bent backwards over the bar with a cocked pistol held to her head. Holding it was Niall Pask, wearing an officer's sash now, but still dirty.

'Smirky,' I said.

'Enough of this,' muttered Peter, leaping up from his chair, he started forward. 'What goes here? Civilians are to be left unmolested by order of the Earl.'

I groaned inwardly and went for my sword, standing

behind Peter as Pask turned to face us. The odds did not look good.

'Well, if it be not Sugar Candy,' said Smirky, waving the pistol in our direction. That was enough to give even Peter pause for thought. Pask nodded to a couple of roughs, who moved to block us from the door.

'So, joined the army have we, Sugar?' he said, in a voice that made it sound more of a threat than a question. 'Who is your friend?'

'Put the pistol down,' said Peter, 'and leave this woman alone. You are supposed to be an officer of Parliament, not a bully-ruffian.'

'What, her?' asked Pask, waving the gun back towards the maid. 'She minds not.'

There was a flash and deafening noise in the confined space, as his pistol went off, hitting the maid in her pretty face. Her head dissolved in a spray of blood, as bone and brain splattered over the bar.

Damnable idiot, waving around a loaded pistol, 'twas bound to cause an accident.

'Bastard! Bastard! Bastard!' I heard myself scream. Peter dived at Pask with his sword, but one of the roughs smashed him in the stomach with a cudgel, and sent him crumpling to the floor gasping for breath. Another one grabbed me from behind, pulling my arm in a lock, and forcing me to drop my sword. Pask calmly walked up to me and held a knife to my throat.

'I think I am going to cut you up, Sugar,' he said.

Then a smash, as a window broke and Pask turned. A musket was pushed in, pointing at us through one of the front-panes.

'I could blow the nipples off your mother's tits at a hundred paces,' came a voice. 'From here,'— damn me, Everard — 'I could fart a shot between your eyes. I think you will be letting Mr Russell and Mr Candy leave now.'

I saw Pask's eyes narrow as he considered his options, then he smiled.

'Of course, Sugar was just leaving.' He sounded amiable as he lowered the knife, but I knew him for an untrustworthy arse-worm. 'Why, we are old friends,' he continued, brushing me down.

I helped Peter up from the floor, picking up my sword, never letting my gaze on Pask drop as we backed out of the Inn. Closing the door behind us, I breathed a sigh of relief, and then Everard scuttled around the corner shouting, 'Run, you fools.'

Peter and I sprinted after him as the door to the inn was wrenched open, and Pask's men filed out behind us. When we reached the square, panting for breath, I checked to see if they had followed us, but none came.

'He murdered that woman.' Peter was still angry.

'Of all the angels in the heavens, where the frig did you come from, Everard?' I asked, kissing his ugly face.

'Damned murderer,' continued Peter.

'Captain Luke, he told me to watch after you, and keep you out of trouble,' said Everard.

'Shit,' I was going to have to explain this to my uncle.

'I am going back, and I am going to have him arrested,' said Peter.

'Have you dung for wits? We go to Uncle Samuel, and tell him what is happened,' I answered testily, grabbing him. The last thing I wanted was to go back to that tavern.

'Sugar?' Everard quizzed me.

'A very poor jest,' I told him, not wanting that schoolboy name following me.

'Oh, I think not,' he replied with a wicked grin, 'I wonder what the rest of the lads will think?'

'Viper.'

We returned to our billets, but Uncle Samuel was with Essex, so we told Russell what had happened. His reaction was one of resignation. 'Accidents and fighting happen, whenever men with guns gather.' He said it almost dismissively, but both Peter and I could tell he was worried. Later, as it was getting dark, my uncle returned with John Hampden.

I recognised him without introductions; I had seen him before out riding. John Hampden, the hero of Ship Money, and leader of resistance to the King. He had not the countenance of a hero, more a middle-aged squire growing stout. His broad face was clean-shaven, and his clothes sturdy and well made. Most men of such stature are fools, puffed up with their own importance. Hampden was not so. He was quiet, a watcher mainly, but when he acted it was with stubborn purpose. He had steel in his soul, but self-control made him abhor abuse of power. Not for him Nicolo's adage of *Accusata - Scusata*[*].

I met them all in my time; the leaders of the Great Rebellion. Hampden was the best of us. As a soldier he was more knowledgeable than all the self-proclaimed experts. At Brentford, he stopped defeat turning into a rout. Cromwell and Fairfax would live to prove their ability in the field, but Hampden never did. As a man to follow, though? Damn me, I would have followed him into hell and back. Cromwell could never inspire that in me — miserable bully that he was.[10]

And there lies the rub. I know first-hand the cruelty of the godly and all they betrayed. But in the early days the zealots were not in charge. When the fighting started it was men like Hampden we looked to. Good men, men to believe in, but when the good men were dead or exiled, then the lunatics took over and they drenched us all in blood.

'There has been trouble.' Uncle Samuel threw his gauntlets at his cot in frustration.

'More trouble?' asked Russell with real concern in his

---

[*]   A reference to Machiavelli 'The ends justify the means.'

voice; I looked up from my billet.

'If it carries on our army will become as odious to the country as the Cavaliers,' said Hampden.

He was right of course; it was the same complaint Peter had made in the tavern. The army was out of control. It was not just the looting of civilians; it was the general standard of the men. Units were undisciplined; our own cavalry had robbed a detachment of troops the day before.[11] Now I ask you, how was it going to help fight the King if you steal your own men's swords? On top of that was the lack of pay that was becoming a general grumble. Officers like Uncle Samuel emptied their own purses to keep the men happy. Others simply did not have the funds. It took all of Essex' diplomacy — not that he ever had much — to get them moving again. The shooting in the tavern was just one more incident; one more little slip into barbarity. However, at mention of shooting, Uncle Samuel turned to Peter and me.

'Now, is this why I have received a complaint from Colonel Hurry about my officers' behaviour?'

Friday Sept the 30th was my last unto you.

That day a company of knights, gentlemen, and yeomen of the County of Hereford, came to his Excellency. They petitioned for strength to be sent speedily to Hereford forthwith. We were commanded to draw out 15 men out of every company in our regiments, in all about 900, with 3 troops of Horse and 2 pieces of ordnance with which we marched (a forlorn hope) towards Hereford.

The weather wet, and the way very foul, we got a little refreshment and marched 10 miles further to Hereford, but 'twas very late before we got there, and by reason of the rain and snow and extremity, one of our soldiers died by the way. It is wonderful we did not all perish, for the cowardly Cavaliers were within four miles of us in this poor condition.

Coming to Hereford, the gates were shut against us, and for two hours we stood in dirt and water, up to the mid legs. The city were all malignants, save three which were roundheads, and the Marquess of Hertford had sent them word the day before, that they should in no way let us in, or if they did, we would plunder their houses, murder their children, burn their Bibles, and utterly ruinate all. Hertford promised he would relieve them himself, with all speed.

Therefore the citizens were resolved to oppose us unto the death, and having three pieces of ordinance, charged them with nails and stones, and placed them against us. We resolved either to enter the city, or die before it, but the roundheads in the city, one of them an alderman, surnamed Lane: persuaded the silly cavalier mayor, (for silly he is indeed) that his Excellency* and all his forces were at hand.

Whereupon he opened unto us, and we entered the city at Bysters Gate but found the doors of the houses shut, many of the people with their children fled, and we had enough to do to get a little quarter. The poor mayor (seeing he was so

---

* The Earl of Essex.

handsomely cozened*) was not a little angry. Hertford with his forces (which had fled from Sherborne) promised to relieve them the following day. Though wet and weary, we were fain† to guard the city.

I took an opportunity to view the city, which is well situated upon the river, with a strong wall, better than any I have seen before, with five gates and a strong stone bridge of six arches over the river; much surpassing Worcester.

In this city there is the stateliest market place in the Kingdom, built with columns, after the manner of the Exchange. The Minster in every way exceeding that at Worcester, but the city is not so large; the inhabitants are totally ignorant in the ways of God, and much addicted to drunkenness, and other vices, but principally unto swearing. The children have scarce learned to speak, and do universally swear stoutly. Many here speak Welsh.

On Tuesday we returned to Worcester, and were received back with much joy. The design had been so desperate, that our judicious friends, never thought to see us again. I am in good health, and by the goodness of God supplied with strength beyond expectation.

The next day, our companies were exercising in the fields at Worcester. One of the Lord General's soldiers shot at random, and with a brace of bullets, shot one of his fellow soldiers through the head, who immediately died.

Friday, a pair of gallows were set up in the market place, for the villain that betrayed our troops, unto the hands of the Prince Robber‡. I have nothing of worth to present you with. There was pillage taken from Sir William Russell, for which I never yet got the worth of one farthing. It(the pillage) is instantly the prey of the ruder sort of soldiers, whose society, blessed be God, I hate and avoid.

---

*   Tricked.
†   Obliged.
‡   Prince Rupert of The Rhine.

I have briefly sent you every days passage since I left London, which I hope you have received. I earnestly desire to hear of the welfare of you, Mrs Elizabeth and your whole family. Send it by this bearer, Thomas Weeden, who weekly visits our army, and is faithful. He lodgeth at the Saracens Head, in Carter lane.

Thus with my love, and service to Mrs Elizabeth, Anna, John, and little Samuel, and my love to all my fellow servants, of both sexes. For the present I rest, but do not cease to remain until death,

Your auntient*, humble, and affectionate servant,

Nehemiah Wharton
Worcester, October 7th, 1642.[12]

---

*   long-standing.

3. Mr Pig, October 1642.

True, a new mistress now I chase,
The first foe in the field;
And with a stronger faith embrace
A sword, a horse, a shield

(Richard Lovelace, *To Lucasta, Going to the Wars*.)

A soldier's life is one spent on the march, tramp, tramp, tramp. I have tramped over all England and half Europe in my time. Boredom and backbiters,* with battles a rarity until some silly arse, with more titles than brains, dives headlong into disaster.

There had been skirmishes around Worcester and Hereford, but our troop had seen nor-hide-nor-hair of a Cavalier. We spent our days riding patrols, and our nights grumbling by the campfires. Wet, muddy, and bitten to buggery, an army of miserable men and women trudged along roads thick with sludge. Hunger was our constant companion as we searched for the King, gnawing at our bellies, and dogging our steps. It was the first time I had gone hungry in my life. I did not enjoy the experience.

'Anything to eat?' I asked Lieutenant Russell for the third time that day.

'Nothing, the supplies are miles behind, perhaps when we get to Stratford.' He looked at my red hat. 'Get yourself a pot when supplies come up.'

'I should have been a preacher,' I said to Everard. 'I would have food instead of fartleberries† then.'

'You are spoiled,' was the only reply.

---

*   Fleas
†   Shit clinging to the hairs around the anus.

The small cottage was a ruin, overgrown with weeds and a collapsed roof. Behind, was a trail leading off through the woods and a small pig enclosure, fenced off with wicker. Unlike the cottage, the enclosure was new, tended, and occupied.

'Is this not looting?' I said. We climbed over the fence into the enclosure, leaving our horses tied up by the cottage. Four pigs, some woodsman's property, had awakened Everard's poaching senses.

'Of course,' said Everard, 'but we have seen no food these three days past, and then only some pottage. I am not refusing a free meal.'

'If we get caught they will hang us,' I said. Although, I was already salivating at the thought of some pork for supper.

'Then we shall have to make sure we do not get caught then,' said Everard, clicking his tongue and walking slowly towards the pigs. 'Look at the size of these buggers, fattened for Christmas and ripe for slaughter.'

'Uncle Samuel would not be happy,' I said, looking around, nervous in case a woodsman should discover us. 'We are supposed to be meeting Mr Blake.'

'Who has not shown up. We will tell your uncle we found the porkers roaming free in the woods,' said Everard. 'And do not go telling Peter either; he has too much of a conscience to keep his mouth shut.'

'And I do not?'

'You are a born scoundrel.'

The pigs were nudging up against him, four of them, expecting food. They must have weighed fifty pounds each.

'So how are we to do this?' I asked. 'That is a lot of pork.'

'Catch one and slit its throat, we can butcher it when we get back to camp.' He scratched one of the nudging porkers above the ear. 'Move behind this one and get ready to grab it.'

I manoeuvred myself behind the pig.

''Tis just like shearing a sheep,' Everard told me.

'When the Devil's-arse do you think I have ever sheared a sheep?' I said, eyeing the hams warily. 'Can we not just shoot it?'

'Simpleton, that would bring anyone near running. Hook your hands under its jaw and pull its head back. I will slit it is throat.'

I moved to hook my arms as he had directed me, but Mr Pig was no passive observer. As soon as I reached forward, its tail lifted, and stinking turd covered me from head-to-toe. I slipped as piggy dashed forward, and landed me face first in more liquid excrement. Everard burst out laughing, as I looked up from the floor.

'Do not start laughing, get the evil monster,' I said. I was determined to eat the damn thing now. It was a battle of wits. Man versus food but the food was winning.

The two of us chased the pigs around, slipping and falling in the rain. The pigs ran squealing away to the other side of the enclosure, but the sound of clapping made us both turn to the fence. Sitting on his horse watching our antics, with a big smile on his face was Mr Blake, dressed in a velvet suit of grey with red facings on the cuffs.

'Oh, gentleman, you really have raised my spirits.' He dismounted, flicking his fine cloak over his shoulder and climbed atop the fence.

I got up from the floor and smiled ruefully. 'The damn thing is mocking us,' I reached up to shake his hand. He looked down at his grey velvet gloves.

'Forgive me if I do not shake your hand, Blandford,' he

said. 'These gloves were rather expensive.'

'Captain Luke said you would have a parcel for us, sir,' said Everard, interrupting.

'Indeed,' said Blake, 'to business. There are despatches here for your uncle,' he handed me an oiled leather pouch. I wiped my hand on my doublet and took it. 'The King is on the move towards Banbury. Make sure to tell your uncle that.'

'How did you find that out?' I asked. 'We have seen no Cavaliers.'

'Did your uncle not tell you? I am Prince Rupert's new secretary,' he smiled again. 'I have his every confidence. Now, however, I must bid you gentlemen good day. I should be back to the Prince before I am missed.' He looked over at the pigs. 'I hope you run your quarry to ground, gentleman, but do not linger; there are Royalist scouts all over.'

Blake swung himself back up onto his mount and turned away. 'Till next time, Blandford,' he waved goodbye and rode off.

I watched him go and then turned to Everard. 'Right, let us get this damnable pig.'

'He plays a dangerous game that Blake,' said Everard. 'Spying on the Prince will get him hung.' He climbed over the fence and turned to walk away to our horses. 'Leave the wretched pigs, we have no time.'

'I wager he knows what he is about,' I said, taking out my pistol and shooting a pig in the back of the head. The crack of the shot echoed around the woods, and Everard looked back at me in horror.

'What, in the name of all that is holy, is wrong with you? Blake just told you there are Royalists near.'

I put away the pistol and grabbed the twitching porker by its hindquarters 'I am not going back to camp without bacon for supper,' I said, dragging it to the fence.

Sadly, my stupidity had not gone unnoticed. I could hear shouts coming through the woods, lots of shouts. I dropped the pig to the other side of the enclosure fence and climbed over. A quick glance behind saw men running down the path towards us, swords in hand.

Everard discharged his pistol at them, and I hoisted Mr Pig's carcass over my shoulders; we took to horse and fled. Everard took aim with his second pistol and fired again. A last look behind as we spurred away, showed riders coming down the path and men climbing over the enclosure fence.

I liked Blake, but that was our last meeting. Everard was right; his was a dangerous game. They caught him out after Edgehill, and snapped his pretty neck.[13]

'The Royalists must be to the north of us still,' said Uncle Samuel. 'If Blake's information is correct. Thank you, gentlemen, you have done well.' He wrinkled his nose. 'Have a wash, Blandford, there's a good fellow.'

'Yes, Uncle.'

'And you came across this pig purely by chance whilst carrying out your duties?' Disbelief written clearly on his face.

'Yes, sir,' said Everard firmly.

'Well then, pork it may be, but I am sure the men will treat it as the fatted calf,' he said, and with that we were dismissed.

'You ever do something that dungwitted again, and I will hand you over to the Royalists myself,' said Everard quietly, after we had left Uncle Samuel's field tent.

''Twas your idea,' I said, as we led our horses back to the rest of our troop.

Mr Pig's arrival was a Roman triumph. Everard butchered him, while I washed in the bitter cold stream running beside our camp. The sweetbreads and liver were put to one side, fried on a skillet, and given to us as the huntsman's spoils.

They tossed Mr Pig into an empty barrel, and scalded and washed him, whilst some others dug a pit. Under Everard's instruction, they put wood to burn down whilst the hog was cleaned. Then staked him out, and set him to roast next to the charcoal.

When Mr Pig was cooked, he was carved out between us, and a couple of platters taken over to Uncle Samuel and Russell. Although the portions were small, the effect on the men was wondrous. One man took out a fiddle and started to play a jig, and the rest of us sat back satiated for once.

It was our last supper.

4. Kineton Fight, October 1642

Fight against them that fight against me,
Plead my cause oh lord with them that strive with me:
And stand up for mine help. Take hold of shield and buckler,
And stop the way against them that persecute me:
Say unto my soul, I am thy salvation.

(Psalm 35.)

The Vale of the Red Horse lies in Warwickshire near the Fosse
Way. A long escarpment on its eastern border runs north east.
In those days, there was the figure of a horse carved into the
southern end of the ridge, but it is gone now. The godly had it
covered in the fifties as un-Christian.

Kineton is a drab little market town, no more than a few
houses and a church, at the northern end of the vale on the
Banbury Road. The Earl of Essex had decided the army
would converge there before marching on. We crossed the
Avon at Stratford, rode past Kineton, and camped in the
fields to the south. It was not raining; for days clouds had sent
torrents to earth soaking the fields, but now it was cold with
a bitter east wind coming down off the escarpment, chilling
the bones.

Our regiment was well equipped; tents were pitched in
the mire, and horses corralled. Others did not even have the
luxury of some canvas to cover themselves. Some of the men
took advantage of nearby barns to hide from the elements but
most slept in the open, huddled around fires, grumbling.

The next morning was overcast and bitterly cold, a
thick frost, maybe even a sprinkling of snow on the hills. It
crunched under my boots as I stamped, trying to bring some
life to my feet. A blessing there was no rain, at least. I pulled
my cloak over my shoulders as our men gathered themselves.
Everard, enterprising as always, had brewed up a nettle tea

so at least there was some heat in our bellies. Peter and I took a mug from the poacher, and squinted, up at the ridge to our east.

'Ours?' said Peter.

High on the ridge there were riders silhouetted against the skyline. I shook my head.

'I think not, damnation, there be thousands.' My voice squeaked with fear.

'What is that ridge up there named?' Peter called over to a nearby local.

'The Edgehill,' came the reply.

We were not the only ones to spot the arrival of Royalist cavalry, and it sent the camp into a frenzy. Shouts of alarm broke out, as men rushed for weapons and armour. I gulped down the hot tisane, grabbed my back and breastplates and, with cold-numbed fingers, tried to tie the straps. Uncle Samuel and Russell had us up on mounts in minutes, forming up with the rest of the regiment in fields to the south facing the Edgehill.

'Well, gentlemen, it seems that our day of rest turns instead to God's work,' said my uncle. 'Make sure to make your peace with him.'

'Any word from the Lord General?' asked Russell.

'He has sent riders to our troops to gather.' Uncle Samuel looked up at the gathering forces on the ridge. 'The longer they wait,' he motioned to the enemy, 'the better it is for us. We have men all over the county coming in.'

That was a relief; I did not relish the thought of charging up that steep ridge with the Royalists pouring fire down upon us. I checked my pistols, making sure the wheel lock mechanism was sound, re-holstered them, then took them out and checked again.

We waited through the morning, watching the enemy host form on the hill above us. Later, about noon, Balfour the Lieutenant General of Horse came past us encased head-to-knee in armour like the rest of his lobsters. He stopped briefly for a few words with my uncle and Colonel Fielding.[14]

'Well, Samuel, Basil, I hope your boys are ready?' He looked up the hill at the Royalist army.

'It is cold but some hard fighting will warm us up,' said Uncle Samuel grimly.

'How far away are Hampden and his men?' Lord Fielding questioned.

'Miles,' replied Balfour, 'Hampden cannot be here for hours yet.' He looked up at the King's army deploying on the escarpment above us. 'Our numbers look similar, but we have men coming in. We just need to hold and wait.'

For all his faults, Essex had deployed us well. On a slight rise facing the Royalist army, with our flank covered by ditches and some scrub bushes. Our position sloped down to a small brook that ran across the whole front. From Dutch experience, he knew the importance of spare bandoliers and powder for his men. So, he had men bring up spare powder and shot for the musketeers. Our regiment, along with two others, took up position on the far right of the Army. The infantry in pike phalanx, with wings of muskets flanking, formed in the centre, with culverins* between battalia. In the north, the rest of our Horse formed up facing the Cavalier right and Prince Rupert himself.

Whilst we had trained in the Dutch manner, we were not good enough to risk complex formations.[15] Balfour instead set up a steady firing line, with Meldrum's infantry to our left, and sent out Wardlowe's dragoons into the ditches and bushes to the right. We waited, half our cavalry absent, cannon still coming up, and the wind in our faces.[16]

If the King had attacked quickly he could have broken us, but true to form, Charles dithered.

Balfour moved through our ranks talking to men, quoting from the scriptures and the psalms, trying to calm us, but the

---

    *   Light Cannon

tension as the day drew on was too much. One man broke down, screaming for the Lord to spare him, and was taken away quietly by a couple of friends. I did not blame him; I felt the same way myself, physically sick, although that could have been my empty belly. The waiting was the worst: not knowing. I checked my pistols yet again, if only to steady my nerves.

The enemy deployed atop the escarpment like toy soldiers on a kitchen cloth. The infantry battalia were laid out in a chequer-board pattern, with a great mass of cavalry on either wing. My brothers Henry and James would be somewhere amongst the Horse. The sound of pipe and drums carried on the wind down to our position, mingling with the drone of praying men around me begging for protection. The stink of fear was thick in the air; a lifetime worth of nightmares. I whispered to Apple, stroking his neck, calming him and myself.

The Royalists slowly crept down the hill, flags waving and drums beating, dragging their great guns into range.

Then another pause, as Essex himself rode up and down the line, giving speech to the waiting men, but too far for me to hear his words. The men cheered as he passed, looking more country squire than conquering general.

Above us the King did the same, I heard later he called us 'rebels, papists and atheists,' for standing against him. For hours we sat mounted in that field, but it was our own cannon that roared out first.

'What in God's name!' Uncle Samuel was furious. 'Why has he ordered the guns to fire? We are still short of men, damn it.'

I heard afterward that a couple of cannoneers opened fire on the King himself. I wonder how much pain and misery could have been avoided, if they had sent him to his maker there and then.

The Royalists had dragged their heavy cannon into a

single battery, just as the hook of the Edgehill curves around towards Kineton, and the enemy gunners soon replied to our opening salvo. With that, hundreds of horses on both sides bolted with their riders, at the thunderous roar of fire and smoke. You will not hear that in the official histories, or the self-serving memoirs by people like Holles or Hyde. Apple himself stood firm, and I thanked God that Russell had shown me how to train him to battle.

The cavalier barrage flew over our heads, or ploughed into the ground in front of us. Our cannonade fared much better; bouncing shot up the hill, like a boy skipping stones, and knocking down Royalists like skittles. For an hour the barrage continued, cannons roaring fire, and acrid sulphurous smoke drifting down the valley, stinging at my eyes, making them water, and choking the breath in my throat.

Through the smoke — to the north — I could see a flurry of activity in the Royalist lines. Their squadrons rode down on Ramsey and our left, but I had more immediate concerns. The pop, pop, of carbines over to our right, was growing louder. One of the men behind me leaned over his horse and retched. The sounds of fighting to our right grew in strength, as did my fear, and I pissed myself; a warm trickle down my thighs.

I confess it freely: I was terrified waiting. So was every man there. So balls to you if you judge me.

Balfour and the Lord General's regiment were taking fire to our front. I watched as men were thrown from their horses, cut down by musket balls. Balfour was canny though, he started to pull them left, behind our infantry to safety. Then with a loud huzzah that I could hear from across the field, the Royalist left wing — already trotting towards us — began a great charge across the scrub. Rolling towards us like a wave of man, beast and metal, crossing hedgerows and ditches, faster and closer with every heartbeat. I could see them close now, make out individual features, see the hate filled faces of my fellow Englishmen.

'Too wide, they are too wide,' shouted Uncle Samuel at Fielding. 'Wheel left to us.'

Fielding could not hear, but Lieutenant Russell did not hesitate, pushing our troopers left.

'That way, that way,' he urged, slapping a horse's rump with the flat of his blade.

I followed Russell and my uncle left, through the smoke blowing into our faces. The Royalist charge was going so wide; it would only catch our dragoons running for the barn and their horses. If we were quick, we could get to the relative safety of our pikemen. We were not quick.

Royalist Horse smashed into us as we tried to move. We did not even fire a shot as our line dissolved into a swirling mass of men and horse. There was a flash of powder in pan as I discharged my pistol, not marking who or what I hit. I felt a glancing blow to the head, and cutting to my right, I felt the shock run up my arm as the sword connected with something, someone.

I could hear myself screaming as we broke through into our own infantry, slashing right and left at enemy and our own. I saw a hand reach up to grab Apple's bridle and I swung at it wildly, cutting it at the wrist, leaving it severed, dangling from the reins, as I pushed through our Foot. The raw infantry broke in turn, running, throwing away pike and musket as they went. All around us was chaos, the Royalist left wing rolled over our flank, and our dragoons were cut up running for their horses. To my side, a trooper went down in a tangle; a sword glanced off my chest skidding off the armour. Then I burst free of the mêlée, digging in my spurs, and slapping Apple's rump to get away from the madness behind.

After a short dash I pulled up, realising there was no one near. I paused, looking around at the battlefield. Wilmot's Royalist troopers, dashing on to Kineton, had thrown our whole right flank into disarray. Most of our regiment, and

Stapleton's, had been swept along with them, barring a couple of troops that now rallied to Uncle Samuel behind our infantry line. Peter was there, still holding our cornet high, but of his father there was no sign.

'You are bleeding, my boy,' Uncle Samuel looked concerned.

I reached up to the side of my head, and the hand came back covered in blood. I could feel two flaps of skin where a sword had glanced off my skull. Then it occurred to me — I had lost my damned hat.

'Barely a graze, Uncle,' I said gamely, though the sight of my own blood had turned my stomach. 'Where's Lieutenant Russell?'

Uncle Samuel was grim, 'I saw him go down in the mêlée, but if it be God's will, he has regained his seat.' Then he looked away as if embarrassed.

Peter was silent, black faced from soot and battle; I could see anger burning in him. I looked away — embarrassed, not knowing what to say — to where only minutes before we had been stood. The broken bodies on the ground like bundles of rags, discarded weapons, and here and there, a horse nuzzling at its rider. It sickened me that Russell could be lying there dead. With the smoke, and the flash of cannon and musket all around, it was a monstrous vision of hell.

I gazed dumbstruck at the horror of war. All this because of a woman? Damn, I am stupid when my cock's been stirred.

The battle had been a disaster. Whatever Essex's plans might have been, they had not worked. Our Horse was no match for the cavaliers, that was a solid gold certainty. Both wings of cavalry had routed from the field, taking terrified infantry with them. From Kineton the sound of musket fire could be heard, as Royalists looted our baggage and butchered our wagoners and the villagers. They murdered women and children even, and before any of you start bleating, I saw the bodies. Do not believe the Tory lies![17]

Through all the insanity, Uncle Samuel remained an island of calm, rallying the broken troopers to his standard, for Fielding's was taken. We moved back up towards the centre of our line where Balfour had his lobsters. We were the only Horse left on the field, a few troops of cuirassier, and our shattered remnants. The Royalist cavalry had swept on past when they had Essex at their mercy, running for the loot instead.

I stripped a pot from one of our dead. Lesson learned, a hat is for whoring or dancing, wear a helmet for battle.

The Royalist Foot slowly marched down the hill, keeping to their checkerboard formation, pausing at hedges, or at officers bawling, dressing their lines. Their flags waving in the breeze, and the drums beat out a steady pace, as cannoneers dragged small cannon down into range. Stood out to their front was Edmund Verney, twirling the Banner Royal like a poxy jongleur. On our left, Holles' infantry had stood their ground despite a battering, but beside them, Essex' own Foot had broken at the sight of Prince Rupert's cavalry. Ballard brought his pikemen into the line, damning their eyes, and calling them 'damned whoresons,' as he stood there with a cudgel, beating them into formation.[18]

Just out of musket range, the Royalist infantry paused and dressed their front, even as our cannon smashed great gaps in them. Then they came on steady, muskets discharging, pikes walking at first then at a charge. From my vantage point on the rise behind the infantry, I saw the phalanxes crash into each other and the push begin. The pikes would lock together, then break off and pull back, before clashing together again like bucks at the rut. All the while, our musketeers kept up a deadly fire on the enemy ranks. This went on for what seemed an age, but could only have been thirty minutes, before Balfour leading his lobsters, charged the centre of the Royalist line, and Essex brought the reserve up to the front.

If my sister had known what she was getting me into I

wondered if she would still have sent me into Tartarus*. Of course she would; she thought it was all God's divine plan.

'You are an idiot,' Elizabeth spat the words out angrily, following me.

'You are not the first to tell me that, dear sister. Is there anything in particular or just general idiocy?'

'Both, you damn fool; you have been rutting with your brother's betrothed!'

'That particular piece of stupidity, and how would you know that anyway?'

'Anne told me.'

'My beautiful little sister.' Vicious little minx!

'Letters arrived this morning, whilst you were dreaming.' The words dripped heavy with sarcasm. 'There has been fighting near Shepton Mallet. Henry was there, he hopes he will be able to visit. The rebels were routed from the field, and he is safe.' She actually looked worried for the overgrown ape.

'Ah,' I grunted. Henry returning home could prove troublesome, best to keep my head down I thought.

'Ah? Is that all you have to say for yourself, Ah?' She slapped me hard across the face.

'Ow!' I yelped.

She slapped again, harder this time, screeching at me, 'I despair, Blandford, I have prayed for you to see the error of your ways, prayed that you would turn away from your drunkenness, and gambling, and stand with the Lord, but now it seems you have added lechery to your list of sins.'

Admittedly, she had a very good point, but I was not about to give her the satisfaction of agreeing.

* Dungeon of torment for damned souls in Greek mythology.

'Truly I am only doing this for your own good, sweet brother. I will save you if I can.' She fixed me with a stern look, her blue eyes blazing with a zealot's fire.

'What prattle is this, you harridan? Doing what? All you do at present is beat me.'

'You must leave, Blandford. When Henry finds out about Sarah he will kill you. The sin of Cain will not deter him; both of your souls will be damned.'

Oh lord, she was trying to save my soul, this could only end badly.

'How is he going to find out?' I said. 'Sarah will say nothing, and even pretty little Anne would not tell Henry. She is not that simple.'

'I will tell him.' She said the words quietly, but each one hit me like a punch in the throat.

'What?' I looked at her incredulously. 'Why would you do a damn fool thing like that; I thought you did not want him to kill me?'

'To save you, Blandford, I must be cruel only to be kind.'

Quoting Shakespeare, whilst decrying theatre as the "devils work" was a petite hypocrisy, but I kept that little snippet to myself[*]. She had a quick right hand.

'There is a holy war coming, dear brother; we must save England from popery. I have letters for you, to Uncle Samuel. Take them to him and he will help you.'

'Move boys, move, God's work is still to be done,' shouted Uncle Samuel.

My time as spectator was over, back once more into the fray. We cantered behind Meldrum's firing soldiers and charged at a gap in the enemy line. We bore down on enemy musketeers, but they fell back, running to the protection of their pikes. I cut down at one as he ran, missing. While Apple would not charge the hedgehog of pikes – no horse will – we

---

*   *Hamlet* Act 3, Scene 4.

rode up to the phalanx, discharged our pistols at close range, then retired to reload. Time and time again but still the Royalists held.

Battle weary, we steeled ourselves as light faded for one last throw of the dice, charging down at the enemy infantry, and they broke. We rode them down, hacking at their heads, as they ran from us like wheat to our scythes. There is exultation at that moment, when your enemy break and flee. I charged a red-haired Ensign with no helmet. Little more than a boy, wielding his standard like a pike, and screaming at his men to hold. He thrust up at me, but Apple swerved and the blade flashed past my face. We turned on a sixpence, and I slashed at the ensign's exposed neck. I half severed his head, blood spraying over me and in my face. As he fell, I grabbed at the colour, ripping it from the pike shaft, and rode back in triumph to our position on the hill.[19]

That boy was the first person I knowingly killed; his death would cause me more trouble than all the others, yet I cannot even remember his face. Just the bright shock of red hair.

Cromwell was with us in that last charge. I do not know when he arrived at the battle, but he was there at the end. Holles knew it as well, despite trying to smear Old Wart Face later. Cromwell was never a coward. He was a cold murdering zealot, but never a coward.[20]

As darkness fell the two lines separated, muskets still spitting out flame in the night. Men on both sides pulled back. It was bitterly cold. Uncle Samuel, watching over the dead, muttered half to himself. '*Go tell the Spartans stranger passing by, that here obedient to Spartan law we lie,*'* then turned away to go to the Lord General.

---

*   Herodotus, *The Histories.*

54

We buried Russell in a pit with the other officers, friend and foe alike, all tumbled in together with little ceremony. I've heard people talk of thousands dead on either side, but by my reckoning no more than a thousand were killed, though more died later from their wounds. The night after the battle was dismal misery. With no fire to warm us, we stood in the field with the cries of the wounded and bodies of our comrades all around.

Essex had convinced himself that we had won a victory. Uncle Samuel was not so sure; he wrote a letter to parliament, urging them to raise more men. The road to London was open for the King to march on, but Charles could not see the opportunity. The Royalists drew off the next morning; quitting their positions on the Edgehill while we watched and then crept to Banbury and on to Oxford.

After a day of funerals, we moved off into the mist, retreating towards Warwick then on to Northampton.

Everard had come through the battle without a scratch, and had acquired a full purse in the process. The wiry poacher's ability to bag a brace of rabbits for the company's pot, and his pouch of herbs and medicines to cure the wounded, made him popular. He had sewn up my face after the battle, and I would rather him than all the leeches and quack doctors in England.

'I was a tailor in my youth,' he told me, admiring his needlework.

'Somehow, I do not see you in a shop cutting cloth.' Everard was a born woodsman, not shopkeeper.

'Hated it; city is fine for some folk, not me, was my Da's idea. Now do not flinch.' I winced as he bit off the yarn. 'Be a bugger of a scar, but your pretty locks will cover it up soon enough.'[21]

I can trace it now, a thin white line barely noticeable. Lucky, given I am bald as a coot.

Peter barely spoke to anyone — lost in his own melancholy.

By the time we reached Warwick I was frustrated and worried. I could put aside the horrors that I had witnessed, and slept soundly enough. Others were broken by what they had seen. Now I do not want to make out I am some sort of Hercules — I am not. Perhaps I am just simple; they say simple men worry less. *Homo est animale rationale** after all. Away from the fight, I put it out of my thoughts, preferring not to brood in silence.

Finally, Peter's mask slipped, and he broke down in tears. I heard him sobbing into his blankets as we lay in our tent near Northampton and did my best to comfort him.

'I saw him fall and I did nothing, I am guilty.' He sat up, eyes red, snot dripping from his nose; I handed him a 'kerchief.

'Guilty? What for? Surviving? What could you have done in that madness?' I asked quietly but surprised.

'I am his son; I should have been at his side.'

'You were,' I reassured him.

'I was terrified,' he said it in a whisper.

'Were we not all?' I said.

Peter looked up in surprise. 'You captured a colour, and it was you who broke the line in the last charge; you were fearless.'

That was not strictly true. Their line had melted as I rode up, and mainly because Balfour had hit them in the rear, but I was not above taking the credit. Especially after the pride my uncle had shown me when I presented him with the Royalist colour.

'You think I had no fear? Holy tits, I pissed myself in terror, and the rest is a blur. I was lucky, that is all.'

This was not false modesty; I had been lucky. I could easily have had my head taken off in that first clash, and a stray musket ball or pike could have left me bleeding my life out on that field like so many others. Russell was a good man and soldier, yet his skill had not saved him.

---

*   Man is a Rational Animal, Porphyry.

'What now?' He asked.

'Now we march again back down the road we came, and see what more the King can throw at us.' I said it with far more confidence than I felt.

'London? He looked distraught. 'Mother, how will I explain this to my mother?'

'You cannot, how could you explain battle to a woman? To your mother? She would not want the detail.' We had found Russell with half his face ripped away.

'I hate him!' Anger now.

'Who?' I asked.

'The damned King, he is the cause of all our woe.'

I held him as he wept. How I conjured words of comfort is a mystery to me, but his weeping was better than grim silence. Had it been me? I would have drowned myself in sack and punks,[*] but Peter was better.

Alea iacta est.[†] At Edgehill, we crossed the Rubicon. We stood against the old order and nothing was ever the same again. Some realised it at the time of course (Cromwell first and foremost) but most did not — certainly not I. It seemed every man was praying for forgiveness, in anguished self-torment, for the sins and savagery of battle.

Some began to question if this really could be God's will, this bloody trial by combat, and their nerve failed them. Others, not daring to think they could be wrong, that the horror was in vain, steeled themselves and grew more determined, more bitter. Once that path was taken there would be no villainy to which they would not stoop, no crime too abhorrent, and step by step we damned ourselves.

The age of the self-righteous man had begun.

---

*   Wine and Strumpets.

†   Julius Caesar, *'The die is cast'*. Attributed by Suetonius.

The King's answer was communicated to both Houses by the Earl of Northumberland, wherein his Majesty calls God to witness his great desire of a peace, and to avoid the destruction and effusion of the blood of his subjects, offering to treat at Windsor, or anywhere else where he shall reside.

This answer was received by both Houses with a great deal of joy, thinking his Majesty's heart had gone alongst with his expression, but it seems it was the least of his thoughts. That very morning (being Saturday, and a very great misty morning, fit for bloody and treacherous design) he sent from Colebrook to Syon, 8 Regiments of his Foot, six pieces of ordnance, and 20. Troops of Horse, and suddenly they fell upon Colonel Holles Regiment quartered at Brentford (being the Red Regiment, those honest religious soldiers, that to their great honour and fame, had fought so courageously and valiantly in the late Battle at Kineton).

They fought with all that force of the King's from 12. a clock, until half-an-hour past three in the afternoon, then my Lord Brookes Regiment came to their relief. At last, the Greencoats, Colonel Hampden's Regiment came and charged them five times over, whereupon they retreated, and the Lord Brookes, with Colonel Hampden, and the remainder of Colonel Holles Regiment retreated to the Lord General.

News of the cutting off the Red Coats (the only terror of the Cavaliers) was carried to the King at Hounslow, who came with great joy on Sunday morning to his soldiers at Brentford, encouraging them to go on, and they should have brave and plentiful pillage in London.

The King glorying at the sight of the dead bodies of our men as he went along, commended his soldiers for their valour in slaying of them. But God who is just, and is the only searcher of hearts can vindicate his honour, and justly punish in due time any that shall take his name in vain, and call God to witness one thing, but intend another.

The King was terrified with the sight of the Earle of Essex and his Army, who faced him and his damned regiments on Sunday morning till two of the clock in the afternoon. Then the King's Army not daring to stir out of the town and their trenches, were forced and scattered with the cannon only, insomuch that the King was glad to make all haste away, and no doubt with a troubled conscience, for that he had consented to such a treacherous, Jesuitical, unchristianly, and unkinglike accommodation, in being cause of the shedding of so much blood, under the signed expression of calling God to witness.

This horrible and unnatural accommodation of the King's, so outraged Parliament, that they voted that there should be no cessation of arms, nor any accommodation, but that the Lord General should revenge this bloody act of the King's and his Cavaliers.

On Sunday, when the Parliament's forces were disposed into a battalia, the King sent a courtier called Dorset White, with a trumpeter, to the Lord General to desire a parley, but the Parliament clapped him and the trumpeter up in the gatehouse, and would not hearken to a parley for the King had dealt so unfaithfully with them.

Even during the very time that White and the trumpeter were coming with their message, and almost at Hammersmith, and before he had delivered his message to the Lord General. The King himself in person (as diverse in Brentford can witness) commanded them to give fire against a pinnace* employed by the Parliament on the Thames near Syon. Played they upon her with ordnance and musketeers for two hours. The sailors in her (having spent their shot) were forced to betake themselves to their long boat, and having laid a train of powder, they blew up the pinnace, and so sunk her, that the King might make no advantage of her guns, and the men got safe away with their boat.

---

*   Riverboat.

This unkinglike design, so to destroy his subjects when the accommodation was agreed unto, hath lost his Majesty the hearts of many of the blinded malignants that stood for him before. For now, they well perceive whereto the fair speeches of his protestations, and invocations lead.

And for the carriage of the King's Army, poor Brentford is made a miserable spectacle. For they have taken from there all the linen, bedding, furniture for beds, pewter, brass, pots, pans, bread, and meal. In a word, all that ever the people have. When the Parliaments Army came into the town on Sunday evening, the innkeepers and others begged of the soldiers a piece of bread.

So, it may be truly said, a great part of the King's Army consists of rogues and thieves. In these barbarous outrages they are cherished, even it is feared by the King himself.

Humphrey Blunden.[22]

5. London, November 1642.

But I did from my Father run, for I will plough no more,
Because he had so slashed me, and made my sides so sore;
But I will go to London Town, some fashions for to see;
When I came there, they called me Clown, and a great Boobee.

(Traditional, *The Great Boobee.*)

London was a wonder to me. The narrow lanes crowded with people, carts, and animals. Streets paved with shit not gold, ramshackle old architecture next to grand churches, crumbling taverns next to smart new townhouses. Every building was a shop-front, and every vice imaginable for sale.

The senses would be assailed. The stink of the tanner's yard or chandler's melting-room; the smoke from ten thousand hearths; the calls of the street vendors enticing customers, or their curses as they were ignored; meat roasting on the spit in taverns, or the peppery assault of an apothecary, with its flowers and musky fruits as you passed by. And everywhere people: Moors and Nubians in their flowing robes, and grim traders from the frozen north with their long beards and cargoes of furs. On the Thames, below the bridge, a forest of masts swayed above ships from every point on the globe. Each step I took revealed a new sight or sound; an Energy of Londoners at their daily tasks. The whole world in one place.

Around the city, the trenches and ramparts that had frightened off the King after Brentford, grew wider and deeper. Citizens marched out every day, moving tonnes of earth, to create a great defensive ring running through Hyde Park and Piccadilly, down to south of the river; Southwark and eastwards. Forts and Bastions with cannon trained on the roads completed the outer defences. If any attacker managed to breach the first layer, they would then face the old walls. Great iron chains were set up in the streets to stop the flow

61

of people and buildings pulled down around the wall to give gunners vantage points.[23]

Peter and I took rooms near Cheapside, in one of Uncle Samuel's properties. We were in the third floor of an old wood built tenement, in a courtyard just off Bread Street. Our rooms were sparse, with a small fireplace, wooden table, chairs, and two adjoining bedchambers. No carpets or comforts to make it homely. The lower floors were used up for storage of some sort. It meant carts arriving at the oddest hours, but I, young buck about town that I was, did not question my uncle's affairs.

Bounding up the narrow stairs one evening — it must have been early in December — I heard conversation in the main room. I paused for a second, eavesdropping. A woman's voice with Peter, perhaps his mother. I fixed on my most charming smile and stepped into the room.

It was not his mother.

'Blandford, well met.' They both stood as I entered. 'This is my sister Emily.'

She was pretty. Tall like a lily, with raven black hair, striking blue eyes, and the palest of skin. She looked nothing like her brother, excepting the small button nose that wrinkled when they smiled. I mocked it on him, on Emily it was captivating. She was smiling now as I bowed and stuttered out a greeting.

'Pleased to meet you, Mistress Russell,' I could actually feel myself blushing.

She brushed a stray hair out of her eyes and curtsied. 'Mr Candy, Peter has told me so much about you.' They both resumed their seats and I pulled up a stool to join them.

'''Tis surely all lies, Mistress Russell.' I could not take my eyes off her. I sat down, missed the stool, and went flying backwards arse-over-tit.

Peter burst out laughing as I struggled back to my feet.

'What, drunk already?' he said.

'No indeed,' I said. 'I've barely touched a drop.' The last thing I wanted was his sister to think I was a soused wastrel. 'Damn stool is unsteady. Your pardon,' I said, realising I had just sworn. Emily bit her lip to stop from laughing and coyly turned away.

'My sister is to go into service, Blandford. I am not sure 'tis seemly,' said Peter.

'When a family needs money it is right that we all make our contribution. Do you not think so, Mr Candy?' she said.

I hemmed and hawed: 'No doubt 'tis very complicated.' I hate walking in on other peoples arguments.

'Not too complicated I am sure,' she said sweetly, looking at Peter. 'With my brother away serving Parliament and father gone.' She paused at mention of Russell. ''Tis left to women to keep families, and homes together whichever way we can.'

'Well, of course, when you put it like that,' I said.

'Plug your ears, my friend,' said Peter. 'She will have you believing day is night if you listen too long.'

'Your servant, Mr Candy.' She stood and curtsied again. 'I think I must return to our mother's house.'

I stood up quickly, knocking the stool over and bowing, too deeply and too long. They both gave me an amused look.

'Buffoon,' said Peter. 'Come, Emily, I will walk with you.'

I bowed again and must have said 'Enchanted, Miss Russell,' three times as they left.

'Pretty woman, your sister.' I said, on his return. I had already resolved to meet her again if I got the chance.

'And not for the likes of you,' he said, laughing. 'Where have you been all day?'

'I saw Uncle Samuel. He desires our presence tomorrow at the Tower.'

The White Tower broods over Eastcheap, sullenly glaring out over the city. We were both quiet as we walked to the prison — a summons to the tower is never to be taken lightly. The butchers' shops that crowd the end of Eastcheap were opening their fronts, but the wares were sparse. In peaceful times the shops would be stuffed full of sausages, hams and sweetbread, with geese and sides of pork, hanging beside rows of fattened capons. These shops were near empty, even with Christmas near, and there were few customers.

At All-Hallows there was a guard of Whitecoats and ammunition store but we marched on past to the looming citadel itself.[24] More Whitecoats checked our passes at the Middle Tower, then waved us through the thick curtain walls.

It is a melancholic place where the past intrudes on the present. Queens and consorts, courtesans and courtiers, the innocent and the guilty; their ghosts haunt the place. Mark me, I speak not of phantoms or sprites, but of the weight of time.

We had been told to present ourselves at the Office of Ordnance and Armoury — in the White Tower itself. After giving our names to a clerk, we were ushered into a large plain room with whitewashed walls, laid out with benches as if for a service. We were not alone, there were about twenty or thirty others gathered waiting. Some I recognised from Fielding's regiment.

Franny Cole was a cornet from Hale's troop who had fought with us at Edgehill. He was of middling height, plain enough with a large mouth. Long brown curls fell down his back, and he looked every inch the gentleman in a fine suit of pea green. Zeal was there, and Sam Brayne, a sandy haired Buckinghamshire boy, both from my uncle's troop, and sitting alongside them puffing away at his pipe was Everard.

'You look well, Franny,' said Peter.

'Morning, gentlemen, have ye any notion what business we are about?' he asked.

'None at all,' I said, whilst Sam and Zeal mumbled their greetings. 'Uncle Samuel told us to be here today, so here we are.'

'Now, gentleman, if you please.' Uncle Samuel had come in quietly from a door at the back. Following him was another thin man, tall, with spectacles perched on his nose, and short hair cropped around his crown. This hushed our hubbub and we turned to look at them.

'I thank you for your presence,' Uncle Samuel continued smoothly. 'Most of you here I already know, some of you have been recommended by your officers to me. No doubt, you can all deduce that you have been gathered here for a reason.' He walked to the front of the room, and turned to face us.

'If we have learned anything from the autumn, it is that we lack information about our enemies' movements. We lack knowledge of their plans and troop dispositions, and without that information we are hamstrung when our forces march to face the King. That, gentlemen, is where you enter the stage.'

He looked us over. 'Parliament has decided to create a new unit, in each association, under the direct command of a scoutmaster. You men are to be the start of that unit for the Earl of Essex under my command. We need men we can rely upon, who can read and write, and who are good horsemen. Men who can keep us supplied with a stream of knowledge with which to combat our enemies. You have all shown, in one way or another, that you can act independently, and have proven yourselves in battle.'

'You want us to be spies?' one man asked.

'No indeed,' said Uncle Samuel. 'You will be scouts, sometimes couriers, and intelligencers certainly, but you will all carry Parliament's commission as officers, and in the main will be attached to the army.'

'What is the pay?' asked Zeal.

'You will receive two pounds a week for your work as a scout, as well as drawing pay as a cornet,' replied Uncle

Samuel. 'Some of you have worked for me as couriers in the past, and know the kinds of danger you will face, but you will be well rewarded for your pains.'

Zeal grunted his acknowledgement.

'I hope 'tis regular and on time; cannot feed ourselves on promissory notes and hot air,' said another.

'On that I can assure you,' my uncle told him. 'Even if I have to use my own purse, you will be paid.'

This was a common enough gripe in the army; pay was always in arrears and never enough when it came. For a dashing blade like myself it was a social embarrassment to find myself short. For others like Zeal, who handed most of his money to his wife and children, if he was not paid they went hungry. Whatever our priorities, the resultant discontent was the same.

Uncle Samuel's assurances seemed to work; he had a good reputation for treating his men fairly, and it was well deserved.

'It is your choice, gentlemen, and no dishonour to you if you choose to return to your regiments.' He looked around to see if anyone wanted to speak. None of us did; the pay was good, and 'twas an opportunity of advancement for us all.

'Then tomorrow morning, gentlemen, you are to meet with Mr Darnelly at the Artillery Garden in Spitalfields,' Uncle Samuel gestured to the man accompanying him.[25] 'We have equipment to be issued and assignments to be arranged. God be with you.' He nodded to us all and they left the room.[26]

Mr Darnelly pointed the pistol at the roundel, and pulled the trigger. There was a flash in the pan, followed almost instantly by a fiery discharge from the muzzle. He paused as the smoke cleared then calmly walked up the range and retrieved the roundel. He had a clean hit in the inner ring just grazing the middle. It would be an excellent shot at fifty paces. At the seventy paces he had set the mark up, it was exceptional.

Zeal whistled. 'That is a mighty fine shot, sir.'

Darnelly smiled and reached into one of the boxes he had brought with him, pulling out a brace of pistols similar to the one he had just used. He passed them round.

'Please examine them. Now, gentlemen, you will notice that the mechanism is somewhat different to usual. It is a flintlock, based on the Le Bourgeoys snaphaunce mechanism, but with some variations that make it far more reliable.'

Peter passed me a pistol to handle, long barrelled — over a foot — with polished wood handle, and steel doglock mechanism; it was a fine piece indeed.

'Look down the barrel please, gentlemen,' Darnelly continued. I looked, noted a spiral of shallow grooves running up the inside of the barrel. I passed it on to the next man.

'That, gentlemen, is rifling; it makes the ball spin, increasing the range and the accuracy considerably. However, they do take longer to load if you find yourself in a battle.'

'That is how you managed such a good shot,' I interrupted him. 'The rifling?'

'Hmph,' he snorted at being interrupted. 'Indeed, Mr Candy, although I should say I am an excellent marksman anyway. Would you care to measure your skill?' He offered me his pistol.

'Why not,' I said, taking the pistol off him and turning to the equipment table for a charge.

'Mr Brayne,' Darnelly turned to Sam and handed him the roundel. 'Will you set up the mark again please, so Icarus can test his wings?'

Sam grinned and ran off to the butts.

I took one of Darnelly's paper cartridges, bit it open and poured the powder down the breech. I wrapped the ball and rammed it down the barrel, tight against the powder charge. I half cocked, poured a pinch of priming powder into the pan, and flipped the frizzen down.

Turning, I looked down the range at the roundel; at seventy paces it looked tiny. I breathed deep and took aim, sighting down the barrel, pulling back the hammer with my thumb to cock. As I exhaled, I squeezed the trigger, and felt the ignition run through the mechanism. The flash in the pan, smoke, and a kickback as the bullet left the barrel in a roar of flame and sulphur.

Sam brought the roundel back, with my mark clean in the inner circle, but not touching the centre like Darnelly's shot.

'Not too bad, Mr Candy, with age comes experience after all,' he smiled at me.

'Indeed, sir,' I answered. 'For a first shot with a new pistol, I am satisfied. After I have used it as much as yourself, I would hope to be much, much better,' I smiled sweetly back at him.

'Hmph,' he snorted again. 'You will all be issued with a brace of pistols,' he pointed to the boxes. 'And with snaphaunce carbines, to go with them. Ah now, this is of interest,' he pulled out a tiny white box, small enough to fit into the palm of my hand.

'Pass it around please, pass it around; here's another one,' he tossed another box out. 'This, gentlemen, is a dry compass in a bone case. This will tell you the direction of north, at any time of day or night. Very useful if you are in enemy held country, and need to get back to our forces.' The little box contained a needle inside, and the compass points marked on the base.

'Ah, even better,' he pulled out a leather tube, 'A telescope, gentlemen, or more commonly a spyglass. Each of you will receive one. Please be careful over there,' he snapped, as one man almost dropped the tube. 'This will magnify your view, allowing you to see distant objects or troops. Useful for counting numbers, or marking down unit flags, without being caught; I am sure you will all agree. It contains two glass lenses, so you need to take care not to break them, else it is useless,'

He pulled out a satchel, 'You will see on this satchel, that there is a pocket to stow the spyglass away safely, and also pockets with a pencil and a journal to record your information. The other pockets can be used as you see fit.' The satchel was well made, double stitched out of leather, with straps to carry on the back, and enough space for some spare clothes as well as Darnelly's spyglass.

'Now, boots,' next out of the box came a pair of well-made high brown riding boots. 'They resemble any other soldiers boot, but observe the heel,' he indicated the sides of the heel, where a couple of nails appeared bent over in the hobbling, 'and twist the small nail there and there...' The bottom of the heel came off, revealing a secret compartment big enough to hide a small document.

'A fair trick for carrying messages if you risk being caught and searched, good, is it not?' He nodded to me, as I was passed the boots and shown the heel.

'Not really my style of boot,' I replied. 'Do you have any in black?'

'Hmph. Yes, your uncle tells me you like to dress well. I am afraid not, but we do have these,' he pulled a plain padded doublet in dark green, out of the box, with cloth buttons up the front.

'A corpse would be better dressed,' I replied. 'No lace and no embroidery?'

'Yes, well,' he replied tersely. 'The dark colours are better for moving unseen about the country, rather than looking like a harlequin.' Everard choked back a laugh.

'It still looks like something my father would wear,' I said.

'Your father's doublets are not reinforced with steel bands, Mr Candy. Good enough to deflect a dagger thrust, I can assure you, perhaps even a musket ball at range. It also has a number of pockets hidden in the lining, which are nearly undetectable. We have it in blue if you prefer?'

'Not really, it is a matter of style not colour; do we get a hat as well?' I asked.

'And we all receive these devices?' asked Everard interrupting.

'Indeed,' replied Darnelly, 'you will work most generally in pairs, scouting out enemy positions. Or you will meet with other agents, in order to courier information.' He went on some more, but the excitement was over for the day and he dismissed us by noon.

An intelligencer I became. It was good money after all and I had my friends around me. Looking back of course, it was a fateful decision that took me to the courts of kings and emperors, and to the battlefields of Europe. It led me to the new world and back again, saw me wounded and near to death, got me imprisoned for treason and knighted by the same Stuart king. Oh, and I knew many beautiful women, even some that I loved. And, knowing all that, I think I would have still taken the same path. I have had a life worth living after all. A life worth writing about.

Sir,

I have only the briefest of moments to write. We are only today returned to Oxford. I am billeted at Holton House and you may send all correspondence to me there.

We are imposed upon the good favour of the Whorwood family, whose scion Brome I know you have some acquaintance with. His wife Mistress Jane is our hostess; Mr Whorwood has taken voluntary exile abroad rather than serve his King, which I think is some measure of the man, as you have in the past suggested.

It is our families shame that B has deserted our true cause. His actions at the late fight at Kineton heap further embarrassment upon us. It is reported that it was his act that killed my hostesses own brother. For which I must make some amends.

Mistress Jane is exceeding kind and gracious despite this, I can only be thankful to God for her sweet disposition and support. She is close to Lord Falkland, and high in the King's favour, so I hope to make some use of her acquaintance.

The withdrawal from London was exceeding hard, the weather and attentions of the Roundheads made it very hot indeed. Their refusal to negotiate before London, despite the King's gracious acquiescence, merely shows to the world their desire for injustice and misrule.

I am made a captain of dragoons, and ride to beat up rebel posts beyond the Thame.* Perhaps I will meet B in the field. He should know that brotherly bonds bind us no longer, even if you still call him son.

If Anne is to come to Oxford she should procure a

---

* The River Thame in Oxfordshire lies to the south of Holton, and should not be confused with the Thames.

71

passport from *Mr Carpenter* at St *Michael's*, who will be able to acquire such[7]. *Mistress Jane* would be happy to make her acquaintance. We are lucky she is so kind in spite of B.

My sincerest regards to you and my sisters, I hope *Elizabeth* is enjoying the preparations for feasting and merriment even in these sad times.*

I remain your son,

James Candy, Holton House, Oxford. Dec 7th 1642.

---

*   Presumably this is sarcastic given Elizabeth's Puritanism.

6. Christmas, December 1642.

When Christmas tide comes in like a Bride,
with Holly and Ivy clad,
Twelve days in the year, much mirth and good cheer,
in every household is had:
The Country guise, is then to devise,
some gambols of Christmas play;
Whereas the young men, do best that they can,
to drive the cold winter away.

(Traditional Ballad, *Drive the Cold Winter Away.*)

Ask any schoolboy and he will tell you that the puritans banned Christmas. 'Tis blackmouth* chatter and anyway most of it happened later. Oh, the theatre had been closed, but plays were still performed in taverns and houses, and they had not banned drinking, or dancing, or music. Uncle Samuel had returned to Buckinghamshire to raise more men, and spend the holiday with his family. I politely declined his invitation; I had plans for Christmas. I bought myself another red hat, and got ready for Yuletide in the city.

Every morning we would gather at the Artillery Gardens and practice with our new weapons. Fencing for me mostly — Darnelly ignored me on the range — and the rest of the day was left free. On the Sabbath, I would accompany Peter and his mother and sister to Mary-le-Bow. Thursday afternoons would be reserved for the sermon in Bread Street, when the whole family would go to listen to different ministers speak. Had Emily not been there my attendance would have been infrequent, but with her presence, the days fell into contented rhythm.

The church sermons were nothing like the dull lectures delivered by the rector at home. Crowds gathered at St Paul's

---

*   Slanderous or deceitful.

Cross, and argued and discussed anything and everything. Personally, I never cared about Bishops or Divines; it was all much the same to me, and whilst I understand *why* decorations might be idolatrous, I never understood breaking works of art. When the Cheapside Cross was smashed I told Everard it was a disgrace; he asked if I was a papist. The whole thing left a fevered atmosphere smouldering in the city. There were riots and marches on Parliament, and apprentices always causing trouble.[28]

We had been paid though — which is more than most of the army could claim — Uncle Samuel had made sure we all had funds for the holidays before returning to Cople. In the evenings you would find me in a riverside tavern taking in a droll,[29] or drinking with my new comrades. Most of them, that is; Peter and Zeal rarely partook, and Everard was always busy running errands for my uncle. The war was never far away of course; it was all anyone ever talked about. Despite that, I was happy.

'Are you coming out with me tonight?' I said to Peter, as we walked back to Bread Street — it was the Thursday before Christmas. 'Some of the others are meeting at the Rose on Cheapside.'[30]

'Who exactly are the others?'

'Franny Cole from Hale's troop, Zeal, and Sam Brayne should be there as well. Maybe a few others as well,' I continued. 'Everard said he would meet us there later. He has some business for my uncle to see to first.' I expected the usual quiet refusal, but for once Peter surprised me.

'Why not?' he said.

The Rose Inn was a couple of hundred paces from Bread Street, down Poultry near the cross. It is not called that anymore; the landlord changed the name to the King's Head when we restored that lying, deceitful, miserly, blaggard to the throne in 1660. A tall brick built building with bay windows, and a large sign of a red rose hanging above the polished doors, I read the writing beneath.

> *'This Tavern's like its sign—a lusty Rose,*
> *A sight of joy that sweetness doth enclose;*
> *The dainty Flower well pictured here is seen,*
> *But for its rarest sweets—come, search within!'*[31]

'Well, that is welcoming; I wonder how much the rarest sweets cost.'

'You can always ask her,' said Peter.

We stepped down into the bar room, a spacious open area, filled with rough-hewn tables and stools. A dozen or more oil lamps kept it bright despite the low hanging beams. The flagstone floor was clean-swept, and a polished wooden bar counter was set up at one end with beer barrels behind. In one corner — away from the fire — played musicians, just a drum, lute, and fiddle, but raucous enough to give the tavern a lively atmosphere. A hog was roasting at the open log fire, being basted in its own juice and dredge,* and turned by a Spitdog in a wheel.

'I love Christmas.'

'Franny's over there, look,' said Peter, pointing through the smoke. We made our way over, squeezing past people at the other tables, to get to Franny sitting near the fire, with the delicious aromas of cooking meat all around.

'What ho, Franny,' I said pulling up a stool.

'What will you drink?' asked Peter. 'Franny, will you another?'

'Hot spiced wine,' said Franny, 'it is a true delight.'

'I will have the same, Peter.' He wandered over to the counter to order us drinks. I saw Zeal and Sam Brayne arrive. Zeal ducking under the doorframe, I called over to them.

People thought Zeal stupid because of his size. He was not, though I knew him to play on it, worked often enough

---

* Flour, breadcrumbs, and spices.

excepting with his wife. Mean bitch, she never fell for his act, but he doted on her, and his ever growing brood of children. Sam was a quiet lad, one of those people who just seem to fade into the background, good with a knife though.

'A Merry Christmas to you, gentlemen,' said Franny, as they arrived. Peter also returned with a jug of spiced wine and flagons. Zeal helped him with the drinks, and poached a flagon for himself, leaving me without.

'Zeal, you sly turd,'

'Do not get all tweak-in-a-tweak*, Sugar.' He called over to one of the serving maids. 'Hey, Pretty, two more jugs of the spiced wine and flagons over here.' She pursed her lips, then turned to fetch more wine.

'Hast swallowed a lemon, lass?' he called after her.

'Best you give her a coin for her trouble, Zeal. Or she'll spit in our drinks.'

'I can give her something for her trouble,' Franny said salaciously. 'Ah, here comes the beautiful lady,' Franny stood up and bowed, as she returned putting the tray on our table. 'Where have you been all my life, darling?'

'Elsewhere by good fortune,' came the riposte, before she turned away with a swish of her skirts.

'A hit, a palpable hit,' said Peter, as the rest of us burst out laughing.

'She's smitten, I can tell,' said Franny to more mirth.

The spiced wine was good, but a powerful brew. I could feel it going to my head with the warmth of the fire so close. I was quite giddy with happiness, and wine, despite the war. In a few months I had made good friends and a name for myself.

When I say a name, I mean as more than a dissolute wastrel.

The music changed to the Wassail; I recognised the version from home. The musicians must have been from the West Country.

---

*   Vexed or angry.

'Wassail! Wassail! All over the town,
Our toast it is white and our ale it is brown;
Our bowl it is made of the white maple tree;
With the wassailing bowl, we'll drink to thee.'

Wassailing at Yule is tame nowadays; it was not so innocent when I was a boy. Now it is groups of churchgoers in their Sunday best. Singing their damned hymns from house to house for cinnamon biscuits and chocolate. Then it was soused rowdiness, a Wassail and a drink, or a broken home. Feeling the effects of the spiced wine, I began to join in.

'Here's to our horse, and to his right ear,
God send our Master a happy new year:
A happy new year as e'er he did see,
With my wassailing bowl I drink to thee.'

A couple of the others were laughing at me, but I carried on nonetheless. Jumping on the table, I tipped my hat back and raised my tankard to the bar room, as I bellowed out the next verse.

'Here's to our mare, and to her right eye,
God send our mistress a good Christmas pie;
A good Christmas pie as e'er I did see,
With my wassailing bowl I drink to thee.'

I bowed to the cheers as the song came to an end, though I suspect most were cheering that I had stopped. There was however, a discordant note that dampened our moods.

'Well, if it be not Sugar Candy.' Smirky Pask and some bullies. 'And his interfering friend.' he glanced at Peter, who stood up.

'Well, if it be not Hurry's troopers, we thought all you craven girls had run home after Kineton,' said Peter.

'Here comes trouble,' said Franny.

I saw a small brown turd fly from the turnspit and hit Franny in the face. Trouble indeed: the dog in the wheel had shat itself. I burst out laughing, lost balance, and fell upon Pask in a clatter of jugs and tankards. Then all hell broke loose.

Pask reached for me on the floor and we started struggling, until Peter smashed him over the head with a stool. Zeal had jumped upon two of Pask's bullies and was giving them a beating. I ducked, as an earthenware bottle flashed past my face, and got to my feet.

The tavern owner yelled, fetched out a club, and rushed with it at Sam Brayne, who stepped back out of the way knocking into a couple more drinkers. One of Pask's bullies grabbed my legs, bringing me back down to the floor. I kicked out with my boots, just as another body fell over me, trapping me under it.

The Lord of Misrule reigned unchecked, as drunks fought with each other. It was a devilish fine brawl really. Then Franny shot the damn dog.

As I struggled to get the unconscious body off, the pretty maid started screaming in terror at the gunfire.

Up went the cry: 'The Watch, call the constables out.' My arms were pinned back and I took a kick to the stomach.

'The watch, call out the watch!'

Oh bugger, I thought.

There was a rattle of keys in the lock, and the door opened. Everyone in the cell looked over expectantly, and the raggedy inmates all shuffled towards the sound. The gaoler entered, a coarse lump of a man, with pockmarked face and untrimmed beard. He was accompanied by my Uncle Samuel and behind them Everard.

'Damn,' muttered Franny.

Uncle Samuel looked at us then to the gaoler. 'Yes, these are my men,' then he turned back to us. 'I am most displeased, gentlemen, most displeased indeed. My Cornet and a chosen man, and you, Mr Cole? A man who holds his commission because of my patronage. I am not impressed with this at all.'

Franny started to say something but my uncle cut him off.

'I will not hear your excuses or apologies, Mr Cole. Actions are what count. It is up to you to seek redemption in your future behaviour. Penitent words are hollow without penitent deeds.'

Everard shook his head at us behind my uncle's back, silently laughing at our sorry looks and unsavoury state. Without even looking at him, Uncle Samuel said in a caustic voice.

'Mocking their misfortune is most unworthy, William. '

Ha! That shut him up.

'Now, gentlemen, I have been called away from an urgent meeting at the House to deal with this. Cole, Miller, I would have thought that both of you had seen the inside of places like this once-too-often already.'

Zeal and Franny looked sheepishly at the floor rather than at tiny Uncle Samuel. A ridiculous sight, given they both towered like giants over his Jack, but I was not laughing as he turned on me.

'Blandford, my own blood behaving in such coarse manner is truly a disgrace to me. I had hoped after your valour at Kineton that you were on the road to redemption. Alas, you still have some distance to travel.'

My uncle's disappointment was worse than my father's temper. I felt a burning embarrassment at his displeasure. My father would have ranted and raved, and I would have ignored him. Uncle Samuel got my attention in an instant.

'Well, gentlemen, I have paid your fines, but make no

mistake; it will be deducted from your pay. I will leave you to explain that to your wife, Mr Miller,' Zeal nodded. 'You are fortunate indeed I was back in the city, and Mr Russell had the good sense to come and find me after you started brawling.' Peter was coming out of it smelling of roses.

My Uncle continued. 'I will expect only exemplary behaviour from you over the next few months, gentlemen. My scouts will not gain a reputation for drunkenness and ill discipline.'

'Yes, sir,' we chorused in sorrow.

'Now, you may return to your quarters,' he looked at the gaoler who nodded. Uncle Samuel turned as if to leave, then remembering something turned back. 'One other thing, gentlemen.' We all looked at him expecting further punishment.

'Merry Christmas.'

I ran up the side streets, across the city, past the wall towards the Strand. It was Christmas Eve and the apprentices were out drinking to their masters health. This would soon mean brawling and singing, already the strains of *We Wish You a Merry Christmas*[32] could be heard coming from taverns as I rushed past; I was late. Turning a corner, I saw her outside the shop; stood there alone — I slowed to a walk. She turned, and seeing me, smiled. Honest pleasure at my approach; it is not often I get that response.

After the death of her father, Emily had taken work minding the shop of an apothecary. The owner, Widow Crosse, was a vast woman, with more chins than a Bishop, and voluminous breasts bursting out of her bodice. A guildsman made the pills, packets, and potions for the customers in the back of the shop, whilst Emily served out front. Russell had left his family provided for with the house in Cheapside, and a small rent from land in Kent, but the family needed Emily's monies.

'Blandford, only just in time, I was about to leave.' The shop had been closed some time; she had waited for me.

'I had to see Uncle Samuel,' I explained.

'It has been a strange day,' she told me, eyes twinkling with laughter.

'Really, why?' Damn me, but her smile was captivating; I could not take my eyes off her.

'Widow Crosse has a new suitor,'

The Widow Crosse had many suitors, none seemed to stay around, perhaps it was her blubberiness, perhaps her whiny high-pitched voice, but there was little attractive about the woman excepting her purse.

'What is this one like?' I asked.

'Scrawny and short,' she told me, 'with a pock marked face. His name is Cademan; he was distiller to the Queen.'[33]

'Really? I suppose business has been poor since the King left for Oxford. Another scoundrel looking to pay off his debts I wager.'

She sighed, 'I feel sorry for her. All Widow Crosse wants is a husband to take care of her.'

'Well, there's a lot of her to take care of,' I said with a grin.

She tapped my arm playfully, 'Be not unkind, she eats to quench her misery, yet food is her the cause of her anguish. I pray this one brings her the happiness she deserves, but to see them together, Fattypuff and Scrawnykins.' She giggled deliciously.

'And you call me unkind?' I said. 'Who is the one making up names?'

We reached her mother's house, and she turned to face me, for a moment I thought she would lean in to kiss me, and my heart started pounding, hammering in my chest, but she just smiled and brushed some fleck of dirt from my doublet, then bade me good Christmas. Turning, she lifted her skirts to cross the muddy road, and disappeared into the courtyard of the house. I leaned back against the wall and started to breathe again.

She made me a better person, I think. We would talk about everything as we walked. She was bright, and funny, and devout. Emily lived for her God, and it infected everything with enthusiasm. I had no thoughts of debauchery; I can say that in my defence. Indeed, as I listened to her arguments — so clearly stated and so captivatingly deployed — she made perfect sense to me. I attended church so as to sit near her, and teetered on the edge of becoming godly.

That is how they get you — through the women. They did it to the pagan emperors and the Saxon kings. Sent them punks to seduce them to the word of Christ. 'Tis passing clever when you think on it.

7. Mercurius Aulicus, January 1643.

The world hath long enough been abused with falsehoods: And there's a weekly cheat put out to nourish the abuse amongst the people, and make them pay for their seducement. And that the world may see that the Court is neither so barren of intelligence, as it is conceived; nor the affairs thereof in so unprosperous a condition, as these Pamphlets make them.

(John Berkenhead/Peter Heylyn -
Mercurius Aulicus, Jan 1st 1643, Issue Number 1.)

I know that my feasting offended both Everard and Peter. Although neither complained directly to me, there was a general air of disapproval when I came home soused. Admittedly, a loud drunk rolling up late at night, interrupting theological discussions with insensible ramblings and puking in the piss-pot, would upset anyone.

By Twelfth Night I was without funds. Drinking, whoring, and gambling are expensive pastimes — more so when you lose — so I returned to Bread Street sober and early. Peter was sitting at the table reading in a fury; Everard dozing in the cot by the fire.

'Have you read this new pamphlet?'

I looked at the front-page. *'Mercurius Aulicus*, yes of course,' I replied. ''Tis everywhere, selling for a sixpence down by the Beargarden.'[34]

'This is what I mean,' he said. 'They are openly selling these lies all over the city. Where do they come from? Why does the mayor not stop it?'

'Well, I suppose a press in the city somewhere, there are enough Royalists around,' said I.

Like everywhere else in England, London was a divided city.

'It must be stopped; these lies will only whip the populace into frenzy,' he insisted.

'Pish, 'tis not that bad, Peter,' I picked up the newsbook. 'Seems even quite amusing in parts.'

'Something must be done,' he said, ignoring my comment.

Something must be done: the words of the parochial Englishman whenever his world is threatened. I suppose I should have stopped him, but really, what would he do? Complain to a few aldermen or a clerk at the Lord Mayor's office. I worried more about where I would breakfast in the morning, or finding some coal to stop the shivers, than chasing down Royalist pamphleteers.

'Read this,' he turned to a different pamphlet. *News from Kineton.'* I understood his fury on reading aloud.

"Between twelve and one of the clock in the morning was heard by some shepherds, and other country-men, and travellers, first the sound of drummers afar off, and the noise of soldiers, giving out their last groans; at which they were much amazed.

But then on the sudden, in the air appeared incorporeal soldiers that made those clamours, and amazingly, with ensigns displayed, drums beating, muskets going off, cannons discharged, horses neighing, the alarm or entrance to this game of death was struck up."

'Oh, Peter, you do not think that you will see your father again? Ghostly battles in the sky, it is just so much arse-gravy.' I went myself to the battlefield years later, in hope of seeing apparitions, and saw and heard nothing. Superstition and wild imagination, is all.[35]

'By all that is Holy, Blandford. I know these for the lies that they are, but simpletons on the streets? They devour the deceit amongst the half-truths and jests, and soon start believing the rubbish.'

''Tis as well, I feared you were set for Bedlam; take no heed of them — there was a story in one about a child in Bristol born with horns and a tail. Nobody believes it.'

He snorted. 'A parcel came for you today,' gesturing to the dresser.

'For me?' That was a surprise; I was expecting no parcel.

'Who is it from?'

'Your sister,' said Everard from his cot. 'Now will you two hush up; I am trying to sleep.'

There was a letter with the parcel — Elizabeth's hand and the exquisitely inked little oak leaf that she drew on all her letters as a sigil — I ripped open the seal.

My Dearest Brother,

It fell upon me to write you with our news since you have been most neglectful in your cLorrespondence. I am confident you long to hear from me, and I hope this will come to your hand quickly.

Our father has been unwell. He has been sick with convulsions and sickness, but the physicians can find no cause for the malady. Anne and I tend to him most conscientiously, and he is still able to direct our affairs. I hope and pray that he will soon recover his full fitness. With his own home burned out by rebel troopers, Rector Carpenter has availed himself of our hospitality, and at least offers Father some companionship.

Your brother's union has been blessed by the Lord; showing the righteousness of their bond! The whole village turned out for the ceremony and the feast that followed. Henry's troopers paraded the couple, and though circumstances of war separate them, she quickly fell with child.

Our resources are much diminished, with our plate being taken for the King by your brothers, and trade is much disrupted. With the coming of war, prices are increased, and many of the men have gone from the estate with Henry. Even so, our God still takes care of us, and has shown his power in preserving us, dear brother. I have made arrangement with Mr Bestney Barker, who has chambers at the Inner Temple, for your keep. A sum of forty pounds is held there for you.[36]

James was able to visit from Oxford and brought word that he saw you at Kineton. I am mightily proud of you serving the godly cause so well, but am eager to hear more. Write me dear brother. We are so far removed from great events and weighty matters, that news only comes to us in trickles. The war seems so distant but I pray that you, and your brothers, are safe nightly. Send me news of your doings, of London, and the places you have seen.

I have enclosed a cake with the carrier, but he is of a base sort and not the usual man. If he does not deliver it, I have told him he will be thrashed.

Pray often, for prayer is a shield to the soul, a sacrifice to God, and a scourge for Satan. You fight for the godly; so be upright, dear brother, and trust in the Lord, for his will is all.

Your loving and affectionate sister,
Elizabeth.

Carpenter's presence at home meant she would be subjected to daily lectures about duty to the King and Archbishop. My father, the sycophant, would lap it all up like a dog at vomit, but neither Elizabeth or Anne would be amused by the rector's groping. That cheered me up.

The rest of her letter showed the madness of civil conflict. On the one hand, she was urging me to do battle for the godly, whilst on the other hoping my brothers were safe fighting for the King. I wondered how she squared that circle. And the marriage? It meant she had not told Henry about my indiscretions. He would not knowingly wear horns at the altar. The affair seemed long ago by then anyway. Like so many in England who lived through it, I divided my life into two parts, before Edgehill and after.

'There is a cake,' I told the others.

'A cake?' asked Everard sitting up.

I cut him a slice. My sister's fruitcake was good; she could cook well. She would have made someone a good wife if she had not been such a nagging witch.

'At least the courier delivered it, Elizabeth was unsure he would, different to the usual one, she says.'

'Fine woman your sister,' said Everard, with his mouth full

of cake. 'Always been decent to me.'

'To you?' I looked at him in surprise. 'When did you meet my sister?'

'Who do you think the normal carrier is? I've been picking up letters and the like, from your sister to your uncle, for a few years now.'

I was incredulous that Elizabeth could have been so clandestine as to carry on a correspondence. Damn, I must have searched her room enough times looking for some coin to steal. It was starting to dawn on me, that my elder sister was more clever than I had ever given her credit. I must also confess that the thought of Everard consorting with Elizabeth, without the family's knowledge, was somewhat unseemly — he was after all a peasant, and I am an hypocrite — 'twas another sign of how the world was turning.

You see, I am a gentleman. Oh, I may be a liar and a thief, and my soul is almost certainly damned, yet I am a gentleman still. I have the right accent, the right clothes and good boots; the perfect air of hereditary privilege. I am used to servants doffing their caps and scraping my boots. Everard — an infinitely better man — was my social inferior, and I never let him forget it. He endured my arrogance, mostly with good humour, and we became friends, but he always hated what I was. The New Israel would be one of equality for all, and he was maddeningly stubborn about it, chanting, *'When Adam delved and Eve span. Who then was the gentleman?'** at me like a monk at matins. He was disappointed in the end, like so many others, and I think that broke his mind.

'Letters about what exactly?' I asked.

'I have no idea,' replied Everard, 'but I know your uncle values her news.' He added going in for another bite.

'Peter?' He looked up from his reading, 'Cake?'

'What? Hum no, no thank'ee, Blandford,' he pushed the papers aside. 'Some wine though.'

---

* John Ball (Attributed by Froissart 1385)

I showed him my letter. 'Forty pounds: I am rich,' and poured him a drink.

'A goodly sum, I am hoping you are going to put it aside, but I fear you will waste it,' he said smiling.[37]

'Well, maybe a new hat and suit of clothes, cloak, some good boots, and dinner at The Bear for us all,' I said.

I like hats, everyone has vices and hats are one of mine, no need to dwell on it.

'A new hat?' said Everard in his drab woodsman garb. 'Not another red one, please. The other one makes you look like a damn cardinal; 'tis embarrassing when we are on parade.'

'Everyone's a critic,' I protested, as Peter burst out laughing.

'I am just a little perplexed as to where Elizabeth has managed to get all this money from?' I said. 'My father ships through Portsmouth and Southampton, not London.'

It was the next day, and we were sat in the shabby office of my sister's lawyer near the Inner Temple. A round little man with white tufted brows, a shining bald crown, and long grey beard. The thick spectacles perched on his nose gave his eyes an oversized aspect; like an owl.

'Ah well, Mr Candy. I cannot tell you anything about your father's industry, but your sister wrote to me some years ago asking me to invest funds. However,' Mr Barker told me firmly. 'Your father has most certainly approved the transactions. I have this letter from him, yes, yes.'

He has most certainly not, I thought to myself, but there was his hand and a letter giving Elizabeth control of the funds.

Forgery and embezzlement are such dirty words, blackmail is another. I am sure you can see where I am leading with this.

'How are her investments doing, Mr Barker?'

'Her main investments were doing very well until last September and the closures, yes, yes, but she still has some income. I hope she will be pleased.'

'Last September? You mean. Oh, this is wonderful,' a grin broke over my face. 'Elizabeth has been investing in the theatre?'

'Yes, yes, your sister owns a share in the Phoenix Theatre,' then he looked concerned. 'That is not a problem, is it, Mr Candy? Your sister is a good client; I would not wish her investments to prove vexatious. Most of my work has come through the theatres over the years. I assumed your sister understood that?'

'No, Mr Barker,' I replied calmly, although inside I was screaming with laughter at my sister's wealth coming from "devilment". 'I am sure Elizabeth will be satisfied. You say she has other investments?'

'Indeed, sir, some rents from a couple of small businesses; a baker's in Eastcheap for instance.'

'Yes, yes,' said Everard innocently. I choked back a laugh, eager not to insult Mr Barker. He seemed a nice enough old sort, and you never know when you will need a lawyer.

'Thank you, sir,' I said shaking his hand, 'If I ever have need of an advocate, you will be the first I ask.'

He smiled, thanked me, and led us back down the stairs trailing dust as he went. Finally, closing the door behind us, we waited for a second and then both burst out laughing.

Somerset House is a huge sprawl of buildings out west with great gardens facing onto the river. In peaceful times it was the Queen's London home, but had been abandoned when she had fled with the King. The only inhabitants now were the pigeons and a couple of French Friars, who spent their time cowering from London's protestant mob.

I got out of the wherry* and took the white stairs up from the river to the garden terrace. A guard was waiting for me, one of Penington's men. I showed him my note, and he gestured down a tree-lined path to an open yard.

I nodded and walked down the path. I had woken late that morning to empty chambers, and an anonymous note telling me to be at Somerset House by noon. I had thrown on my new cloak and hat, and taken a wherry from the Bridge, along the river, to the Queen's palace.

At the end of the path there were more guards, dressed in red and black this time. One of them pointed to the chapel — the Queen's catholic chapel.

'Her Ladyship awaits you there, sir,' said the guard.

Again I nodded in silence, and walked up to the chapel doorway. I pushed open the small inset entrance, and stepped into the nave of the chapel, all fluted columns and arches, its floor dabbled reds, and greens, and blues, by the great stained glass windows.

The chapel would have given Everard apoplexy, filled with saintly icons, and bright painted walls, with a carved rood screen covered in gold leaf, and behind, candles flickering at the jewelled altar. Perhaps, I should have been disgusted by such flagrant papist symbols, but above the altar, instantly fixing my gaze, was the most fantastic painting.

A life-size Christ, crucified, reached up to the carved ceiling, anguished eyes gazing heavenwards. It upset my newly found facade of Puritanism. The realism of the image was astonishing; I had never seen the like; painted by someone who understood how torment and pain rack the human form. The saviour's mouth grimaced in the agony of death, his limbs twisting from their sockets. The colours so vivid and bright

---

*   Clinker built riverboat.

I felt I could have walked right into the picture, and stood with the legionaries and women at the messiah's feet. I was lost in the painting, astounded by it, and did not notice the woman enter the chapel. How long she stood, watching me enraptured, I do not know. In the end, she coughed politely to gain my attention.[38]

At first I did not recognise her, but she stepped out of the shadows, and the sunlight caught her face. The beautiful and nameless matron from Syon House. Dressed for riding this time, her dark auburn hair tied back, but face perfectly made up. She wore a long wine coloured doublet, buttoned up the front, covering deep skirts and boots. A wide brimmed cavalier bonnet was tilted on her head to complete the outfit, and a crop held tightly in her hand.

I bowed quickly, saying. 'My Apologies, Milady. I did not hear you come in.'

'Pray, do not apologise; it is magnificent, is it not?' She skipped up the steps — past the screen — and walked behind the altar, reaching out to the picture, and sacrilegiously brushed a gloved finger along the base of the cross, to where painted rivulets of blood ran down the canvas.

'Yes,' I agreed. 'It is a marvel indeed.'

She turned to face me and placed one hand to her chin as if contemplating, then: 'Her Majesty would be most distressed if something were to happen to it.'

I did not know what to say to that. Frankly, I was surprised such a work — wondrous as it was — had survived so long. Some philistine was bound to rip it down sooner or later. Me? I would have sold it for a king's ransom and retired on the funds.

'Your friend Mr Russell has been looking for the Aulicus press, I hear,' she said.

I looked at her incredulous. Peter had been asking questions for a few days, but with no result. A wild goose chase as far as I was concerned. We knew that the newsbooks were smuggled into the city from the East End by washerwomen, but nothing else.

'How did you know that, Milady?'

She smiled at me. 'I always believe in following the exploits of promising young men. Perhaps, you should question your business partner as to the whereabouts of the press.'

That was even more confusing. 'Business partner? I have no business partner, Milady.'

'You own a share in the Phoenix Theatre, do you not?'

'Ah no, not me. My sister Elizabeth.' This woman knew far too much about my affairs for my liking — no matter how beautiful.

'I hear that Mr Beeston of the Phoenix can always find information for a price. Perhaps he could help you in your quest.'

'Pray, madam, might I know your name?' The lack of introduction had gone on for far too long. Damned rude if you ask me.

Again with the mysterious smile. 'Oh, I think that for now, Sugar Candy, you may simply call me friend. Now, there is a boat waiting to take you back to the city. I am sure you have some people to speak with. Good day to you.'

I bowed again as she left the chapel, leaving me with my unanswered questions. She was enticing and beautiful, certainly, but my belly told me the pretty lady was trouble. One last glance at the painting, then I left the chapel and took the wherry back to the bridge and home. Peter was there when I arrived, frustrated after more fruitless investigations. I told him of my encounter, knowing that he would be enthused about the information, regardless of whence it came.

'Well then, we should ask your sister's lawyer about this Beeston,' said Peter. 'I remember him from the stage. He always played the villain.'

Mercurius Aulicus 7 Jan 1643:

By an express sent from the West Country, the fortunes and success of Sir Ralph Hopton, were this day made known unto His Majesty. In which it was declared, that having possessed himself of Powderham Castle, and lying now before the City of Exeter with part of his forces, and yet leaving no fewer than 1500 men at Milbrooke, some at Saltash, and some at Torrington. He hath appointed Sir Bevil Grenville, and Colonel Godolphin with their Regiments to seize Topsham, the Sea-town to Exeter, which bred so great a fear within the rebel city, that diverse of the people got over the walls by night, and fled away.

For the regaining of which place, the governor of the Topsham Sir George Chudleigh, having committed most of the well-affected persons, and with much inhumanity, compelled some of them to pay twenty pounds a week, some ten, some five, for the maintaining of the war; conspired with some corrupt inhabitants on Wednesday the 28th of December to fire the town. Then whilst the soldiers laboured in the quenching of it, he with his forces out of Exeter might regain the same.

But notice being given of his design; our soldiers placed some musketeers within the hedges, and lodged others within the covert of their breastworks, and gave him such an hot welcome at their first approach, that they retreated with more haste then they marched thither.

Within a quarter of an hour, they made head again, but were received so stoutly by the Cornish Forces, who with much eagerness discharged upon them, that they retired with great confusion; carrying back with them a cart laden with dead bodies, besides those which they brought back on horses, and seven which they had left behind at the town. The Cornish having lost but one man, and but four of them only hurt, one of which was shot in at the mouth, and out at the ear, which wound is thought will prove mortal to him.

The Cornish had good store of pillage, good buff coats,

a beaver hat, many swords, twelve muskets, and a scarlet coat lined with plush; Yet, when the enemy was come back to Exeter, it was reported by them that they had the victory, and thanks were given to God for that happy day.

Never were men so thankful, as some have been lately, for being beaten so often, and so thoroughly beaten.

John Berkenhead/Peter Heylyn.[39]

8. The Cockpit, January 1643.

I am no haunter of the plays, to pick poor people's purses,
Nor one that, every word he says,
doth coin new oaths and curses:
If I do run on tapsters' scores, to pay them I am wary,
Let others spend their means on whores,
I love mine own vagary.

(Traditional, *A Light Heart's A Jewel.*)

The crowd roared as two gamecocks were thrust into the pit. The noise was thunderous within the Phoenix. Over two hundred people were crowded around the galleries and stage; shouting wagers, baying for blood.

My sister's theatre was no roofless stage in the round. This was covered, with pit in front of the stage and semicircle of stall, and three levels of gallery. Brick and stone, wood and velvet, rough benches below, opulent seats above.

The raised stage had more seating, and tables with food and drinks, whilst a small dirt circle was marked out in the pit for the contests. Two small boys jumped in behind the birds, waving caps, and driving them into battle. I had put half a crown on the red, but already regretted the decision. The speckled cock's head thrust forward as they circled each other, feathers sticking out and wings flapping. Red looked too cautious.

Wagers were still being shouted down to the Pit Master, as gentlemen, knaves, even the odd masked woman of quality, screamed at each peck or scratch.

Red's handler nudged his charge, urging the bird to fight. Then he skipped back around the dirt circle as the bird struck. Pulled feathers from Speckles' neck fell to the ground, and Red, crowing now, circled, looking to attack again.

Perhaps I would win my wager after all. I moved to the side to get a better view, past the archway, down into the pit itself.

'I cannot see him,' Peter shouted in my ear.

'Perhaps he has not yet arrived,' I yelled back, keeping my eyes on the spectacle below.

Speckles looked a disorderly mess, struck by Red over and over again. I should have wagered more than half a crown. I looked over to the Pit Master wondering if I could get another bet on.

'This is vile entertainment, setting God's creatures against each other.'

'The Romans did it.' I looked away from the fight.

'That is no justification, the Romans crucified our Lord.'

'Will you stop worrying; Barker told us Beeston would be here.'

A night's baiting was a rare treat, and I did not want Peter dampening the mood by being a venerable killjoy. It was not that the godly hated fun, most were happy enough, but they were always so damn moral. In those days everybody went to the ring, from prince to pauper, although now it is out of fashion amongst the quality.[40]

Speckles finally launched into an attack, the crowd shouted, leaping from their seats. I stood up and stretched my neck to see. Red was pinned under a crowing Speckles. Damn! I had missed the finish and lost the bet.

The spectators drifted away, some grabbing drinks and food, others checking the birds for later bouts.

'There he is.' Peter pointed to a figure, in red, on the other side of the cockpit.

'Are you sure 'tis he?'

'I saw him on the stage before the closures.'

'Let us see what he has to say for himself then.' The crowd were coming back to their places ready for the next bout.

We left our seats in the gallery, and went down to the crowded stalls. He was sitting, watching as the pit was raked over and made ready. Peter tapped the man on the shoulder, and whispered something in his ear.

They came over to me. Beeston was dressed all in scarlet, with greasy black ringlets, bunched, cascading down his back and staining his falling band grey. He was actually wearing make-up; caked in the damn stuff. His face an emotionless mask because of it. The two thick gold rings in his ears made him look like a sailor.

'My name is Septimus Hutchinson,' he said. 'I am the proprietor, at your service. What is your desire?'

'Your name is William Beeston. You are the manager, not proprietor, and this event is illegal,' said Peter.[41]

Beeston looked at one of the lackeys who had followed him over. Big bastard, I did not fancy a tangle in this crowd.

'You are well informed, sir,' he said. 'Hutchinson is merely a stage name for when I tread the boards. And who might you gentlemen be?'

'We are interested in information, sir,' said Peter. 'Information is one of your services, is it not?'

'Information comes at a cost,' said Beeston. 'What is it you fine young gentlemen wish to know?'

Peter looked at me then back to Beeston. 'We wish to know where to find the Aulicus press.'

'That is very costly information indeed.'

'Well, Mr Beeston, that is where I come in,' I said. 'I am your business partner.'

That made him laugh. 'I thank you, but I have business partners enough.'

'And I fear that you utilise my theatre for illegal purposes,' I carried on. 'My name is Candy, nephew to Samuel Luke, and I would like to know where my share of this event is?'

The look on his face was a sight; his mouth drooped so much it cracked the paintwork. Uncle Samuel was Scoutmaster General for Parliament, and his name would have been enough I think. Elizabeth's share in the theatre was but a garnish.

'What do you want?'

'Just the information,' I said, 'and some monies to be paid to Mr Barker on time next month.' I looked over at the crowd. 'I am sure you can afford it.'

'The Devil's Tavern,' he said, then turned to leave.

'The money, Mr Beeston?'

'You will get your due.' He walked away.

From Drury Lane it is a straight walk down Fleet Street into the city and home; well lit, with guards and gates, and people still about on business — safe enough from footpads and bashers. New gives way to old; stone and brick are followed by wood and plaster, blackened by age and smoke. Then over the Fleet — a stinking drizzle of excrement — and into the city at Ludgate. I babbled happily to Peter about my evening's winnings as we walked, but he, lost in thought, said little.

After passing under Ludgate, and the squad of men from the Trained Bands, Peter pulled me right, down towards the river into the dark rabbit warren of alleys and narrow lanes that back onto Fish Street. Old wooden buildings lurched drunkenly over muck-covered cobbles, the overhanging eaves forming gloomy tunnels through the night.

'We are being followed,' said Peter, pulling me along.

'What? Where?'

'Do not look: there are two behind. They have been marking us since the Phoenix and followed us back to the city. When we get to the next corner follow me.'

At the next corner we both took off like hares, sprinting down towards the river, then cutting along Fish Street, and turning into the southern end of Bread Street. At the gates of St Matilda's, we stopped to catch our breath for a second.

'Do they follow still?' I asked.

'No, oh wait,' two men came running round the corner into the street after us.

We both turned to run for home, only yards away, but a man in dark leather breeches and coat, sword in hand, stepped out from the church gates, as the two behind caught up. Three against two. Bugger!

'You boys are in trouble,' said Dark Leathers.

One of the bashers swung at me with his cudgel, making me step to the side, as Peter drew his sword and stepped up to Dark Leathers. I faced off against the two ruffians with clubs— watermen, by their bare feet and barrel chests. I waved my steel, making them back out of reach, but there was no room for manoeuvre in the narrow street. To get at me they would have to come in a rush, and at least one of them would be run through. Neither looked excited by that prospect. To my back I could hear the clash of blades as Peter fenced with Dark Leathers in front of the church gates.

The watermen paused briefly then, in unspoken agreement, attacked. One ran blindly into my steel, the weight of his own charge driving the blade into his chest. He fell groaning to the ground, as the other smashed into me, pushing me up against the wall. Cudgel pressed flat against my chest as he raised a dagger to strike at me.

Unable to move my sword to get at him, I leaned my head forward and bit the tip of his nose off. He staggered back, screaming, hands reaching up to his gnawed proboscis. Spitting out blood and gristle, I stuck him in the belly, silencing his cries with my steel. Turning to Peter and Dark Leathers I could see that they were evenly matched, but there was no room to get at him. I stamped on one of the groaning watermen, and dropped my sword, to load my pistol.

Fingers shaking with nerves, I fumbled at the powder and shot, spilling some as I rammed it home and added the primer. I raised it to aim at Dark Leathers, just as he ran Peter through the side. My friend slumped to the ground with a moan; I pulled the trigger — flash-in-the-pan — a misfire.

Dark Leathers looked at me, ready to attack, but breathing heavily from his duel with Peter, and bleeding from a cut to the shoulder. I think he was ready to go for me, till out of the darkness a screaming banshee charged him, swinging a bucket at his sword, and throwing him backwards. I threw a quick prayer of thanks for my deliverance to the heavens, and grabbed up my sword ready to fight. Dark Leathers was not waiting around; faced by me, and a pail-wielding bundle of rags, he turned and ran towards Cheapside.

I did not follow, instead rushed to Peter, struck out prone on the cobbles. There were bruises to the head, but the bleeding was coming from a wound at his side. We were close enough to home. I called over to the bucket swinger.

'Help me and there's a shilling in it for you.'

He nodded and came forward. He seemed strong enough, but with beard covered face and wearing rags. Together we hoisted Peter up and carried him back home. I hammered on the door of the tenement, until Everard opened it smoking his pipe.

'What has happened?' he said.

'We were attacked; he has been stabbed.'

Everard looked at the wound, ''Not deep, blood loss is the worst, look how pale he is. We must fetch him upstairs, Blandford.' Between us, we carried him up the stairs and onto the cot by the fire.

'What is your name?' I asked the bucket man.

'Jacob, sir.' he touched a dirty forelock. 'You mentioned a reward, sir.'

Everard interrupted. 'Water, Blandford, I need boiling water. Throw a handful of salt in there as well,' and he leaned over to tend to Peter.

Jacob rushed to get a fire set and water started without any questions. A shilling is a fortune to a man in rags.

I watched as Everard cut away Peter's doublet and the

shirt underneath. He took one of my new shirts and ripped it into strips. When the water was boiled, he carefully cleaned around the wound, wiping away clotted blood. He looked up at me.

"'Tis shallow, skidded off the ribs, but I need to sew him up.'

Slowly and carefully, he sewed the wound together, then took some herbs from one of his pouches, made a green mush with some vinegar, and slapped it onto the wound. Peter groaned but did not come around.

Jacob washed up well; shaved, and in a set of old clothes, boots and a bonnet of mine. I was quite proud of the transformation. He claimed to be an old soldier fallen on hard times; a mercenary from Germany, but knew the chores of a domestic well enough. Grey-haired but still strong, he quickly made himself useful. Everard called it a vanity, but I hired him on at sixpence a day to be my valet; a gentleman's gentleman.

The door opened and Everard came in. We had heard the downstairs door, and tramp on the stairs; Jacob had a hot bowl of stew waiting and reached to take his wet cloak as he arrived.

'You are not my servant, friend,' said the sanctimonious turd. 'We are all brothers to the Lord.'

Pish! William Everard was a rude poacher not a prophet, and I noticed he took the stew happily enough.

'Did you find anything?' Peter asked from his cot by the fire.

'Oh 'tis the Devil's Tavern right enough,' said Everard, between spoonfuls of stew. 'I watched them load up carts with bundles of newsbooks and cover them with laundry. They must have a press in the back by the river.'

'What is the Devil's Tavern and why have I not heard of it?' I asked.

'Because you spend your time south of the river whoring, drinking, and gambling,' said Everard, 'but for smuggling, thieves or pirates go to the Pelican in Wapping. Sir Samuel will not be back in London for a few more days, and you two have stirred up a right hornets' nest.'

'What did Darnelly say?' asked Peter.

'He has gone to the country with his family, like everybody else of worth. I told an officer in the Whitecoats about Beeston's little gathering; so at least that will be closed down.'

'Killjoy,' I muttered.

'Then what do we do about the press?' said Peter, ignoring me.

'We deal with it ourselves,' I said. 'This information is the gift of providence is it not?' That raised an eyebrow from Everard, but I carried on before he could protest. 'We get Zeal and some of the boys together tonight, and take a boat down to Wapping.' I must confess I saw a chance to win some glory and leapt at it.

Everard paused for a moment and I thought he would argue. Instead he just nodded, 'I will get myself over to the boys in Aldgate, and see how many we can get back here tonight,' he said.

'Tonight?' asked Peter, concern on his face. 'I will not be ready tonight.'

'Must strike while the iron is hot, Peter. You will have to go to your mother's; 'tis too dangerous to leave you here alone.' I could see he was disappointed, but we had no choice. If we moved quickly, we could close them down permanently.

Everard gathered his sword and pistols, took his cloak off Jacob, and left to fetch Zeal and the others.

'You have changed,' said Peter quietly.

'I have?' I looked at him in surprise. 'In what way?'

He smiled, 'That spoiled young brat with a clever tongue, running away from home, is turning into an officer and perhaps a gentleman.'

I laughed, 'You flatter me. I share not your impossible sense of duty to Parliament.'

'Oh bugger Parliament,' he said, wincing as he shifted his weight.

'Well, that is a very cavalier attitude to take,' I quipped. It was a poor joke but popular at the time, and it made him laugh.

'Bastard, do not make me laugh, my side hurts.' He groaned, then in a quiet voice, 'now what, Blandford?'

I tried to reassure him. 'Now? Now we wait for Everard to get back with some of the boys, then we go down that tavern, and kill the shit-breeches who did this.'

Sir,

I send to you news of a great victory out of the west by God's grace.

Yesterday morn, I led my troop from Boconnoc towards Liskard in the van of My Lord Hopton's column. We sighted the rebel forces under Lord Ruthven about nine in the morning. The rebel army, many thousands strong, drew up in a fair position on a hill and prepared for battle.

For two hours and more we exchanged fire from musket and ordnance and the battle was exceeding hot. The Millner boy was hit in the head and killed outright from small shot. I convey my sorrow to his parents, for he was a sturdy lad and pious in conscience.

About noon we made a great charge uphill against the enemies host and drove all before us. The Cornish Foot, brave and defiant boys, made good work of it, and the Roundheads fled in great distress to Lostwithiel, but the town proved no refuge for them, declaring instead for the King.

We captured near two thousand rebels and march on. Soon I predict we will be home and able to free you from the misery of puritan governance.

I have received word from James that Blandford serves with Uncle Samuel. I confess I am not surprised, yet disappointed. These are sad days indeed when brothers must face brothers.

I wish for you to be duly diligent with my spouse during her confinement. My duty requires me to be absent at this time, which causes me much anguish. Elizabeth writes often, but I would remind you of your words at my marriage, it ill befits us all if my wife is diminished in resource, especially now.

I remain your most humble and obedient son

Henry Candy.
Saltash, Cornwall. 20th January 1643.

9. The Devil's Tavern, January 1643.

I will tell of whores attacked, their lords at home,
Bawds' quarters beaten up, and fortress won,
Windows demolished, watches overcome,
And handsome ills, by my contrivance done.

(John Wilmot, 2nd Earl of Rochester, *The Disabled*
Debauchee.)

It was peaceful, with moonlight, and the soft dip of the oars speeding us across the water. We headed to the river centre, away from the great ships at anchor, and followed the flow of current east. The others were quiet in the boat, but as we neared Wapping and The Devil's Tavern, I whispered some encouragement to them.[42]

'These boys are bullies and ruffians, lads, not soldiers. Show them your steel and they will not dawdle, I wager.' A poor speech I know, but there were a couple of laughs from the boat.

'At least you wear not a bubbie on your head this time, Sugar,' said Sheldon, another from Uncle Samuel's troop, to more chuckles.

'Lesson learned,' I whispered back, pulling my pot on and tightening the strap under the chin. 'Fine hats for wooing, helmets for hewing,' I looked over at Zeal beside me, whispering a prayer to himself, his face white. 'Ready?' I said.

'Aye,' he replied.

I felt the wherry ground on the gravel foreshore, I jumped out followed by the others; we ran to the steps to the side of the inn. Three stories high, with balconies; a bare walkway ran along the side to the street front, and a door on the walkway led into the back room. The windows at the ground level were shuttered; there was nobody on guard. I went up the steps carefully, noting the crack of light coming from the back room shutters, and crept around to the side door.

I could hear the murmur of voices from within. The others were climbing up from the foreshore; I pointed a couple of lads down the walkway to the tavern front. Everard and two of others silently swung themselves up onto the balcony.

Zeal and I went to the side door, both of us had sword and pistol in hand, I took a deep breath, and kicked hard at the lock — it held. There were raised voices coming from inside as the bolt was drawn back.

'What the buggery is going on?' came the question, and the door opened a crack.

Zeal barged into the door, and charged on into a small dimly lit room. I followed on behind. Inside, an old man sprawled on the floor as Zeal struggled with Dark Leathers.

I could see two more with cudgels coming from the back room.

I raised my pistol shouting, 'Yield, you whoresons or I shoot.' Just as the old man on the floor recovered his senses and dived at my legs, knocking me over. My pistol discharged as I hit the ground striking him in the stomach, and Sheldon, jumped over me to help Zeal.

I could hear the clash of sword and explosion of pistol shot coming from outside as I hauled myself to my feet. The old man, writhing and rolling from the hole in his belly, reached out with bloody hands to grab my leg. I stamped on him and lunged at Dark Leathers, sticking him in the stomach. He collapsed, blood seeping out from the wound. Sheldon had fallen to the floor, dead or unconscious I did not know. I ran to help Zeal, his head gashed and bloody, against the last two Cavaliers.

'You would do better to surrender,' I gasped, thrusting at one with my sword, and then pulling back as his cudgel came down to smash it. He stepped back, ducking into the cellar, as Zeal brought the hilt of his sword down on his friend's crown with a crack, and sent him crumpling to the floor.

I pushed past into the back room, lit with oil lamps and

containing a small press, and only one Royalist. Zeal followed me.

'Yield,' I shouted at the Cavalier. 'You are under arrest.'

'Balls to that,' he said, drawing a pistol on me and pulling the trigger.

I flinched, half turned away — and nothing; the bastard had misfired. I thrust at him with my sword, but he skipped behind the press, throwing the pistol at my head and putting me off balance. As I ducked, Zeal flew past me, smashed into the press, and tried to tip it on the Royalist. I jumped to the side as it crashed down to the floor, forcing him back round to face me. I slashed at him, opening a great gash from shoulder to groin. He fell to the floorboards and lay there in a swift growing pool of his own blood.

Finally a pause; I looked around me: a broken press and copies of the newsbook fluttering to the floor. He was still alive, but I had seen the look of death before. He looked at me with eyes surprised.

'You are the boy,' he gasped the words out, '...Bonduca is going to...' He coughed, blood in his throat, and died.

Who the holy titties is Bonduca? I thought, but no time to rest; there was still fighting to be done. Outside, and from above, I could hear the clash of swords and shouts of battle. Zeal checked Sheldon's prone body.

'Dead,' he said with a sigh. 'Lord bless him, he saved me; how are you, Sugar?'

'Unharmed,' I said. 'You?' I looked at the cut on his head.

'I am good, these others,' he gestured to the bodies on the floor, 'are all dead, but for the old man and he will not be going anywhere soon.'

'Well then,' I said, 'let us see how the others fare.'

We went back outside; there were men above me fighting on the balcony, but immediately to my left Everard was struggling with a man in a skullcap. I stabbed the man in the back, and jumped round to face anyone coming along the walkway from the street, but none came. The body of one of the ruffians had been thrown off the upper balcony, and his head had cracked open like a melon, the brain spilt over the stone floor. I retched and Zeal charged past me to the street.

Shouts and the sound of fighting still came from the upper levels. I took a deep breath and raced behind Zeal with Everard following, expecting any moment a sword or shot to send me tumbling down. Instead, as I came out to the street, I ran into a group of green-coated soldiers. Zeal, stood with hands raised, and sword dropped, and three muskets levelled at me.

'Right, and who are you, Dandyboots?' asked one. Everard slammed into me from behind, knocking me to my knees in front of them like a postulant at prayer.

'Cornet Candy,' I replied, getting to my feet when they raised their glowing matchlocks.

The street was full of people: musketeers herding patrons of the inn together, passers-by watching the raid. The tavern was smashed up, with a few bodies lying about; one screeching trull clawing at the prone body of her man. I sighted John Hampden on his horse overseeing the arrests, with a pale Peter beside him.

'Should you not be at your mother's?' I asked Peter when I joined him.

He grimaced. 'When Jacob brought me there, she told us Colonel Hampden was back. I thought you might need some help. So out I crept when she went to church.'

'Well done, Candy,' Hampden jumped down from his horse. 'Well done, indeed,' he repeated. 'We have cut off one of the Hydra's* heads this evening.' he grabbed my hand and pumped it enthusiastically.

'Indeed we have, sir,' I replied. 'The printer is alive but unconscious downstairs.' I led him down to the battle around the walkway, ignoring the broken head, and showed him the fallen press and the stacks of newsbooks.

---

*   Many headed serpent from Greek mythology.

'Organised by whom, I wonder?' He prodded the unconscious printer with his boot. 'Perhaps this odium will tell us when he awakes.' He smiled at me. 'You are making a name for yourself, young man. A colour at Edgehill and now this. No hat though? I am almost disappointed. I will be telling your uncle; I think he will be pleased with your work tonight.'

You must understand that even a few words of encouragement by a man like Hampden would puff anyone up with pride, myself included. He was a hero to us all; more of a leader of Parliament than Pym ever was, and a better man to boot.

He led me back up to the street, where watchmen and Greencoats were carting off all from the tavern. My boys gathered, hoping to get a sight of the great man. A couple of the boatmen had been injured, but only Sheldon was dead. Hampden gave them each a silver half crown, then dismissed us with polite thanks.

'Gentlemen,' he told Peter and me as an afterthought, 'you must come to supper. I will send my man to arrange it,' and waved us off.

The thing about the Hydra is when you cut off a head, two more grow in its place, and the blood and breath are poison. That is what the pamphlets were. Hydras, ever increasing, breathing poison into men's hearts, turning brother against brother with their flights of fancy; all penned by troublemakers and malignants. A thirst for information gave the pamphleteers power over men's minds.

A censor may have his part to play after all; it keeps the journal-writers honest.

I turned to the men, where Everard was gathering half crowns from the troopers.

'William?' I asked.

'For Sheldon's wife, cannot ask the boatmen but...' he shrugged.

'No,' I said, reaching into my doublet for my purse. 'Keep your coins, boys. Send his wife this, there's five pounds or more in it.' Then, I turned away so they could not see my face. Now the rush of battle had passed, I wanted only to weep.

Mercurius Aulicus, 8 February 1643.

There came good news from Sir Ralph Hopton, and the rest of those noble gentlemen in the west. It being certified from thence, that they have gotten Plimpton and besieged Plymouth, and that the Earl of Stamford's soldiers do not only refuse to fight, but flee from him daily, which puts the town to a necessity of yielding, if it be not yielded before this time.

And also, that Sir Bevil Grenville with his forces went towards his own house at Bideford in Devonshire, and hath got possession of the same; by means whereof, if is conceived that he will quickly master Barnstable, being already master of the Haven there, and consequently the mouth of Severn.

John Berkenhead/Peter Heylyn

The Kingdomes Weekly Intelligencer, 8th February 1643.

From the west, It is said Sir Ralph Hopton, now also Baron of Glassenbury, still hangs as a cloud over Plymouth, but it dispels every day, by reason both Exeter and other parts of Devon, send to the assistance of that Town. It was reported that Captain Chudley was taken prisoner by the Hoptonians, which was a misreport, but it is most certain that Mr. Godolphin a Commander in the Army of the Cavaliers is slain.

Richard Collings.

Brother,

I send you greetings from Oxford and news that by the King's grace I am made knight bachelor after the recent action near Cirencester. I have sent the same to our father. It was hard fighting till we fired the town and smothered the rebels in smoke, they fled in disorder and we were victorious.

I was presented at court to His Majesty and honoured by him. The first of our line to hold such. I can only hope that you will soon emulate me in the King's service.

I have received news from Carpenter that your wife is with child and send you my congratulations and felicitations.

I say this to you in fair warning. Have great care in that which you send to our father. Carpenter believes that much is astray, and carriers cannot be secure. Trust nothing that comes from Elizabeth. When we meet in person, I will give you a fuller account of what I have found.

This only I say. Our traitor brother has grand designs around him that concern us both. With God's grace we are forewarned and thus forearmed.

Sir James Candy.
Holton House 9th February 1643. [43]

10. The Codebreaker, February 1643.

There was Division and Subtraction made,
And Lines drawn out, and Points exactly laid,
But none hath yet by demonstration found
The way, by which to Square a Circle round:

(Margaret Cavendish, *The Circle of the Brain Cannot be Squared.*)

'You cannot come dressed so,' said Peter.

'What is amiss?' I twirled around showing him the black embroidery on the back of my doublet. My new suit had cost a pretty penny.

''Tis very bright,' he said.

'I think not!'

'Scarlet?'

'Scarlet and black,' I pointed out the slashed sleeves as I finished buttoning the front, and tied my falling band. 'And the breeches are black.' Jacob handed me my cloak and gloves.

'With scarlet ribbons,' said Peter.

'I think the Master looks most gentlemanly,' said Jacob.

He had spent the morning putting a shine on my boots, so I gave him my most benevolent patrician smile, and turned back to Peter dressed in his Sunday finest. A suit of darkest blue velvet and a tall felt hat.

'You look like a preacher,' I said.

'This is no party; we go to sup at Hampden's.'

'So, there will be other guests,' I said. 'Maybe women; I want to look my best. With my cape off the shoulder, embroidered brocade, and new unconfined breeches, I am the very height of fashion.'

I turned to Everard, smoking his pipe in the corner. Feet

up, boots off, a big toe poking through his vamper*, and a flagon of ale in his hand. He looked every inch the rustic he was. I gave him a flourishing bow.

'What think you, William?'

'You look like a Spaniard,' he observed, then farted.

'Philistine,' I said, standing up. 'At least we are to go in a hackney, I do not wish to get daubed in filth before we get there.'

'Bring back some cake if he serves it,' said Everard. He and Jacob looked set for an evening of backgammon and beer. The two had become fast friends over a pipe and a beer these last weeks.

'Your uncle should be here anon,' said Peter, pulling on his gloves. 'Please behave tonight, drink not overmuch. Put not your knife in your mouth, and no rude tales. Especially not the Turk in Lesbos one, which I am certain is not physically possible.'

''Tis not,' I said. 'I have tried.'

'You are an incorrigible rogue. This meal could be important for us, we both want advancement, especially if you are to ride home in triumph, and break you sister-in-law's heart.' He grinned at me.

Absence makes the heart grow fonder — of someone else†

Hampden had been as good as his word, and given a glowing report to Uncle Samuel of our conduct, and extended an invitation to supper. Uncle Samuel, now a Colonel of Dragoons as well as Scoutmaster-General for the Army, had offered to take us. As very junior officers, it was an honour to be invited, and we had been speculating for a week on the identity of the other guests. I must confess, I was hoping for some merriment and a good feast, whilst Peter just wanted to meet John Pym.[44]

The hackney arrived and we piled in; my uncle sighed

---

*   Stocking

†   Francis Davison, *A Poetical Rhapsody.*

when he saw my fashionable dress.

'At least you are not wearing the red monstrosity, but need you dress like a popinjay?'

'I wish only to present myself well, Uncle.'

'Vanity is a sin, Blandford.' That shut me up; I am always the loser in an argument about sin.

It is a myth that the puritans dressed in sombre black. I have seen Cromwell himself, dressed like a Frenchman in a fine brocade, drunk and dancing in the Palace at Hampton Court. Uncle Samuel though? Well, he thought I looked ridiculous in my fashion (who does not look so at nineteen) but I doubt he really thought it sinful.

The hackney trundled on through the streets, with us all sitting in silence. Outside, Londoners hurrying home through the muddy streets after work, pulled their cloaks around them in the cold, barely noticing the people they passed. We arrived at Hampden's mansion in good time. An old three-storey building with a great hall and arched monastic windows. Taken over during the dissolutions, I would wager. It backed onto St James Park, though I doubt Hampden ever partook of its notorious services.

'Tis consecrate to prick and cunt.[*]

Ha! I still cannot believe Wilmot got away with that verse. He wrote me into it of course; I am the first knight of the elbow and the slur. I did not mind that so much, he only did it to embarrass Waller, and Waller as you will discover deserved the taunts.[45]

We went through to a wood panelled antechamber, where green-liveried servants poured water over our hands, and

---

[*]   John Wilmot, 2nd Earl of Rochester, *A Ramble in St James' Park*.

held out clean linen cloth for drying. Good manners then dictated keeping our hats on at the table; strange how fashion changes. Now men have started wearing flea-ridden periwigs on their noodles to cover baldness, hats have stopped being worn inside.

I walked into the great, curtained hall where the other guests were gathered. It was bright from the light of dozens of candles on brass chandeliers, with a polished wooden floor and roaring coal fire to give a toasty feel. I noted Bulstrode Whitelocke amongst the throng. I say throng, there were only ten or so there and only two women, one of them Hampden's mouse of a wife.

The other made me stop in surprise. Not only was she dressed in brighter colours than myself, but perched upon the arm of a gentleman that could only be John Pym. That would be enough to make me gape, but she was also the beauty from Syon House; my unnamed friend from the queen's chapel. I finally got my introduction. The Countess of Carlisle, Lucy Hay — Pym's mistress — a right saucy punk.[16]

'Well, Mr Candy, you fellows have done well for yourself since we last met. Breaking up a Royalist conspiracy, I hear.' As if she had nothing whatsoever to do with it.

I played along and bowed, and scraped, as a good little courtier should, then stood by my seat.

Peter and I were placed at the lower end of the long table. A fine green linen cloth with a damask pattern woven in covered the table, and silver plates, salts, casters and saucers, knives and spoons. Most people had already seen their plate melted down for the war.

Hampden took his place at the head and spoke to us.

'A prayer for peace I think would be apt,' he said. 'Oh God, source of all holy desires, right counsels and just actions, grant to your servants that peace which the world cannot give, so that our hearts may be wholly devoted to your service and all our days, freed from dread of our enemies, may be passed in quietness under your protection.' He spoke in a beautiful tone. 'Please, ladies, gentlemen be seated.'

We sat and I draped my napkin over the shoulder, as the servants heaped the table with food: a pork brawn in a tart mustard sauce.

'The boar comes from my estate,' Hampden told us. I heaped my plate, despite a frown from Peter. 'It has been force-fed to improve the flavour.'

We were in illustrious company: Hampden and John Pym sat next to him, with the Countess alongside. What a Royalist ravilliac* would give to be in the kitchens tonight, I thought. Both Harleys were there, father and son, and miserable as always. I liked Edward; he was about my age, and honest and loyal if morose, but he took after his mother by all accounts. Robert Harley was one who played both sides of the table. I never liked him even if he was close to my uncle.

A studious looking young man in spectacles and skullcap was introduced to us as Reverend Wallis.[47] He gave me a glance of acknowledgement, but went back to the book he was holding.

The war hung over the meal like an oppressive unseen force. I had hoped for some gay company, some laughter, but the atmosphere was heavy with gloom. The only bright light was Lucy Hay.

I watched as she made eyes at every man, even Uncle Samuel, and they all loved it. Vivacious and charming, laughing at their jests, a touch of the arm here, a lowering of her long eyelashes there. She turned herself into the hostess of the party, even with Hampden's wife sitting right there, in an act of beautiful seduction. I caught her eye at one point, and she gave me a knowing smile, as if a sharing of some private joke. Then she leaned forward, and told me I was wearing Percy colours of red and black.

---

*   Assassin. Francois Ravilliac murdered Henry IV of France in 1610.

Damn, now I think back, she was working me like all the others, and like the others, I fell for it.

'There is word of more atrocities in Ireland,' said Pym.

'Yes,' said Hampden 'Oliver told me; even said he pitied the Irish their trials.'

'Pity the Irish?' asked Pym. 'I did not think your cousin capable of such a thing.'

'Not pity so much,' replied Hampden. 'More what you or I would call contempt.'

I nearly choked on my drink at that; even then Cromwell had a reputation for stubbornness, and consuming hatred for the Catholic Irish. He proved that well enough to Clio* without my testimony. I turned to the studious reverend next to me, briefly considered one of my jokes, but instead asked what book it was that so absorbed him.

'A book by Hobbes,' he told me. 'A scholar living in Paris, and of great interest. Indeed, this phrase sums up, to me, our present condition. *Bellum omnium contra omnes,'* he quoted.

'The war of all against all?' I asked, trying a quick translation in my head.

'Very good,' he told me. 'Although I am not certain Hobbes is correct, I shall look forward to his work.'[48]

'Here,' he said pressing the small tome on me. 'You must take it, Mr Candy, is it? Yes! No, no, do not protest. I have several copies; colleagues send me the same manuscripts all the time, and I am oft left with spare.'

'Show him your cipher trick,' Whitelocke said to him across the table.

He sighed: 'It is no trick, Bulstrode, as I keep explaining to you. It is simple mathematics.'

'Pish, show him anyway.'

The reverend called for a piece of paper and a pencil and wrote on it:

Cdmmvn pnojvn

---

*   The Muse of History

'This is a coded phrase familiar to you,' he said. 'Can you see what it says?'

I stared at the page and sought out its meaning.

'Bellum omnium?' I asked.

'Excellent,' said Wallis, 'but how do you know.'

'Bugger,' whistled Whitelocke.

'The number of letters in the words is the same as the Latin phrase you used a few minutes ago,' I said.

'Very good,' said Wallis, 'but if I were to use the same method to encrypt a phrase you did not know, how would you work it out?'

'I do not understand,' I said

'Neither did I,' said Bulstrode. 'Made my damned head hurt. Give me the law instead, far less vexing than mathematics; no offence, Wallis.'

'There is a pattern beyond the amount of letters, but we can use the phrase we do have to find that pattern,' said Peter,

'Indeed,' said Wallis 'So can you see the pattern?'

Our dishes were cleared away and a course of kickshaws* filled up the table. Peter pulled the paper to him and worked at the code. My suggestions were met only with stony looks, so I gave up, but Wallis watched him appreciatively.

'Pound says he will not get it,' Whitelocke said to me,

'No gambling in my home please, Bulstrode,' Hampden told him, but I tipped Bulstrode a wink anyway. I had faith in Peter's intellect to solve the puzzle.

'You have moved the letters by one, so B becomes C, and E becomes D, and so on' said Peter finally, to approval from Reverend Wallis.

'Yes, very good, Mr Russell. The conceit in essence is simple and easily broken, but think now, if a hundred symbols were put for words and phrases as well as letters. The more complex the cipher, the more symbols used, the more difficult

---

* Puff pastry stuffed with different fillings, either sweet or savoury.

to break, but none are impossible. The King's grandmother, poor foolish woman, used one little better than a child's bauble.'[49]

'The Reverend is assisting me with my new role as Scoutmaster,' Uncle Samuel told us.

'Let us hope Essex appreciates it,' snapped Pym.

Fruit and cheese were brought and talk turned to the sorry progress of the war: suers for peace against firebrand republicans; the inaction of Essex, the obduracy of the King, and 'neath it all, the unspoken fact that Lucy Hay's brother was now leader of the Peace Party, and an agitator for settlement. Then, midst the miserable discourse, came the word that shook and haunted me those weeks past.

'We still have no word of who this *Bonduca* is, or if we have a traitor?' The countess asked Reverend Wallis.

'None whatsoever,' replied Wallis, 'but it must be someone close to the King's court.'

'That is the name the tough in the Devil's Tavern used,' I said interrupting.

'What is this?' asked my uncle. He had asked for my account of the night, but I had neglected to tell him the name. Not knowing what it meant, or even if I had been mistaken.

'After I pinked the last tough, Uncle. As the life left him he told me "*Bonduca*" would avenge him, or get me, I think.' The actual words were fuzzy after a few glasses of claret.

'It helps us not,' said Wallis. 'Whoever Bonduca is, he has been orchestrating more than just the newsbooks. Too much information gets back to the King in Oxford. Information seeps out through disgruntled members of the peace party, but military plans also.'

Pym brought an end to that conversation, suddenly leaning forward, racked with coughing and convulsions. The countess leaned forward to help him, and after a minute or so, he sat back and composed himself, but the rest of the table looked on concerned. I noted how thin he looked compared to the woodcuts that flooded the country. I thought it must have been the strain of the war, but realise now that it was the cancer taking hold in his stomach.

Pym's fit marked the end to the evening. Hampden rose from his place followed by his wife and the rest of us. There were hackneys and carriages waiting outside to take us back to the city. After thanking Hampden and his tiny silent wife, we climbed into the hackney, but not before Whitelocke begged a seat back to the city.

'Much appreciated, Samuel,' he said, settling back into the seat opposite me. I considered pestering him for the pound, but had a feeling he would call the bet void.

'When do you return to Oxford, Bulstrode?' asked Uncle Samuel as we trundled along.

'Oh, in a week or so. We shall see what proposals His Majesty has thought up this time. I begin to think it but a futile exercise in debate.'

'Would you like some new assistants to serve you on your next trip?' asked my uncle.

'Hmm, what do you mean, Samuel?'

'Well, these two gentleman are rattling around London, stirring up trouble with their boredom, whilst the army waits on the Earl of Essex' pleasure. Perhaps a visit to Oxford would be good for them,' he tapped his nose.

Whitelocke saw the gesture. 'Well, if you think it is a good idea, Samuel. I have no objection to the boys tagging along. As long as they keep out of trouble,' he looked sternly at the two of us.

'Oh, of course, I will be sure to impress their duty upon them, of that you can be certain, Bulstrode. Now, where are your apartments? Up near Camden, I believe? Well, we will take the road round the city and carry you there before going on to Cheapside. No, no do not protest, I insist.'

Whitelocke had not actually looked like protesting and sat back in his seat.

My Dear Heart,

I hope Parsons has arrived to give you tidings of my landing in England. I expected every day to go to York, which has prevented me from writing to you, but so many difficulties have arisen, that I have already been here nine days. What has retarded me, has been the difficulty finding wagons to carry the ammunition and my baggage.

It would have been much safer for the whole army to march with me, and to leave nothing behind us. I hope that in a day of two I shall set out, but shall leave half the army to guard the ammunition and the other half will march with me.

We have to do with enemies who are very vigilant; therefore we must be on our guard.

I will not repeat that I am in the greatest impatience in the world to join you. I hope that it will not be difficult for you to believe, after all that I have done to secure my return, and also that you have equal desire to see me, which I would fain believe, notwithstanding all the tidings I found current about you at my arrival.

You pass for a dangerous creature and I am,
Entirely Yours.

Henrietta Maria, Bridlington 22nd Feb 1643.

11. Oxford, March 1643.

The Parliament must willing be,
That all the world may plainly see,
How they do labour still for peace,
That now these bloody wars may cease.

(Traditional, *When We Enjoy Sweet Peace Again.*)

Oxford had become London-by-the-Cherwell. The students may have run home to their families, but the Royalist diasporas of war gathered in Oxford to look for salvation. The court and various entourages were set up in the college halls and churches. Privy councillors, secretaries, officials, and their families, squeezed into every building. Fashionably dressed ladies walked in the college gardens and there were masques, and balls, and dances, and dashing officers singing for their paramours in the street. All whilst the good people of the city grimly watched on. Their wealth taxed away and their labour enforced to construct great defences outside the decayed city walls. While the rich play, the poor suffer, as is the way of the world.

Inside the ring of forts and ditches, the city was overloaded with people, and not just the court. Soldiers were billeted in every house — at cost to the owner — and every day the drilling recruits would march down the High Street, and out to fields by the Cherwell for manoeuvres. With so many people, 'twas inevitable that disease soon followed. None of us relished our time in the city.

The one bright moment for me throughout, was to kick Everard down the stairs one evening. I had left Jacob in London, to my regret, and Everard played the servant — much to his distaste — and got in my way. Treat him as he deserves, Uncle Samuel had said, and so I did. He was not impressed.

The peace commission was the last chance for a settlement before the start of the campaigning season, but discussions were not going well. The King — believing his fortunes to be on the rise — was truculent and evasive. Peter and I were not privy to the meetings and had discovered nothing of worth for Uncle Samuel. Instead I spent my time in the Spotted Cow,[50] drinking watery beer and listening to the prittle-prattle of the disgruntled populace. The low hanging beams and heavy smoke gave the tavern a choking, oppressive atmosphere. None of it good for the humours*.

'There is plague all over the city, the sooner we are gone the better,' Bulstrode said, as we sat drinking ale a couple of days after our arrival.

'Plague is everywhere,' I shrugged. 'What was the King's response to the petition?'

He said he, 'w-w-w-would consider it,' replied Bulstrode. 'In the meantime we are all packed into this plague pit, awaiting His Majesties pleasure.'

'Do you think he will agree to the proposals?' I asked him.

'The King? No, not from his demeanour. The last time we played this charade, his Majesty met us in the gardens of Christ Church, and interrupted Northumberland incessantly when he tried to read out the document. Then he flounced off to play tennis with his nephew; he seemed more interested in talking to Waller.'

'Perhaps the King likes his verse,' I said.

'Do you? I think they are worse than bum-fodder.'

'True, but it would not improve them to tell him,' I replied. Indeed it does not. I've tried, but for some reason my criticism always makes poets blood boil.

'Well, when Waller came to present himself to the King, his majesty lavished him with praise and attention telling him, "Th-th-though you are the last, yet you are not th-th-the worst, nor least in my f-f-favour," as pompous as you like,' he told me laughing. 'I am sure the sly bastard is up to something.'[51]

---

* The four bodily fluids it was believed affected temperament.

His laughter was cut short by Peter's breathless arrival: all in a whirl, throwing off his hat and cloak, and ordering wine.

'I have just seen your brother,' Peter told me. 'He looks like enough as to be your twin.'

'Not hairy and apelike?' I said.

'No, he looks much like you.'

'Bugger, that will be James,' I told him. 'He's the clever one; where was he?'

'On the High Street, I called him Blandford twice before I realised my mistake. The look he gave me. I thought he was going to call me out for a second.' The words came out from him all in a tumble.

'What did he say?' I asked, trying to seem outwardly calm, but inside my heart was pounding.

'Told me I was mistaken, and if I was seeking you to look amongst rebels and traitors, not men of honour.'

'A problem?' Bulstrode asked.

'That gave me pause for thought. 'Probably,' was the only answer I could honestly come up with.

'Ah,' said Peter with a worried look coming over his face.

'Ah?' asked Bulstrode.

'Well, when he called us traitors and rebels, I told him I was with Parliament's commission, and Blandford was my compatriot, and acknowledged as a man of honour.'

'And?'

'And he's outside wishing to speak with you,'

'We truly need to talk on discretion being the better part of valour,* Peter,' I said standing up. Bulstrode started loading a pistol.

'Is he alone?' asked Bulstrode.

'No, he has a woman with him.'

'Cannot kill him then,' Bulstrode told me. 'What are you

---

*   A famous proverb from *Henry IV*, but it is not original
       to Shakespeare, and has been traced back as far as, *The*
       History of Jason, (circa 1477) by William Caxton.

going to do?'

Strange, I thought. These men look at me confident in my ability, but my brother knew me for what I was. Confrontation with James had always ended badly for me as a child, and I was scared this time would be no different. Any respect I had earned would soon disappear in a flash.

I walked through the bar room out to the flagstone courtyard by the side of the inn. Standing outside, talking to the King's guards, was my brother looking every inch the cavalier dandy (a love of fine clothes is a family trait; I should remind my tramp of a nephew about that), and with him a tall flame-haired woman. Striking, but not a great beauty, her face pockmarked from smallpox and with hard eyes. Richly dressed in blue silk though, her tangled red curls fell loose around her bare shoulders. She must have been cold with no shawl but bore it well. I've seen her type before, I thought to myself—dangerous, like Lucy Hay.

'Well met, brother,' I said, without enthusiasm.

'Well, here is the rogue,' replied James, breaking off from his conversation with the guard. Both of our hands went to our swords.

'What is your wish, James?' I asked, resigned to a confrontation or even violence, but strangely, now I had seen him, without the fear that had always gutted me as a child.

'Oh, fear not, Blandford,' he sneered, seeing my stance. 'You are under the King's protection here. I only regret I did not kill you at Edgehill, instead of just cutting your hat.'

'That was you?' My hand went to where he had cut me, which raised a malevolent smile I knew well enough from our youth.

'Give you a haircut, did I?' He asked.

'Bastard,' I replied. 'That hat cost me a pound, but I doubt you are here to repay me for it. What do you here, James? I see little we need talk about.'

'Do not deceive yourself; I am not interested in a worm

like you, brother. Mistress Whorwood wished to see the cornet who murdered a poor printer in London Town. Oh yes,' he said seeing my look of surprise. 'Word of your exploits bullying innocent old men reached us here.'

'I did not bully him, James,' I said. 'I shot him and stamped on his face, then arrested him for sedition and libel, and 'twas not murder. He was still alive last I heard.'

'You were wrong, Sir James. You said your brother was a dullard,' the lady leaned in, 'but I find him quite amusing.' She smelled of red apples, I remember that.

I flashed her a smile and a bow. 'Forgive my brother's manners, Milady, he failed to introduce us properly. I am his younger and infinitely more pleasant brother.' I had determined to needle him by now. She curtsied, and then it struck me.

'You called him Sir James?' I said. I looked at him: 'Sir James?' and I started to laugh.

'Well, and what diverts you so, treasonous oaf?' asked my brother.

'Well,' I said, wiping mock tears from my eyes. 'I wager Henry was frothing at the mouth when he heard of your knightliness,' then I threw a little bow at him. 'A merry recompense for pissing the bed until you were nine, is it not?'

'You, pug-faced* runt,' he started forward, but the King's guards quickly stepped in to dissuade him.

'Now, sir, you know what we said. We cannot have you beating him. On the King's orders, none of the commission is to be harmed.' That made me relax.

'Well, Milady,' I said, 'you have met the monster. Do I live up to my reputation?'

'Oh, I think you just might, Mr Candy, yes, you just might.'

I had no idea what that meant, so turned back to my brother. James still had murder in his eyes, but with armed men standing vigil, he was not fool enough to go at me. Had

---

    *   Deceitful or dishonest, from Puck.

it been Henry, I could have goaded him into doing something stupid, but James was too quick witted to trap like that.

'Our father is not well.' That stopped me in my tracks.

'So Elizabeth's letters tell me,' I said. That was a slip, and I knew it. James noted it; I saw the flash of realisation in his eyes.

'I suppose she writes to the Dwarf as well?' he asked slyly.

'I know not,' I said, wondering how to turn the conversation away from Elizabeth.

'Anne wishes to join me here in Oxford.' He suddenly changed tack.

'More fool her wanting to come to this plague-hole,' I told him. 'What has that to do with me?'

'You set yourself against your entire family, brother, by standing against the King. You could still come back to us, to your family. I know the King would forgive you, welcome you, even.' Damn, he even managed to look sincere, but I knew him better.

'You have been set against me since I was born, James. Now you complain that I stand on the other side? Had you stood for Parliament, I would be taking the King's shilling now. The thought of fighting alongside a pimple like you sickens me. You are a wart, a boil, a vile pus-filled bubo, now be gone.' That stung him, I could see from his face, flushed red, how angry he was.

'We are your family.' He was persistent, at least.

'You are deluded, brother,' I said with venom. 'Family? I am a third son; I mean nothing to our father, and you are merely a spare. When Henry's brat is born, if a boy, you will not even be that.'

'Now, Sir James,' said the woman, 'I think it is time we leave before tempers become, well, too heated.' She looked at me. 'Farewell, Mr Candy. My regards to your uncle the Dwarf. I will be watching your progress with some interest, I think.'

'Please to call me Blandford,' I said sweetly, whilst wondering what the devil she was talking about. ''Till next time, James, Mistress Whorwood.' I nodded to her, turned my back on them both, and walked back into the inn. Bulstrode was waiting inside the doors, pistol in hand.

'Is there going to be trouble?'

'Not tonight,' I said, 'At least I do not think so.'

'Who was the redhead?'

'Said her name was Whorwood, heard of her?' He shook his head.

'So what did they want?' Peter asked back at the table, as I called for more wine. Some of the other commissioners had come down to see what the fuss was. Old Selden, Waller the poet, book in hand as usual, and some others all crowded around, as I sat gulping at my wine.

'I am not sure, other than to needle me,' I said, unbuttoning my doublet and shirt at the top — I needed to breathe easily.

'The woman was handsome,' Peter said. 'His wife?'

'No,' I said. 'James told me her name was Whorwood.' We men we are all alike, my brother could have cut me down, but it was the woman they wanted to know about.

'Oh, I know of Mistress Whorwood,' Waller suddenly said, then nervously continued as we turned to look at him. 'Or at least I know of her husband Brome. They have estates near Oxford; a good family,' he added.

'Good families are on both sides in this divide,' Selden said gloomily. 'Good people being killed every day and I see no prospect of reconciliation with His Majesty.'

'Was there something you wanted, Edmund?' Whitelocke asked the poet brusquely.

'No, no, perhaps not,' Waller replied. 'Forgive my intrusion,' he added and left to sit in the corner and read his book.

'That was not civil, Bulstrode,' chided Selden quietly.

'Well, I do not like him,' Bulstrode told him. 'He looks

and acts like a weasel, with his pointy little nose constantly twitching. It sets my damn teeth on edge just to look at him.'

Selden smiled half-heartedly, 'You judge him to harshly, my friend; I am sure he means well. However, gentlemen, I will bid you good night as well, I think. I have letters to write.'

I sat there in silence for a while with Bulstrode, whilst he gave Peter a gloomy account of the negotiations with the King. Though with Waller sitting there reading, I noticed he kept his voice low and the insults light.

'Let it not trouble you overmuch, Candy,' he said to me, suddenly interrupting my contemplation.

'What, Bulstrode?' I asked confused. I had not been listening, turning over the meeting with my brother in my head.

'Family,' he said sadly. 'I know it can be hard to see those you love arraigned against you. My mother's family serve the King, my cousin Richard fought against us at Edgehill.' He sighed. 'Family always know to stick the bodkin where you are most fleshy.' He called for more wine.

'You have that right,' I said. 'I need a piss.'

I struggled to my feet still shaking from my encounter with James. I needed air; the room was too smoke-filled. I pushed past the crowd by the bar, out to the privy, quickly relieving myself. Splattering my boots with piss, I cursed. Then stepped out into the moonlight, into the clean air, breathing deeply and clearing my head. Fresh air helps me think.

For a moment I stood there, pondering. Would James question Elizabeth? Then again, what was Elizabeth's role in all of this? Was she really a spy? She had certainly been sending information to Uncle Samuel — an informer then — would James suspect her of that from my comments?

Of course he would. He was a clever bastard.

I went back inside, someone had picked up a lute, and Bulstrode was singing. He had a good clear voice, although his choice of song was melancholy itself.

'Trust not a civil foe,
Which under colour wisheth good:
for ere thy self dost know,
by craft he seeks to have thy blood.
The Snake in grass doth grovelling lie:
Till for revenge due time he spy.
The leering Dog doth bite more sore:
Then he that warning gives before.
fine flattery, fair face:
Much discord breeds in every place.
fire, and shot, must be too hot:
for those which have their God forgot.'[52]

It was too close to the bone, and I suspect Bulstrode knew it. I had had enough, no more wine, no more singing. I went to bed exhausted and collapsed into my billet, little more than a straw mattress thrown on the floor, in the room I shared with Peter.

'I've found him Henry!' James reached under the bed, trying to grab at my hair. I punched at his hand. 'You shall suffer this time, you little thief.'

Henry came into the room; I could see his feet, minus one boot.

'Where is the little bastard?'

'He's under the bed,' said James, reaching for me again. I bit his hand. 'Damn!' He drew back.

'Where's my damn boot, you runt,' Henry had gone around to the other side of the bed and reached for my legs. I kicked out at him.

'I touched it not,' I screamed. 'It was James; why do you always blame me?'

'Little liar,' shouted James.

'Because you are a thieving little shit-breech,' said Henry. He had his riding crop and swung it under the bed. I pulled my legs up away from

it.

James reached under the bed again, punching out at me—I crawled up towards the top of the bed. To no avail. He grabbed my hair, and dragged me out from under the bed.

James held me down as Henry raised up the crop.

'You are going to get a thrashing to remember this time, thief.'

He struck down at me, hitting square on my face, I could feel a welt rising up under my eye. I curled up into a ball, as he struck down again, then again, and again.

I climbed up to the attic, hidden away from the others. I looked down at Henry's new boot and cut into it with my knife. A petty act of vengeance, but it made me feel better. I winced from my bruises and placed the boot with the rest of my treasure. Some of James' silver buttons, the boot from Henry, and a buckle from his other pair. A tortoise shell comb, even some of Anne's ribbons, taken more through irritation than spite. Nothing from Elizabeth: she had only had the bible worth stealing, and even I thought that a blasphemy too far.

I awoke hours later, Peter snoring beside me. Bladder full, I reached for the piss-pot and relieved myself. It was late; the inn was quiet as a tomb, and for a while I lay there turning over the meeting with James in my head, but a noise in the corridor drew my attention. Voices, a door closing, and the murmur of conversation; it made me curious. I crept up to the door and opened it a crack. There was no light in the corridor to see by, so I felt my way along the wall in darkness. The voices were louder, at least one was.

'A play by John Fletcher? For what purpose?' It was Edmund Waller's whiny tone.

'Keep it safe,' came another tired voice. A woman, I knew that voice as well but could not place it.

I crept closer to the door, trying to catch more of the

conversation.

'And what if it goes awry, what then?' Waller said.

'It will not, as long as you hold your nerve. Pour yourself a drink and be calm,' came the reply. 'Keep the book safe, you will know when you need it. Until then, do not contact me again, Edmund.' There was something I did not catch and then: 'When this is all over your debt will be paid. What more could you ask for?'

'As long as I still have my head, that is.' Waller snapped back

'Then do not lose it meantime,' she replied. I heard a chair being pushed back. I quickly tip-toed back to my room, closing the door, but leaving the tiniest crack open so I could peek out to catch a glimpse of the woman Waller had spoken to. The door opened, illuminating the corridor, and she swept out, a shawl covering her face, but I recognised the dress. I had seen it earlier, sky blue silk, my brother's companion Mistress Whorwood.

I woke Peter, putting a hand over his mouth so he did not start, and told him what I had seen and heard.

'Well, what does it mean?' he said, sitting up.

'I know not. Why would she give him a play?'

'How much are his debts?' asked Peter. 'Waller is supposed to be fabulously wealthy.'

'Copies of plays do not sell for that much.' I replied, 'Happen 'tis no financial debt, but a debt of honour, perhaps?'

'And we know not which Fletcher play? Shame,' said Peter.

'Why?' I asked.

'Do you remember what Reverend Wallis said about encoding messages?'

'Some of it,' I said. You seemed to understand it better though.' That was true, as Bulstrode had said, Wallis made my head hurt.

'What if the play is the cipher for their codes?' he said.

'So we could break their letters?'

'No,' replied Peter. 'Not if I understand Wallis. We would need the key as well.'

'Key?' I asked.

'The variable Wallis talked about, so you know which act or scene to turn to, or which page number.'

'So knowing the play would be no use then,' I said, deflated.

'Oh, I would not say that,' said Peter. 'Whatever Waller is up to, the people in on the plot will need a copy of the play as well. You see?'

'No, you make my head hurt.'

'Possession of a play by John Fletcher makes people a suspect.' He sighed. 'If the theatres were open we could find out more about his plays, which ones have been published and the like.'

'We might know someone,' I said, 'when we get back to London.'

'Beeston?'

'Beeston,' I agreed, 'but Barker as well. The old lawyer has been around long enough to remember Shakespeare. I am sure he will know about Fletcher's plays, and he's more trustworthy than Beeston.'

'Here is to the King making up his mind about Parliament's proposals, so we can get out of Oxford soon then,' said Peter.

'Amen to that.'

The Kingdome's Weekly Intelligencer Sunday 5 March 1643.

There is certain news come out of Yorkshire that the Queen is still at Bridlington where she first landed, and that her ammunition is landed.

The four ships which did ride at the mouth of Newcastle Harbour, having notice of it, weighed anchors, and came before Bridlington into the bay, and shot at the small vessels that were landing the ammunition, and did execution upon them. The Popish Army playing with their great ordnance upon those ships all the while without prejudice, and in the night arose a great storm, which scattered the said ships, and two of them lost their masts:

There are two causes conceived to make the Queen still reside in that unhealthy harbour. The one is, that is she should go to York with the safe conduct, her ammunition would be at the mercy of the Lord Fairfax's forces. Another is, that when her arms and ammunition landed is fitted with soldiers, Her Majesty intends to visit Hull, which is not much out of her way. Some houses have been burnt in that part of the county where Her Majesty is. Yorkshire had affliction enough by the sword of the Popish Army before Her Majesty came, and it is their increase of misery to have fire added to the Sword since she landed.

It is further informed from thence, that the Lord Fairfax in duty and respect to Her Majesty, sent Sir William Fairfax (a brave gentleman) to Her Majesty, to acquaint her that the Parliament had an army on this side of York, to oppose the Popish Army under the Earl of Newcastle. Therefore, if Her Majesty should be misled by that lord into any other danger, he thought good to desire Her Majesty to withdraw her person, but (it is said) Sir William Fairfax is detained prisoner.

Richard Collings.

12. Beaconsfield, March 1643.

Not able to endure the sight of day,
But self-affrighted tremble at his sin.
Not all the water in the rough rude sea
Can wash the balm off from an anointed King;

(Shakespeare, *Richard II*, Act III, Scene II.)

The court was a pale imitation of the splendour of Westminster. The Great Hall of Christ Church, with its high vaulted roof and brightly painted beams, was decked out in tapestry and cloth of gold. Thronging with courtiers, and soldiers, and clerics. Beautiful women dressed in their finery, hid behind jewelled fans, and made eyes at their beaus. The throne was set up on a dais at the far end of the hall, shrouded in light from the great arched windows, with the Royal Standard displayed behind. The whole scene devised to accentuate the divine aloof majesty of a monarch.

I admit I was impressed by the pomp and display—not unaided by Mr Inigo Jones; Royalty always hides its false face with theatre, to enchant the mob and distract from its iniquities. To those who remembered the days of peace though, however great the display, however magnificent the spectacle, it was a diminished court and a diminished crown.[53]

The negotiations were a farce. The King thought he was winning the war, so why talk? Day after day passed and Bulstrode returned from Christ Church frustrated and despondent. I went but once to court, and saw the King in audience. He did not impress me. I met him again over the years, and a more courteous fool you would be pressed to find. Yet, for all his prickly dignity, he exuded weakness and vacillation. Charles the Martyr? The last gasp of self-justification. He conveniently forgot his own letters proved how faithlessly he approached the propositions. Charles Stuart was not fit to rule a chicken coop, let alone a kingdom. Only at his trial managed he to muster some glimmer of substance, and by then it was too late.

He dismissed the commission with a stammer and a sneer, and sent us back to London at the start of March. Oh, the talks would drag on some more, but it was clear the King could not be trusted. I remember some of the commissioners walking in miserable procession back to the inn. Anyone still harbouring hopes of peace had seen their dreams shattered. The Commons sit in Oxford? Pah![54] Even Denzil Holles, who desired settlement at all costs, was disheartened. Only Waller was different: neither discouraged nor disappointed but oddly exhilarated. Strange for one who had seen his dreams of peace dashed.

I watched the poet carefully after his meeting with Mistress Whorwood, wondering what he was up to, where his loyalties truly lay, but I had found nothing I could report to my uncle. Already, menservants were rushing back and forth. Everard among them, helping make ready for our return to London. Now the talks had proven fruitless, there was little reason for us to remain in Oxford.

'He toys with us!' Bulstrode exploded once we back were inside the inn.

'He has distracted us with empty words, whilst the Queen returns from France with money,' said Selden, even gloomier than usual.[55]

'There is always a chance,' said Holles.

'Only if the King is prepared to negotiate with us in good faith, and that man has no faith in us at all. He would have us all twitching on the end of a rope if he could. Surely you can see that now, Denzil?' Bulstrode asked him.

'He is your King, sir, and beyond our reproach.' Waller suddenly butted in, weasel nose twitching.

'Oh, go to the devil, you pompous prig! What are we doing here then?' For a moment I thought Bulstrode was going to strike the cringing poet, but he composed himself as Selden put out a calming hand.

'Let us see what Parliament thinks, Bulstrode; there is no need to argue amongst ourselves here.' Selden looked around at the others. 'The sooner we are back in London the better.'

'My apologies, Waller. I am as disappointed in spirit as you and Holles,' Bulstrode said. Then he bowed stiffly and left with Selden following on close behind.

That was the odd thing though, Holles looked disappointed enough, and I think he genuinely believed peace could be negotiated with the King, but Waller still had that strange smile on his face. He looked around for a moment after Bulstrode had left, and then noticing me watching, hurried off upstairs. I followed on to my room to stuff my few belongings into my satchel ready for the journey back to London. I must confess to relief at our departure, for between the plague, my brother, the King, and the overcrowding, I had a poor opinion of Oxford.

I've been back since and it was worse; full of poxy students quoting poetry, thinking they are damn clever, and never buying the drinks when their turn comes around.

Within an hour, the whole lot of us were packed, ready to move, and eager to be leaving Oxford. We were provided with a cavalry escort by the King, as far as Beaconsfield; there to be met by an escort of dragoons sent by Essex to protect the commission.

Apple whinnied, fresh from the stable, and I whistled, happy to be free of Oxford—but the day was not yet done. As we approached Beaconsfield from the north, we veered off the main road around the town itself to our lodgings for the evening. The soldiers sent by Parliament to meet with us were nowhere to be seen, leaving us unguarded, as the King's escort clattered back down the road to Oxford.

Most of the commission were to stay with Waller at his manor near Beaconsfield. The servants, the clerks, Peter and I were sent to the Ship Inn to the north of the town, a grim reminder of the war welcomed us: a forest of half-rotted heads, putrid flesh falling from the grinning skulls, stuck on pikes beside the entrance to the inn.[56]

'Welcome to Hell,' said Peter, as we dismounted.

Waller was still with us at that point. Northumberland and Bedford and the other Lords had gone on to the estate, but Waller wanted to make sure we were settled. Bulstrode was with him, angry at our dragoons' absence, and loudly demanding to see the innkeeper. Said innkeeper, was a giant of a man, red faced from wine and the heat of the kitchen, with a haystack of a black beard and lazy eye.

'Who is in command here?' Bulstrode bawled at the man, 'Where are the troops set here by Parliament?'

I liked Bulstrode, he was generally fun loving and no ranter, but when he got angry, he got loud.

'Begging your pardon, sir,' the innkeeper said in an insolent tone. 'Captain Pask is in charge of the garrison here. He was meeting with the couriers who came through this morning bringing word of your arrival. He is in the town now; I can send the boy with a message if you would like?' He said it without any enthusiasm.

'If you please,' said Bulstrode, 'and be quick about it, man. 'Tis damned important!' He shouted as the innkeeper slowly waddled off to send for the absent officer.

Pask? Damn! John Hurry's bullyboy lieutenant was the last person I wished to see, excepting perhaps his foul-breathed chief. I decided to make myself scarce, so hid in the common room. A small sandy haired boy came and asked if I wanted food; I, half-lost in my thoughts, nodded and ordered wine as well.

He brought back a bowl of steaming hot mutton stew, with a loaf of fresh baked bread. It smelled delicious, but I barely noticed. I poured myself a goblet of sack, pondering my family. They really were a bodkin in the flesh, as Bulstrode had called it. Absently I dipped some bread into the stew and chewed on it.

I turned the events in Oxford over and over. Had I placed my sister in danger? I had let slip to James that she wrote to me. That worried me, Elizabeth was a nag, but she at least cared about me, which was more than I could say for the rest.

I knew now she passed information to Uncle Samuel, and if either of my brothers suspected as well, there would be trouble. I resolved to write and warn her as soon as I returned to London.

Then there was Mistress Whorwood—who was she? What was her role and why was she meeting with Waller late at night? It all screamed of a plot, but how was my brother involved, or Waller? Was Fletcher's Play a codebook as Peter had suggested, and if so what was the key? And which play was it? There were so many questions and nothing to answer them with.

Within minutes Pask had arrived, I could hear him apologising to Bulstrode. I had not forgotten that murdering bastard, or the poor serving maid in Northampton, nor my night in the Compter at Christmas for that matter. Now, it seemed we were under his protection.

I wondered whether Uncle Samuel would be satisfied with our mission. We seemed to know even less than before about whom the traitor was. It could not be Waller himself, he was too much of a coward to risk his head without connivance. He also did not have access to the Earl Essex' plans, although I was certain he was involved. Someone else was feeding information back to the King. Someone else was pulling the strings, making us dance and twist like marionettes.

Bulstrode came into the barroom. I looked up to call him over, but felt something amiss. My legs were numb—I tried to move—they responded not. 'Poison!' I gasped, heart hammering in my chest. I could barely breathe, my arm started going into spasms, and I knocked the bowl of stew over, and fell when I tried to stand up.

When my eyes next opened, it was night. Lamps were burning, and Peter's face loomed over me.

'Blandford, are you awake?' he asked.

I grunted, my throat burned and I felt weak as a babe, stinking of stale sweat, but there was no fever. I was just weak, and I needed a piss badly.

'He is awake, Bulstrode,' said Peter. 'Thank the Lord.'

I reached for the piss pot and relieved myself, falling back with my head on the bolster.

'Asclepius can wait for his cock* it seems,' said Bulstrode. 'How do you feel, my friend? I thought we had lost you.'

'Like a Borgia in the morning,' I replied with a rasping voice. 'I need water.'

'I see your humour is not diminished by a brush with death. I am not sure whether to be thankful or to cry.' But he smiled, even so.

Peter held a glass to my lips, 'Small beer,' he said. 'Sip it, do not gulp.'

'What happened?' I asked, after drinking my fill, letting

---

* A reference to Socrates' last words after taking Hemlock as punishment for corrupting the morals of the Athenian youth, *'Crito, we owe a cock to Asclepius. Pay it and do not neglect it.'*

my head fall back on the bolster.

'You were poisoned,' said Peter. 'In the stew. The serving boy confessed, said he was paid half a crown to do it. The boy ran as soon as you collapsed. One of the dogs ate the dregs after you and dropped down dead.'

'I barely touched the stew,' I groaned, my head was pounding.

'Be thankful,' said Peter. 'You could have ended like the hound; it did not look pretty.'

'Everard was quick,' said Bulstrode, 'mixed some Venice Treacle[57] with beer, and got it down your gullet—you were vomiting all night.'

'All night? How long have I been out?' I asked.

'Two days,' said Peter. 'After you collapsed, Bulstrode had you brought up here.

'The boy?' I asked. 'Where is he now?' They looked at each other at that.

'Found dead yesterday morning, they locked him in the cellar overnight,' said Bulstrode. 'Hung himself it seems.' He did not sound convinced.

'So we cannot find out who paid him?' I asked,

'No,' Peter told me, 'convenient is it not? Pask's guards swore they heard nothing, for all they can be trusted. Why would the boy poison you though?' he asked. 'No offence intended, my friend, but there are more important people in this affair than Sugar Candy. Could it be your brother?'

I shook my head. 'Poison is not James' way; he would want to humiliate me first. He would have to prove to everyone how clever he is; this is too anonymous for him. Pask would happily murder me, I wager, but he did not see me, or even know I was with the commission.' With that, I started vomiting into a bowl, a horrid black, vile, stinking mess. They waited until I had composed myself.

'Could it be Waller?' Peter asked. 'Could he have found out you heard him and Mistress Whorwood t'other night?'

'From whom?' I replied. 'Only you knew. I think he would be more likely to murder Bulstrode after being cooped up together in Oxford, not me.'

'Waller is too much of a coward to dabble in murder, and poison is a woman's weapon,' said Bulstrode. 'Although the boy was clear it was a man who gave him the powder and money. Perhaps the family of a jilted love?' he suggested, only partly in jest. I thought of Emily and shook my head.

'I think not,' I said. 'Not recently anyway. How did the boy know who to poison?' I asked. 'I had never seen him before.'

'Give it to the one with the golden hair and a red hat, he was told,' said Bulstrode. 'You were not hard to find sitting in the bar room.'

'I need to get a different coloured hat,' I said, only half in jest.

Peter laughed. 'It has rather become your signature. Why, I do not think I would recognise you in a plain black one.'

'Recognise me? I would as soon the poison take me, than dress like you in Birchin Lane drab,' I told him.

'His temper is not improved,' Peter observed to Bulstrode.

'Well, perhaps we should tell him the rest of our news then,' said Bulstrode, grimacing.

'Good news, I hope?'

'Is it ever?' said Peter.

'The rest of the commission left this morning,' Bulstrode told me, 'With Pask's men as escort. So, we are left here with hostile locals, and John Hurry's troopers all over the county stirring things up. I did not dare risk moving you, and Pask said he could not leave any men to watch over us.'

'Smirky's a dirty huffler. He would happily leave us to the Royalists,' I said. 'So what do we do then?'

'We get out of here with all speed. Can you ride?' asked Bulstrode.

I nodded. 'Even if you have to strap me to my horse and lead the way; where is Everard?'

'He had to go on with Waller and the commission; else he risked discovery. You are lucky he was there when it happened, with his bag of powders and pills,' said Peter.

Perhaps Everard had discovered more about the traitor whilst working for Waller. If it was the poet behind the poisoning, I swore he would pay.

'So when do we leave?' I asked.

'For now you sleep some more,' he told me. 'We have a few hours, then we leave before dawn,'

'To London? Damn, that is a devil of a ride,' I said.

'No, to Windsor it is but ten miles,' Bulstrode smiled. 'Small mercy I know, but Essex is there with the army. Nevertheless it will be a hard ride even if we are not stopped by royalist troops.'

Fortune always dictates that I finish thus, wounded and lost in enemy territory. Sometimes I wondered, why me? But generally, it all boils down to the same thing. Being in the wrong place, at the wrong time, with the wrong damn hat.

Dear Heart,

Though ever since Sunday last, I had good hopes of the happy landing, yet I had not certain news therof before yesterday, when I likewise understood of thy safe coming to York. I hope thou expects not welcome from me in words, but if I shall be wanting in any other way(according to my wit and power) of expressing my love to thee, then let all honest men hate and eschew me as a monster. Yet, when I shall have done my part, I confess that I shall come short of what thou deservest of me.

I am making all the haste I may to send my nephew Rupert to clear the passage between this and York. In the meantime there is a design upon Berwick Castle.

Yesterday there were articles of cessation brought me from London, but so unreasonable that I cannot grant them. Yet, to undecieve the people, by showing it is not I, but those who have caused and fostered this rebellion that desire the continuance of the war and universal distraction. I am framing articles fit for that purpose. Both which by my next I mean to send to thee.

Will Murray doth write to me to make Hamilton Duke which I think fit to be done, but I would have the have the thanks of it. I am now confident that Hamilton is right for my service. Since the taking of Cheshire, there is nothing of note of either side. What little news there is I will leave to others.

Only this I assure thee that the distractions of the rebels are such that so many fine designs are laid open to us, we know not which first to undertake. But certainly, my first and chiefest care is, and shall be, to secure thee and hasten our meeting.

So longing to hear from thee, I rest eternally thine,

C. R.   Oxford 12th March 1643

13. The Charcoal Burner, March 1643.

*And went to him, and bound up his wounds,
pouring in oil and wine, and set him on his own beast,
and brought him to an inn, and took care of him.*

(Luke, 10:34.)

In the twilight before dawn, we snuck out of the inn like thieves, saddled our horses and made our escape. The town still slumbered, but come daylight, our leaving would be discovered, and out in the open we were vulnerable. Windsor lay ten miles to the south through woodland and the grey drizzle. With luck, we would reach it with a couple of hours of riding. The country around us was supposed to be under Parliament's control. However, Royalist raids and ambushes were commonplace, and our own troopers were as much hated as the King's for their looting.

'We pass through woodland most of the way, then over the Thames at Eton and we are home and dry,' said Bulstrode. 'We go cautiously though, couriers have been taken in these woods by Royalist scouts. Have no fear,' he added cheerfully seeing my look. 'In a few hours we'll be in Windsor Castle having a bath and drinking sack.'

'A nice posset for me, and bed.'

'I went to school in Eton,' Bulstrode said. 'The Mermaid Tavern opposite the Castle had a cook that made the best hashed hare* you have ever tasted.'

'I have no taste for food either, with my stomach so tender, Bulstrode,' I said.

'Pish to you, I am famished,' he said. 'I hope the cook is still there.'

We trotted along at a fair pace, and looming trees did shield us from the weather. For nearly an hour, we saw

---

*   Rabbit stewed in wine with nutmeg and lemon.

nobody. As it began to get light, I dared to hope that we would make Windsor without mishap.

'Behind us,' I looked as Peter pointed. Five riders, rounding a turn in the road a hundred yards or so behind. When they saw us, they spurred their horses and shouted.

'There they are!'

'Damn, go off through the woodland,' Bulstrode shouted. We all kicked our horses into a gallop and I followed Peter, jumping over a ditch to get into the cover of the trees. Bulstrode was coming on close behind me. I was a better horseman than either of them, but I was still suffering from the effects of the poison and in no fit state for a fight.

Trees flashed past in a blur as I leaned over my horse's neck, and gave him his head; a quick glance behind showed that the riders were following us through the woodland, and they were closer.

'Split up,' shouted Bulstrode. That was a fool's plan, but things were happening too fast to question, and we all went off in different directions. I slapped Apple's rump and rode, not marking which way I went, seeking only to escape. My horse and I thundered along at a fair pace, jumping fallen trees, and bushes in our path.

Soon, I was woefully lost. I drew Apple up, and listened for the sound of pursuit; there was nothing. After a moment of thought, I pulled Darnelly's compass from my satchel. At least I knew which direction Windsor and safety lay. Without it, I would have been wallowing in a shit-bucket of trouble. I paused and loaded a pistol, cursed my poor luck, and prayed that the powder was dry.

For close on quarter an hour, I weaved my way carefully through the woodland; seeing neither hide-nor-hair of anybody, till Apple started pricking his ears. I pulled up again and listened out for my friends.

'Blandford, Blandford,' I could hear the shouts. It must be Peter and Bulstrode I thought, directing my horse to the calls.

We pushed past some bushes, but I kept my pistol at the ready. I rode into a clearing expecting to see my friends and found instead one of my pursuers there on horseback calling out my name, the bastard!

'Over here! I have him. He wears the hat.'

I shot the swine, taking him in the chest and spinning him around, throwing him from the horse.

I threw my pistol in its holster, and galloped away; there were more shouts and the crack of shot. One of them was quick, he got on my tail and nothing my horse or I could do would throw the bastard off the scent. We swerved and ducked past trees and over ditches. I let Apple lead, he was more surefooted than I, but the cavalier was drawing level, sword in hand. He swung at me; I pulled on the reigns to avoid the slash, and he missed. I dashed off in a different direction with him crashing on behind.

Both of us were swept from our saddles by a low hanging branch and the horses galloped on. I hit the ground, rolled, and came to my feet quickly. Drawing my dagger I dived on him; he struggled against me, but I was on top, using all my weight to subdue him. I shoved a gauntleted hand into his mouth to choke him as we struggled. He bit down on me, but I ignored the pain, stabbing at his eye with my other hand.

I drove the knife into his eye socket, ignoring the pop! as it punctured eyeball and bone, and pushed through into his brain. He shook for a few seconds and then was still.

I paused and listened for the sound of the others, but the woods were quiet. Searching the body proved fruitless. There was nothing of value, not even some coin. His clothes were sturdy, but coarse, with good boots though. He was just some poor trooper, I guessed.

That left me with no idea what to do next. I was without horse, and had only sword and dagger for protection. One course of action was clear though: I threw away my hat. I like red and I like hats, but it was not worth dying over. And then a disturbing thought finally broke through into my noggin: someone actually wished me dead.

That introduced me to a world of fear. People trying to kill me in battle was already enough, without dealing with assassins to boot.

I had also lost my compass in the scramble, and with the sky grey and full of rain, I had no idea which direction to take, but staying with the corpse was no choice at all. I cleaned my dagger on the tough's clothes and started to trudge away, as swiftly and quietly as I could.

I trolled about* those woods, sodden through from rain, hair pasted to my face, dripping down my doublet. Exhausted and terrified, I jumped at every sound. Once or twice, I heard someone crashing through the trees nearby, and shouts, but I hid, not knowing if they were friend or foe. I sat in a bush for hours, straining at every sound, fearful of being found. As it grew dark, I smelled wood-smoke on the breeze; someone was close. I drew my sword and crept forwards out of the bushes, whispering a prayer to myself—the idea of a divinity is always more amenable when danger is near—swearing to mend my ways if only I found safety.

In a clearing surrounded by stacks of coppiced wood was a little stone-built house with a thatched roof. Smoke was coming from the chimney and I could smell food. A forester or charcoal burner, I thought. Despite that logic, the word "Witch" kept flickering in my head. It was getting dark, there was no way I could survive the elements in my state. I had no choice.

Damn, I will bed down with the devil himself if I can have a spot by his fire, I mused. From prayers to profanity in a matter of yards. I am a fickle fellow.

I walked around to the front, noticing the shutters closed on the windows. Cautiously I went up to the door and knocked.

I heard a dog yap, and shuffling from within, followed by bolts being drawn back. A voice called out something

*   Wandered.

unintelligible. Finally, the door opened just a smidgen, and the flared muzzle of a musketoon* was thrust out.

A bearded gargoyle of a man confronted me. Short and dirty, with a bulbous purple growth all over the front of his face instead of a nose: a clear sign of the Spanish Disease.†

'What do you want?' He thrust the muzzle at me, a small terrier growling at his feet.

'I need help, please can you hide me. I have coin.' There could be no mistaking the desperation in my voice.

He looked me over taking in my sodden state: hatless, muddied, bloodied and with sword in hand.

'Best you come in, then,' he said it slowly as if remembering the words, pulled me inside, and looked around to see if I was being followed.

Inside the house was a mere room. A broken down bed covered in blankets, a table, and a couple of chairs next to a fire. From the rafters of the low hanging roof hung all manner of odds and ends, pots, and pans, onions even; in one corner a barrel of what I assumed was ale. It was hot from the large fireplace, a pot bubbling away with some kind of stew. I remembered my hunger but also my manners, and recent experience with stew made me wary.

'You can put your sword away, lad. I do not invite people into my home only to murder them,' he said to me. Then looking at the yappy little terrier: 'Now, Pepper, mind your manners, we have guests.' For a moment, I had a vision of my father slamming the table back at home.

'Thank you,' I said, sheathing my sword. Apart from his face, he was a shamble of filth, ragged doublet, leather breeches, and stinking of wood smoke.

He waved away my thanks, putting down his musketoon. 'Hungry?' I nodded. He went over to the cauldron and ladled out a bowl of the stew, then reached into a cupboard, pulled

---

*   Blunderbuss
†   Syphilis, the Spanish called it the French Disease.

out some black bread and tore me off a hunk. It was cabbage soup with leek, potato, and bacon.

He watched me as I devoured the food; I made no pretence at manners, gobbling it down and licking my fingers. 'More?' He asked, as I wiped the bowl clean with bread.

'Yes, please.' It was the best meal I ever had, soothing my tender stomach and warming from the cold.

He took my bowl and ladled another helping of stew and bread for me. This time I took in the flavour, well seasoned, tasty and, from what I could tell, not poisoned.

'You are a soldier?' he said.

'Yes, of sorts.'

'Of sorts? Either you are or you are not, lad.'

'I am,' I said, 'but not a very good one, I fear.' He laughed at that, a gappy toothless smile.

'Why?' he asked.

'Why what?'

'Why are you a soldier?'

I half-smiled. 'I wanted fame and fortune,' I said, 'and was swept along, in a manner of speaking.'

'And now?'

'Now, it seems, fame and fortune are a bit more difficult to catch than I imagined.'

'I heard about the war last time I went to village,' he said.

'Do you go there much?' I asked. 'This place is quite solitary.'

He gave me another gappy smile. 'You are the first person I've seen since Christmas. I will most likely go to the village at Easter in a couple of weeks.'

'Are we near Windsor?' I asked, trying not to look at his face.

'Aye, about five miles o'er that way.' Five miles was not too far if I could avoid trouble.

'I will show you the way in the morning,' he told me, starting to stack up a pipe. 'This filthy weather is set in, and 'twill soon be too dark for travel.'

I fumbled for my purse to give him some coin, but he put up a filthy mitt.

'Do not insult me, lad, 'tis my Christian duty to help you. As did the Good Samaritan.'

'What are you doing out here on your own?' I asked, although judging from his face, I had a fair idea.

'Charcoal burning. I've lived out here alone nigh on fifteen years now, but I was a soldier like you once. When I was young and had a face.'

A timely reminder that a night in the arms of Venus can lead to a lifetime on Mercury, and a pox-racked body.

'Why were you a soldier?'

He laughed at that. 'They said the pay was good. I thought I would get enough to marry my sweetheart. By the time I got home, she had married someone else.'

*When such a spacious mirror is set before him. He needs must see himself.**

'The carts come in August to pick up my burn and pay me. I go into the village then for church, but I do not think the vicar likes it; he minds not at all, if I am absent most Sundays.' He chuckled to himself. 'I have my bible, and with the Lord's creation all around me, it is as good as a church— better, maybe.'

'Is that not heresy?' I said.

'Is it?' He turned his eyes on me, and for the first time I noticed a fierce intelligence.

How to answer that. Of course, it was heresy to some but I would not condemn him for it. For myself, I was never a radical. Cromwell told me once that he fought for toleration, and I think he even believed it. It is as good a cause as any to hang your hat on in a war of religion. Nowadays of course, a man need not hide away in the woods because of his faith. We are oh-so tolerant in England (as long as you be not

---

*   *Anthony and Cleopatra*, Act V, Scene I.

Jewish, Catholic, or a Turk). Even a smidge of atheism is now acceptable. I wonder what King Oliver would say to that?

'My face ain't so particular for company is it? Fret not, lad, I saw you staring. The stares was why I came away to live on my own.'

'Your pardon; I did not mean to stare.' I had not realised I was.

'No mind, if I you had a face like mine I would stare.' The terrier jumped into his lap. 'Old Pepper here do not notice, and the Lord God do not notice. Even if I cannot turn a pretty lady's head without turning her stomach any more, I am not lonely.'

'I fight for Parliament against the King,' I told him, wondering if that would change his stance.

'Sides do not really matter too much, lad, the war is a long way from me,' he paused. 'Well was, till you came-a-knocking.'

'Your pardon again.'

'It is of no matter, lad, as I keep telling you. In the morning I will see you on your way safely to Windsor, and life will go back much the same as before.'

'When were you a soldier?' I asked.

'I was in Cadiz in twenty-five,' he told me, 'and Bohemia before that.'

Cadiz had been one of the King's early military misadventures. He must have seen the look on my face because he chuckled.

'Old age is a bastard sneak; it steals your strength and saps your faculties,' he said.

I did not understand him then; I do now of course.

We sat in silence after that for a while. The Charcoal Burner puffing away at his pipe. The glow from the bowl as he sucked on the 'bacco lit the room. When he finished he grabbed up some blankets, and told me to make up a bed by the fire, whilst he knelt and prayed, then lay down on his filthy bed. My blankets were dirty and probably louse ridden, but I was exhausted and fell asleep quickly.

I was with Emily; she was laughing at a jest then leaned in to kiss me. My hands fumbled with her bodice struggling to free her glorious little titties. I could feel her lips on mine, her tongue in my mouth, lapping away at me with her stinky breath—damn dog, ruining my dream.

I pushed Pepper away from my face and sat up. It was still dark and raining, but the charcoal burner was already up. There was a smell of bacon frying in a pan.

'You want some breakfast, lad?' He asked.

'Yes, please,' I said. My stomach was groaning with hunger and I ached from falling asleep in my damp clothes. I forced myself to stand and stretch, rubbing my legs, to bring life back into them.

After a breakfast of bacon and bread, he led me through the woods; we followed the twists and turns of animal tracks, with Pepper at our heels. Finally, after about an hour, we reached the tree line and in the distance, I could see Windsor Castle rising above the floodplain. There was a couple of miles walk across fields, and over hedgerows to Eton Bridge, and then I would be safe.

I turned to face the charcoal burner, pulling my purse out to hand to him.

'Put your money away, lad. You will need it more than I.'

'How can I thank you?'

''Tis no matter; 'twas payment enough to have company for a change. May your God go with you.' With that, he turned and walked back into the woods, with his terrier following behind. I watched him go in silence, a strange little man that had probably saved my life.

It was only afterwards I realised he never asked my name nor offered his.

I thanked God for my deliverance and followed the hedgerows down across muddy fields heading for the castle in the distance. In my weakened state, I had to pause often, cursing my boots that were better made for riding, and scraping off the mud that collected on the soles like glue. Climbing over a gate, I followed a lane for a few hundred yards, before cutting across the fields once more.

'Well, if it be not Sugar Candy,' came a man's voice.

I started, looking around. There, perched in a ditch by the hedgerow, carbine in hand, was a figure wrapped up in cloak and hat. A scarf covered his face. My hand went to my sword.

'Who are you?' I recognised the voice, but could not place it.

'Your uncle has had men out looking for you all night since Whitelocke got back. They picked up your horse this morning. Lucky for me I found you.'

'Thank God,' I said. Finally, I could start to relax; I was safe.

Then he shot me.

Dearest Elizabeth,

I have arrived in Oxford, the travel was exceeding difficult, but with the passport procured by Mr Carpenter we were unhindered. At present I am lodged at Holton with James, and Mistress Jane and her family.

I must tell of the most fortunate occurrence which has quite transformed my prospects in Oxford. I am to be appointed companion to Miss Margaret Lucas, younger sister to Sir Charles Lucas, and she is exceeding young, here at court.

It is no onerous task for she is said to be quiet and pleasant, yet I hope that we can become friends for court is wondrous. Miss Lucas is to be Lady in Waiting to the Queen and I companion to such. It is a splendid affair.

I find myself quite delighted at the prospects of such employ, unsought but for the intervention of the Countess of Carlisle, who I happened upon during my journey to Oxford. At her insistence, I presented myself to Sir Charles in the hope of a position, and with her approval and encouragement was granted such.

I must confess James seemed most displeased with my appointment. I hazard he wished for me to wait upon him like a servant instead of advancing. His cloud is dissipated however in the sunlight of the court. It is so bright and happy, I could scarce believe that such miserable times are abroad, for all is gaiety and joy here.

I must have funds, for if I am to continue the good standing I have thus enjoyed, I must sustain myself in sufficient style. Please present my hopes to Father, and persuade him that my presence in Oxford does nothing but improve our standing.

Goodnight sweet sister, I will write again soon.

Anne.

March 9th 1643

Post Script: I write this in haste before the carrier departs. I have word of Blandford. To my dismay, James has informed me that he was killed in fighting near Windsor, but we have had no confirmation as yet.

I hope and pray that he is not taken, but fear it is as James insists.

A.

14. Windsor, April 1643.

Smiling, she chides in a kind murmuring noise,
  And from her body wipes the clammy joys,
When, with a thousand kisses wandering o'er
  My panting bosom, "Is there then no more?"
She cries. "All this to love and rapture's due;
  Must we not pay a debt to pleasure too?"

(John Wilmot, 2nd Earl of Rochester, *The Imperfect Enjoyment.*)

I stared out of the window, down to the fields beside the Thames. A regiment of infantry were drilling; new recruits who could not hold their pikes straight, and musketeers without muskets standing aimlessly in the drizzle. It was little wonder we were losing the war.

In happier times my room would have been occupied by some royal lackey, but the rich furnishings and paintings had been stripped out and sold, leaving only the pale impression of their occupancy on the walls. The bed was good, well strung and wide, but a month of inactivity left me feeling like a caged bird.

The wound itself was not too bad, the bullet had bounced off one of the steel bands in my doublet and lost most of its force, but still it made a mess of my shoulder. Darnelly was, of course, overjoyed at his doublet's effectiveness. I received a smug little thank you note from him.

To be shot is to be hit with a hammer. No pain at first as you are thrown to the floor by the force of the blow. Then comes a white-hot agony, throbbing, emanating from your wound. You can feel your blood boil, burning as it seeps out, and with it your life.

The would-be ravilliac escaped; the arrival of Peter and troopers stopped him from finishing the task, but he ran for a horse. That was not comforting; the thought of him being out there, waiting to attack me again, fairly had me wetting myself in fear.

Whilst I sulked, ate gruel, and annoyed the servants, England burned from war. The commission had gone back to Oxford to plead with the King to see sense, all to no avail. The different sides manoeuvred their forces like chess pieces in anticipation of the Spring. As long as both sides held out hope of absolute victory through force, there could be no negotiation, no peace. A war that nobody had wanted was now a war nobody dared to stop.

In the West Country the Cornish had started their great advance towards Bristol, my brother Henry among them, under General Hopton. The newsbooks were full of tales of atrocity: the usual bile of baby-killing and rape that was still unbelievable to me. My innocence did not have much longer to last; it would die in a privy in Reading.

'Black' Tom Fairfax and his father fared little better in the north; the Royalists held Newcastle and York, and had established a strong garrison in Newark. Without help, father and son could not hold out against the Royalist numbers— not even the Holy Ghost could save them. The Queen's return from France with gold and weapons had only boosted Royalist hopes further, and though I was not to know it then, her return would have a profound impact upon me.

Bulstrode and Peter had both come to see me in the first week of my incarceration, but had now left Windsor: Bulstrode to Oxford taking Sam Brayne with him, Peter with the rest of the scouts to Reading. The Earl of Essex, reinforced by the London Trained Bands, was preparing for the new campaign. Reading—held for the King after our retreat from Edgehill—was the gateway to Oxford and the midlands, and our first step.

I threw myself back onto the bed and picked up the letter from Elizabeth. Jacob had brought it from London with a box of receipts and complaints from Barker about lack of monies from the Phoenix.

My Dearest Brother,

Still you have not written, Blandford, causing much concern to your family. I can only hope that you are well, and have not succumbed to some grievous disease incapacitating your fingers.

She started with sarcasm that boded well.

Our father is now bedridden with a palsy that comes and goes, but still the doctors can find no cause to the disease. With Anne now availing herself of the pleasures in Oxford, I am left to nurse him alone. Henry has found time to visit only once, while Sarah is now great with child and has gone to her family in Farleigh for lying in.

Ha! That left Elizabeth alone waiting on Father and the rector. Serve the sneaky harridan right.

Uncle Samuel informs me that you still have not visited our Grandfather in Cople, or our cousins. This is most remiss of you. Your ill manners can reflect upon all of us.

Well, I did actually feel some guilt over that, but nagging me was not going to help.

The Cavaliers raided Trowbridge this week making off with some horse after a distraction had been raised in the market-place by a preacher calling out 'For the King, for the King.' Rumours of Prince Rupert abound in the village. Have you seen the Prince? It is said his dog "Boy" is a demon, and protects him in battle.

Most of the male servants have now left with your brothers, only the old men tend to the estate. Mercifully, the Roundhead garrison have left us alone, despite Henry and James serving the King. Others have not been so lucky, Royalist estates are raided for coin and plate.

The monies for the year-end have been poor; the war has disrupted business, and your brothers raid our finances for their own purpose. I have accounted another sum for your allowance with Mr Barker for this quarter. I do expect a response this time, brother, else I will be forced to withhold such allowances in future.

Remember, dearest brother, what blessedness accompanies prayer, when you are wearied, when cares corrode you, and fears disturb you;

when infirmities oppress you, go unto the lord your God and feel peace.

Your loving and affectionate sister,

Elizabeth.

I crumpled up the letter and threw it to the floor. I had already read of the attack on Trowbridge in the news books, and if she was frustrated at home waiting on our father, I was frustrated at the tedium of Windsor. The money though would be welcome, if I was ever allowed out to play again. Coin is always welcome. "No money; no cunny," call out the whores of Gropecunt Lane; as true a phrase of love that I have ever heard.

A knock on the door shook me from my contemplation. Lucy Hay swept into my room, dressed in rose coloured damask, draped in lace, and wearing a spectacular hat. I do like hats.

'I see the invalid is still abed.'

I struggled to get out of my cot.

'Oh, do not rise; you've been having some adventures I hear.' She settled into a chair beside my bed, took off the hat and let her brown ringlets fall free.

'Yes, Milady,' I said meekly.

'So, how are we feeling today?'

'I am much better thank you, Milady,' I said. 'Hopefully I can go back to my friends soon.'

The Countess of Carlisle smiled at me, 'Indeed? Well we still do not want you to over-exert yourself now do we?'

Her gloved hands were toying absently with the edge of my blanket. 'Such a pretty face,' she leaned forward cupping my face with one hand, whilst the other slipped under the covers. Not knowing what to say, and in a strange combination of anticipation and terror, I said nothing at all.

'Poor boy, your mother died so young. You have missed the tender ministrations of a woman,' she said.

My mother died when I was a child, and I am certain her hand never dallied where the Countess of Carlisle's now played.

'Oh, you are eager.' She kissed me, her tongue darting fire in my mouth, as she lifted her skirts, and jumped astride me as if I were a docile pony.

This was only going to end one way, and I am certain your imagination is more vivid than my pen; besides, there are some memories an old man keeps to himself.

Afterwards, I lay silent but puffed up with pride at cuckolding Pym. That should have given me pause for thought, instead I wondered if I was ready to go again (at nineteen I could stand to attention in double quick time, and even now the thought of Lucy Hay makes my flaccid manhood stir).

She was a beautiful woman and with powerful connections. Buckingham's punk first, until Buckingham put her aside for the Queen of France. It was rumoured that in a fit of spite she had stolen the queen's diamond necklace—I can believe it. She had bedded Strafford until Pym had him executed, then she went and seduced Pym! I wonder what her former lover's shade thought of that. Well, she had more tricks in the bedchamber than her wizard father had potions and spells, and I—like so many others—was blinded by her charms.[58]

She picked up Elizabeth's crumpled letter from the floor.

'Your sister still writes to you and sends you money I see. What does the leaf mean?' she pointed to the little oak leaf that Elizabeth drew on all her letters.

'Elizabeth being clever,' I said.

Lucy turned her big brown eyes on me and I near swooned at the loveliness, but it was still a little early for my passions to rise again. I lay my head back on the bolster and explained. 'When we were children she would run away and hide in a hollow old oak tree on the estate. She thinks we never knew but I did; she used to keep the books father had forbidden there. Ever since then, she has used the oak leaf sigil.'

'Books?'

'Nothing worth stealing.' I let my hand drop to her bubbie, fondling it, and hoping to rouse her desires again, but it seemed the debt to pleasure had been paid.

'Well, Mr Candy, perhaps it is time for you to be up and about.' She pushed my hand away. 'I cannot dally in bed all day even for one as pretty as you.'

She kissed me gently and rose from the bed, brushed down her crumpled dress and petticoats, and swept out again with merely a wave and another glorious smile, leaving me dumbfounded in silence.

She was right of course; a month of inaction was more than enough. My wound was nearly healed, although it still twinges like buggery in the mornings, so the next day I got out of bed, dressed and went to see my uncle.

Windsor Castle had been ransacked; if it was valuable and could be ripped out and sold, it had been. The deer herd was wiped out as every man wanted a taste of venison and there was an armed camp in the Great Park. Trees had been torn down to provide fuel for their fires. I followed Thames Street round the curtain walls of the castle, down to the bridge over the river. Ale vendors and bawdy houses had taken over the buildings facing the wall, giving the town a riotous air as they catered to the new recruits.

'Are you sure about this, Master?' said Jacob, looking concerned.

'Yes, yes indeed, do not fuss.' I was in good health, just a little out of puff after so long inactive.

My uncle was set up in Eton College, so we crossed the bridge following the High Street to the school. I gave Jacob some coin and told him to see what food there was in the town. I wanted mutton, not gruel, and a bottle of sack to wash it down. His arrival had been a pleasant surprise, and having an extra pair of eyes on me felt safer with an assassin abroad.

There were guards on duty at the entrance; soldiers billeted in the buildings facing the street. I asked a trooper directions, and he pointed me across the quadrangle to some red-bricked chambers.

The antechamber set aside for my uncle's new secretary was a spacious room, clean whitewash, and a row of chairs along one wall. The secretary sat behind his desk and in one of the chairs was my fellow scout Franny Cole. I had not seen him since we started our training with Darnelly.

'Well met, Franny. What are you doing here? I thought everyone was out near Reading.'

'Morning, Sugar, I was coming to see you later and share a bottle of sack. I bring reports for your uncle, if *Malvolio* over there ever deigns to let me see him.'

I looked over to Mr Samuel Butler. Oh, he's famous now; the darling of the Tories. Then, he was merely a disgraced clerk throwing himself on my uncle's mercy. It makes his dirty lies in *Hudibras* worse somehow. After they buried him in Covent Garden, with all his honours, I went and pissed on his grave.

He was short and chubby, already balding at the crown, with lank sandy hair dangling down his back. I guess he could not have been more than thirty, but seemed older, with protruding lip that made him resemble some Hapsburg degenerate. Jammed behind a plain wooden desk covered with papers and quills and ink. The only ornament in the room was a rough portrait on the wall behind him. Butler ignored my entrance and carried on scribbling.[59]

'What is amiss?' I asked in a lower tone.

'He is a petty little official, with a jumped up sense of his own importance, and no measurable sense of humour,' said Franny, not bothering to moderate his voice.

Butler looked up, sighed, and turned to a piece of paper,

scratching a line through whatever was written on it. I went over to his desk. He carried on writing, ignoring me for a minute, until I coughed.

'Yes?' He asked in a tired tone, not bothering to look up.

'I am here to see my uncle,' I told him.

'You do not have an appointment, do you?' He looked up.

'No, I fear I do not,' I said politely.

'Then you will have to wait; your uncle is a very busy man. He cannot just drop everything because some people think they are important,' he said, turning to glare at Franny.

'Very well,' I said. I had nothing else to do so waiting did not bother me. I went to sit back with Franny.

'That man's a shitling,' he told me. 'I asked him who painted the monster on the wall and he went off like a firecracker.'

I took a closer look at the portrait on the wall, and I use the term portrait loosely. Some woman I assumed, although I would not stake my life on it. One eye was higher than the other, giving her an odd squint, and hair that looked like a blob of black paint perched on the top of the head. It looked more a daub by a child.

'Maybe 'tis of his mother,' I said.

'He told me he had painted it himself. I told him he was lucky to have a job as a clerk then. I've been waiting ever since,' said Franny. 'Four other people have gone in whilst I've been sat on my arse. The only thing that damn picture is worth, is for kindling on a fire.' His voice got louder as he spoke. Butler gave him another vindictive glare from his desk, and then turned back to his papers.

After only a few minutes of waiting, the door to my uncle's office opened, and a stout, hook-nosed man strode out, flushed with anger. Middle aged, running to fat, and with thin straight hair swept back to disguise his bald crown.

'Get out of my way, damn-your-eyes,' he swore at Butler, kicking his chair, and strode past us, making Franny grin at the secretary's discomfort. 'Damnable Rebels.'

Butler looked over at me. 'Mr Candy, your uncle can spare you five minutes now. I am sure Mr Cole can wait a bit longer.' He smiled sweetly, as Franny's grin turned to a scowl.

'Go on in, I will see you afterwards,' he said, glaring back at Butler.

I walked past Butler, through the door behind him, into my uncle's office. He was standing with his back to me, staring out of the windows to the army training in the fields outside. I coughed politely.

'Blandford, my boy, how are you feeling?' He said, turning to me.

'Much better, Uncle,' I said.

'Mr Butler is still keeping Cole waiting, I see.' He smiled. 'It will do Franny no harm. He is too cocksure at times; it will be the death of him if he is not careful. Now then, what can I do for you, my boy?'

'I am bored, Uncle, can I go back with Franny to the scouts?' He burst out laughing at my moan.

'Happy news indeed after my last guest, who is frankly one of the most spotted fellows I have had the misfortune to be acquainted with.' He sat down behind his desk and smiled.

'He did not look too happy,' I said. 'He kicked Butler's chair on the way out.'

'That was Sir Edmund Sawyer, he was declared unfit to ever sit in the House in twenty eight. Now he is trying to escape a debt of £500 that he swindled from a widow. He will be in Oxford sucking up to the King's council by tonight; they are welcome to the odious liar.'[60] He shrugged, 'I have been keeping you here for a reason, my boy, and I needed information and did not dare risk you if it would draw attention. A scout is useless if he is being watched.' He beckoned for me to take a seat.

'I am being watched?'

'It seems you have attracted the attention of some

important women, my boy. First the Countess of Carlisle takes a hand in the newsbook business...'

'The Countess is on our side, isn't she?' I interrupted; his tone worried me, especially after my recreation the day before.

He laughed again at that. 'The Countess is a Percy. She is neither fully on our side or the King's, nor is her brother. The Percys are only truly for the Percys.'

'I do not understand,' I said. I always feel a bit dirty when I realise I have been used, and there was a glimmer of realisation now.

'Her family were lords of the north when the Stuarts were nought but gatekeepers to Scottish chieftains,' my uncle told me. 'King James imprisoned her father, and Northumberland has seen his influence ignored at court. I believe they would be happy to see the King humbled, but not so happy perhaps to see Parliament's pre-eminence. And, she may be Pym's mistress, but she is also the Queen's favourite, and the Queen has returned from France.'[61]

'You think Lucy Hay wants me dead?' Surely that could not be true; it would make her some kind of monster.

'No, but she takes too close an interest in your affairs for my liking,' replied my uncle. 'However, I do not think we can say the same of your brother's companion.'

'Mistress Whorwood? Why would she wish me harm?' This was all becoming far too complex for me.

'You fought well at Edgehill and took a colour,' he said.

'So did at least twenty other men that day,' I said. 'Arthur Young even took the King's colour.'

'It is not so much about you, more about the person you killed in taking the colour.'

'The red haired boy carrying the ensign?'

'Exactly. His name was James Maxwell; his mother was the old queen's laundry woman. He has a half-sister from his mother's first marriage. You have met her; her maiden name was Rider, but she married an Oxfordshire gentleman—Brome Whorwood.'[62]

'Bugger! Well, the red hair fits.'

'Indeed.' He took his spectacles off, leaned back and looked at me. 'It seems Mistress Whorwood was none too pleased with your action at Kineton. However, she has had more than just revenge on her mind.'

'What else?'

'She is Lord Falkland's agent.[63] Her contacts move money for the King. Not just money though, she has a network of informers passing secrets to Oxford. From the information you gave me, it is probable that she has been plotting with Edmund Waller for the King. Her washerwomen were certainly behind the distribution of the *Aulicus* in London. When you shut down the printers in Wapping, you further enraged her I fear.'

'I have a habit of upsetting women,' I said blithely. He gave me a half smile and continued.

'However, now she has revealed herself and that was foolish,' he said. 'In our business, my boy, it is better to walk in the shadows than to reveal yourself. Mistress Whorwood gave away an advantage for no other reason than to meet you. Engaging as you are, it was not worth it.'

'Zounds, had I known that, I would have tempered my courtesy in Oxford. What of Elizabeth, is she in danger?' I had told him of my meeting with my brother, and my slip of the tongue regarding Elizabeth's letters.

'The West Country is under Parliament's control for now, but the Cornish are advancing,' he said. 'At the moment, Elizabeth is safe in Hilperton, but I must confess I have placed her in danger. I assure you, Blandford, that was not my intent.' Uncle Samuel looked quite mournful at that.

'She has always been a meddler, Uncle. I am sure she would have found trouble without our help.' Although, in my mind there was a growing fear that I had put my sister in danger, rather than my uncle.

He smiled and leaned forward. 'Your sister is an intelligent woman, Blandford. She is very much like your mother. When Elizabeth wrote to me a few years ago, I confess it was like having my own sister back again. I allowed her to gather information in Wiltshire, on local doings, and enjoyed her news. She has a rare insight and before long was providing vital intelligence from the west. Your father's business contacts gave her access to people with money and power,' he paused. 'It is no secret I was against your parents' marriage, Blandford. I felt my sister married beneath herself, but your father was charming and handsome and she was besotted.'

'My father charming and handsome? Are you sure you have the right man?'

He laughed again. 'Ah, the curse of children to never know their parents. In his youth, Christopher could charm anyone. It is why his business has done so well; he is a consummate salesman. He became a drunk after your mother died.'

That was food for thought. Perhaps the apple does not fall that far from the tree after all.

'So what of Elizabeth now?' I asked.

'For now she is safe; if things change I will ensure Elizabeth is brought to London, whatever your Father says. I promise you that, my boy.' I am sure there was a glistening in his eyes as he said that, but he turned away and looked back out of the window.

'I shall give thought on sending you back to the scouts with Franny, my boy. Tell Mr Butler to let him in now; they both have had their fun.' With that, I was dismissed. I went back to the antechamber.

'My uncle says he wishes to see Franny now, Mr Butler.'

He looked at me with disdain, 'Indeed? I shall send him in presently.' Franny was right; the man was an arsehole.

'I will see you in a bit,' I said to Franny as I walked past. He nodded as Butler finally called him over to go in and see my uncle.

I walked slowly back up the hill to the castle and my billet, thinking of my parents in their youth. I had no memories of my mother; she had died when Anne was born.

Jacob still had not returned from his errands about Eton, so I threw myself onto the bed and lay staring at the ceiling. I had gone into this war with no real convictions, no real beliefs other than my own amusement. Now, I was marked for death by assassins. That should have been enough to send me running, but instead I was indignant. Before, I had risked life and limb for promotion, for wealth; now it was become a matter of survival.

My Dear Heart,

This afternoon, I received letters from you by Tom Elliot, to which I have nothing to reply, except that I shall certainly never find anything to blame in what you are pleased to do. I only tell my opinions and submit, but I will wait till I see you, for I am afraid lest my letters be explained after another fashion that that which I intend.

Only I cannot refrain from saying this word to you that there is something about disbanding armies which I do not like. I will only say to you en passant, that if you do it before this perpetual parliament is finished, all is lost.

This bearer will tell you tidings from the place whence he comes. Wherefore, I have nothing more to say. Percy is with me, I think him very faithful, and that we may trust him.[64]

Our army is gone to Leeds and at this time are beating down the town. God sends us good success: our affairs are in very good condition in this country; besides eleven garrisons that we have in Yorkshire, our army marches seven thousand effective footmen, two thousand five hundred Horse and one thousand dragoons—all very resolute; twelve pieces of cannon and two mortars.

Entirely Yours,

Henrietta Maria, York 9th April.

It was advertised this day from Reading, the Earl of Essex having drawn together all his forces, and caused the bridges over the river of Loddon (which he had formerly broke down) to be set up again, was marched with all his army towards that town, intending to assault the same, and that he was already come within the sight of their works, to the great joy of all the garrison, who have long desired to see his Excellency, and try the metal of his soldiers: whose brave exploits are so much talked of in the weekly pamphlets, though not heard of otherwise.

For the particular, some of their newsbooks tell us of a former visit bestowed upon that town by the garrison of Wokingham, eighty of which are said to come the last week very near the town, and to tarry a great while there in expectation that some of the Cavaliers would have showed themselves: but finding none so hardy as to issue out, they went to one Master Halsted's house, not far off the town, and were there set upon by two troops of Horse that followed after, whom they charged so valiantly, that they soon routed them, and took nine of their horses, and returned in triumph to Wokingham.

A tale as manifestly untrue, as that Prince Rupert plundered Birmingham before the battle at Edgehill, and got there so much money and plate as paid his army; or that the rebels issuing out of Manchester, had beat the Earl of Derby, not far from Wigan, that last week they took 1500 of his men, 1000 Arms, many pieces of ordnance, in goods and money twenty thousand pounds, and made the Earl himself flee into the steeple; or that the Marquesse of Worcester is held prisoner in Cardiff Castle, and the Lord Digby killed at Birmingham; or that every one of Prince Rupert's Dragooners are double armed, that is to say, with a musket before, and an Irish whore behind; or that Sir William Waller when he came first to Tewksbury (after his beating up of the Lord Herbert's quarters) took 25 of His Majesties horse, with their pistols, carbines, and other arms, and

16,000 pounds in money; or that there are two fleets of Danes, and Dunkirkers now at sea, under English colours, for the invasion of this realm.

All which besides many other petite falsehoods, are most impudently are affirmed for undoubted truths in the London newsbooks which came out this week.

John Berkenhead and Peter Heylyn.

Sweet Elizabeth,

I can send to you since our last such joyous news (if it has not come to you already) for which I can only thank the Lord our God. Blandford lives! I had word from my lady the Countess of Carlisle, that he was only injured in fighting near Windsor. Mistress Margaret says that whilst righteous joy at his survival is no dishonour, it is best to not display such in present company.

Mistress Margaret is exceeding bright, but too shy and bashful. She hides away too much, but we are become friends. We travel north to meet with Her Majesty in York in the company of Prince Rupert himself. And he is very dashing indeed. James rides with us, but he is kept busy with his troops, and is still in much dudgeon about my appointment. Mistress Margaret says that Madam Whorwood is not so high in favour now that Her Majesty has returned, and James is much reduced because of that.

Please give my sincerest love to Father. He is well I hope? I had word from Henry that he hoped soon to be in Wiltshire. My Lord Hopton drives all before him in the west. Perhaps soon this great divide will be over. Mistress Margaret is not so hopeful, she says it will last years and years, but I am not so melancholic.

I will write again soon dearest Elizabeth, when I am arrived in York.

Anne.

Newark, 16th April 1643.

15. Reading, April 1643.

When all my joys are thus complete, the Cannons loud do play;
The Drums alarum straight do beat,
Trumpets sound, horse away,
Awake I then, and nought can find but death attending me,
And all my joys are vanished quite; this is my misery.

(Anonymous Ballad, *The Loyal Soldier.*)

I crawled on my belly in the mud, seeking a better view of the Cavalier column. At least a regiment of dragoons, some infantry, and five carts. The commander was careless; no outriders or scouts, but we did not have any troops north of the Thames able to intercept them. I waited for the column to pass, noting the numbers down in my journal. Once they were out of sight, I scrambled back up to the copse where I had left my horse, and then rode towards the siege lines around Reading. Uncle Samuel would want to know about the column, before they could do any damage.

The army had left Windsor in the middle of April with me in tow. It was not like the march to Edgehill when hope still drove us forward. Now, there was only a grim resignation to continued battle. I travelled in comfort this time, with a servant, and victuals, and bottles of sack, determined to avoid the squalid hunger of the previous autumn. Jacob seemed happy enough to follow me on campaign. I had assured him that there was no need for him to fight, but I noticed he went armed with pistol and short sword, and handled them like a veteran.

A reliable servant is a rare jewel; if you find one keep him close. I gave thanks more than once for Jacob's service.

The Earl of Essex determined to take Reading, before advancing onto Oxford. We swept around the town encircling it from the west. Hampden's Greencoats took

Caversham Bridge over the Thames, sealing the city off from reinforcement. Essex offered the Royalists a chance to surrender, but Governor Aston declared he would, 'Hold the town for the King, or starve and die in it.' Aston, a catholic, was a damn fine soldier despite his faith, but without help from the King in Oxford, Reading was doomed.

A great square of ditch and rampart had been thrown up around Reading. Earth and gabion reinforced the old abbey walls facing the Thames, then ran south to the drowned floodplain of the Kennet. Forts and redoubts completed the defence. The Thames protected the whole northern flank of the town, but also stopped reinforcement; south and west, our trench-lines and gun emplacements, kept up a constant fire. Our cannoneers targeted the church towers and spires, pounding the town. Every day, wagons of powder and shot, and supply, came down the road from London to keep the guns roaring.

Reading was invested from all sides. I arrived at Caversham Bridge and showed my pass to the guarding pikemen.

'Any news from the north, Sugar?' one asked me.

'Nothing of interest,' I said, and clattered across the bridge.

Essex had set up Headquarters at a manor owned by Daniel Blagrave, one of Reading's members of Parliament. An old moated grange built out of sandstone, with an ancient guardhouse. It was well fortified and made a perfect headquarters. The large grounds and outbuildings provided accommodation for the staff, and servants, and us scouts. A thick drizzle had started up by the time I arrived at the manor. I stabled Apple and walked to the house; my face was well enough known by the guards at the bridge that they waved me through. Uncle Samuel would not be happy if he knew that, but in my bedraggled state I really did not care. I crossed over the moat and up the steps into the large hallway.[65]

Butler was set up in there with a desk. I will admit to his efficiency and value to my uncle. Yet, he disliked the scouts, and we did not like him much either, the officious prick-weasel. Unsurprisingly, he was not impressed with my information, or my wet clothes dripping on the flagstone floor.

'Your uncle is with the Lord General and cannot be disturbed,' he told me.

'I realise that, Butler. I do not ask to go in, only pass this note to Uncle Samuel. There is a Royalist column to the north.'

'Your uncle will want to hear the report in person. You will have to wait.'

'Why are you being so damnably difficult? It would take a couple of seconds of your time.'

'I am not being difficult; I am following orders. Your uncle and the Lord General are not to be disturbed.'

'Yes, I understand that, but both will want to know this information.'

'Which is why you can wait over there until they are ready.' He gestured to some chairs set up along the wall.

'You really are a pillock*, Butler, do you know that?' His jelly chins wobbled indignantly, but he ignored me. I went and threw myself into one of the chairs in a huff.

I sat waiting in my muddy wet clothes for an hour or so, until Uncle Samuel came down the stairs with Essex, Hampden, and Phillip Skippon commander of the London Trained Bands. I had seen Skippon at Turnham Green, but close up realised just how tall he was, especially with Uncle Samuel bobbing around at his waist height. I jumped to my feet.

'My Lord,' I bowed to Essex, but held out my hand with the notes ripped from my journal, to show I had a message, before Butler could stop me.

'Ah, Candy, what is this?' He took the paper.

---

*   Penis.

'There is a Royalist column to the north, Milord. I was sure you would want to know of it.'

Essex showed the list to Uncle Samuel and the others.

'Are these numbers correct, Blandford?' asked my uncle.

'Yes, Uncle, I counted them myself.'

'Send Hurry and his bully boys along the Thames to the east,' said Hampden to Essex. 'It might keep them out of trouble.'

'Yes, John, I think you have made your point about Colonel Hurry already,' said Essex, looking irritated.

'Thank you, Blandford,' said my uncle, 'you are dismissed. Try to get yourself out of those wet clothes and some warm food inside you.'

I bowed, leaving them talking, and ignoring Butler, headed outside to my billet. Crossing back over the moat, I took Apple round to the stables and left him in a stall with some mash. The big old tithe barn that the scouts had made their home was full of baggage, noise, and the stench of men, but it was dry. I could hear the arguing voices as I arrived: Peter and Zeal bickering.

There was a smell of warm food, so Jacob had been cooking. He had become our *de facto* cook and seemed to enjoy keeping us all warm and fed. He was busy about camp as well, making sure he knew the best hawkers and vendors to keep us supplied. I was certain he made some coin on the side, but did not begrudge him.

'He's a witch,' said Zeal.

'He's a charlatan. Witch? Foolish fancy.' said Peter, from his bedroll on the floor.

'He's a witch,' insisted Zeal.

'Who?' I asked.

'William Lilley, the astrologer,' said Jacob, laughing. 'Zeal says he is a witch.' He got up and took my coat and hat off me.[66]

I sat on a bench to take off my boots and looked over at

Zeal. 'He's a damn charlatan. Have you been giving him money, Zeal? You know your missus will rip your balls off.'

'No, he's been reading those damn books again,' said Peter. 'Lilley has made a prediction that Reading will fall and the King will lose the war.'

Jacob handed me a pottage—stew or pottage were all we ever ate—I took the bowl gratefully though, and handed him my boots to clean and dry.

'Whitelocke believes in him,' Zeal said.

'Whitelocke has more money than you, he can afford to believe in him,' said Peter. Do you really believe in witches?'

'You've met his wife,' I said. 'Of course he believes in witches. This food is good, Jacob.'

'Thank you, Master.' He handed me a fresh penny loaf.

'You two think yourselves so damn clever,' said Zeal. 'I am going for a drink. He saw my face. 'Enough what my wife would say, I know already. And witches do exist,' he said to Peter.

'We have wine, Zeal,' I said.

'I want a damn beer,' he replied, grabbing his cloak. He stalked out to find himself a drink from one of the hawkers.

'I will see to your boots, Master.' said Jacob, following him.

I picked up the copy of the *Mercurius Aulicus*. It was full of the usual mix of lies, half-truths and jokes. Both sides were printing them now, but the Royalist rag was still the most popular. The Perfect Diurnal, The Parliament Scout, Mercurius Rusticus, Civicus and Brittanicus, and other colourfully named newsbooks all vied for attention. The more outrageous the claims made, the more copies a pamphlet sold.

The Aulicus had a story about Hurry and the other Scots officers defecting from Parliament and joining the King. It was spurious drivel. I knew Hurry's boys had been looting a manor in Mapledurham because I had seen him bawl at Pask for not getting a good enough haul of loot. I sighed and put it down. Peter had picked up a small book, probably some religious tract, but I did not want a sermon, so threw myself onto the blankets and straw that made up my bed.

We were lucky, close to Headquarters, with a fire and fresh supplies. The rest of the army fared rather worse. Down at the entrenchments, the men had no cover from the elements. With few enough tents, most slept under hedges. When it rained, they got wet and stayed wet. At least I had a change of clothes and a warm billet.

The boats emerged out of the morning mist heading upriver towards Reading. At least twenty packed to the brim with musketeers and supplies for the beleaguered garrison. Uncle Samuel had sent me with a troop of 'goons along the river to check on the Cavalier column. It had been difficult enough to find cavalry with enough beasts to mount a patrol. Half of our Horse were without horses so to speak. I had finally drummed up a troop, and their Scottish officer, and led them out to Caversham, then east along the Thames towards Sonning. An outrider had spotted the boats on the river heading towards Reading.

'A nice ride in the morning for the troop you said,' grumbled Captain Strachan. 'Now we have a fight on our hands. We must face the Amorites at our own Waters of Merom.'*

I glanced over at the dour Scot. 'You can hardly blame me. Hurry was supposed to be guarding the river to the east,' I said. 'How, in all that is holy, did they get those boats?'

'We have not enough to stop them,' said Strachan, looking down the line at his troopers. Fifty or so men with carbines crouched along the riverbank, waiting for the boats to come

* Book of Joshua 11:8

into range. The boats cut against the current, making good time.

'At that speed they will be at the Kennet and into Reading in half an hour,' I said.

'Well, let us see if we can delay them a while,' said Strachan standing up. 'Pick 'em off, boys; go for the officers!' he shouted to our waiting ambush.

Carbine fire ripped through the quiet of the morning, sending up splashes in the water around the flotilla. Here and there, a man fell back into his longboat, or dropped into the water. Return fire was quick in coming from the boats, and Strachan ducked back down as musket balls whistled through the undergrowth. I took a careful aim at one of the finely dressed Cavalier officers, discharged my pistol, and watched with satisfaction as he tumbled backward into the river.

After reloading I ran, half crouched, along the bank to keep apace with the boats, but we were drawing heavy fire from the river. I fired a shot at the rowers and then pulled back beyond the riverbank as Strachan shouted to withdraw. I paused to help one trooper with a wound bleeding from the leg. One glance was enough to tell me he would lose it, and probably his life under the knife.

'Thank you, sir,' he said slumping to the floor. I cut away a piece of his breeches, tying it off tightly above the knee to try to stop the blood. The shinbone was shattered and poking through the skin. It must have been agony, but he bore the pain stoically as I dragged him out of range.

'We'll ride ahead a bit and try again,' Strachan told the rest of us as we gathered around him. 'This time try and concentrate our fire on the lead boat.'

We went back to our horses, and galloping further upriver, set up another ambush just before the mouth of the Kennet joins the Thames. Once the boats reached the Kennet they were safe, covered by cannon from the walls of Reading. Some of us lying, some crouched, we waited for the lead boat to heave into view. As it inched closer, I could see the Cavaliers preparing for our volley, ready to respond. Again, Strachan stood up, waving his sword and shouting, 'Open fire!' as the boat came into range. There was a roar as the volley rang out, buzzing musket shot around the lead boat. I began to reload, as the muzzle flash from enemy muskets exploded in reply.

Men were falling around me, but I squeezed the trigger, discharging my pistol once more. The men in the lead boat were ducked down behind the gunwales, but the others coming up behind fired their carbines at us. We were taking heavy casualties for little gain. Just as I thought that, there was an almighty explosion, throwing me to the floor with its force. My ears rang with the shock of it, deafening me. The lead boat had disintegrated; the supplies of gunpowder had somehow ignited.

To this day, I have no idea how it happened. You cannot just shoot at a barrel of powder, and expect it to go bang. It will not go up—I've tried. Somehow in the fire-fight, a spark must have got into a barrel and the whole thing had gone boom.

Boat and body parts were spread across the river, shrouded in smoke and mist. I sat in stunned silence, so did everybody, paused in horror at the explosion. Whoever was in charge of the convoy was quick though, he had them shooting back at us, whilst others rowed like galley slaves to get to the Kennet and safety.[67]

'Fall back,' I could hear Strachan shouting. So I scrambled back up the riverbank, out of sight of the Cavalier muskets.

What was left of the troop gathered together again around Captain Strachan. Out of sixty troopers who had ridden out that morning, almost a third were dead or wounded, and all for little gain. If that boat had not have gone up, it would have been a disaster. As it was, we could see the rest of the Cavaliers row up the Kennet, into Reading and safety.[68]

'Gather the dead and wounded,' Strachan told his men, 'and let us get back to Caversham Bridge. We have done all the good we can here.'

'The Lord General will not be happy,' I told him.

The dead and wounded were thrown in haste over the back of their horses: everybody anxious to get back to our own lines. The trooper I had helped earlier was still alive, but barely conscious. He groaned as he was thrown over his saddle and led off. He was dead by the time we reached Caversham. Strachan was a good officer, and he saw to his men first, getting the wounded off to the surgeon—much good it would do them—and the dead to the Pastor. After they were settled back, he turned to me.

'Let us go to your uncle, and see what he has to say about this.'

Butler did not even try to stop Strachan as he strode in to my uncle's office. The fat bastard would make us scouts wait on his pleasure, but not an angry captain of dragoons. Uncle Samuel was furious; I had never seen him so vexed before. Normally so calm and controlled, Hurry's failure made him throw a glass against the wall, shattering it.

'I beg your pardon, gentlemen, that was remiss of me,' he said, as if shocked by his own anger. 'Governor Aston will be cock-a-hoop at the supplies of powder. It will lift their morale as well. Hurry has just prolonged the siege by a week or more and given the King time to raise a relief force.'

'Prince Rupert besieges Lichfield,' said Strachan.

'Then let us hope Lichfield can hold, and Reading falls, before the King can make his move,' said my uncle. 'Thank you, gentlemen. I will need to go to the Lord General now.' He dismissed us and left to see Essex and break the bad news.

'What now?' I asked Strachan.

'I need to see to the burial of my men,' he said, brusquely. 'We go west in a couple of days to join with Waller near Bristol.' He half smiled. 'I cannot say it was a pleasure, but good luck to you, Candy.'[69]

I shook his hand, took my farewell, then went back to the barn. Most of the boys were out, but Jacob stood as I entered, to take my saddlebags, and Franny (who I had not seen for a week or so) was sitting in the corner in his cups. Zeal was lying in his cot mumbling to himself, sweating so much his hair was plastered against his face. I looked at him in distaste and turned to Franny.

'When did you get back, Franny?'

'This morning, I've been stuck listening to his groaning and moaning ever since.' He gestured to Zeal.

'What is wrong with him?'

'Headache, he says, has a bit of fever too, Master,' said Jacob. 'Probably still suffering from last night; he stinks of ale and a night spent in a tavern.'

'You see the boats get in earlier?' Franny asked me.

'Yes, I was with Strachan and his troop. One of the boats exploded, but the rest floated into Reading, as happy as you like. Thank you, Jacob.' He handed me a cup of wine. I sat down next to Franny.

'Will help them not,' Franny told me. 'There is fever in the town. 'Tis only Aston, the papist turd, who has kept them going. He's been hurt though, hit by falling masonry.'

'Where did you get that snippet?' I asked.

'Spoke to one of Aston's maids in Reading. Pretty little thing, I told her I would rescue her when Reading fell,' he said.

'How in God's name did you get into Reading? I thought you had gone south to Basing.'

'Waded through the drowned pastures; she's your uncle's contact in Reading, so I stayed there till last night, and came out the same way.'

'No guards?' Jacob asked.

'A couple, and there are cannon covering it. Easy enough for one man to sneak in, but no good trying to assault that way; you would be cut down in the flood,' he said.

'You take some damn risks, Franny,' I said.

'Sir Samuel caught me thieving on his land and gave me a choice. Told me I could be a sneak for him and the Lord, or he would string me up there and then. Running the odd risk for him is better than a stretched neck. He's a good man, your uncle.'

'True enough,' I said.

Half the men there had some tale to tell of how Samuel Luke had saved them. Everard the poacher, Franny the thief, even Zeal had half killed a man in a tavern brawl before turning to God and my uncle's service. We all wondered what Butler's secret was, and why he had been dismissed from the Countess of Kent's retinue.

'Any word from Russell? If the King decides to march his army south we might have some trouble,' said Franny.

'Peter went north towards Oxford. He will not be back for hours yet.'

'Let us get a cook on then,' he said, pointing to a sack he had with him.

I looked in the sack. 'Where did you get these from, Franny?' I asked, holding up two dead chickens. 'There are men down at the siege lines that would kill for a couple of birds like this.'

'A load was delivered earlier when I was reporting to your uncle. Butler was too busy fussing about the carter's filthy boots, to notice me swipe these two and walk off. 'Twill not harm him,' said Franny. 'If he gets any bigger his arse would not fit under his desk.'

'Uncle Samuel would not have taken his service if he was beyond redemption.'

'Even Samuel Luke can make mistakes. I have met the like of Butler before, and seen the way he looks at you.'

'The way he looks at me?'

'Like a Spartan looks at his boy.'

I laughed at that.

'Well, 'tis your balls Butler will have a squeeze on if he finds out you thieved these, not mine,' I said. 'Jacob, what do you think you can do with these birds?'

'Stew, Master, I have some potatoes and onion to go with them.'

I grimaced. 'That will be a nice change.'

Zeal's mumbling was getting louder, Franny picked up a boot and threw it at him, 'For God's sake, Zeal, hush up, will you?' he said.

Zeal sat up in his cot, looked at us both, bloodshot eyes glazed over. 'There is no King saved by the multitude of a host: a mighty man is not delivered by much strength.'* He hissed at us, and then fell back in his bunk.

---

*   Psalm 33.

This day, came news by an express, that Prince Rupert had taken the close at Lichfield. The particulars these: On Thursday last he sprung his mine, and made a reasonable breach, and whilst some of his soldiers did assault the breach, others should at the same time, in another place, attempt the scaling of the walls. But, the Scalado* failing, and the service at the breach being very hot, His Highness also having been much pressed by several letters to return with speed unto the court, he was content to give the defendants such conditions, as would not otherwise be granted.

That Lieutenant Colonel Russell, who commanded in chief within the close, on the surrender of the same, should depart thence with 80 Horse, with men upon them, and arms belonging to the horsemen, as also with 80 muskets, and colours flying. All other persons being permitted to go where they pleased. That for their safe conveyance thence, the Prince should give them a free pass, and furnish them with eleven carts to carry away such goods as did belong to any of the officers and soldiers, with themselves to the city of Coventry. All prisoners taken on each side within the county of Stafford, since the Lord Brooke came into the country, should be immediately released.

According to which agreement, the close was yielded up on Friday, April 21, together with the ordnance and ammunition, all sorts of arms except the horsemen's arms and muskets before mentioned. All such treasure which had been formerly conveyed in thither, and did not properly and of right belong to the soldiers there, was to be left to the disposing of the victor.

John Berkenhead/Peter Heylyn.

---

*   Someone who gains entry by a ladder.

16. Caversham Bridge, April 1643.

Adieu, farewell earth's bliss, this world uncertain is,
Fond are life's lustful joys, death proves them all but toys,
None from his darts can fly; I am sick, I must die.

(Thomas Nashe. *A Litany in the time of Plague.*)

Reading was burning. I could smell the foul smoke on the wind. I got myself up a tree and took out my spyglass. For days, our gunners had been targeting the steeple of St Giles' church that dominated the town. Once visible for miles around, as I watched, it collapsed in on itself like a house of cards tumbling to the floor, sending up billowing clouds of dust. The Royalists deserved it; they had used the tower as a gun platform. To the puritan cannoneers in our trenches, it was already defiled.[70]

I sighed; I had bet on it lasting another couple of days. That was a pound I owed Bulstrode Whitelocke. Well, he would have to wait; we had not been paid since leaving Windsor. With every day that passed, and no sign of coin on the horizon, even Hampden's Greencoats had grown restless. I climbed down the tree, mounted Apple, and turned back to Caversham Bridge.

Whitelocke had arrived at Reading with other Members of the Commons to survey the siege, and report back to their committees. Whitelocke at least did his job. He took time to talk to the soldiers as well as the grandees. He was a good man like that; he took his responsibilities seriously and always tried his best. I think at heart he was frustrated:—as an Anglican made leader of the Presbyterians. He should have been a natural supporter of the King, but he saw Charles I as a tyrant, and the King did nothing to dissuade him from that.

As I clattered over the bridge at Caversham, I could hear cheering from the gun batteries. Gad! The gunners would be drunk tonight, which meant fighting and arguments. Apple and I picked our way past the main camp, southwest of the town.

The abject misery of the ordinary soldiers at the siege lines improved my mood. *It is pleasant, when the sea is high and the winds are dashing the waves about, to watch from the shores the struggles of another.* I think that was Livy, and he is right[*]. Someone else's misfortune always makes you feel better about your own. That is not a lack of empathy, but an excess of it.

After a couple of days in the open, I wanted my bath and drink back at the barn. The poor bastards in the trenches were wallowing in mud and filth. Disease was rampant, and half the army was sick with bellyaches and the shits. I turned Apple down the Bath Road and headed to Blagrave's Manor, stabling him with some fresh straw and oat mash. I walked over to the barn, hoping Franny or Peter would be there, I wanted conversation and sack. Peter was there, and Jacob as always, but the barn stank of sickness.

'Zeal has a fever and he's been shitting himself all day. Some of the others are just as bad.' Peter told me as I arrived. 'His shit is green!'

I looked over to where Zeal lay shivering and drenched in sweat.

'It looks like my mother's pea soup,' said Peter.

'It does not smell like it, Christ alive, that is foul.' I covered my face. 'Are you certain 'tis not the plague?'

'Gaol Fever[†] says the leech; he says it is all over the army,' said Jacob.

Peter frowned. 'I wish Everard was here. He would have something to help them.'

'He is still in London watching over Waller,' I told him. I missed William as well. He was a calm head when we needed one, but Uncle Samuel kept him in London.

---

[*]   Blandford is mistaken, it was Titus Lucretius Carus (Lucretius), *De Rerum Natura*.

[†]   Typhus Fever

'I doubt he is happy, stuck in the city working for that weasel.'

'I would rather be in London than here,' I said.

'I would rather be anywhere than here,' said Peter.

'What is that damn-awful smell?' said Bulstrode, coming into the barn.

'Zeal,' Peter said. 'He's sick.'

Bulstrode looked over at Zeal. 'If I had a dog that stank like that, I would shoot it.'

'Gaol Fever, the Leech says,' said Jacob again. 'Half the others have it as well.' He gestured to the other men lying around.

'He will probably live. You owe me a pound by-the-by,' Bulstrode said to me, palm extended.

'Well, when you Members of Parliament see fit to pay us poor soldiers, I can pay you.'

'A fair promise,' he said, putting his hand away 'Well, gentlemen, I have need of a scout; there are letters that must be taken to Windsor.'

'I have been out all night,' I said, 'Peter can take them.'

'Gladly,' said Peter. 'I am happy to do anything to get away from this shithole.'

Tired as I was, and despite the sickness around me, I still wanted a bath and drink. I had Jacob pull the large wooden tub used for cider making outside into the spring sunlight; soon after, I lay back in the hot tub with my feet dangling over the end, and a cup of wine in my hand.

'I never thought I would get such pleasure from bathing,' I told Jacob, as he boiled more water.

I sat there for near half an hour just soaking and watching people. I was contemplating getting out and dressed, when I sensed consternation spreading through the camp: men rushing around, shouts, and the palpable sense of panic.

I called over to a russet coated guardsman, 'What is amiss?'

'Lichfield has fallen,' he told me. 'Prince Rupert is coming.'

The King called his nephew back to his side and marched south from Oxford. He thought the defenders would sally out to meet him and catch us in the pincer, but we had picked up his messenger, alerting Essex to the plan. When Rupert and the King approached, we waited for him at Caversham Bridge. The Lord General's own regiment of Foot and Uncle Samuel's dragoons with a brace of culverins set up covering the crossing.

'Why do we not just blow up the bridge; we have enough powder?' I asked.

Caversham Bridge was a long narrow crossing made of stone spanning the Thames. There were buildings at both ends, packed full of musketeers. On the northern bank the land rose up to high ground overlooking the bridge, but we had pulled back to the Thames. We had pikemen covering the Reading side, whilst half of the dragoons were dismounted along the south bank with carbines; the rest of us mounted as a reserve.

'Because we will need it afterwards to move north,' Bulstrode explained patiently. 'If the defenders in Reading sally forth though, we shall have trouble. I just thank the Lord we caught the King's messenger.'

'I just hope he was the only one.' said Franny.

'What the hell is that noise?' said Bulstrode, turning in his saddle. There was wild cheering breaking out all over the camp and siege lines to our rear.

'Maybe the Royalists have surrendered.'

'That is folly, Blandford.'

Ha! I was right. Within minutes, Peter rode up with a wide grin over his face. 'A white flag, they have hung a white flag out from Reading. The town has surrendered.'

'I told you so, Bulstrode,' I said smugly; then an explosion rocked us. Peter was thrown from his rearing horse and I struggled to control my own. Explosions from cannon fire threw the pikemen guarding the Bridge into a panic. The King and Prince Rupert had arrived. Peter climbed back into his seat, and we watched the red-coated Royalist musketeers rush forward to attack.

'The cannon are up there on the hill,' Bulstrode had his spyglass out, and pointed to the flash of cannon muzzle on the high ground overlooking Caversham. 'They have the range on us.'

Uncle Samuel rode down the line of dragoons, near three hundred of us, as Royalist musketeers dashed onto the bridge. There was fighting in the houses on the other side as they evicted our troopers. Finally, our two culverins responded, pounding the dense ranks of Royalists running over the long narrow crossing.

The Cavaliers were faltering, as our dragoons added carbine fire to cannon shot, and the Lord General's pikemen charged to meet the oncoming rush.

Despite the initial surprise, the Cavalier musketeers crowded together on the bridge made an easy target. They were so tightly packed together crossing that it was impossible to miss, and impossible for them to fire back.

'Look, they are stopping,' I said.

'No,' said Bulstrode, 'look over there,' he passed me the spyglass. 'It is the King himself.' Charles was there, armoured head to toe, on horseback, urging his men to attack again. Alongside him, was the man who gave us all nightmares, Prince Rupert of the Rhine.

The Royalists were driven on by the sight of the King, charging across the bridge once more, despite our musketry wreaking bloody murder in their ranks. This time it looked as if the charge would carry the day, with our pikes wavering as the Royalists crashed into them.

'Charge,' shouted Uncle Samuel, ordering the trumpets to sound as he threw the mounted reserve in.

'C'mon, Blandford,' shouted Peter as I kicked the spurs into my horse's flank.

At first, I felt nothing on my helmet in the tumult as we charged down to the bridge, but in seconds a deluge of hail fell. The stones rat-tat-tatted off my armour, and drove straight into the faces of the Royalist infantry on the bridge. Faced with charging horsemen, being picked off by carbines, and now assaulted by the elements, the Cavaliers broke and ran.

Afterwards there were those who said it was 'divine intervention,' that God himself, had sent the hailstorm to spread fear into our enemies. Cromwellian rhetoric that grew stronger as the war went on. Old Wart Face used the line so often that it lost all meaning. Anyway, if the weather was a sign of God's will, then what were the days of downpour that followed? God's will left us all wallowing in the mud like pigs-in-sties.

We clattered over the bridge chasing the fleeing musketeers back up the hill, cutting at them as they ran. To stop defeat turning into a rout, Rupert led at least three troops of cuirassiers to meet us. The chase turned into a swirling melee of cavalry as the musketeers scrambled for safety.

I avoided a sword thrust and cut back, then crashed into a soldier on his feet, who reached up to grab my horse's reins. I smashed my sword hilt into his face and he fell back. Rupert's charge had halted us in our tracks, and he was canny enough not to take it too far, falling back once his infantry were clear. Then the Royalist cannon started up again, and Uncle Samuel called the withdrawal.

It had been a bloody skirmish, but the King had failed to break into Reading. Essex sent more troops and cannon, freed from the siege, to reinforce us at the bridge. Seeing this, the Royalists realised that the relief of Reading was a broken dream. They drew off their cannon first, followed by infantry, as Rupert's cavalry watched us from the hill. By mid-afternoon, our own cannon had been brought into range of the hill and the Cavaliers withdrew to Oxford.

The end of the siege saw us in a happy mood as we fell back to Blagrave's manor. Casualties in Uncle Samuel's dragoons had been light, although the infantry had taken a beating. The crossing itself was undamaged, but it bore the scars of the fight: pockmarks of musket shot peppered the stonework. Following the hailstorm, the clouds had cleared and the day was bright as we stabled the horses. There were high spirits, laughter, and jests as we walked back to the barn.

'I care not overmuch for soldiering,' said Bulstrode.

'You are Deputy Lieutenant of Buckinghamshire, and my member in the commons,' Franny pointed out.

'That is why I am here; I can hardly ask men to go to war without sharing in the tribulations.' he replied. 'War is too much of a wager; give me politics or the law any day.'

'Politics is but war by peaceful means,' said Peter.

We arrived back at the barn in good spirits. The King beaten, Reading had surrendered; the siege was over. There were only a couple of other scouts sitting around the fire. Zeal's cot was empty.

'Where's Zeal?' I asked Sam Brayne.

'Dead,' came the reply. 'Hundreds have been taken with it; disease has killed more than the King.'

We buried Zeal in the gardens of the manor, under an oak tree on his own, not in a pit. The few scouts in camp attended, as did Uncle Samuel and Bulstrode, even Butler. Though I think Uncle Samuel had ordered his presence. Gaol Fever is a damn awful way to go. I've seen so many strong men have the life sucked out of them, and it has killed more soldiers than all the battles in history. Zeal was the first of our little company to be taken, and it weighed heavy on us.

The same day as our pitiful funeral, the Royalists signed the Articles of Surrender with Essex. Zeal's wake was accompanied by the drunken cheers and singing of our victorious army. The Royalist garrison marched out of Reading the following day, to the sound of drums beating, and with their trumpets blowing.

'Mayhap we will be paid now Reading has fallen,' said Peter.

'If they wait a bit longer, there will be few enough left to pay,' said Franny.

'Essex let them off easy,' I said.

'Not much choice in that,' said Franny. 'If they had sallied forth when the King attacked Caversham, it would be us surrendering.'

'Essex lost his nerve,' I insisted. 'We would do better with someone like Hampden in charge.'

'Hampden is too loyal to challenge Essex,' Peter said. At the moment, he keeps the peace between Essex and Pym. We can ill afford Old Robin in a huff. Now Reading has fallen, the road to Oxford is open.'

'If Essex has the balls to take it,' Franny said. 'And disease does not kill us all first.'

'Letting them take their cannon is a mistake,' said Peter.

We agreed, and watched the four cannon being dragged past by a team of horses. The wounded Royalist Governor Aston had been carried out first, on a red litter, followed by the enemy sick and wounded, then the rest of the garrison. They marched out, proudly displaying their colours, to the beat of drums and tootling of their trumpets. The Royalist garrison snaked past our silent brooding army, and turned north to Caversham; the scars of the fight on the bridge clear for all to see, as they took the road to Oxford.[71]

The greatest part of this present day was spent in expectation of the success of Reading. His Majesty, finding some hesitation in the Earl of Essex to make good the Articles of Agreement, had commanded some of his forces, which had been sent back to Oxford, to return unto him. But at the last, news came that the town was surrendered, according to the Articles of Agreement on the part of His Majesties soldiers, though most shamefully broken by those of the Earl of Essex.

For after our two first Regiments were passed their guards, the rebels most perfidiously fell upon the rest (their officers and commanders looking on, and giving way unto it) plundered their wagons, searched their pockets, took from them many of their weapons, and trusting to the proverb, that change was no robbery, would needs exchange both hats and cloaks with them, whether they would or not.

Nor was it strange, or contrary to expectation and their usual practice, that they who formerly had cancelled the bond of natural allegiance to their Lord and King, should think themselves discharged from all obligations made to private men. And it is worth the observation, that when complaint hereof was made to the commanders of the rebels, of a manifest breach of the agreement, the answer was made, that they had two independent regiments in their army raised of volunteers, which would not enter into the action, but on this condition, that they should be under no command but of their own immediate officers.

Therefore, whatever injury had been committed, it was done by those volunteers, and not in their power to remedy. A device full of impudence and baseness, both to frustrate all contracts and agreements both now and hereafter, and yet to save themselves from the imputation of breaking covenants. If men were all so dull and simple, as not to see through such poor disguises as their villainies.

But to proceed, His Majesties soldiers came at last to Wallingford in safety, the next day to Oxford; where, and in the villages adjoining, they were disposed of by His Majesty, to refresh themselves.

John Berkenhead/Peter Heylyn

17. Murder, April 1643.

Hell hath no limits, nor is circumscribed in one self place,
For where we are is hell, and where hell is must we ever be.

(Christopher Marlowe, *Doctor Faustus*.)

When a town falls to a marauding army, there is always trouble. Reading was no sack—Drogheda and Wexford spring to mind—but Essex lost control of the troops. He should have stopped them entering the town, but he was like a puppeteer when the strings to his toys are cut. Once the Cavaliers had left for Oxford, to our jeers and catcalls, the soldiers flocked to the town. Taverns were smashed open and men, drunk on stolen wine, began looting the houses. Rape and murder were close behind.

'Right, gentlemen, I have a young maiden to rescue, if anyone wishes to join me in the town,' said Franny.

'Has she not gone with Aston and the rest to Oxford?' I asked.

'No, she is a good little Roundhead; I promised her I would come when the town fell, and reward her for her information.' He gestured at our soldiers crowding into Greyfriar's gate. 'This rabble would not care if she is for King or Parliament.'

'What need have you of us, then?' asked Peter. 'Two is company, three is a crowd, so they say.'

'Three isn't always a crowd,' I said.

'Your stories about the Turk in Lesbos do not count,' said Peter.

'Will you two make haste,' said Franny. 'She has a sister.'

'Well, if she has a sister how can I resist.' I said, picking up the pace a bit. 'What are you going to do, though, Peter?'

'Keep you two out of trouble, I expect,' he said.

'You can talk to the grandfather, it will keep him out of our way,' said Franny.

'I see, so you two get the pretty maidens; I get the old man.'

'I made no claim the sister was pretty,' said Franny. 'Now come on.'

We walked into Reading from the Grey Friars Gate with the other troops streaming into the city. Before the war I had visited Reading with my father. The clothiers and merchants had built fair houses, and wide streets, and it was a prosperous town. No longer.

Smashed grey roof-slates and rubble filled the road; cobblestones had been pulled up, leaving great scars in the paving. Everywhere lay the discarded dross of the besieged. The neat flint-stone shops that had lined the main street to the Friary, ripped and broken by cannon shot. Houses burned out, barely half left with any roof at all. The rain had kept fires down to a minimum, but buildings were smashed open and stripped of anything of value. Any resistance by the owners had been met with violence. What owners there were of course, with half the populace gone; dead or departed, I did not know.

'How do you do it, Franny?' asked Peter, as we stepped past two soldiers fighting in the mud. 'I mean, pretty boy there I can understand,' he gestured at me, 'but you are not what I would call handsome. Some might even say homely.'

'Confidence, my friend; *possunt quia posse videntur*,'* said Franny. 'And always tell a woman she's the most beautiful in the world. Flattery sets their quims all-a-quivering.'

Taking a right turn inside the gates, Franny took us away from the looting, down a road towards the river Kennet. Reading Minster had a great flintstone chequered tower that dominated the town north of the Kennet. The top of the tower was broken—another target for our cannoneers—and the buildings around it burned and abandoned.

We turned by the minster, before we reached Seven

---

*   They can because they believe they can. Virgil, *The Aeniad.*

Bridges over the Kennett. Fire had torn through the district, leaving only blackened skeletons of the buildings collapsing into the muddy brook alongside the river. This part of the town should have been filled with busy brew-houses and laundrywomen, but was deserted; not even a stray dog to disturb us.[72]

'I came in over there.' Franny pointed to the river. 'Crawled along the bank and waited for the sentries to pass, then ran for it. C'mon, over here.'

He led us over to a row of small broken down houses, wood-built, two storeys high and as yet undamaged. A couple had boarded up shop fronts, but Franny went down a side alley between them to a door. There was a shuttered window to the left looking out into the alley. He knocked three times. There was no response.

'That is strange,' he said. 'I told her to wait here.'

'Perhaps you are not as good a lover as you think, Franny,' I said, although he looked worried.

'I think we both know that is not true,' he replied, banging the door this time and calling out, 'Martha! Martha!'

'Nobody is coming, Franny,' said Peter. 'Look at this.'

We both turned to face Peter, he had his eye against the crack in the shutters; he stepped back and gestured to Franny. Franny looked through the crack.

'Christ preserve us,' he said.

'What is it?' I asked,

'Bodies on the floor,' replied Franny.

'Kick the door down,' Peter said to me. 'There's been murder.'

I took a boot at the door kicking the lock in with one blow, throwing it wide open.

There were bloody footprints trailing towards us, and the house was dark inside and quiet as a graveyard. I stepped into a scene of horror, with Franny with Peter behind. From the tools and wood shavings, the room was some kind of woodworker's shop. Two bodies lay in the middle of the floor, an old man, and a young woman. Both had been trussed up, with their hands behind their backs, and throats slit. A pool of dark clotted blood lay around them. Bloody spatters covered the floor and walls.

That was not the worst of it though. Hanging naked from the rafters, against the wall, was the body of another woman. She had been hung from her arms and beaten, the welts still visible on her discoloured skin. On her forehead, she had been branded with a T, and around her neck was hung a board with the words, *'Et pumilionum admonitionem'*. She had been raped, her private parts slashed with a blade. Her throat had been slit and blood had washed down her body pooling on the floor beneath.

Peter started retching but I was struck dumb by the sight of her hanging corpse.

'No!' cried Franny in shock, and choking. I put my hand out to hold him. I could feel him shaking, but he composed himself quickly, looking at the board around the girl's neck.

'The evil bastards made her suffer. What does the Latin mean?' he asked.

'To the Dwarf a warning,' I told him. 'T is for traitor I would guess. They must have discovered she had been helping us.'

'Let us away from here,' said a white-faced Peter.

I cut Martha down, and Franny tenderly covered her with a blanket he had found. We went back out in the alley, closing the door behind us, and breathing the fresh air deep into our lungs to clear away the stench of death.

There is something monstrous in mankind; a duplicity in our nature that drives men to commit such deeds. It is not a rare evil; I have felt it myself. War is not just battles, and sieges, and soldiers. It is hatred, and murder, and savagery. We are fragile creatures, in mind and body, and it does not take much to break either.

We walked back to the gate at Greyfriars in silence, unable to speak. The town around us was still in uproar, looting and drinking had got out of hand, but we passed by, barely noticing. I was filled with a burning anger. We had seen too much of brutal death that year. That poor family were but another atrocity in a growing war of insanity.

There were a group of drunken soldiers set up just inside the gates, who had smashed open a tavern, and were stopping any civilians trying to leave the town. A line of carts and people, desperate to get out of Reading, were being searched by a troop of our dragoons. With dismay, I recognised their officer.

'That is all we need, Smirky damn him,' said Peter.

Pask and his bullies had found a mark; they had stopped a rich coach evicting the family, a couple with children and servants, and had started to strip everything of value. The well-dressed father tried to step in but was knocked to the floor by one of Smirky's men; he tried to rise, but was knocked down again by the butt of a musket. I half-expected Peter to step in as he once had in Northampton, but after what we had just witnessed? They were Royalists after all, and we had just seen their handiwork.

The man's wife shrieked, and started begging for help from the people around her. They turned away, none wishing to risk Smirky's attention, as they tried to escape Reading. She fell to her knees in tears as the troopers continued robbing the coach. A strongbox full of silver was found under the seats in the carriage, much to Smirky's delight. We tried to move past the whole scene, none of us wanting to be caught up in the brigandage. It was then that Pask made a bad situation worse.

The couple had a daughter, a pretty, dark haired little thing, still a child, surely no more than twelve. Drunk on the discovery of the silver, as much as wine, Pask called her over, demanding that she be searched. The poor child was terrified, and cringed back in fear from him, but he reached for her, ripping at her bodice, exposing her barely formed breasts and leering.[73]

Something inside me snapped. I have done some terrible things, but I have never violated woman or child. Smirky was no better than the Cavalier bastards who had tortured Franny's maid. I ran up, and before Peter or Franny could stop me, grabbed Pask by the shoulder, swung him round, and punched him square on the jaw. I knocked him down on his arse before he could think. Smirky's men did not stand around to watch him get beaten. I was grabbed from behind as Pask got up. Franny and Peter had their pistols out pointing at him.

'Leave it, Pask, or we fire,' said Franny. The problem was I knew their damn pistols were unloaded. The bluff stopped Pask from killing me outright, which was one thing at least.

'Well if it be not Sugar Candy; interfering as always. This is official business though. I can have you all on a charge.'

'We do not answer to you, Pask. We answer to the Scoutmaster General,' said Peter.

Something rang in my head, the way Pask had called me 'Sugar,' I had heard it before. I made up my mind at that point, but first another voice from my past came back to haunt me.

'You can answer to me, I think,' came a gravelly tone from behind. The bullies turned me to face him, but I had already recognised the Scots accent of John Hurry.

'I answer to my uncle,' I told him defiantly.

'So many interesting family connections you have, boy. However, I have command here and hold the Lord General's warrant.'

'Sir Samuel will hear of this.'

'Run away and tell him then,' said Pask. I glared at him, but Hurry grabbed my hair and pulled it back, before I could tell Pask to be damned.

'The damn homunculus will not be around to protect

you forever, Sugar. Watch your back; you have made enough enemies already, without making one of me.' Then he threw me to the floor.

'These goods are confiscated in the name of Parliament. Any attempt to stop that is treason,' he said to the crowd.

'Rape isn't confiscating goods,' I said loudly from the floor.

'Shut your damn mouth,' said Pask.

'Make me,' I said, he started forward, but Hurry kicked me in the face instead, making me spit blood.

'Take him away from here,' said Hurry, to Peter and Franny. 'Else I let my boys on him, dwarf uncle or no.' They pulled me away from the tavern towards the gate. I did not mention recognising Pask's voice. I probably should have, but I had already decided to settle that score myself.

We arrived at the manor, striding into Butler's office to see Uncle Samuel. The secretary was sitting in his usual position guarding access to my uncle; his face fell when he saw us.

'Do not begin your complaining, Chubby,' said Franny, as Butler got to his feet.

'What is it?' asked the secretary.

'There is trouble, Mr Butler,' said Peter. 'We need to see Sir Samuel.'

Now for all of his faults, and they were many, Butler did not argue. Perhaps he saw the look on my face, but he ducked into my uncle's chamber, quickly returning, and sent us in.

Uncle Samuel was seated, writing in his journal; he looked up as we walked in.

'Well, gentlemen, how can I help?' He saw my bruised face, 'Blandford, what has happened—have you been fighting?'

'Bad news, sir,' said Franny. He told Uncle Samuel what had happened with Martha, and then what had happened at the gates with Hurry and Pask. My uncle closed his journal.

'There is no indication who sent this warning?' he asked, looking at the bloody board I had retrieved. We shook our heads.

'How could they have found out about Martha, sir?' asked Franny.

'That is a good question, Mr Cole. One I fear I have no answer to,' replied my uncle. 'I will need to ask Mr Darnelly to look into that as a matter of urgency. The Lord General was the only person we had told of a contact in Aston's household. Nobody else in the army knew. She must have been discovered somehow, but by whom?' He mused half to himself.

'Thank you, gentlemen. Go back to your quarters, stay away from Reading and Colonel Hurry. I will see the Lord General anon to see what can be done about the rioting. Mr Cole,' he looked at Franny. 'I need you to take some despatches to Darnelly in London.' Peter and I turned to leave.

'Blandford.'

'Yes, Uncle.' I paused.

'Steer clear of Hurry; he is not be trusted,' he reiterated.

'Yes, Uncle.'

Lead me not into temptation, oh Lord, I thought to myself. I can find the way without help.

Peter and I got out of the manor leaving Franny with my uncle. As he turned to walk to the barn, I walked away.

'Where are you going?' he asked.

'I need air; I shall walk to clear my head.'

'Do you wish me to come?'

'No, I wish nought but my own company for a while.'

He looked concerned. 'Do nothing foolish, Blandford.'

'I need only air, Peter,' I reassured him.

So, I am a liar; you already knew that.

I walked straight back to Reading, going through into the gates just as light was fading. The flow of people fleeing the town had slowed. Those who could, had got out, even if they had been robbed on the way. The rest were stuck with our pillaging army. Inside the gates, Pask's men were still at the tavern, deep cut and stumbling. I pulled my hat down, walked around to the rear, to the privy, and hid in the shadows, watching who went in, waiting for my prey. The privy itself was a badly built shack lit by rush light. There was a long drop to a cesspit below, and piss-buckets for tanning.

A couple of hours passed, but I was patient. I watched the drunks go in and out, pissing, shitting, and farting, then staggering back to the inn for more ale. Then I saw him; he was alone. My luck was in.

I walked into the privy behind him. Smirky was standing in the darkness taking a piss; he did not turn around as I entered.

My head was pounding as I walked up behind him, knife in my right hand. I grabbed his hair with my left hand, and yanked his head back. In the same movement, I drew the dagger across his throat, cutting as deep as I could and ripping the jugular. There was a gout of black blood as his hands flew up to the torn neck.

I pushed him to the floor, and watched as he thrashed around, blood guttering in his throat, shocked eyes bulging. Once he fell silent, I lifted the wooden covering to the cesspit, and tipped his body headfirst below. Pulling my cloak over my bloodied hands and clothes, I turned, left the privy, and walked out of the town gates back to my billet.

It was murder, cold and bloody; I do not deny it. However, if anyone deserved it, Niall Pask did.

I hurried back to the manor and headed to the barn. It was empty save for Peter. All the others were celebrating the fall of the town.

'What in damnation has happened to you?' he asked,

seeing my clothes and bloody hands.

'Pask.' I said.

'Are you mad? You went back there? After what your uncle said! You are lucky he did not kill you.'

'I killed him.' I said it quietly, pouring water on my hands to clean off the evidence.

'What the hell?'

'He was the masked man.' I told him. Peter looked shocked at that.

'What! The one who shot you in Windsor? How do you know that?'

'I recognised the voice; the way he called me, "Sugar Candy".'

'So you murdered him? Why did you not tell your uncle?'

'He deserved it,' I said, washing my hands clean of the clotted blood. Peter looked aghast.

'He may have deserved it but...' His voice trailed off.

I sat on my cot looking at my hands. I felt no remorse; I felt nothing at all. The rage that had boiled in me as I stalked Pask had gone; I just felt empty. I turned my back on Peter, rolled over and went to sleep.

18. The Bookseller, May 1643.

WITS, like Physicians, never can agree,
When of a different Society;
And Rabel's Drops were never more cry'd down*
By all the Learned Doctors of the Town,
Than a new Play, whose author is unknown:

(Afra Behn, *The Rover or Cavaliers Banished.*)

For two days, the army was out of control. Then, on the Sabbath, the soldiers filed into the three churches to beg for forgiveness. I was long gone. I cannot be sure that Peter told my uncle about Pask, but the next day, Uncle Samuel sent me to London with despatches and bade me remain. I counted it good fortune to be away from army, war, and all the death. Smirky's body remained undiscovered: doubtless some poor soul took fright when they emptied the cesspit. I sought not to dwell on it, but Jacob and I rode back to London in silence, and a vision of Pask sinking into the shit did intrude most frequently on my thoughts.

Reading changed me. I became harder, not so quick with a jest perhaps, and full of an impatient energy. I had been a reluctant revolutionary—well, no longer. Reading convinced me that Charles Stuart was no king but a tyrant. If nothing else, England needed rid of him, and I have never wavered from that belief.

After taking the despatches to Darnelly, and stabling our horses at the Tower, Jacob and I walked the mile back to Bread Street. The rooms we had shared with Peter and Everard in the winter were cold and empty. Jacob made up a fire with a bit of coal left in the scuttle, but did not light it. I told him to get some food and wine on credit, so he left for

---

   *   Patent Medicine of similar reputation to Snake Oil.

the shambles* to see if he could pick up some end-day scraps. It was late in the afternoon, but I decided to visit Barker's chambers to collect my allowance.

The walk to the Temple took me out west, so I cut through the churchyard of St Paul's to reach Barker's chambers. The old cathedral dominated the skyline in a way the damn papist dome never will—even without the spire. The churchyard always thronging with people: gossips, cutpurses, whores, and pamphleteers all crowded in. I ignored the crowd of hawkers, went past the squad of Whitecoats guarding Ludgate, and followed Fleet Street to the Temple.

After banging on the door to his shabby offices, the window above opened, and his head popped out.

'Yes, yes?' Then he smiled when he saw me looking back. 'Mr Candy, well met indeed. I am on my way, yes, yes.' He came down and opened the door, looking delighted to see me.

'It is good to see you safe, at least,' he smiled. 'Come up, come up.' I followed him upstairs to the jumbled chambers.

'You look older, Mr Candy,' he said, concern in his voice.

'I do?'

'You have gained some wrinkles. Yes, yes, and you look as if you have not slept in weeks.'

'The last few months have been eventful,' I told him after a pause.

True enough: I had been poisoned, shot at, and hunted by ravilliacs. Let any man try that without gaining a few lines.

'Please sit, sit, Mr Candy. May I offer you some refreshment?'

'Thank you, Mr Barker, some wine. I have only today returned to the city.' I took a seat and sat back.

'You were at Reading, Mr Candy? The newsbooks are full of stories of its fall.' Like everyone he looked eager for news.

'Yes,' I replied. 'It is not something I wish to speak of.'

'Of course, of course, forgive me. You have come for your

---

*   Meat or fish market.

allowance?'

He was disappointed, I could tell, but he could get his information from the newsbooks like everyone else. If I told him the truth of what I had seen, I doubt he would have believed it, and why scare innocents with horror?

'Yes, please,' I said.

He smiled, 'I shall fetch it now.' He poured me a goblet of sack.

'I do have another question, Mr Barker, which you may know the answer to.' He paused to look at me.

'Anything, anything, Mr Candy, something of the law?'

'Actually, something of the theatre. I am looking for a playbook.'

'Oh, indeed, Mr Candy, well John Rhodes' shop, near the sign of the bible in Charing Cross, is the best place to acquire literature; yes, yes.'

'Would he have plays by John Fletcher do you think?'

'Ah, sadly you may be out of luck, Mr Candy. Fletcher's plays have not been published to my knowledge, no, no. Rhodes will know better of course.' He sought quickly to ease my disappointment by adding:

'I do have some tidings for you however. I have received letters from your home in Wiltshire.'

'From my sister, Mr Barker?' I asked as he took out a strongbox.

'Indeed, yes, yes, congratulations are in order, Mr Candy. The good Lord graced your brother with a baby son. Mother and child are doing well; so your sister writes.'

Well, that was some news indeed; poor James would be devastated. Henry's death in battle meant nothing now, and James's hopes of inheritance were rapidly diminished. The thought of his discomfort made me smile. Barker misread it completely.

'It is a blessing that families can still care for each other, even when on opposite sides of this great divide,' he said. I did not disabuse him of his fantasies; I had started to do the mathematics.

'When did you hear of this, Mr Barker?'

'I received news a fortnight ago,' he said. 'They have called him Christopher in honour of your father. I am sorry; I did not think to forward the news.'

'No matter, my friend, I must set aside some of my allowance to buy a gift for my new nephew, and for the mother,' I told him with a straight face.

Have you worked it out? *Copulati sunt?* When did they marry? The child was a month early at least.

Yes, I know; my idiot great-nephew could be my idiot grandson. He is still an idiot.

I begged my leave of Mr Barker and pondered what to do next. Charing Cross was not far, just up the Strand. I planned to visit the bookseller to find that damn play, but first there was someone closer.

Locked heavy oak doors blocked the main entrance of the Phoenix. I walked around the front of the theatre, to the stage door at the back, and hammered on it. The hatch opened and the face of a painted courtesan appeared.

'Yes?' she asked sleepily, yawning.

'I need to see Beeston,' I said.

'Who seeks him?' she asked.

'Candy, I am Beeston's partner.'

'Ooh, the Golden Scout; well, you are pretty enough.' The hatch closed; I could hear the bolts drawn back, and then the door opened. Underneath the woman's face was the slender, half-naked body of a young man in a shift.

'You are a boy,' I said.

'Only by day, dear-heart. By night I am Ophelia, or Helen

of Troy, or whomsoever you want.' He winked. 'Follow me.'

He led me into the theatre, to the space behind the stage, filled with boxes, and clothes, and scenery, all of it covered in a thin film of dust. From woodland scenes, or castles, and mountains, to the rigging of a ship. Along the walls, there were costumes from prince to pauper; wigs, and dresses, and grotesque masks, hanging alongside wooden swords and spears, even a suit of armour painted black. By all accounts, Atlas had taken the world, given it a shake, and tumbled the contents backstage at the Phoenix. The boy gestured to a room off on one side. 'Beeston is in there.'

I paused before the door; there were voices coming from inside; I knocked.

'One moment, please.' Beeston's voice. I waited until finally, the door opened, and Beeston was there, open-shirted and stinking of sack. There was nobody else in the room, just books and papers and clothes. It looked like Beeston was sleeping here.

'I was just practising my lines,' he said as if in explanation. Then he recognised me. 'Oh, 'tis you.' He sat back down.

'When you die, they will crack off your make-up for a death mask, like old Queen Bess,' I said, as I entered the room.

'What do you want, Sugar?' A bottle of wine was sat on the table in the middle of the room. There were two goblets and two chairs. Practising his lines my hairy arse.

'Information, Mr Beeston, that is all.' I sat down and picked up the sack. 'Spanish?' I said. 'Expensive, I hope you are paying my sister's rents to Mr Barker on time.'

'The last time I gave you information, I got a visit from the Mayor, and a rather profitable venture for both of us got closed down.'

'The last time you gave me information, I was waylaid in the street and my comrade stabbed,' I pointed out.

He shrugged. 'That was nothing to do with me. You were

poking your nose into powerful people's business. I cannot be blamed if they got upset. 'Twas none of my affair.'

'Your affairs are mine, Mr Beeston, and mine yours. We are, whether you like it or not, business partners,' I said. 'Only my uncle's influence stops this place being confiscated, and you turned out in the street.'

'I have other business partners, you know.'

'D'Avenant is in York with the Queen, I am here,' I said cheerfully.

'What information do you want this time?' he said, after a cold glare.

'I want some information about a play by John Fletcher. That is your field of expertise, is it not?'

He looked at me for a minute, in silence, eyes appraising behind the powdered mask. Then half turned in his chair and spoke to the curtains.

'Come out, John. If anyone can help us this addlepate boy can.'

From behind a curtain stepped a grey haired man, middle-aged, and dressed in puritan black. A worried expression fixed upon his thin face.

'Are you sure?' asked the man.

'Appearances can be deceptive. He is the Dwarf's nephew,' said Beeston.

'He looks more popinjay than puritan.'

'I am a constant disappointment to my family,' I said. 'And who might you be, sir?'

'I am John Rhodes the bookseller. Are you truly the Dwarf's nephew?'

'Know you the name of the play I seek?' I said.

He nodded.

'Have you a copy?'

He nodded again. 'At my shop in Charing Cross. At least it was, but I was attacked there two nights past; I have not been back. We need your uncle's protection.'

'Get me the playbook and I give you my word you will be protected,' I said. Hoping that Darnelly would back me up on that.

''Tis not just the play,' said Rhodes.

'What else?' I cared not for the tone in his voice; it made me nervous.

'I have a list of those gentlemen in the city who have copies.'

'In your shop with the playbook?' I asked.

'Yes, that is what they want.'

'I am not surprised,' I said. 'Why have you not gone to the authorities with this? Mayor Penington would have rewarded you.'

'Penington is the beslubbering, fool-born turnip that closed the theatres. Why would we go to him?' said Beeston. 'He has made paupers of us all, the dour-faced killjoy.'

'Fairly spoken,' I said. 'We will need a hackney.'

'Ophelia!' Beeston bellowed. 'Get us a coach.'

The shutters on the shop were closed, but the lock had been broken and the door lay open. Leaving Beeston and Ophelia in the Hackney, I drew a pistol and stepped into the street.

'I assume you did not leave it in this state?' I said to Rhodes as he joined me.

'No,' he said. I let him lead and then followed him into the shop.

It was dark inside. Rhodes fumbled around for a lamp, as I watched the street and Strand for signs of pursuit. Quiet, most people already abed. He got the lamp set, dimly illuminating the scene. The shop lay ransacked; books and papers scattered across the floor. A desk in the corner had been overturned and smashed, and stationary wares of inks, quills, and paper emptied from a box then dumped.

'Did they find it?'

'It is still here,' he replied, then lifted a floorboard in the corner and pulled out a small box.

'Then bring it and let us be away.'

He looked around at his broken premises. 'My poor shop,' and blew out the lamp.

'Come, you are not yet safe.'

We climbed back into the hackney and I tapped the driver. 'Get us to the Tower quick and safe, and there's a mark in it for you.'

'Right you are, Master,' he said, snapping the reins and getting the carriage moving.

The shouts started almost as soon as we moved off, followed quickly by the crack of pistol shot. The driver whipped the horses up into canter—about the best we could hope for—and we rolled down the strand. I stuck my head out the window to look back, and almost took a shot to the head. Splinters from the frame cut into my face, as the ball thudded into the carriage. I ducked back in.

'I hope you can use that,' I pointed to the sword at Ophelia's side, loading my second pistol. I noticed Beeston loading a brace of his own, fumbling as the coach jarred over the cobbles.

'It is not real,' said Ophelia.

'What?' I said.

''Tis of wood; a stage piece, nothing more.'

'Well, what is the damn use in that?'

'I, sir, am an actor,' he said in a haughty voice. 'Not a ruffian.'

The thud of someone landing on the back of the coach ended that conversation. I discharged my shot above and behind, striking that assailant through the thin wooden roof, and tossed the spent pistol into Ophelia's lap.

'At least tell me you can load that?' I said, as Beeston fired a shot out of the window.

On the other side, a horseman jumped onto the coach, and reached in through the window. Rhodes and Ophelia cringed back as I shot him in the face with my second pistol. Ophelia hurriedly started to load one pistol, Rhodes the other. Beeston discharged his second, then ducked back inside as three or four rounds smashed into the carriage. The driver, shielded up front, screamed at his horses, stirring them up into a run.

We clattered down the Strand with the Royalist agents in pursuit, some running on foot, and at least one left on horseback directing the attack. They came on in a rush, discharging pistols as they came. Splinters of wood and glass sliced through the air. Beeston, cut under one eye, wiped away blood as Ophelia and Rhodes huddled on the floor, clutching each other in terror. At Temple Bar Gate, two others were waiting for us.

'The damn driver's been shot,' shouted Beeston, opening the door, and swinging himself up to the front.

I discharged my reloaded pistol at one, as we passed under the arch, but that was my last shot. There was no time to load again. Ophelia screamed as the door on the other side was wrenched open, and a Royalist jumped in. He went straight for Rhodes in the confined space. Ophelia scratched at his eyes, trying to protect the bookseller. I pulled a dirk and stabbed the Royalist in the back, pulling him off the bookseller, and stabbing down again, and again, dark blood staining my hands. Then I kicked the body out of the carriage door, and watched it roll in the street as we drove on past.

That was the last attack. We crossed the Fleet, with Beeston driving the horses, into Ludgate, and the squad of Bluecoats guarding the entrance to the city.

The pursuit had pulled back before coming in range of the guards' weaponry. Beeston slowed the carriage and I jumped out. Bluecoats with raised muskets, and a guard commander. Another young boy caught up in the war, his officer's sash proudly tied around his coat, pimples on his face. He raised his pistol.

'What is going on, sir? I must warn you I am empowered by Parliament to...' he started in a barely broken voice.

'I am Samuel Luke's lieutenant and I need to get to the Tower,' I cut him off.

Fair play to the boy, he simply nodded and detailed men to escort us through the city to the Tower. With an armed guard, the attackers were melted back into the night. We drove through the city, down Canon Street all the way to the Tower. I breathed more freely once we passed under the foreboding battlements.

'The playbook and the list, if you please, Mr Rhodes.' I said, looking at the bookseller.

He pulled out the box, slid the lid open, and handed me a plain white booklet. Cheaply printed, I thought, scanning the cover.

Bonduca.
A Play by John Fletcher.

My Dear Heart,

It is but two days since I wrote to you by a man of my Lord Newcastle, which I do not fail to do twice a-week. I fear that some of my letters are lost, for I get no reply to one I wrote by Will Murray's man, which gave you a very exact account of all we were doing here, and many other things which I thought it necessary for you to know.

In my last, I answered you, touching what you wrote me about the west, for you would no longer be able to have any assistance from the North or from Wales, nor from Ireland by Chester. Ashburnham will add to this some reasons that he has given me in his letter. He will tell you them, for he will remember them, they are the same that I could say.

Only, that I would add here; I hope now that the ammunition is arrived, you may stay at Oxford on the defensive till I can arrive. To this effect, I have sent Jermyn to Lord Newcastle, to press him to give me nine hundred men who are coming from Newcastle and Berwick, that have no arms. If that succeeds, I doubt not of bringing you four thousand men, well provided with the equipments of a little army, in spite of all hindrances there are, which are not small, for our general and all the gentlemen of the country are against it.

This army is called the Queen's Army, but I have little power over it, and I assure you that if I had, all would go on better than it does. The Duke will have told you all that passed here at their departure, about my journey.

I had written it you since; I fear that my letter is lost having had no reply. As soon as Jermyn is returned, I will send you another messenger, and by him an absolute resolution about what I will do. This will be in two days.

I have sent so many despatches into France and Holland this week, that instead of complaining, you should pity me. Then you must not forget the letters I have written to our army here, as well as the impatience I feel to set off, and the diligence I use for that.

When I see you and can tell you all this, you will say that I am a good little creature, and very patient. But, I declare to you that being patient is killing me, and were it not for the love of you, I would with the greatest truth, rather put myself in a convent than live in this manner.

Adieu my dear heart.
York, 14th May, 1643.

Post Script: I have received two of your letters, one dated the 7th, and the other the 10th. As to the excuses you make for having opened one of my letters of Wat Montague, I am offended that you should believe I have any secret from you, that I would not tell you. No, I swear to you I have none. I beg you tell Culpepper and Ashburnham that if I do not write, it is because I have written all I have to say to you.

I am very weary of writing.
H.M.

19. Emily, May 1643.

Madam shall I tie your garter,
Tie it a little above your knee?
If my hand should slip a little farther,
Would you think it amiss of me?

(Traditional, *Oh No John.*)

I received fury in place of praise: Darnelly was enraged. I had expected at least a modicum of gratitude for the playbook and list of traitors. He quickly disabused me of that notion, as I sat in his office in the Tower later that night.

'Have you any notion of what you have done?' he asked.

'Your pardon, sir,' I said a trifle peeved. 'I thought I acted as an intelligencer should.'

'You gave no thought at all. You should have brought them straight in, but instead caused a street-fight in the middle of London, that will be in the damn newsbooks by tomorrow night. What is more, you have put at risk our agents around Waller.'

'You have a list of traitors, and Reverend Wallis can use the book,' I pointed out.

'Names we already knew, and who were being watched. Names that now will go into hiding, and with more care for their safety. You have given them warning. As for the playbook, Reverend Wallis informs me that without the key it is useless. A fact he also mentions you were aware of.'

'Ah.' I had not forgotten. If I am honest, I did not really understand it.

'Rhodes and Beeston are known to us already and the other one. What is his name?' He looked over to a grey-haired clerk standing to the side, with a sheaf of papers in his hand.

'Ophelia?' I said.

'Ezekiel Fenn,' said the clerk glaring at me. 'He plays

women and is a known Royalist sympathiser.'[74]

'I did not know he was a Royalist sympathiser,' I said. 'He seemed such a sweet girl.'

'They are all Royalist sympathisers, you dunderhead,' snapped Darnelly. 'We closed the theatres remember? The only reason they did not hand the playbook over to Waller and his friends was to extort some gold. 'tis not Beeston's turdlets that interest us, but the greater bowel movement.'

'Blackmail sounds like a scheme of Beeston's,' I conceded.

'We shall have to keep them all in the Tower until we have dealt with Waller,' said Darnelly. 'I have half a mind to deduct their keep from your pay.'

'What pay?' I said.

Darnelly sighed. 'Go back to your chambers, Sugar Candy. I do not want you running around the city causing any more problems. Find yourself a good whore and waste your energies on her until you are summoned, there's a good fellow.' He dismissed me with a wave.

I left the Ordnance Department in a sour mood and wondered what to do next. I had a purse full of coin and time to escape from the war. Despite Darnelly's advice, I knew one thing.

I did not want a whore.

I stepped down into the apothecary, its dark wooden shelves stacked with bottles and ampoules from floor to ceiling offering wonderful perfumes of flowers and musk. Emily stood behind the polished counter, but a look of horror crossed her face when she saw me.

'Peter?' she said. I realised what her fear was.

'No, he is well. My apologies, I should have given you

warning I was back in London.'

She burst into tears, gave me a clout or two, and burst into tears again. I offered her my kerchief.

'You should have sent word; you gave me such a fright,' she said, between sniffs.

'My apologies,' I repeated.

'When did you get back? Is Peter with you?'

'No, he is still in Reading but well. He came through the siege without a scratch.'

'There have been terrible stories, disease killing half the army!' Her eyes were wide with fear.

'Oh, it was not that bad,' I lied, thinking of Zeal. 'You should not believe the newsbooks,' but I held her close to me nonetheless.

Widow Crosse waddled into the room from the back of the shop, and was not impressed that I was not a customer.

'Emily! Such behaviour for one of your family. And with a Roundhead officer no less,' she said, huffing and puffing for want of breath.

Emily turned to face her: 'Your pardon, Mistress Crosse,' she said. 'Mr Candy has just brought me word of my brother in Reading.'

'Your affairs are for your own time, Miss Russell,' the old whale said, emphasising, "affairs". 'I expect those working here to conduct themselves in a respectable fashion.' Time for me to step in and use my charms, I thought.

'Please forgive me, Madam,' I said, flashing my most delightful smile. 'The fault is mine; I did not think of propriety.' It was to no avail.

'That is as may be, sir, but I have a shop to run, and Miss Russell work to do.' She glared at me with piggy little eyes.

'Indeed,' I replied, 'then I shall take my leave so that I inconvenience you no further.' I said it politely, all the while thinking what a fat bitch.

I bowed to them both and doffed my hat, before backing

out of the shop. Once outside I went to the Mitre opposite and sat with an ale by the window, overlooking the street, and waited for Emily to finish work.

So, my days fell into a routine. I would wake late and break my fast in one of the food stalls by the river; sometimes, I would send Jacob to buy the Aulicus or one of the other newsbooks, and waste my afternoon in an inn drinking small beer.

In the evenings, after she finished work, I would stroll with Emily from the shop in the Strand back to her mother's at Cheapside. Afterwards, I would go home to my empty chambers, drink sack and sleep. I ventured to the Beargarden once, but with the theatres closed, Southwark had lost its lustre. Whores did not interest me, and I was tired of games of chance. Only Emily brightened my days, she filled my waking thoughts, and haunted my dreams.

Gad, I sound like a simpering fool, worse, a poet, but the sentiment was true in heart.

There was one incident of note in the weeks that I waited on Darnelly's pleasure. At the Saracens Head, I was expecting news from Peter and I hoped to surprise Emily with it.[75] Jacob and I went down to the tavern and spoke to the Post Master but nothing new had come in. As I was leaving, a drunk started pushing me, perhaps to roll me for coin, and pulled a knife. Jacob was quick, and smashed a bottle over his head before he could use the blade and I was unharmed. Some watchmen dragged the fellow away, and gave him a good beating. Shaken, the two of us went back to Bread Street.

It could have been just another rough in a London tavern, there are enough random killings in the city, but I took it as a certain reminder that Mistress Whorwood had a long reach.

I became more wary, only venturing out to the Tower, or for my walk with Emily, and always with Jacob in tow. It was after one of those walks at the end of May, that we returned to Bread Street, but the door to my rooms was unlocked. At first I was cautious until I recognised a familiar odour of pipe smoke billowing down the stairs. I raced up them three at a time.

'William!' He was sitting at the table smoking his pipe, all dressed up in a blue and red footman's rig. He rose as I came rushing in.

'Hullo, Sugar,' he said, as I gripped him in a bear hug. Jacob followed into the chamber with a smile on his face.

'Damn, it is good to see you, Everard,' he said. 'It has been months.'

'And you, friend,' said Everard taking his hand.

'Let us have some wine.' I grabbed a couple of wooden goblets and a half-empty bottle. 'Why these rags?' I asked him. 'You look like a blackamoor houseboy.' I shook the bottle, and sent Jacob out for more.

'Ha! 'Tis bloody awful, is it not? I am Waller's footman still.'

'Still?'

'Not for much longer, the weasel has been unmasked.'

'How did he manage that?' I poured out some wine.

'We have him plotting to raise a rebellion in London. He plans to arrest Penington and Pym, and take over the tower.'

'Isaac Penington? The Lord Mayor? He's the arsehole who closed the theatres. I hope they shoot the turd. He has cost Elizabeth and me a fortune.'

'Sadly for your theatre 'tis all a fancy.'

'You have cozened him?'

'No, the plot is real enough; they even have the King's commission to raise troops in London,' he said. 'No troops though and no money.'

'I knew he was up to something when we were in Oxford,'

I said.

'It seems the plan was dreamt up then by some of the King's less practical advisors. You helping Beeston and Rhodes fretted them, so they brought it forward.'

'I thought my help was less than appreciated,' I said.

He grinned at that. 'Darnelly would never confess to it, but you uncovered a couple of people we had been looking for. Thanks be, for I hate this city, it chokes me.'

'Did Wallis crack their codes with the playbook?'

'No, but they all have a copy and it tells us who Bonduca is, does it not?'

'Really? Who?'

'Mistress Whorwood. The conceit of a red headed warrior queen pleased her well enough, it seems, to choose that play. She had a copy printed up special for the plotters by Rhodes.'

'Damn, she has a high opinion of herself, does she not?'

'I hear she is quite persuasive, close to the King, close to Lord Falkland his secretary as well,' he said.

'Close?'

'As close as you and one of your whores get, but I wager she does not sell it.'

'I am a reformed character,' I told him.

'Really? How so? Or have you found God?'

'Do you want some more wine?' I reached for the bottle.

'Surely you have not lost your heart to some Southwark punk?'

'No, of course not, but with the theatres closed and baiting banned, Southwark has become dull. I've been living a quiet life since upsetting Darnelly.'

'I never thought to hear you say that. Perhaps the gallant* has turned gentlemen.' There was a big grin on his face.

'Perhaps,' I said laughing. 'Although Darnelly keeps telling

---

* According to Dr Johnson, 'Gallant' had two meanings. Normally associated with a 'splendid man,' it was also used to refer to, 'A whoremaster, who caresses women to debauch them.'

me to keep my head down, so carousing over the river strikes me as a bit conspicuous.' I chose not to tell him about Emily.

'Wonders will not cease; I am sadly still sceptical,' he said to me. 'However, I had best be off. I am running an errand for Waller, must return,' he said draining his cup. 'Darnelly requires you to be at the Tower tomorrow morning. I shall return later tonight and have a proper drink, some of the others should be here by then.'

Jacob came back up the stairs at that point with sack and a pie, and looked sorely disappointed at William's departure. I sent him straight back out again to get more provisions. I planned to give the Scouts a welcome back to the capital.

I loved them all, you see. Peter, Franny with his ready smile and acid tongue, quiet Sam Brayne, even Everard, with his disapproval of my vanities and puritan idealism, was like a brother to me. Brothers-in-arms we were, after all. We fought for each other as much as any ideal. And I watched them all die, one-by-one, in bedlam or battle, and with them the dreams and hopes of a better England.

Ach, I become melancholic.

'Forgot you the key?' I said, as I opened the door. Emily was standing there.

'Emily? I thought you were Everard, what is wrong?' She put her hand to my lips.

'Say nothing,' she said, and then she led me to the rooms upstairs, and turned to face me.

'But,—'

'Hush,' she kissed me and led me to the cot in the corner of the room. We fell onto the bed together, her hands fumbling at the buttons to my breeches as she kissed my face. My hand slipped between her legs as she parted them lifting her skirt. I lay on one side with only one hand free to explore her body as we kissed. She smelled of the shop, lemon scents, and musk. I could feel myself growing hard in my breeches, as she slipped her hand inside, gripping me.

'Whoreson! False friend!'

Peter was stood by the doorway with Everard behind. Emily pulled her skirts down but too late. Peter enraged, grabbed Emily, pulling her off me, and pushed her towards the door.

'Get home,' he shouted at her. Then turned to face me.

'How now, Peter,' I said, trying to be reasonable.

He knocked me down, cutting my lip. Emily shrieked at him, but he threw her aside and jumped on me, beating me around the face. I struggled with him, pushing him off me, trying to stand. Emily ran from the room. Everard, the bastard, just sat on the table and started packing his pipe.

'She's my sister, damn you.' Peter screamed at me.

'It is not as it seems,' I said between the blows, but he was not listening. He was also stronger and hit hard. At least I had the practice of enduring beatings from my brothers to help me.

'You have enough whores to visit without dragging Emily into the gutter, I thought we were friends. How could you?' He stopped beating me, and stood up leaving me bloodied and battered on the floor. I could feel my left eye starting to close up where he had caught me.

'Is that your plan, to make a whore of my sister?' he said.

'Am not I good enough?' I asked, spitting out some blood and getting to my feet to face him.

'Good enough? You blaspheme, drink, and gamble. Of course you are not good enough for her, you bastard.'

'Balls to you then.' I spat at him. He knocked me down again.

He stood over me. 'If you go near her again I will kill you,

Blandford, that I swear.' He turned and walked out of the room. I heard him stamp down the stairs and the door slam behind him. Everard sighed, blowing out a cloud of smoke and pointed his pipe at me.

'They say the brain is the thinking organ, Blandford, but with you? 'Tis your cock.'

Dear Elizabeth,

I have received your last dated the 25th April. I am overjoyed at the birth of my son, and the continuance of our line, yet saddened Father has not written. Is he so unwell that the birth of a grandson has passed him by?

Much has passed since I was last home, but I hope I will soon be able to visit and welcome my boy to the world. He is to be named Christopher after our Father, perhaps that will shake him from his lethargy.

Troubling news of Blandford has come to me from James and Anne in Oxford. I must confess I can scarce believe what I am told is the truth. On this I will speak more upon my return.

We have won a great victory in the west to secure Devon and Cornwall for the King. Despite the rebels holding a strong position, and more than twice our number, the charge of the Cornish Foot carried all before it and the rebels fled in confusion. Next we march into Somersetshire and then to you. There is little the rebels can do, for no army now stands against our advance. Soon Bristol will fall and the War will be over.

His Majesty has commanded that we are to ride for Somerset to join with the Marquess of Hertford and Prince Maurice and secure that place for the crown. When conditions permit I will ride on to Hilperton.

I must finish now, but I say only this, His Majesty is King by God's will: to refute that is to refute the true religion. Do not damn yourself or your family with Presbyterian flirtation.

Your brother,

Henry.
Stratton, 18th May 1643.

20. Waller's Plot, May 1643.

The Sun most pleasing blinds the strongest eye
If too much look'd on, breaking the sight's string;
Desires still crossed must unto mischief hye,
And as despair, a luckless chance may fling.

(Lady Mary Wroth, *Can pleasing sight misfortune ever bring.*)

We rose well before dawn; I had not slept. After Peter had stormed out, Sam and Franny arrived looking for a billet. About ten scouts in all had been called into London. Jacob made up a breakfast porridge for us, but I could not eat it; I felt sick. Sam told me that Peter had already resigned from the Scouts, and asked to be returned to the Regiment.

'You should have told him,' Everard said. 'Seducing your friend's sister behind his back is just not done, Blandford. 'Tis what distinguishes us from the French.'

'Pretty girl though,' said Franny. 'You have good taste.'

'Do not encourage him, Franny.'

'Well, how do I mend this?' I said.

'Firstly, you stay away from his sister and wait for Peter to calm down. Then hope that he forgives you.' Everard told me.

'But I did nothing.'

'That is only because we arrived first. We found them with her skirts over her head, and his hands buried between her legs,' He told Franny and Sam for the third time. Both burst out laughing again.

'It is not funny,' I muttered.

'I think it is damned entertaining, *friggus interruptus* so to speak,' said Franny.

'I think I might actually be in love with her.'

'He thinks he might be in love with her,' Everard cuffed me. 'You are a dozy turnip.'

He was probably right. Had I gone honestly and openly

to my friend, I think he would have welcomed me. Instead, I behaved like a true debauchee, and I lost her and him, at least for a time.

After breakfast, the four of us walked to the Tower, to meet with Darnelly and deal with Waller's conspiracy. The plotters were to seize the Tower, and its magazines, and release the Earl of Bath. The Earl was to take command and free Archbishop Laud[76]. The King himself was going to lead a force of three thousand men within fifteen miles of London. It was abject fantasy.

The Tower was controlled by the Lord Mayor, Isaac Penington. He was an odious scab of a man, but efficient. Even if the plotters could have scraped together some men to fight, the trained bands, and cannon of the Tower, would have made it suicide. That was patently clear as we walked through the gates at the Middle Tower, between two curtain walls bristling with musketeers and cannon.

Penington's Whitecoats would assist with the arrests. Plotters across the city were to be rounded up, and their homes searched. Members of the peace party in both Houses of Parliament were being taken in and questioned, as Pym used the plot to discredit the tremblers and end vacillation over the war.

The other scouts and constables were already waiting at the Tower when we arrived. There were greetings and smiles, but I was subdued and sat waiting for Darnelly in silence as they talked.

'Quiet please, gentlemen,' said Darnelly, coming into the room looking cadaverous as ever. Everyone quickly took a seat. 'We much to arrange before we can make these arrests under. Now, you will be acting in pairs, with a squad of Whitecoats, in case any of them decide to fight their way out.'

'Not Waller,' whispered Everard. 'He be too much the coward.'

'Firstly,' Darnelly said. 'The King's commission was

233

smuggled into the city two weeks ago by Lady D'Augbiny. The note is now in the hands of a linen draper called Richard Chaloner from Holborn. Candy, you will go with Everard and arrest Chaloner. Tear the house apart if needs be, but find that commission.'

'Yes, sir,' I said.

'No complaints or suggestions?'

'No, sir?'

'How very refreshing. Chaloner has two daughters, Mr Candy. Do try and keep your hands to yourself,' he said to general mirth.

'He knows already?' I whispered to Franny.

'Everybody knows.'

'How the frig does everyone know?' I asked.

'I told them of course.'

I glared at him.

'Brayne, you take the arrest of Waller's brother in law, Tomkins,' Darnelly went on. 'His house is in Fetter Lane near Chaloner's. I believe a man called Roe has been your contact in Tomkins' household, Everard?'

'Aye, sir, said Everard.

'Take him in as well then, Brayne, so as not to arouse suspicion. Cole,' he looked at Franny, 'you can come with me, we may need some of your skill with locks at Waller's.'

There were more orders, people across the city were being rounded up whether they were involved in the plot or not. Facts did not really matter; Pym wanted a conspiracy to discredit the peace party, so he got one. If Waller had not had me poisoned, I might have felt sorry for him.

Chaloner's home was in Holborn, near Hatton House. A fine

house with four floors, whitewashed walls, and sash windows. The shutters still closed at ground level at the early hour. An arched gateway led into a small courtyard, well-tended with flowers, and steps to a main door on our right as we marched through. Everard nodded to the sergeant who hammered on the door.

'Open up by order of Parliament.'

The door opened a crack, but the sergeant smashed into the door with his shoulder, forced it wide open and pushed his way inside. Everard and I followed him, pistols in hand. On the floor was a woman, thrown back by the charge, staring at us dumbfounded.

It was a large hallway, with stairs to the left. We ran up them, followed by a couple of soldiers. The woman started to scream as Whitecoats trooped into the hall and dragged her to her feet.

On the first floor, there was a long corridor leading to the back of the house, but it was silent. The stairs went on up another floor; I nodded to the two soldiers to start searching the rooms. A door slammed higher up, so Everard and I ran on. I was panting for breath by the time we reached the third floor.

'You are getting fat,' he said.

'I lack a little practice.'

Another corridor leading to the rear, but this time a door was open, and standing at it was a tall, thin man, with mousey hair. He was dressed in a nightgown and held pistol.

'Give it up, Chaloner, the house is taken.' Everard told him as I caught my breath.

He thought about it; I will give him that. After a pause, he flipped the pistol and offered the butt to Everard. I shouted for a couple of troopers who came rushing up the stairs.

'Am I under arrest?'

'By the order of Parliament, Mr Chaloner, for High Treason,' Everard said. 'Take him downstairs, gentlemen, and hold him. Who else is here?'

'His wife and daughters, sir, and some servants who we are holding.' One of the troopers said.

'Good, start searching the rooms for papers then.' They led Chaloner downstairs, whilst I poked my head into the chamber he had come out of. It was a small study room with a desk and chair, panelled walls lined with bookcases. The shutters on the windows had been thrown open, and sunlight flooded the room. I blinked as my eyes adjusted to the glare.

The bookcase had more than twenty books, and even more pamphlets. There were poems, a few plays, and Royalist journals, a copy of Holinshed's histories, and an English translation of *Don Quixote*. Hardly an inspiring library but I took the last down.

'This is said to be entertaining.' I tucked it into my doublet. 'Nothing else that is interesting. Check the trunk,' I said. 'I will search the desk.'

A small walnut desk in the Italian style sat in the corner. The drawers were stuffed full of papers. I started looking through them as Everard searched the trunk.

'What a damn awful picture, what do you think it is?' Everard passed me a small painting; a swirl of distorted blotches.

'Oh, I've seen these before,' I told him. 'My brother has some, is there a silver cylinder anywhere?'

'Umm, yes, here,' he took it out of the trunk and passed it to me.

I placed it in the middle of the image: 'Look at the reflection.' An image of a bearded man was clear in the metal, King Charles.

'By the Pope's cloven hooves, I've never seen anything like that,' said Everard.

'Well 'tis a disappointment,' I said.

'What is wrong?'

'My brother's pictures were always of naked ladies.'

'Addlepate!' he said. 'Here's something else. A box of pomegranates, what would a merchant need these for?'

'Pomegranates?' I asked.

'Hand bombs, look.' He showed me a box full of small iron spheres with a short match coming out of the top. 'These would not be much good against the Tower's battlements.'

'There's nothing else here,' I said. 'These papers are all to do with his business.'

'How do you know that?' He put the box of grenados down.

'I've seen enough of my father's accounts, suppliers' dockets, shipping receipts and the like. We can take it all in for Darnelly to pore over, but there's no commission from the King.'

I looked at the table and pulled the carved drawers out, looking underneath them, then got on my knees and looked underneath the table. I stood up and called one of the troopers from his ransacking.

'Go and find me an axe.'

'Yes, sir.' he ran downstairs, and soon returned, bearing a small hatchet.

'What are you about?' asked Everard, a quizzical look on his face.

'That will do,' I said, taking the hatchet off the soldier. I turned to the desk, and brought the hatchet down with a smash in the centre of the polished walnut surface, and again, and again, until I split the wood, ripping it off the frame. Underneath was a small compartment, with a booklet, and parchment with a list of names.

'Did you have to smash it?' said Everard. He was happy to smash works of art in a church, but some cheap table bothered him.

'Sometimes they have secret compartments,' I said. 'I was not going to waste time trying to figure it out. *Bonduca, a play by John Fletcher,*' I showed him. 'Well, evidence he is in the plot but no commission.'

'What is the paper?'

'A familiar list of names, most of the commission to Oxford; a cast of traitors and malignants.' I passed it to him.

'Not all are usual. Northumberland is here and Bulstrode?'

'Bulstrode is no traitor,' I said, looking. 'I know what he thinks of Waller well enough, and Hampden is written there as well. Do you really see him plotting for the King?'

'It could be any number of Hampdens, there is no initial, but there are enough names here to cause trouble,' said Everard.

'Darnelly will still want the King's commission.'

'Well, if it be hidden we must just tear the house apart before him until he cracks. If he thinks his family are going to lose everything he might speak up.' Everard said. 'I am tired of his fiddle-faddle.'

Downstairs, the family were held in one room. Chaloner stood to one side with a couple of Whitecoats guarding him. Soldiers were ripping off the patterned panels from the walls, looking for concealed documents. A strongbox full of coin, and plate, and papers had been found in the cellar, along with wine, and was already on the cart to be taken to the tower. Chaloner looked distraught, aghast at what was happening. I could not see why he just did not give the commission up. It could not save him, and it would stop his family being left destitute, their house destroyed, and wealth stolen.

I saw him glance over at his womenfolk; something Darnelly said struck me. I turned to his wife and daughters, dressed in their nightgowns and embroidered robes.

'Ladies,' I said. 'Lift your skirts if you please.'

'Really?' said Everard looking at me.

'How dare you, sir,' the wife started shouting at me. I ignored her; the eldest girl had gone white.

'Lift them, ladies, or I will lift them myself and be none

238

too gentle,' I said.

'Enough!' Chaloner finally broke. 'Mary, let them have it.'

The eldest, a pretty buxom thing, pulled up her nightgown showing off some white thigh, and a small box strapped to the top of her leg. She took it off and passed it over to me. I slid the box open and took out a folded piece of parchment. The seal and signature were clearly emblazoned at the bottom. It was the King's commission.

'Why did you do it, Chaloner?' I asked.

'It came from Waller.'

'The man is a weasel; why did you trust him?'

'Waller said that we could be a moderate party here in London, stand between the two parties, and unite the King with Parliament.' He shrugged. 'I hoped to stop the fighting.'

'We all hope for that,' said Everard.

'The Kingdoms are bleeding, if we do not put a stop to it now, all hope is lost.'

'Miserable traitor, take him to the Tower, Sergeant. Take his daughter in as well.'

'Everard!' I said, shocked. 'We have no need of her; she was no part of the plot.'

'Very well,' he said gruffly, 'leave her.'

Chaloner gave me a glance of gratitude before he was chained up and led off by the Whitecoats. Everard and I followed, leaving behind a ransacked house and broken family.

''Twas not like you,' I said to Everard.

'A pretty wench lifts her skirts, and you are all over her, like a dog on bitch in heat.' Then he stopped and sighed, 'I know, I was angry with him; the girl was not to blame.' He looked at me. 'I will talk to Peter when we go back to the army. He will forgive you eventually.'

We arrived back at the Tower with our captive, and the commission, and took both down to the Flint Tower, where the plotters were being interrogated. The royal captives they had hoped to free would never see these dark chambers, I concluded. It was certain to be Chaloner's last home though.

Was it so different from the Plowdens and Smirky? Different motivation perhaps but the result was the same. Another family destroyed by the war. To those women, I was not an officer doing his duty. I was always the monster who tore their father, and husband, away to his death. I met the youngest years later. She looked at me as if I was Lucifer himself, dancing at the gates of Hades.

'Waller burst into tears when Darnelly told him he was under arrest for treason.' Franny said.

'The man is a snivelling wretch, worst employer I have ever had, and a coward to boot,' Everard said. 'Where is he now?'

'Still down in the cellars with Darnelly, squealing like a stuck pig. Did you get the commission?' asked Franny.

'Yes, after a search,' I said.

'Darnelly will be satisfied perhaps, the miserable curmudgeon,' he stopped himself. 'Best you take it down to him.'

'I am having a pipe, you take it,' Everard said to me.

The interrogations were taking place in the cellars of the Flint Tower deep in the complex of the Tower of London. They had an oubliette down there, and supposedly a rack, and other implements of torture, but I never saw them. They did not need them for Waller, he was so wracked with terror he could not stop blabbering. When I knocked and went into the cell, he cringed away from me. Darnelly smiled.

'Ah, Mr Candy. Well, here is the man who had you poisoned; what do you think we should do with him?'

'Take him outside and hang him, sir, if you please?' I said.

Waller, eyes white in terror, started whining. 'It was Whorwood who wanted you killed, not I. Pask was the one who gave the boy the poison, and sent word to Oxford you were laid up at the tavern, not I, please,' he started begging. We both looked at him with contempt. Although, I felt more justified in dumping Pask head first into that cesspit.

'It was in Oxford that you took this plan to the King, was it not?' Darnelly asked.

'I did not make this business, I found it. Falkland and Mistress Whorwood conceived it, and Crisp,' he added. 'Sir Nicholas Crisp was behind it.' Darnelly wrote the name down with an evil grin.

Look, with a spot I damn him.[*]

'Did you bring the commission, Candy?' he leaned back in his chair and glanced at me.

'Yes, sir, and this list,' I handed them to him.

'We intended only to abate the confidence of the rebels with public declarations, and to weaken their powers with opposition to new supplies. There was to be no killing.' Waller wittered on.

'The commission does not say that, Mr Waller. Nor this list of names,' Darnelly showed him the list we had found at Chaloner's. 'The Earl of Northumberland? Portland? Are you saying they were involved too?'

'Yes, yes, both of them, and Lord Conway as well. Alexander Hampden would carry the messages between us and the King in Oxford. Nobody thought to stop a Hampden,' he added.

'What of Whitelocke? His name is here as well.'

'Whitelocke would not hear of it, I went to Selden's room one night in Oxford and Whitelocke was there. I talked in general terms, but he damned my eyes at such an idea. I dared not tell him all,' said Waller in tears.

---

[*]   Shakespeare, *Anthony and Cleopatra*. Act IV Scene I

'You can go now, Mr Candy.' Darnelly dismissed me.

I left the oppressive dungeon quickly, passing the cells of other plotters. Waller had given up powerful people. The plot had influential supporters, even if without chance of success.

'Was he still crying?' Franny asked.

'Like a baby,' I said.

'Well, we have some time before going back to the army, by my reckoning,' said Franny. 'Whoring over the river?'

'I am staying out of trouble,' I said. 'No whores and no drinking; I've lifted enough skirts for today.'

'No damn fun then. There's little point in making yourself miserable, Sugar. *Carpe Diem* so they say; you could be shot by a Cavalier tomorrow.'

'My thanks, that is truly of comfort when I have Royalist assassins after me.'

'All the more reason to get drunk then.'

'Let him be, Franny,' said Everard. 'Probably best we all keep our heads down for a bit after this morning's work. Penington will have the city under curfew whilst tempers are high.'

Pym may have been dying of canker, and it was by then clear something was badly wrong, but he was as verbose as ever. I watched him deliver a speech in the Commons denouncing the conspiracy. Ranting of 'blood and violence,' warning the other members that these plotters would have, 'our swords dripping with each other's blood'.

Pish, as if they were not already.

The moderates were gelded; the whole peace party reduced to impotence, as they scrambled to prove their loyalty. With Waller throwing accusations at anyone to save his skin, it was all too easy. The poet delivered his abject confession in the House, and then he paid ten thousand pounds to go into exile. Chaloner and Tomkins were not so lucky, they were both hung as traitors.

Pym forced everyone to sign a covenant, declaring their

innocence. He drafted it to include a vow to support, "*The forces raised by the two Houses of Parliament, for the defence of the true protestant religion and liberty of the subject, against the forces raised by the King.*" Once it was signed, the members were trapped; there would be no more talk of peace. They called it a "Sacred Vow and Covenant". Fine words, but all they meant was war to the bloody end.

This day there also came a punctual information of the success which had befallen the Marquess of Hertford and Sir Ralph Hopton since the conjunction of their forces. There had been a report on Sunday that the Marquess passing by the town of Dorchester, and Sir Ralph Hopton leaving forces to block up Exeter, were to meet that night, and with their joint power take some course for the reduction of Somersetshire to His Majesty's service.

And it was certified this day, that with their whole forces, amounting to 9000 men and upwards they drew towards Taunton, a town of great command and consequence in those parts of Somerset. Their coming struck such a terror into the inhabitants, that they desired to be admitted to His Majesties favour upon such conditions, as should be agreed upon betwixt them.

Which were in fine to this effect; that the inhabitants should be free from plunder, and imprisonment, that the town and castle should be delivered to His Majesty with all the ordnance, arms, and ammunition, which was found therein, and that the people should afford the army free quarter and a whole weeks pay. This being condescended and agreed upon, His Majesty's forces took possession of the town and castle. They found 6 piece of ordnance, 500 arms, 19 double barrels of powder, a tonne of match, with bullet, and other things thereto proportionable.

The news whereof being brought to Bridgewater, a town of great importance also, which hitherto had held on the rebels side; they sent unto the Marquess to desire that their submission might be taken on the like conditions: which being yielded to, they gave up the town, and in the same 8 piece of ordnance, with ammunition, arms, and other necessaries proportionable to so many ordnance.

By means whereof His Majesty is already master of the most part of that county, there being but few places in it which are able to resist in the least degree, and the most active and considerable of the rebels being fled to Bristol, as their only sanctuary in the west.

John Berkenhead/Peter Heylyn.

21. John Hurry, June 1643.

The cuckoo's a fine bird,
It sings as it flies;
It brings us good tidings.
And tells us no lies.
(Traditional, *The Cuckoo.*)

'Twenty thousand pounds of gold, I could travel the world with that.' I watched the carts roll past, tarpaulins covering the strongboxes packed with coin, all destined for the army in Thame.

'You would not get very far,' said Everard. 'Every soldier in the army would be out to carve your pizzle off.' He was dressed in his old rustic rig; the clothes he had been fain to wear whilst spying on Waller, now consigned to a trunk in Bread Street.

We had run courier between Thame and London for days. Essex begged for money and men, whilst Parliament made excuses. After the fall of Reading, Essex had marched the army north to Thame, just five miles to the east of Oxford. He remained perched there for a week, like a desperate man staring over a precipice, and wondering whether or not to jump.

With every failure, morale worsened; Essex was losing the war. St John and Harry Vane harangued him in the Commons, and he was pilloried by the London newsbooks. In the north, the King had strengthened his grip; the Cavaliers chased "Black" Tom Fairfax and his father, all over Cheshire. In the west, the Cornish advance drove all before it, threatening Somerset and my home in Wiltshire.

Essex had spread the army out in hamlets and villages all over Buckinghamshire. Lonely garrisons of raw recruits, disturbing the locals, and easily picked off by Cavalier raids. Whenever he concentrated our forces to move against the

246

King, the Royalist response was swift, as if forewarned. Whispers of treason abounded, which only increased the sense of panic.

Parliament, faced with the disintegration of discipline and loss of the war, had finally released funds to pay the army. Twenty thousand pounds, guarded by a regiment of infantry, slowly crept towards Thame.

'This money will save Essex' bacon.' I said.

'As long as it keeps me out of that choke-hole, I am happy,' Everard said.

'I like London.'

'That is because at heart you are an idler and a wastrel,' he said.

'Thank you.'

'Candy, Everard.' The Lieutenant Colonel of infantry called us over. A white-haired Londoner with the Trained Bands, and a decent sort.

'Sir?' I said.

'Get yourself to Thame as quick as you can,' he passed me a note. 'Give this to the Lord General. As long as we make good progress we should be in Chinnor tonight.'

'Yes, sir,' I replied and turned to ride away.

'Peter is in Chinnor,' said Everard.

'I wonder if he has calmed down?'

'I doubt it,' said Everard. He looked around, 'I will stay with the column, just in case anything happens. If we make good time, we should make Thame by tomorrow night.'

'There will be sack waiting for you.'

Uncle Samuel was late, Colonel Hurry was missing, and the Earl of Essex in high dudgeon. The hot summer weather did not improve tempers; only Hampden remained calm.

That morning, Essex had sent nigh on three thousand cavalry to Islip, to beat up the enemy's outlying pickets. It had not been a success. Faced with Royalist cavalry and ordnance, they turned and rode back without a shot being fired. I had arrived, with good news of the army's pay, after the miserable return from Islip. Now it seemed my uncle and John Hurry were missing, and High Command a pottage of fear and gloom. Essex' staff sat around an oak table in the manor's study, despondent at the ever increasing failures.

'Where is your uncle, sir?' The Earl asked me for the third time.

I shrugged but said nothing; it is always the best policy when a superior is having a tantrum. Essex glowered at me, but motioned to Quartermaster Dalbier to continue.

'We need eleven tonnes of oatmeal a day just for the soldiers, we receive barely six,' said Dalbier. 'The local populace is hostile because the men are billeted on them, stealing their food. We have to...'

'What is the point of a Scoutmaster if the enemy know our every movement, and we know nothing of theirs?' The Lord General erupted again, cutting Dalbier off and looking over at me.

Bastard, I thought. It was not as if I was to blame for Uncle Samuel's absence.

Dalbier stood back, face flushed at being interrupted yet again. There was also a sharp intake of breath, from Stapleton and a couple of others around the table, at the insult to my uncle. The others were silent; Essex did not like being contradicted, but Hampden had the balls to call him to account.

'The garrisons are too spread out, Milord,' said Hampden, 'and too weakly defended. We should bring them in.' It was the same argument Hampden had been begging Essex to take heed of for days.

'When the army gathers there is always trouble over

money and outbreaks of disease. I have them spread for a reason. It keeps grumbles about pay down, and the fevers at bay.'

'If the King or Rupert were to raid, Milord, these meaningless garrisons would not be able to hold them.'

'They would hold long enough for support, Hampden,' Essex cut him off. 'Hurry's dragoons can run post between them. The alarm would be raised quickly enough. As it is we have disease; I cannot risk many more men or horses dead from the fevers.'

'So, where is Colonel Hurry, Milord? You put too much trust in the man. Need I remind you, it was his failure to secure the riverbanks that led to Reading being reinforced?' Hampden said. 'Now, he is absent when summoned.'

'And where is Sir Samuel?' shouted Essex, losing his temper again. 'Stop nagging at me, Hampden.' He looked over to me. 'Go and find your uncle, Mr Candy, and inform him that I desire his presence at his earliest convenience.'

Squeaky bastard plied his sarcasm with venom.

I left the meeting and went outside, took my horse's reigns from a waiting footman, and swung up into the saddle again. Damn, my arse was sore. The Earl's headquarters were in a manor to the south of the town, owned by Viscount Wenman, one of the commissioners to Oxford in the Spring. It would take a mere quarter of an hour to reach my uncle's billet, but Apple and I had been on the road all day, and we were both tired.

Uncle Samuel had set up in the rectory near the church. That he was so far away from Essex was a sign of the growing distrust between the senior officers of the army. The fall of Reading had been a disaster. The strong army that had left

Windsor in April was reduced to a hungry diseased mob. Essex was like Pyrrhus without the wit or the victories.

The churchyard had been turned into a camp when the army had arrived at Thame, followed by the habitual smashing of glass and images. There were only a few Greencoats around when I arrived. Opposite the rectory, was a long timber frame tithe barn. Red brick built like so much of Thame, with herringbone patterns and space enough to house us and our horses. I took Apple and stabled him in the barn alone. Everyone else was absent or on duty. Even Jacob, who would normally be awaiting my arrival, was missing.

The scouts were one of the few units kept mounted. Other regiments and units were rapidly becoming infantrymen by default. That is not good for an army; it is bad for morale to see cavalrymen sitting without steeds, and poor supply will cost you a war. I've seen the best forces destroyed through lack of horses or fodder. And the army under Essex was not the best.

I hurried over to the rectory but only Butler was at my uncle's billet, sat behind his desk eating cold chicken with his fat fingers.

'Where is Uncle Samuel, Butler?'

He paused in his feast, and looked over at me. 'He went over to see Colonel Hurry about an hour ago.'

'He's supposed to be with Essex.'

'Not that I know of; he was waiting on despatches from Tetsworth, and wanted to check some of the outlying garrisons.'

'Well, the Earl wants him now.'

'You will have to go and find him then,' he said.

'Too much trouble for you to get off your lazy arse and help, I suppose?' I did not wait for a response, turned, and went to fetch Apple back on the road.

Hurry's regiment were set up as pickets on the Oxford Road, on the outskirts of Thame. Some of them would have been Pask's bullies, but I did not let that worry me too much. They had been quiet since Smirky's demise in a privy. I took Apple from his stall, despite his look of utter disgust, and rode to the outlying pickets.

After Pask's treachery had been revealed by Waller, it had seemed obvious to me that Hurry would be involved, but Uncle Samuel had found no evidence. Other than looting and pillaging, the foul breathed monster was clever enough to cover his tracks, even when his lieutenant was exposed. Without evidence we could not confront Hurry, and the Earl of Essex had confidence in him, which made our task more difficult.

The guards at Hurry's billet were lazing around when I arrived. Most were raw recruits, filling the gaps in the army left by disease and battle. It was supposed to be a regiment of dragoons, but the lack of horses meant half the men lounged around wasting their time, instead of riding picket as they were supposed to. Their equipment looked ill kept and unpolished.

God help us if the Royalists attacked.

'Where's the Colonel?' I asked a shabby looking young soldier-boy smoking a long clay pipe. He looked damn young, barely sixteen, certainly not one of the veterans. You may make comparison between kettle and pot, yet at nineteen years old, I had already seen my share of battle and death, and was old past my years.

'I know not, sir. He rode out with your uncle an hour or more ago.'

'How do you know who I am?' I asked, curious. I had avoided Hurry's camp in Thame.

'You are in the newsbooks, sir.' He handed me a well-thumbed pamphlet.

'*The Parliament Scout*,' I read the title. 'This is new?'

He turned one of the stories, 'There you are, sir. It is in *The Perfect Diurnal* as well.'

I read the story, it was a vague telling of the fight on the Thames when the Cavalier boat had exploded, but there was a passable description of me. The phrase, "Golden haired Apollo," played to my vanity. The newsbooks had been calling me the Golden Scout for months now, ever since the Devil's Tavern, but they always got some detail wrong. This time they gave my rank as captain and named me my uncle's second. I had a vague memory of a drunken conversation with some scribe in London. Uncle Samuel would not be impressed; he kept telling us to 'walk in the shadows,' and I had managed to get my name, and description, in the newsbooks again.

'Bugger,' I said.

The boy looked at me quizzically.

'I wish I had a captain's pay,' I told him, as if in explanation.

'I would settle for my trooper's pay that is owed, sir.' he said.

I laughed at that: 'So would I; at least it is coming. Parliament have released the funds to pay us at last.'

'So I have heard, sir. Believe it when I see it, though.'

'Well, I have seen it,' I said. 'It is in Chinnor. Where is Colonel Hurry's billet?'

The boy turned, and pointed me over to the small cottage Hurry had set up in. I strode over, opened the door, and walked in as if I owned the place. The few troopers there said nothing, barely noticed me in fact, just carried on with their conversations. It did not occur to me that he should not have known about the pay, or that perhaps I should have kept silent, but I was not thinking properly.

Looking back, I do not think my words changed what happened, but you can never be sure.

It was filthy inside Hurry's billet; just one room. The poor owners had been thrown out, and it now stank like a tavern. The furniture was sparse, with only a couple of chairs, and a bed made up in the corner. One thing caught my attention though; there was a large chest pushed up against the back wall. If it had been the owners, it would have been smashed open; it had to be Hurry's.

Now that was when my curiosity started to get the better of me. Dare I open the chest? It was bound to be locked; it did not stop me trying though. My heart started pounding, I checked in a crack in the door to see where Hurry's men were; a couple outside talking but not close.

Creeping back to the chest I studied it for a second, and then kneeled in front of it. Holding my breath, I tried to lift the lid; it was locked. I paused and looked at the lock. If Franny had been with me, he would have cracked it open in seconds, but I did not have his skill. I slid my dagger between the lid and the lock, to click back the mechanism. I essayed a jimmy or two, but slipped and there was a loud crack.

I froze, listening out, expecting any second that Hurry's troopers would come rushing in, but nobody did. I had broken the lock; damn, there was no hiding that. Well, in for a penny, in for a pound, I lifted the lid. It was full of papers, clothes, and some coin. I rummaged through the mess, until tucked in the bottom corner I found what I was looking for. *Bonduca, A Play by John Fletcher.* Hurry was the traitor. I sat back on my heels triumphant. At last, we had the bastard.

The implications for Essex and the army were serious. Hurry had been trusted by the Earl, and had been privy to all of his plans. It was no wonder the force sent to Islip that morning had been met by overwhelming force. Not if Hurry had been feeding information back to the King. Worse, was the fact that Parliament had finally released the funds to pay the army. If news of the gold convoy had got back to the King, the pay column was in trouble, and when a young trooper knew it was on the way, it was certain the King would as well.

I heard voices at the door, a familiar Scots tone, deep and gravelly. I turned as it opened: Uncle Samuel, and behind him Hurry, stood staring at me on my knees in front of the chest.

'Blandford?' my uncle looked surprised. I lifted the playbook to show him, but Hurry was fast. Taking one look at me, he knew his secret was exposed. With a cry of rage, he pushed into Uncle Samuel's back, throwing him into the room, and slamming the door shut. I jumped to the side to avoid Uncle Samuel pitching into me; instead, he went headfirst into the lid of the chest, cutting his forehead. I got to my feet, and helped him up. He looked at me, blood streaming down his face.

'His playbook?' he said.

'Yes, Uncle.'

'Well, do not just stand there, let us get after him.' Uncle Samuel drew his short sword and motioned for me to do the same. He pulled the door open only to be faced with two muskets pointed at us.

'You are under arrest, sir. Colonel Hurry has gone to fetch the Earl, and told us to keep you here.'

'You damn fool, let us out,' I said. I could see Hurry mounting his horse and starting to ride off down the road at a gallop.

'Calm yourself, Sugar,' said the other one. 'When the Colonel gets back with Old Robin, then we can sort it all out.'

My uncle glared up at the guard, pointed to the disappearing John Hurry, then in a haughty tone he said,

'My good man, if Colonel Hurry is indeed going to fetch the Earl of Essex, perhaps you can explain to us, why he is now riding west towards Oxford?'

It is reported for certain, that Colonel Hurry, the Scottish man, hath now fully discovered the (ever suspected) treacheries of his false heart, by turning Apostata. For he hath deserted the Parliament's service, and is run away to the Cavaliers at Oxford. This man was well beloved, respected, and confided in, insomuch that he hath been employed in services of consequence, which how slightly he hath performed, and ill requited, is now conspicuous and obvious to all observers of these times. It seemeth that Oxonian promises, and hope of vain preferment, is more prevalent with him, then the true honour and reputation of an heroic and noble soldier.

William Ingler.

22. Midas' Curse, June 1643.

*"Demasiada cordura puede ser la peor de las locuras,
ver la vida como es y no como debería de ser."
"Too much sanity may be madness. And maddest of all,
to see life as it is and not as it should be."*

(Miguel de Cervantes Saavedra, *Don Quixote*.)

We galloped back to Headquarters, reaching Wenman's manor towards three or four o'clock. Hurry would already be halfway to Oxford. It had been but an hour since the Earl had sent me out to find my uncle, and the recriminations in command were still ongoing. Uncle Samuel strode into the middle of the meeting without ceremony.

'Where have you been, Luke, and where is Colonel Hurry? The pair of you have been most tardy,' said the Earl, ignoring the cut on my uncle's forehead, and his bloodstained falling band.

'Colonel Hurry is on the way to Oxford, and I am here thanks only to God's providence and my nephew's wit.' There was a clear note of hostility in Uncle Samuel's voice.

With his reply the meeting dissolved into pandemonium as all present assailed my uncle with questions. Essex tried to assert himself.

'Silence!' He screamed, bringing some semblance of order to the table. 'By Christ's wounds, what mean you, Luke?'

'Colonel Hurry has betrayed us.' My uncle threw the copy of *Bonduca* onto the table. 'He rode to Oxford this afternoon, taking details of all our dispositions to the King. Since he knows about the gold wagons, we can only assume that the King also knows there are twenty thousand pounds on the road to Chinnor.' Uncle Samuel looked Essex straight in the face. 'We are undone, Milord.'

'Where is the column now?' asked Hampden, as Essex sat

ashen faced in silence.

'It left High Wycombe this morning, sir,' I said. 'I rode on to bring word. They should be in Chinnor tonight.'

'I have three troops of dragoons at Chinnor,' Uncle Samuel said, 'and there are infantry with the column.'

'I will ride down to Stokenchurch, then on to Watlington,' said Hampden. 'If we can alert some of the outlying garrisons, we might counter any raid. Milord, do you concur?'

Essex roused himself. 'Do that, John,' he said. All charming now, no doubt thinking he could send Hampden off somewhere. 'There are troops at Wheatley who can hold the river crossing over the Thame. Sir Samuel, ensure that gold gets to Chinnor safely. If we lose the army's pay, the war is over.'

He dismissed us, turning to his other officers and starting to rearrange garrisons. Hurry's treachery threw all his plans into chaos, and he was being forced to act.

I followed Uncle Samuel and Hampden outside to the stables. Once in the seclusion of the stalls, my uncle confronted Hampden. For weeks, the newsbooks had been calling for him to take the leadership of the army. Now, Uncle Samuel took the same approach.

'This cannot go on, John. Old Robin is too timid to have command,' Uncle Samuel said quietly. 'We are losing the war.'

'What would you have me do, Samuel?' Hampden said. 'Take control of the army myself? You have been reading too many pamphlets, my friend.'

'You know that is what I would urge. The officers would follow you, and the men believe in you,' said Uncle Samuel.

'And what of Parliament, Samuel? What of Parliament's wishes?'

'What of Parliament? If the King wins the war, then what Parliament wants will not matter a jot. The army needs leadership if we are to gain victory, and Parliament needs us to win.'

'An army is a powerful thing, Samuel,' said Hampden. 'An army unfettered by control of the House would be a sword pointed at the nation's throat. Essex is our lawful commander set by Parliament. It is our duty to be his loyal officers.'

'We are both loyal officers and members of the House; we could assume the authority,' insisted Uncle Samuel.

'That is sophistry, Samuel. If I should set myself as General regardless of the will of Parliament, why then I would be as much a tyrant as the King. Indeed, what could stop me becoming King if I so decide?'

'You would not do that, John, I know you.'

'Perhaps I would not, Samuel, but once the precedent is set what is to stop another taking such action? Can you ever trust an unfaithful wife not to stray again? Soldiers are as fickle women, my friend; they may follow me now, but what if the pay were late again? Or food supplies held up? Or plague took hold? Come, we have enough to worry about making war on the King. Would you make Lucius Brutus[77] into Gaius Caesar as well?'

He smiled at his jest, but it was a dark prophecy.

'Find the wagons, Samuel, and I will check the garrisons to the south. If Rupert comes that way, I will hear of it and stop him.'

Uncle Samuel looked primed to argue further, but after a short pause just said, 'God go with you then, my friend.'

'And you, Samuel.' They clasped hands before Hampden took to his horse, and rode out for Watlington. Uncle Samuel began pulling on armour and gestured for me to do the same. I sighed; when I was ready, he glanced over.

'Come along then, Blandford, Let us go search for Midas' curse.'[78]

Chinnor lies about five miles to the south of Thame. It is a small village, along a straight chalky road. By the time we reached the garrison billeted there, both of us were coated in white dust thrown up from the road, and baked by the late afternoon sun. My throat was parched and my arse sore, and when we arrived in Chinnor, the pay column was nowhere in sight.

The three troops of dragoons billeted in the village were raw recruits. Green boys from Buckinghamshire who had signed on to Uncle Samuel after Edgehill. They had a new standard, black with bibles, and brand new equipment, but no experience. I thought little of them; they were worse than Hurry's bullyboys. Peter was a troop commander here, though I had not seen him on my way to Thame earlier. At least one of the officers would be competent—even if he was enraged at me.

I begged a serving of stew, that proved thick with gobbets of fat but no meat that I could discover, some ale to quench my thirst, and we waited in Chinnor until it was nearly dark.

I had finished the ale, and saw one of their officers talking to Uncle Samuel, and then walking away. I knew that bowl of a haircut. 'Peter,' I called over to him. He turned and saw me, our eyes met for a second, but he turned his back and walked away.

Uncle Samuel came over to me. 'We need to find that column; they should have been here hours ago.'

'What did Peter say?' I asked, hoping for some sort of forgiveness.

'He's worried about the troops here, their morale is low. We need to be drilling them, not leaving them idle in these villages.'

'Oh.' I must have sounded disappointed.

'Not everything is about you, Blandford. Now come, we need to find the money.'

Uncle Samuel and I followed the road south, searching

259

for the pay column. Picking our way slowly in the darkness up through the woodland, we climbed up to the chalky hills above Chinnor. We carried on along a small ridge past a couple of small hamlets, no more than a house or two. To the east, the land fell away from the road into thick woodland, until finally as we turned down off the ridge we saw lights below. Fires had been set up, with a few hundred soldiers huddled around. There was a line of wagons, ten in all, motionless along the road with them.

It was the pay column, halted at the bottom of a climb, just as the road turned, three miles short of Chinnor and safety. Torches were held around the front wagon and a cluster of wagoners and soldiers. Nobody stopped us as we rode up; no guard and no urgency.

The first wagon was tilted on one side, its precious cargo beside it in the dust. Lying on the ground in the dirt, strapping up the axle, was Everard and the driver.

'Why are you not in Chinnor, William?' called my uncle as we rode up.

Everard looked up and spat. 'These wagons are damn useless, Sir Samuel. The axles cannot stand the weight of the coin. It was fine on good roads, but these chalky strips of potholes-and-ruts, are ripping them from the frame. We've had three go since High Wycombe, and in the dark more will fail.'

'We cannot leave the gold in the open, with Rupert's troopers abroad looking for it.' Uncle Samuel said. 'Get the column off the road and under cover.'

'It is going to take at least another hour before this one is ready to move, sir,' Everard said.

'Spread the coin out among the other wagons for now,' said my uncle, 'and bring that wagon on after. We get the rest off the road and into the woodland. They can head into Chinnor tomorrow. Who is in charge of the infantry?'

'The colonel is over that way,' Everard gestured to where

infantry were huddled smoking pipes. Uncle Samuel trotted over to get the soldiers busy, driving the pay wagons off the road and into the thick woodland.

'It is wonderful to be away from the city with creation all around,' Everard grinned at me, his face covered in shit.

'You find this fit sport, do you?' I shook my head in disgust. 'Covered in dung, in the middle of nowhere, with not a tavern in sight, and you are happy?'

'Breathe that air, Blandford,' he said. 'Smell how fresh it is?'

'The only thing I can smell is you. How long till dawn?'

He looked up at the sky. 'A few hours, I think. Was Peter in Chinnor?'

'Yes.'

'What did he say?'

'Nothing, just turned his back on me,' I replied.

'He is still angry then?'

'It looks so, does it not.'

'I told you he would be. Do not fret yourself, Sugar; allow him time.'

'I hate that poxy name.'

'I know, 'tis why I use it; call it your penance.' He smiled at me.

It took less than an hour for us to drive the wagons and oxen off into the woodland. The infantry doused their fires, with a little grumbling, until it was pointed out to them that Cavalier troopers were searching for us. That made them move a bit quicker. In the darkness off the road, with the men sitting silently, we could hope to avoid any Royalist scouts until dawn.

Sound carries further in the darkness. Before dawn, the noise of battle struck up to the north.

'Fighting at Chinnor,' Everard said to me.

'By good fortune the axles broke,' I told him. 'It could have been us there.'

'Providence, not fortune.' said Everard.

Uncle Samuel came over to us. 'I need to know what is happening, the colonel will hold here with the gold. You two come with me.'

Both of us ran to get our weapons and horses ready. I was exhausted; I had not slept for over a day, and my muscles ached from the riding. Everard had armed himself with breastplate and pot, and the three of us headed back towards Chinnor and the sound of fighting.

We went back up to the road just as dawn broke. Another cloudless day, growing brighter by the minute, as we rode towards the sound of battle. Turning off the track, we headed down through the woods until after a short descent we came in view of the village. By the time we reached the tree line, it was clear that Chinnor was burning. It was not a happy sight. The flames leapt from the houses, and the screams of the poor souls burning carried to us.

'Christ preserve us,' muttered Everard. Uncle Samuel and I were silent.

We paused on horseback surveying the carnage below. Houses were on fire, but the sounds of fighting had died away. The Royalists had moved on after destroying the garrison, and finding the gold missing. The three of us rode towards the flames, noting bodies on the ground. There were some wounded men, and a few still standing, stunned at what had happened. Over two hundred men had been billeted here; only a handful were left alive amongst the bodies. We dismounted walking through the horror. It was like a slaughterhouse on feast day.

Even from a distance, I could see it was him. I recognised his coat, smouldering from the fire, and the bloody stupid haircut. I turned the body over, hoping, praying that I was mistaken. Please let it be someone else; please let him still live. It was Peter.

Everard found me later, cradling his body, tears streaming

down my face, heaving in shock, and barely able to breathe.

'Come away, Blandford.'

'I cannot leave him here in the dirt.'

We carried his body into one of the houses and laid it out on a table. I was in shock; warfare gives us terrifying testimony to the fragility of life. Mostly soldiers deal with it through dark humour and casual indifference. When it is someone close though? Then the madness of Mars hits the bone.

'What happened?' I asked.

'Prince Rupert hit them while they slept. Most woke up to die, the rest surrendered.'

'And Peter?'

'The officers tried to hold out in the house, Rupert had it set alight, and gunned them down when they fled the flames,' Everard told me.

'That is murder,' I said.

'You need to be ready to ride. The Royalists are heading to Watlington; Hampden is there with more men. We might be able to free the captives and regain your uncle's colour.'

I looked at him, his voice calm, as if the death of Peter were of no matter. His face betrayed him though; the streaks of tears had run through the dirt.

'Come, Blandford,' he said softly. 'Let us make the bastards pay.'

My Dear Elizabeth,

I received the monies that you have sent me and thank you for it. I have bought some beautiful cloth and hope to make a fine dress but there are no needles here so I will await our return to Oxford; we are at Newark still. Her Majesty has come out of the north, and Mistress Margaret and I have been presented to her. The Queen was exceedingly gracious and kind and she accepted Mistress Margaret as Lady in Waiting.

Is it a sin to enjoy such felicity? With war and pestilence all around I should be melancholic. Mistress Margaret says that great misery begets great happiness, perhaps this is what I feel.

The newsbooks are full of Blandford and the arrest of poor Mr Waller. They call B the Golden Scout; it would be a rare delight, were it not Parliament that he serves. Mistress Margaret says, that there are grand designs about him and we should have a care who we speak to on the matter.

Mistress Whorwood was much embarrassed by Mr Waller's arrest. There are whispers that it was her design and she persuaded the King to support it. B has only enraged her further I fear. Yet, now the Queen is returned, perhaps there can be some reconciliation. Her Majesty says that she desires only peace and an end to this perpetual parliament.

James has returned south to Oxford in haste. His closeness to Mistress Whorwood makes him somewhat distasteful to Her Majesty which is no surprise. There are rumours about how high in Mistress Whorwood's favour he is. I sought word with him before he left but he took me for a foolish child.

I will write again soon, there is a great feast today to celebrate Her Majesty's arrival, and our presence is commanded. Mistress Margaret does not wish to attend, for she is exceeding shy with strangers, but I am quite giddy with the excitement.

Farewell dear Elizabeth. Please write soon; I so look forward to your letters.

Anne.
Newark, 18th June 1643.

23. Chalgrove Field, June 1642.

I have seen him in front of's Regiment-in-green,
When death about him, did in ambush lie,
And whizzing shot, like showers of arrows fly,
Waving his conqu'ring steel.

(Captain John Stiles, *Elegy on the Death of that worthy*
Gentleman.)

I was silent during the short ride to Watlington, my thoughts
sorely taken up and troubled by Peter's death. To my shame,
I confess my grief was in part a loss of hope: for I realised
any I had for Emily had died with him. I knew she would not
look at me again without seeing her dead brother, nor I her
without seeing him and feeling a burden of guilt. We rode on
to the sound of gunfire, the snap of carbines could be heard
up ahead; there was no time for misery.

We reached Watlington in good time, but the Royalists
were already moving on. They headed for the river crossing
at Chiselhampton. Laden with booty and prisoners they were
making slow progress, but in daylight it was clear that their
numbers greatly outweighed our few troops.

'I have sent to Essex for more men,' Hampden told us
as we arrived. Dalbier had joined him in the night, tired of
Essex' whining. They had taken command as Rupert tried to
slip past the garrison after burning Chinnor.

'What did Old Robin say?' asked Uncle Samuel.

'He is splenetic*,' said Dalbier. 'Your news about Hurry
had him all-a-fluster. Now word of the attack has him terrified
that Parliament will dismiss him.'

'I hope they do,' I whispered to Everard. 'The man is
scared of his own shadow.'

'Stapleton is bringing support, they started mustering as

---

*   Melancholic.

soon as he received word.' Hampden said.

'Stapleton is a good man,' my uncle said. 'How many men is he bringing?'

'Two regiments of Horse and some dragoons,' Hampden told him. 'More than enough to frustrate Prince Rupert before he escapes. If we can delay him now.'

'Will Stapleton get here in time?' came a clipped voice; it belonged to the German mercenary Major Gunter, who had proved himself a good and able officer.

'If we can delay the Prince,' Hampden repeated. 'He can only go as fast as his slowest musketeer. If God wills it, and time allows, we may yet catch him.' His quiet confidence infected us all, for despite the odds and the slaughter at Chinnor, the men were in good spirits.

We were still badly outnumbered, but Hampden led us in an attack on the retreating Cavaliers. A great hedge divided us from the Royalist force, keeping us apart, so we duelled from a distance with pistol and carbine as more troops came to join us.[79]

I took aim at one of the brightly dressed Cavalier officers, over fifty metres away. Sat on my horse, on a rise behind the hedge, I could just about see over it to fire. I squeezed the trigger, and saw him sway back from the force of the blow. The ball must have bounced off his breastplate. He noted me watching from over the hedge, made a mocking bow, doffed his hat, and rode on.

'Bastard,' I said, and started to reload.

'Good mark, though,' Everard told me.

As more troopers from the outlying garrisons started to come in, there was word of the column of Cavalry under Stapleton coming to our aid. It was close and would swell our numbers to match the enemy. Perhaps Hampden would be proven right, and we would catch Rupert and the Cavaliers, before they reached the safety of the river crossing.

We carried on, slowly moving north, picking off any stragglers, but were still divided from the enemy by the great hedge running between us. Too thick to push through, and too high to jump; far from engaging the enemy at close quarters, we received only the jeers and catcalls of the Royalist troopers on the western side instead.

'If we can slow them down, we can stop them at the bridge,' Major Gunter told us.

'We cannot get at them through the poxy hedge,' said Everard.

'The hedge thins out, and then ends up ahead; there's a manor and some open ground,' said Gunter. 'Rupert will have to turn there and face us, if he is to stop us catching his infantry.'

Even with seven or eight troops of cavalry and a hundred or so dragoons, we were still well outnumbered by the Royalists.'[80]

'Where's Stapleton?' I asked.

Gunter frowned. 'Not here yet. 'Twill be too close for my liking.'

Hampden sent the dragoons into the hedge on foot, to harry the Cavaliers with musketry. Rupert was a canny bastard though; he could see us being reinforced, and drew his cavalry off onto a small rise. The great hedge still lay between us, but ended after a short distance on our right flank. We drew up behind the hedge with Horse covering its northern end, and more reinforcements mustering at a small manor house a few hundred yards to our rear.[81]

It was a good defensive position; Rupert would have to come around the hedge to attack us, stopping him from using his advantage in numbers. That is if Rupert had been a normal commander. He did the unthinkable. After being stung by our dragoons sniping, he charged the hedge.

'Satan's imps, he's mad,' Everard said.

In truth, madness had little to do with it—for he had an excellent seat. He bore down upon us in magnificent fury, and jumped the hedge. Rupert always tried the unexpected and nearly always won. If his uncle had listened a little harder to him, King Charles would have won the war. Was it fortune or providence that our King was an idiot?

I could hear Rupert shouting, 'damn insolence,' and 'impudent traitors,' in his thick German accent, as he leaped the hedge, hacking out at our dragoons. Dressed in bright red with silver lace, with no helmet and hair flowing, he made a perfect target. More than one man fell trying to stick him. About a dozen of his bodyguard followed him at first, throwing our dragoons into a panic, sending them fleeing in terror. At the same time, other Cavalier troops came around the northern end of the hedge, crashing into our right flank. Our men on the right held, but more Cavaliers pushed over and through the hedge to face our front. Rupert paused to collect his men, and then came on at us at a full gallop, swords pointed in charge. We stood to receive them as at Edgehill, stopped with carbines and pistols ready. We just had time to discharge our shot at close range before that first wave hit us.

To everyone's surprise, we stood our ground. It was the first time that had happened; normally they swept us away in a tangle. For once, we matched them: it did not last long.

I discharged my first pistol into the face of a Royalist at point blank range, the muzzle nearly touching his nose as the gun went off. He fell away; I felt his blood and brain spatter me, and he dropped from sight. I slipped the pistol back into its holster and drew my second, just as my horse reared at the Cavalier riders pushing into us.

It was Hampden's presence that steadied the line, but Hampden was hurt in that first clash, shot in the shoulder. He turned away; face white, with his head hanging down. Resting his hands upon the neck of his horse, clearly in pain, he was led away by one of his men.[82]

Beside him, Uncle Samuel went down, unhorsed in the charge. Everard and I struggled to get through the mêlée to help him. Cornered by three Cavalier horsemen, he despatched one with a pistol shot, then ducked and stuck another with his porker* in the groin. He dropped to one knee as a sword flashed above his head, spinning on the balls of his feet. I took the man with a pistol shot above the eye, as Uncle Samuel grabbed hold of my saddle and swung up behind me.

'Get us out of here, Blandford, if you please,' he shouted in my ear.

For all his small size, he was lightning quick, and with his short sword a menace. I knew that from the few times we had fenced in practice. I had just seen the skill save his life.

We rode to the rear of the fighting; Hampden's loss meant Dalbier had taken command. He had reformed some of the cuirassiers and after reloading, we readied for a counter charge on Rupert and the Cavalier centre. The two lines crashed together again, but our charge did not have enough force against their numbers.

I tried to get to Hurry who was at the head of the Prince of Wales' regiment. The fight was close and brutal with no quarter given. I pressed the muzzle of my first pistol against the metal corselet of one Royalist, discharging it into his back and killing him outright. I drew my second to shoot at Hurry, ducking back as a sword was thrust at me. That put my aim off, and my shot hit his horse in the head. He recognised me as I drew my sword, and his horse collapsed to the floor, but I could not get to him.

Our initial momentum had slowed, and now the weight of Cavalier Horse started to push us back again. Hurry was struggling with one of our troopers, but I was hard pressed to defend myself. Faced with Cavalier troopers thrusting at me, I parried and pulled back on the reins to draw Apple away. I took a glancing blow to my leg, that cut through the boot

*   Short Sword

leather; I saw the blood stain my torn breeches but felt no pain.

I fell back from the mêlée to reload my pistols again, but I heard my name through the crash of battle. Strange how a single voice can cut through a cacophony. My brother James. I pulled Apple up and turned, spying him less than thirty feet away, bloodied sword in hand.

He pointed the sword at me, dug his spurs into his horse's flanks, and charged. I did the same, meeting him almost at full pelt. Our swords crashed together, sending a shock down my arm, and stinging my fingers. He stabbed down at Apple, and cut him in the flank, causing him to rear up. I kicked with my left boot, out of the stirrup, catching the wretch right under the chin. It threw him back, but I nearly unhorsed myself as Apple plunged to the earth again.

He screamed and slashed with his sabre at my head, but I ducked and smashed him in the face with the basket hilt of my sword. I felt his nose crunch, despite the guard on his helmet, and he let out a yowl of pain. Ha, broke the bastard's nose. He wore a crooked beak for the rest of his life.

A rider collided his horse into Apple, and for an instant, I was distracted as I sought to wheel back. When next I looked, James had been swept along in the fighting. I could see him a way off, but there was no way to get back to him. Bastard! That is the second time he has tried to kill me, I thought. Third time pays for all.

Again, I fell back to the banners at the centre of the battle, reloading my pistols. Uncle Samuel, made horseless once more, yet stood discussing the situation with Dalbier as if on an afternoon ride, rather than amidst a vicious battle.

'We must retreat, Samuel,' Dalbier said. 'Lest we be hemmed in by them.' Uncle Samuel took the reins of another spare horse, mounted and took the whole scene in. The line was starting to crack on both flanks, as the superior numbers of the Royalists began to tell. He nodded in agreement to

Dalbier, and soon our officers could be heard shouting above the din.

'Withdraw, withdraw in good order.'

It did not fall out like that. Rupert led another attack on our line and we broke. We were all driven along, even the reserve standing near the manor were caught up in it. We scattered, every man for himself, fleeing over the chalky fields. I stayed close to my uncle and Everard, and the Cavaliers did not pursue us far. Rupert had learned his lesson after Edgehill, so drew his men back before they were spread out over miles. Then he calmly led the cavalry off down the road, following his infantry to the river crossing at Chiselhampton.

We fled for at least a mile, galloping as fleet and far as we could, before we ran headlong into Stapleton's relief force. Only a regiment, not the army promised, but enough to turn the tide if he desired. He did not desire. Whilst those of us fleeing the battle gathered ourselves, Stapleton drew up his regiment and watched the Royalists fall back to safety. Essex was left with another defeat to digest.

More skirmish than battle: no more than a hundred killed and all over in a quart of an hour. Major Gunter died, pierced through with stab wounds. The rest of our troops had been scattered, but our little triumvirate rode with Stapleton back to Thame. We followed Hampden; he had withdrawn there after his wound and then collapsed, so the doctors were summoned.

'How did Hurry escape?' Franny asked. We were in the barn, near the church in Thame.

'Two troopers gave him the chance to surrender after his

horse was killed,' Everard told him. 'He offered his parole then shot one and stole a horse to escape.'

'That is raw.' Franny looked over to my cot, where I was pretending to read the Don Quixote I had taken during Chaloner's arrest. 'How has Sugar taken it all?' he whispered.

'I can hear you whispering, you dolt.'

'My apologies, Sugar, Peter was a good friend to us all. Devil's own way to die, made worse by Hurry's treason.'

'No matter, Franny,' I smiled sadly at him. 'First Lieutenant Russell, then Zeal, now Peter. This war is damn costly in friends' lives, but I trust I shall have the chance to face Hurry again.'

And when I did I would kill him, that much I had determined. I loved Peter and his death demanded a reckoning.

'Perhaps Essex will listen to Hampden now,' said Everard, 'and bring the garrisons in. Hurry has given the King all our deployments.'

'The King has offered Hampden his own physician to tend his wounds.' said Franny. 'I heard it from a contact in Oxford. Doctor Giles, the parson of Chinnor, was ordered to offer his assistance.'

'Not out of honour I would wager,' said Everard. 'Only to try and put Hampden in his debt in some way. I saw Whitelocke afterwards, he'd been in to see Hampden, said they sent the messenger away.'

'How is he?' I asked Everard.

'Who, Whitelocke? Smug. His wife has had another daughter, and he's happier playing politics than he is playing soldiers.'

'Not Whitelocke, Hampden. How is Hampden?'

'Not too bad. He took a bullet in the shoulder; it stuck between the flesh and collarbone. The doctors have pulled it now, though, and Sir Samuel has spoken to him as well. Through God's mercy, it is more likely to be a badge of honour than any danger to his life.'

Fateful words, Hampden was dead a few days later. He died on his wedding anniversary. A bitter pill for his wife to swallow, to lose a stepson and now a husband in the space of a few months. That thought only drew my mind back to Emily, and Peter's mother. Uncle Samuel had already written to them, but I had no words to write that could give comfort. No words that I thought they wanted to hear.

I made the newsbooks again for saving my uncle's life, but this time he saw to it they changed my name to "a servant", I never saw the hundred pounds reward either.[83]

Newsbooks and their lies, they talked of Hampden giving a damn speech at his death. A diatribe directed against the King and his wicked counsellors, for the sake of his "poor bleeding land". What a crock of shit. He was raving and unintelligible with fever when he died. It was a sorry end to a great man, and a disaster for England.

24. Homeward, June 1643.

There was three men come out o' the west

Their fortunes for to try,

And these three men made a solemn vow,

John Barleycorn must die,

They ploughed, they sowed, they harrowed him in,

Throwed clods upon his head,

And these three men made a solemn vow,

John Barleycorn was dead.

(Traditional, *John Barleycorn*.)

I mourned Peter in a dirty little brewhouse on the edge of Aylesbury.[84] Filthy straw on the floor, and stretched hide windows darkened by smoke that made it gloomy even in daylight. Its main attraction for me was a Welsh punk by the name of Megan. We had finally received our back pay, some of it at least. The wine vendors, food sellers, and whores that follow every army were making a fortune.

I hate the mornings. Waking with a sore head and tender stomach after passing out drunk, puts one off. In fact, I try to avoid them as much as possible. It is far better for me to wake when the sun is high, and thank the Lord for the night to come. Unfortunately, Butler did not give me the chance. He brought news, kicking open the door, and then kicking me.

'You are wanted.'

I opened my eyes, shielded them from the light, and looked up to see Butler's moon-face staring down at me.

'You are not,' I moaned. Megan muttered something in Welsh, and buried her head into my shoulder.

'Sir Samuel wants you. It is pressing, so awake and arise.'

'Butler, you dim-witted-fart-of-a-man, close the damn door,' shouted Franny, to the giggles of his strumpet.

'It stinks like a sty in here,' Butler said, 'and these whores should not be allowed.'

'Bugger off,' I reached out and grabbing the nearest object to hand, threw *Don Quixote* at him. I missed.

He sneered at us. 'Look at the two of you, vanity, pride, and arrogance. You are the truest characters of ignorance.'

''Tis the pot calling the kettle black,' I said, sitting up. Megan rolled over onto her stomach, cursing us all.

'That is funny,' said Franny. 'Who did you steal it from?'

'The book I just threw at him. Now I tell you, Butler, take it, read it and for the love of God, find a sense of humour.' He picked up the copy of *Don Quixote*.

'Perhaps I will,' he said pocketing it. 'Your uncle said he wants you now, Candy.' Then he turned and walked out.

'You had better go,' said Franny, pulling the blankets back over himself and his trull.

'I wonder where he's sending me this time.'

'I know not; I care not,' said Franny as the girl started giggling again. 'Close the door on your way out.'

I looked down at Megan's naked body and slapped her arse, 'Right then, my lover. Time for us to arise.'

'Bastard,' was the only reply.

I threw on some clothes, locating my breeches under the bed after a brief search, scraped my hair back, then splashed some water on my face to freshen it. Blinking, I stepped out into the sunlight and walked over to the house used by my uncle. Butler was back at his desk reading the book as I entered.

'Go right in,' he said smugly. 'Sir Samuel is waiting for you.'

I walked into the small room Uncle Samuel had set aside as an office. As always a table, covered in papers and maps, sat in front of him.

'You sent for me, Uncle?'

'Yes, my boy, come in,' he gestured to a seat.

'I have news from the west.' He picked up a small paper and passed it to me.

Elizabeth Candy is taken, imprisoned by the rector in her father's house and accused of witchcraft.

'Is this a jest?'

'No jest, it was left in a letter cache near your home. Sam Brayne picked it up on his way back from Bath. The Royalists are advancing, it would be timely to bring Elizabeth out of harm anyway, but this message,' he paused. 'Something is clearly not right.'

'What do you mean, Uncle?'

'It is not written in code in the first instance. Only your sister used that cache, and only ever in code since your unfortunate encounter with Hurry last year. Even when she knew the carrier, Elizabeth was careful. It is not from your sister, so who wrote it, and how did they know your sister used an oak tree for the cache?'

'But Elizabeth a witch? It is ridiculous. Although I can believe anything of the rector.' Something gnawed at me, but I could not put my finger on it.

'Indeed, I want you to find out what has been happening, Blandford. Bring Elizabeth home, your father too if needs be, but I want to know who used the tree.'

'Yes, Uncle.'

'It is the second time one of my letter caches has been compromised in the space of a week. Once is unfortunate, twice is suspicious.'

'When do I leave?'

'Today, take Everard and Cole with you,' he handed me another note. 'This is a warrant signed by the Earl, commanding anyone to assist the bearer and not to hinder your passage.' I took the paper and turned to go.

'Blandford,' he fixed me with a piercing gaze.

'Yes, Uncle?'

'I think you have indulged your melancholy enough now. Do not dishonour Mr Russell's memory by dragging it out any longer.'

'Yes, Uncle.' Feeling guilt in a way only my uncle could ever arouse, I left to find Everard and break up Cole's tryst with his punk. Homeward bound after so much time away. I ran to the stables, my hangover gone.

Jacob had packed up his pots and pans onto a horse, and stood with Franny and Everard, dressed in a cloak and hat for travel. Before I could question what he was doing, he spoke.

'If you do not have me with you, Master, who is to do the cooking, and 'tis better to be on the road with you than stuck here with the disease. Besides, it is not right you go home without your servant.'

I could not argue with that, and there was no harm in another pair of hands.

'I can cook,' protested Franny.

'No,' said Jacob. 'You really cannot.'

Everard shrugged. Taking Jacob was a risk, but the thought of Franny's burned bacon or lumpy porridge decided the matter. Jacob was good enough with his weapons to defend himself, and had proven his use more than once.

'Where did you get the horse?' I asked Jacob.

'It is Mr Butler's,' he said innocently. 'I was sure he would not mind.'

That sealed it; the four of us took to the road in good humour. We had to take a great swing south then west to avoid Royalist territory. It was at least two days hard riding, in the heat, to get to Wiltshire.

The road back home was a journey through my past year. We rode to Windsor first, to avoid Royalist patrols from Oxford, then turned west to Reading. Neither Franny nor I wanted to stop in the town. It held far too many dark memories, so we skirted around it. It was warm and the weather good, so we camped that night in a field rather than find an inn. England had been broken by the conflict, and strange taverns were too much of a risk to travellers.

We passed the place where I had first been ambushed by Smirky and pitched into adventure. I did not mention it to the others; they were thoughts I did not want reminding of. The dark things you do stay with you. It is the light that fades.

We arrived in Marlborough near noon on the second day and stopped to water the horses. I had visited the town often as a boy. My father had contacts there. I had planned on speaking to them to get local news before moving onto Hilperton, but I was disappointed. Marlborough was a ruin. The houses burned out and my father's contacts gone. What people that were left scrabbled around in their broken homes.

I should not have been surprised. I had seen Reading after the siege, and I had seen my share of devastation, but this was home. Cocooned in the east with the army under Essex, the reports of war elsewhere had seemed so distant. To see those places I had grown up with, played in as a child, now burned out was a grievous blow. I had forgot how war was everywhere in the three kingdoms. I walked back to the square where the others were watering the horses. Only Franny and Everard were there.

'Where be Jacob?'

'Gone to rustle up some ale and pie,' said Franny.

'In this place?' I looked around gloomily.

Jacob was not long in coming back. He had bought pies for us all and a casket of ale, but also some information.

'There are Royalists to the south of us in Devizes,' he said. 'The vendor told me our boys are all north of the Avon with General Waller. It looks like there will be a battle soon.'[85]

'We should take the Chippenham road then,' I said. 'We avoid the forest as well that way. Come, we can eat as we ride.'

Franny took a bite out of his pie, and climbed up in the saddle. 'Let us get going then,' he said, with a mouthful of crust. We clattered out of Marlborough and took the road west.

The bridge over the Avon at Staverton, is really two narrow crossings onto an island in the centre of the river, with a sharp turn in the middle. There was always talk about widening it. No parapets meant that carts were always tipping off, something my father had complained of when it was his cloth being soaked. We had troops stationed there, watching the river crossing, but the Royalist army was close and they were scared.

'I care not a whit what yon bit of paper says,' said the Captain in his thick Wiltshire accent. 'I can spare no musketeers. My orders be to hold the bridge, and I have few enough men as it is. Damn Cavaliers be everywhere, beating up any of our troopers they see. T'other side of the river is trouble, and I will not send my boys in. There bain't no cavalry here. Strachan's 'goons are s'posed to be coming, but we ain't seen 'em yet.'

'So, you deny us, do you? The Earl will hear of this.'

'Earl of Essex has no 'thority in the west. If ye want some men, do not axe I. Ye can go to Bath and axe General Waller hi'self if ee's got any spare. Otherwise ye head over alone.'

''Tis only a couple of miles.' General Waller was the poet's cousin, I doubted he would be disposed to help us.

And it would not take ye long,' he said. 'Tell ye what, I

280

shall move the cart away for ye to cross over, nice and easy.'

I wondered whether to point out, that with the lack of rain, the Royalists could wade across the river with little difficulty. A barricade over the bridge was not going to help. I started to feel sorry for him; he had a company of musketeers and the whole Cornish army coming for them.

'I know you, your name is Long, is it not? Your family live in Whaddon?'

'Aye, and I know tha an all. Fair hair, blue eyes, and pompous; got to be a Candy, I fancy. The youngest of the brood, are ye not? The one with the stupid name.'

That brought me down to earth.

A prophet is not without honour, save in his own country, and in his own house. [*]

'There's naught to be gained by arguing here; they are not going to help, and it grows dark,' said Everard. 'If we make haste, we can be there and back quick enough. A squad of infantry will only slow us down.'

'Very well,' I turned, but Long grabbed my arm.

'Tell ye what, Candy. If Strachan's dragoons come down 'ere, I shall tell 'ee where ye be off to.' He shrugged, 'that be the best I can do. Some boys at the crossing in Bradford, ye might have luck with them.'

'Thanks, Long, and good fortune.' There was no point in blaming the fellow.

'Right 'en me laddos,' he said to some troopers. 'Put'ee o'er there,' pointing to the cart.

They moved the cart out of the way and waved us off as we crossed over the bridge. It was late, and the light was fading. It was the first of July, and almost a year since I had ridden that way.

We rode down the marsh road from Staverton to Hilperton, turning off into fields before we got to the village. My eye took in every little change; they were not for the

[*]   Matthew Chapter 13, Verse 57.

better. More fields lying fallow than was natural, and it was empty of people. Normally at this time of year, people would still be abroad, drinkers in taverns at the very least, but all were absent.

I've heard people say that their homes looked smaller when they returned after time away. I did not see that. Despite the changes the war had wrought upon the place, I was the one transformed. It was dark by the time we paused in a small copse of beech trees at the turning to the Hall.

'So what is the plan?' asked Franny.

'Jacob and I go in on horseback, you and Everard cover us on foot.'

'You need allow us time to get into position,' said Everard. 'Take my horse for your sister. If it goes easily we can pick up another. Tie Franny's over there.'

'How long do you need?' I asked.

'Count to three hundred then ride up. Unless you hear a gunshot, then come in at a gallop.'

Jacob and I waited, while Everard and Franny took their carbine and pistols, and scuttled off towards the Hall. I tied up Franny's steed, then silently counted down from three hundred, and added another fifty to make sure. Then we rode back to the lane, and turned into the drive. There was a light in an upstairs window, my father's bedchamber, and a couple of lamps glowing downstairs. Apple pricked up his ears, recognising his old home, and gave a whinny as we trotted into the courtyard. Jacob, leading Everard's horse behind, had a pistol in his other hand.

I dismounted from my horse; the house was silent. I looked at Jacob and he shrugged back, so I turned and walked to the front doors. Once, I would have thrown them open and walked in, shouting for servants, but I paused; it was my home no more. I banged on the door with my fist.

There was a flash from a muzzle at an upstairs window and I heard Jacob curse. There were more flashes from muskets, and the door opened before me. I went for my sword, but was not quick enough, there was a pistol pointed at my face.

'Welcome home, brother.' The gargantuan monster of my childhood.

Henry was waiting.

25. Elizabeth, Hilperton, July 1643.

Beat down our grottos, and hew down our bowers,
Dig up our arbours, and root up our flowers;
Our gardens are bulwarks and bastions become;
Then hang up our lute, we must sing to the drum.

(Sir William D'Avenant, *Ladies in Arms.*)

'Has war deprived you of your wits?' Elizabeth scowled at me.

'I was actually coming to rescue you,' I said mildly.

'A rescue, sir? What manner of rescue is this? Did you not think to spy out the land, before riding up like a contented squire at the county fair? And into so clear a trap as this, Blandford.' She shook her head at me in disgust.

'Will you two be silent!' shouted Henry, sounding every bit like our father throwing a tantrum. His men were all over the estate; he must have had twenty or so in the grounds.

My arms had been taken, and I now sat under guard with my sister and Jacob. The three of us, at the table in the Hall's oak panelled parlour, whilst Henry paced around. I tried to catch Jacob's eye, but he kept his face down, so I turned to Henry.

I studied my brother, studied the changes that war had wrought. He looked bigger; if that was possible. More muscular, and a narrow waist, not the lump of brawn he had been a year before. Still hairy though, a full beard sprouted untamed from his face, whilst his thick blonde curls sat bush-like around his head and shoulders.

'What fixes your gaze so?' he asked.

'I wonder, Henry, how much more hair it takes before we cease to call you a man, and begin to call you a monkey.' That earned me a slap across the face; the split lip was worth it.

'Captain?' one of his troopers came into the room. I recognised him, one of the workers from the estate. I could not remember the name.

'What is it, Corporal?' The soldier looked at me and then gestured outside to Henry. My brother followed the man out of the room, closing the door behind him.

'Where is Father?' I asked Elizabeth, as soon as the door clicked.

'Upstairs abed; he barely moves since the palsy returned. He has asked after you, Blandford,' she said, with some sincerity. I turned away.

'Your pardon, Jacob.'

'It is of no matter. I am sure we will find a way out of our predicament,' he spoke with confidence, but I noted his subdued look.

The door opened again and Henry came back in. He looked furious; his fists clenched.

'How many men have you got out there?'

'None.'

'Tell me no lies! How many?'

I said nothing.

'You may be wanted alive in Oxford, Brother, but make no mistake, I will happily slit your throat if you answer me false.' He saw the look of surprise on my face. 'Well, what did you expect from cuddling up to Parliament's Scoutmaster? The Golden Scout,' he sneered. 'Your vanity knows no bounds. We have had an informer in your house for months.' Then turned to Elizabeth, 'and you, betraying your king, and bringing even more shame to the family. I could happily string the pair of you up.'

'He has two men in the grounds armed with carbine and pistol,' said Jacob. 'I am your informer, and the Countess wants him unharmed, not hung.' He shrugged. 'Do what you will with your sister.'

Everybody turned to look at Jacob in stunned silence for a few seconds, then Elizabeth turned to me.

'Brother, thou art a fool,' she said.

'You may be right,' I said, glaring at Jacob.

'Be silent!' Henry picked up the pistol, pointing it at me. 'You have proof of this?' he said to Jacob.

'In my bags,' said the Judas.

'You whoreson,' I said.

He looked at me coldly; in an instant changed from the faithful servant I had thought him.

'You traitor,' he said.

Henry called for the corporal who came running back into the room.

'Take this man to his horse and let him get what he needs from his bags,' he said, pointing at Jacob. 'If he tries to run, kill him.'

Perhaps there is a plan to this, I thought; some design or ruse that Jacob had conceived. Well, I hope he knows what he is doing then, I decided. He got up and left with the corporal. He was not gone long. He returned carrying a small pouch and took out some parchment and handed it to Henry. My brother read it in silence, then looked up at Jacob.

'This is Her Majesty's seal and hand?'

'It is indeed,' said Jacob, 'and here a note from the Countess of Carlisle.'

There was no ruse, no design. Bugger!

'Explain,' said Henry.

The door opened again before Jacob could answer, and the red-nosed, white-haired rector, Mr Carpenter came in. The rector was a man I had despised since boyhood, with his endless hypocrisies. He looked to Henry.

'The gunfire has wakened him; he wants to know what is happening.' I noticed a fresh scar running down the left side of his face.

'What a happy reunion this is,' I said to Elizabeth. 'What happened to his face?'

'I cut it when he tried to rape me,' Elizabeth said glaring at Carpenter.

My dear indomitable sister, I think I had actually missed her.

'Witch, you cast some spell upon me, to seduce me from the path of the righteous,' said Carpenter.

'Elizabeth and seduction are two words that do not really

go together, Rector,' I said. Even Henry saw the funny side of that, the corner of his mouth twitched.

'You can mock, boy, but you will soon be wishing you were dead when they get you to Oxford for questioning, and then I will see the witch hang,' said the rector.

'Touché.'

'Mr Carpenter can explain,' said Jacob. 'If you show him the Countess's note.'

My brother passed Carpenter the note then sat in one of my father's comfortable chairs.

'Explain then, Carpenter,' he said. He seemed calm, although I am sure the situation was taxing his tiny brain.

'Her Majesty wishes for the Golden Scout to be in Oxford when she arrives with the King. His presence there as captive would embarrass a certain gentlewoman who has displeased Her Majesty,' said Carpenter.

Henry looked at me then at Jacob.

'The Countess of Carlisle placed me in his service months ago,' said Jacob. 'I was watching him and his friend at first, then when I helped him from an attack, he offered me a position.'

'Thrice times fool,' muttered Elizabeth.

'Why was I not taken in Oxford? I asked.

Henry nodded, leaning forward.

'Her Majesty had only recently landed in the north. The Countess had not informed her of the King's, ahem, indiscretions, shall we say,' said Jacob. 'I had been ordered in the meantime to keep you alive. Had I been in Oxford you might not have been poisoned or shot.'

Women! Sly, sneaky, devious, manipulative women. Now, I am no misogynist and have enough honour never to have raised a hand, but really, was my young life to be decided on the whim of female jealousies? What was it Congreve said? *Heaven has no rage like love to hatred turned, nor hell a fury like a* *woman scorned.*[*] It also explained how the Royalists had found Franny's maid in Reading, for Jacob had been privy to that information.

'Who is this gentlewoman who has so displeased the Queen?' asked Henry.

I knew well enough who it was before the answer came.

'Mistress Jane Whorwood of Holton,' said Jacob.[86]

Henry burst out laughing. 'Oh, that is rich, with one stroke I can rid myself of this nuisance and embarrass James to boot.'

'The Countess thought you might see it like that,' said Jacob. 'She should be here soon with men.'

'Does Father know?' asked Henry.

'No,' said Carpenter. 'He has no knowledge of it. I felt it best to keep your sister's treason and the design from him. The shock could kill him in his weakened state.'

He always said I would be the death of him, I thought.

'Good,' said Henry. 'Now the two of you can leave. Blandford and I have family matters to discuss. You can have what is left when I am finished.'

Jacob got up to leave, but Carpenter started to say something. Henry cut him off.

'Get out, Carpenter; go see to Father. This is between Blandford and me.' Henry turned back to me as the rector and Jacob left the room. Damnation, he looked angry, crazed even. 'Did you do it?' The words came out in a whisper.

'Did I do what exactly?' Although I had a fair notion of his meaning.

'Did you fuck my wife?' He screamed at me picking up the pistol again.

'Why on earth would you think that?'

'James told me you had.'

'And you believed him? More fool you to fall for his lies.'

'You are the runt of the litter; you are the one who lies.' He

---

[*]   William Congreve, *'The Morning Bride.'* Act III Scene III.

pointed the gun at me again.

Then it dawned on me. Something I had never even considered, he actually loved his wife. He was smitten with the little strumpet.

'The child was born early,' he said.

'Lots of children are born early.'

'Is that what this is all about?' asked Elizabeth. 'You assault your family on the word of gossip?'

'Why would James lie?'

'Why would he lie?' I rolled my eyes. 'Surely you are turned simpleton, Henry? James covets this house, the estate, all of it. Your son,' I said the word deliberately, 'takes all that away from him. I have never had any illusions over my inheritance.'

'Anne says it is true!'

'Anne? Christ's tits, Henry. Anne has less wit than a sheep. She would say whatever James told her to.'

'You are an imbecile, Henry Candy; this has nothing to do with the war,' Elizabeth said. 'A typical man: always worried about love's lesser organ. Is it big enough? Is it hard enough? Am I any good? Is your marriage bed so barren that you blame others for your failings?' she laughed at him and I eased back in my chair, in awe at my sister in full flow.

'Men!' She snarled the word, 'I despair at them. You all think you are so clever, so quick witted, and we are supposed to laugh, and smile demurely, and let you ruin everything around. Have you any notion what it is to be ruled by such addlepates, such empty fellows?'

'Women are the weaker vessel, Elizabeth. They cannot be expected to understand weighty matters,' said Henry dismissively. Even I was not stupid enough to say that to my sister when she was in a slapping mood.

'Not understand? Not understand! Oh, I understand well enough. What do you know of our father's business, or the running of the house and estate, either of you? I am the one who sees to the books and runs the home. Some families are lucky they can send the fool of the brood into the church. Such a shame we cannot do that with you two. Our poor father left with three idiot sons, the schemer, the scoundrel, and the swine.' I assumed I was the scoundrel.

'We cannot be ruled by the monstrous regiment, Elizabeth. Women should know their place.'

'Oh, save us from the monstrous regiment,' she mocked. 'Well, you are all doing a wonderful job ruling at the moment are you not? Civil War? Plague and murder? Give me the monstrous regiment instead!'

'I am in command here, and I will not be berated by a woman and a traitor to boot!'

My sister stood up clenching her fists. Henry flinched back; she had slapped him as much as me over the years. I waited for the volcano to erupt.

The explosion came, but not from Elizabeth. The House was shaken as a roar ripped through it. Elizabeth screamed, thrown to the floor; pictures fell from the walls and clouds of dust billowed around us. Then silence, until outside the shouts of men and calls of 'Fire! Fire!' could be heard. This was my chance; I jumped from my seat.

'Do not even think it, Brother.' A pistol pointed at me. He was quicker as well, not just leaner. I preferred him slow and fat. 'You have not yet answered my question.'

'Which question was that? Faith, you have asked so many, I have quite lost count,' I backed away from him until I met the wall. I could smell smoke.

'I know you for a poxy whoreson who would not think twice to put horns on me.'

'I told you the truth, Henry. Our brother James has invented all for his own ends. If you disown your son and kill me, then Sir James has only you in the way of inheritance.' I stressed the word 'sir'.

Whilst my brothers had always presented a united front

when it came to me, I knew there was no love lost between them. James's elevation to knighthood must have rankled; Henry sneered at my mention of it. Elizabeth got back to her feet but he ignored her.

'Sir James, pah! He thinks he is so damn clever. Well, 'tis my house and my damn estate.'

'So what are you going to do with me, Brother?' I noticed how hot the wall at my back had grown to the touch. He turned away from me; above the shouts outside, we could hear the pop of carbines and the arrival of horses. Henry walked to the door, reached out for the handle, but then flinched back.

'Damn, 'tis hot.' He grasped again and yanked the door open.

What happened next was beyond understanding, although I have seen the phenomena since. As he opened the door flames erupted all over us, licking around the doorframe. Henry was thrown backwards by the explosion, and tendrils of fire thrust in at us, scorching me. A thick black smoke billowed into the room, choking off the air. I dropped to my knees to try to breathe, and so did my sister.

'Now is the chance,' I said to Elizabeth. 'Get the windows open.' The house was on fire; flames in the Hall. I could see the staircase burning through the blackened doorway. Elizabeth rushed to pull back the shutters and I checked Henry. The bastard was still alive but singed. I went over to help Elizabeth with the sash window. She gave me a withering look.

'Fetch your brother.'

We opened the windows, as another explosion erupted, flames leaping up around us catching on Elizabeth's dress. I picked her up and threw her out of the window, out of the fire. I turned to my brother still lying unconscious on the floor. I confess I thought about leaving him there to roast like a hog. Instead, I shouldered him and pushed his dead weight out of the window, then clambered out behind him to safety.

I pulled Henry away from the burning house. Around me, a battle of carbines between his troopers, and the arriving horsemen had broken out. Once we were clear of the fire, I looked back at the Hall.

Elizabeth screamed, and pointed. At the large upstairs window, there stood a human torch, hammering at the glass. The rector, engulfed in flames, lit up against the frame. He howled in agony, until the glass shattered in its lead, and he tumbled burning to the ground. I gasped, my father was in that room. I ran back to the Hall to save him.

At the front of the house, staggering out of the great doorway, came a figure smouldering from the explosions. Jacob, blood streaming from a head wound, but a short-sword in his hand.

I grabbed a long piece of wood blown from the house as he saw me. I swung at him, and he just managed to step aside, then weakly raised his sword but I battered it away. He fell to his knees, and I struck him on the side of the head, crushing his skull. Leaving him dead or unconscious, I ran up the steps to the doorway, but the flames beat me back. There was no way to save Father.

I turned away from the heat, leaving Jacob lying prone on the floor, only to be faced with two Roundheads on horseback pointing their carbines at me. Falling to my knees, I cried out my name, and tears streamed down my face.

Jacob was dead; I killed him. My brother escaped, running off into the darkness when he gained consciousness. Strachan's dragoons weren't going to waste time looking for him. Henry knew his way around the estate well enough. Most of his men were killed, a few ran, we took no prisoners. There was no saving the hall; the fire was out of control as we rode away. The glow lighting up the night sky, as my father's grand residence burned to the ground.

'Where be Franny?' I asked Everard who had turned up with the dragoons.

'Couple of Strachan's troopers took him back to the bridge.'

'Is he hurt?'

'Shot in the bum.' He grinned. 'Now he has two arseholes.' That made me smile.

'Your pardon, Sugar.'

'For what?'

'For the house,' he gestured behind. 'I told Franny to start a little fire in the kitchens as a distraction. I did not think it would go up.'

'They must have had powder stored,' I said. 'Think no more on it, William.'

'Did you find out who used the letter cache?'

'Carpenter, but it goes deeper than that.' I briefly explained to him about Jacob and Lucy Hay as we rode back to Staverton Bridge, away from the fire and the Cavaliers that would soon be swarming to it.

At the bridge, Long and his men were already starting to move out. The barricades abandoned as their column snaked westwards. A few torches left burning cast a gloomy yellow light as they departed. Franny was waiting for us, a jug of cider in his hand, breeches bloody from his wounded arse.

'What is happening?' I asked Strachan. 'I thought you were going to hold here.'

'The Cavaliers have moved on Bradford. We have to fall back there to stop them taking the crossing over the Avon.'

'I do not know how to thank you.'

'Ach, laddie, what was I going to do when Long told me my old comrade would be in trouble? Like Caleb, you are rescued from the land of Canaan, and the fury of the Amalekites.'[87]

He really did speak like that. It was worse than listening to Milton, but he knew enough of my uncle to know our work.

'Well, what are you to do now?' Strachan continued. 'Will you be coming back to Bradford with us?'

That gave me pause for thought. 'No, we'll ride up north to Chippenham, and take the London Road to the east.'

'Well then, we shall be off. Good journey, Mr Candy.' He tipped his hat to me and rode off with his troop, westwards to battle. I walked back over to where Everard and the others had our horses. We had begged a spare pony from Strachan for Elizabeth, one taken from Henry's troopers.

I took Elizabeth's hand; we had not spoken of our Father. We were orphans without a home; the flotsam and jetsam of war.

'What now?' asked Everard.

I paused, glanced at Elizabeth, 'London,' I said. Elizabeth nodded.

'Well, how am I going to get there?' Franny broke in. 'I have a bullet-hole in my bum.'

'Perhaps a cushion, Mr Cole?' suggested my sister.

Everard started to chuckle. Elizabeth looked over and at first, I thought that she would start to scold him, but instead she began to laugh. I joined in and the three of us guffawed at his discomfort. Franny looked at us in outrage.

'It is not funny. 'Tis damn painful, let me tell you.'

Which just made us laugh all the more, and a sorrowful sight we must have been: soot-stained and bloody, wiping tears of laughter from our faces. Finally, we composed ourselves.

'Well, gentleman, we have been granted the gift of providence. 'Tis only proper that we should give thanks for our deliverance.' Elizabeth looked at me. 'Then you can wash your face before we set off.'

I groaned, but we knelt and prayed with her like dutiful little choirboys.

'Mr Everard,' she turned to him afterwards. 'If you can

find some padding, we can try to protect Mr Cole's buttocks.'
She waited for a second, but when we were slow to move, she
clapped her hands like a little princess.

'Jump to it, gentleman, please.'

We jumped.

She carried on like that all the way back to London. Over
a hundred miles of nag, nag, nag.

Cross Deep, Twickenham 1719.

All, all of a piece throughout; Thy chase had a beast in view;
Thy wars brought nothing about; Thy lovers were all untrue.
'Tis well an old age is out, And time to begin anew.

(John Dryden, *A Secular Masque*.)

The magistrates say that I am a disgrace. Mr Pope is famous.
Mr Pope is rich. Mr Pope has important friends. Mr Pope! Mr
Pope! Mr Pope! I paid the Cleland boy half a crown, to shove
a lump of ginger up his horse's arse[88]. I did not expect the
damn thing to bolt down Cross Deep, overturning carts, and
stalls, and leaving destruction in its wake. I should have paid
the boy more to buy his silence. So, I have been bound over as
a public nuisance. Confined to my home, like a criminal, with
no friends to speak out for me.

Everyone I ever knew is dead. All my friends, all my
enemies, I have outlived them all. It is a hateful existence.
There was a time, when the only invitations I received were
to funerals, but even they have dried up. I used to attend the
graves of the people I despised in glee, triumphant in my long
life, but who is left to dance on mine? There will be none who
knew me at my wake. Everyone will be sombre and whisper
kind words, but they will only think of an old man, they will
not remember me.

Remembering my history is a morbid pastime; a grim
fascination with the already departed.

Do you remember your grandparents? Did they tell you
their childhood dreams? What about a generation higher,
your great grandparents? Four men and four women, eight
lifetimes joined in you. Do you know what made them laugh
and love? Do you even know all their names? No, I thought
not.

Three generations, a hundred years, and we are forgotten

296

by our own blood. Infamy or rank may keep the memory alive a little longer, but still the candle will splutter and fail. In a few hundred years, even the great and good, are reduced to a dry entry in some dusty tome. We become scribbles in church registers of deaths, and births, and marriage, but there is no sense of life there.

It may be that I am lucky having my legacy immortalised by a poet, even one as poor as Butler. I will be remembered as a fool and a puritan with only his verses to stand as my testimony. Does it even matter?

My great nephew is getting married; perhaps I will last long enough to see it. He be a jelly-brained dunderhead, only sniffing around when he wants some gold. He is in for a shock; I have not even a pot to piss in. My pension will end when I die and the house is leased. The next generation can make their way in the world without my help.

Tomorrow, and tomorrow, and tomorrow.

I wish Alexander Pope was dead. The swine wants to build a tunnel under the road to his pansy* garden, a grotto he calls it. That will mean months of excavations with dust, and rubble, and more damn noise. I came here to die in peace, sunk in my dotage, but the bastard has awoken me.

It is good to be alive.

---

* Memory Garden rather than the modern connotation.

Appendix: Religious factions in the Civil War.

The different religious factions during the English Civil War are often confusing. The Elizabethan religious settlement had encompassed a middle way, between the austerity of Puritanism and the pomp of Catholicism. The Anglican Church had been a compromise between the two competing extremes, and had changed little under James I. Whilst there had always been recusants, (people who refused the Anglican Church) in the catholic section of the population, in the Seventeenth century there were increasingly recusants from the Protestant congregation. When Archbishop Laud implemented his reforms, he further alienated many who saw them as a return to the idolatry of Rome. This led to a fracturing of the Elizabethan settlement, and a number of competing groups vying for control of the English Church.

Anglicans were a group that followed the King's prayer book, and supported the reforms of the archbishop. Whilst they would not consider themselves catholic, they accepted ritualistic elements of faith which appalled puritans, such as icons, statues, incense, and altars. They made up the majority of the population who, despite antipathy towards Catholicism, regarded the Elizabethan settlement as a successful compromise. Blandford's family, other than his sister Elizabeth, were typical Anglicans and unsurprisingly Royalist in outlook.

Puritans is a catch all term for those who felt the Elizabethan settlement had not gone far enough, or who had been alienated by Laud's reforms. They wished to reform the church and clear away any remnants of Catholicism. The Stuart Kings failure to address their concerns, led some to leave England for the New World. Oliver Cromwell himself, planned to sail for the Americas in the 1630's. Those that remained, became a vocal opposition to Charles I rule. However, there was a wide range of competing ideas amongst the puritans. A variety of Calvinists, Lutherans, Anabaptists, and later groups such as the Quakers, added their dissenting voices, as religious control broke down during the Civil War. Politically, they tended to fall into two camps: Presbyterians and Independents.

Presbyterians believed that there should be no established bishops, and opposed the feudal Episcopalian system. Favouring instead a national church on the Scottish model, with no bishops, and elected representatives. James I and Charles I passionately opposed the abolition of bishops, regarding them as vital in the administration of the country. James I declared memorably: *No bishops, no Kings.* The Presbyterian faction in Parliament, was powerful in its opposition to Charles, but also later came into conflict with Cromwell and the army. The military was filled with much more radical and independent dissenters.

The Independents believed in local congregational control of church affairs, with no wider hierarchy, no bishops, or national structure. They were heavily represented in the army, especially after the reforms that led to the creation of the New Model Army. Cromwell and the other army grandees were ostensibly independents, and this led to the break with Parliament at the end of the first civil war. Despite their stern reputation, Cromwell and the Independents were surprisingly tolerant in religious matters (except if you were an Anglican or an Irish Catholic). The readmission of the Jews in 1656 is theologically consistent with the Independent view, if not necessarily an example of a caring tolerant Cromwell, that some would claim.

Catholicism was very much in a minority in Stuart England, although there were influential nobles who wanted a return to loyalty to Rome, and a re-established Roman Church. Certainly, after the Gunpowder Plot in 1605, the

Catholics were seen as the enemy within. Always relentlessly persecuted by both sides, they tended to support Charles I during the war, hoping for concessions from the King, and his domineering Catholic wife Henrietta Maria.

Blandford himself would certainly have been brought up as an Anglican, and would have attended church services at least once a week as a boy. Once in the army he was exposed to more radical preachers and independent dissenters, and he attended sermons by famous firebrand preachers of the time. Whilst not considering himself an atheist, he was certainly more influenced by Enlightenment ideas than religious devotion. The breakdown of authority and central control during the Civil War saw social bonds collapse. This included religious bonds, freeing many people from theocratic control for the first time.

Authors Note.

The novel is based on information taken from extensive sources. Some of these included: Samuel Luke's Journal, the Memoirs of Bulstrode Whitelocke, Denzil Holles, Prince Rupert and Edward Hyde, collections of letters by Brilliana Harley, and Nehimiah Wharton, copies of original newsbooks, such as the Mercurius Aulicus and Parliament Scout, and contemporary poems, ballads and plays.

Secondary sources included work by Christopher Hill, CV Wedgewood, Dr John Adair, Tristram Hunt, Dianne Purkiss, Antonia Fraser, Brigadier Peter Young, and Richard Holmes. I have also taken account of up to date research in Battlefield Archaeology and work on the Battle of Edgehill website, The John Hampden Society website, English Heritage website, and the British Civil Wars website.

All dates are given according to the Julian calendar. During the Civil War, the Julian date was 10 days behind the Gregorian calendar. Years are numbered from 1st January which was the method used by Blandford in 1719, although many 17th century writers numbered the year from 25th March.

I must give my wholehearted thanks to those that have helped me in my research and completing the novel: Nicola McLaughlin, James Smallwood, John Bayliss, Nigel Williams, Nicola Williams, Elaine Guilding, Serena Jones, Emma Holt, Robert Peett, B. Lloyd, and everyone at Holland House Books. All the mistakes are mine!

Notes

1   John Hurry (died 1650) was a professional soldier who had seen service in Germany during the Thirty Years War. He returned to Scotland in 1639 to fight in the Covenanter army against Charles I. In 1641 Hurry was involved in a Royalist plot to kidnap three Covenanter nobles, known as the 'Incident'. However, he betrayed his fellow conspirators and exposed the plot, forcing Charles I to accept Covenanter demands, and abolish bishops in the Church of Scotland. This in turn emboldened the Presbyterian faction in the English Parliament. With the likelihood of war in England, Hurry took a captaincy in Parliament's army in June 1642.

2   Sir Samuel Luke of Cople (1603 - 1670) was famously short, and described in the Royalist press as a *deformed hunchback* or *grotesque*. Blandford makes no mention of any deformity, and his description tallies with non-Royalist sources, and two surviving pictures in the National Portrait Gallery. Luke and his father were prominent members of the Presbyterian faction in Parliament. He has long been identified as the character of *Sir Marmaluke* in Samuel Butler's poem *Hudibras*. The poem was similar in structure to Don Quixote, on which it was based, but was far more personal and vindictive in its attack on Puritanism, and Luke in particular. It was fabulously popular in its time, and Butler's metre was praised by Blandford's later neighbour Alexander Pope. Blandford has already identified himself as *Sir Marmaluke's* dim-witted squire *Ralpho*, although, Butler's portrayal of him as a dogmatic puritan seems somewhat wide of the mark.

3   The skirmish at Marshalls Elm was fought on the 4th of August, and was one of the first engagements of the Civil War. Roundhead forces were put to flight easily, with few casualties on either side. Henry Candy does not, however, mention the tense standoff that occurred in Wells a couple of days later, which led to a Cavalier withdrawal to Sherborne. The military situation was

not as favourable to the cavaliers as the tone of the letter would suggest. Wiltshire was strongly in favour of Parliament in the early months of the war. The Wynne-Candy Archive, contains a number of letters and pamphlets from the period that were available to Blandford in 1719, and included in his memoir.

4   The theatres were closed by Parliament at the start of September 1642. It was deemed too frivolous *to indulge in any kind of diversions or amusements in such troublous times.* It is unlikely that Blandford saw the last performance, as he states. Whilst he is frustratingly vague about the date, it could only have been the first week of August 1642. It seems (from the lines quoted) Blandford saw a rehearsal for James Shirley's play *The Court Secret,* rather than an official performance. The King's Men (made famous by Shakespeare) were certainly rehearsing *The Court Secret* when the closures happened, and the play would not be properly performed on the London stage until 1664. Pepys wife commented that it was, *'the worst that ever she saw in her life.'* Isaac Penington(1584 - 1661) was the mayor who ordered the closures. A rabid puritan, he was Colonel of the Whitecoats (London Trained Bands) and Lieutenant of the Tower of London. A supporter of the republic, he was arrested for High Treason at the Restoration, and died in the Tower in 1661.

5   Parliamentary infantry had been issued with uniform coats before Edgehill, but the Royalists, without the resources of London, were less matched. Blandford's observation that the infantry regiment wore red coats, means that it was probably Denzil Holles Regiment of Foot, as Blandford later mentions Holles' chaplain Obadiah Sedgewick.

6   It is possible that Lieutenant Russell was Thomas Russell of Cheapside although neither Blandford or Samuel Luke give his first name. In 1638, he held a lease on a tenement in Mary-Le-Bow churchyard and an adjoining shop. Russell's children are not recorded in the baptismal register, although this is not unusual for some of the godly.

7   Robert Devereux, 3rd Earl of Essex (1591-1646) was
Parliament's senior commander in the early stages of the Civil
War. He had married Frances Howard at the age of 13 but the
marriage was never consummated. Howard sued for divorce on
the grounds of impotence after she began an affair with Viscount
Rochester. The divorce made Essex a laughing stock at court.
After the divorce, Howard (now Lady Somerset) was tried along
with her new husband for the murder of Sir Thomas Overbury.
Essex, sitting as juror, pressed the King to send his ex-wife to the
scaffold, but the sentence was suspended. In 1630, Essex married
for a second time, but the paternity of his short-lived child was in
doubt. The couple divorced quietly in 1631. Essex's military career
before the Civil War was undistinguished. He served in the Low
Countries and Germany and later commanded a regiment of
Foot in the disastrous Cadiz expedition(1625). In 1642, he was, as
Peter Russell states, Parliament's most senior noble and the logical
choice to command the main army. Despite Blandford's personal
antipathy and poor opinion, Essex was very popular with the rank
and file who nicknamed him *Old Robin.*

8   The White Hart that Blandford mentions is probably in
Whitton in Middlesex. Only a cottage and outbuildings in 1635,
it quickly developed into a large building with rooms to let, and
stabling for twelve horses. With much of the army stationed on
Hounslow Heath it was close to Blandford's billet. It is still open
today and is a popular haunt with rugby fans during the Six
Nations, given the proximity of Twickenham Stadium. Only some
of the seventeenth century building remains, however.

9   Obadiah Sedgewick (1600 - 1658) was from Marlborough,
and his Wiltshire accent is correctly noted by Blandford. In
1642, he became Chaplain to Denzil Holles regiment of Foot,
and accompanied them on the Edgehill Campaign. Sedgewick
published his sermons, and various other polemics, between
1639-58. He was a strict Presbyterian and powerful orator, whose
views on idleness and delinquency were well known. Blandford's
description of his sermon against profanity certainly matches
other sources, although the last words are from the *Book of James.*

Sedgewick became a member of the Westminster Assembly of Divines in 1643, and supported the League with Scotland. He was opposed to the idea of independent congregational control of the church, and the religious toleration proposed by Cromwell and the Independents. Despite this, he seems not to have fallen out with Cromwell during the protectorate, and retired from his clerical positions in 1656 due to ill health. He died in Marlborough in 1658.

10   John Hampden (1595 -1643) was without doubt the hero of the Parliamentary faction. His stance against Ship Money had brought him national fame in the 1630s, and Blandford's physical description is accurate. Contemporaries of both sides praised him for his honesty and good character, and his death in 1643 robbed Parliament of a potential leader.

11   Blandford's description of the ill discipline of the Roundhead Army match with other historical sources. The shooting of a maid in Northampton was recorded, but the only new detail Blandford provides us with is the culprit. The officer that caused so much trouble by looting his own infantry was Nathaniel Feinnes, an ancestor of modern explorer Ranulph Feinnes, and actors Ralph and Joseph Feinnes..

12   The letter is a transcription of Nehimiah Wharton's, but it differs somewhat from the original held in the National Archive. Considerable detail is missing from Blandford's version, although the main facts remain unchanged. Letters were very much communal sources of information during the War, and were often censored then printed for propaganda purposes. Nehimiah Wharton's letters provide ample testimony to the behaviour of the army in Northampton and the Edgehill campaign. Wharton was a sergeant in Denzil Holles regiment, who sent detailed descriptions of the Edgehill campaign home to his Master in London. Wharton's letters survive in the National Archive and were transcribed in 1854. Sadly, the letters come to an end just before the Battle of Edgehill, so we do not have his account of the battle, and Wharton is not heard of again. It can only be assumed he was one of the many casualties in Holles regiment.

13   Blake's letters were discovered two days after the Battle of Edgehill, when Prince Rupert raided the Roundhead baggage, and captured the Earl of Essex's carriage and correspondence. Blandford provides us with some interesting detail about Blake, a previously obscure figure. He is the first witness to link Blake to Samuel Luke's intelligence network. He also gives us some idea of exactly how the letters were sent to Essex from the Royalist camp. The importance of intelligence during the civil war has often been overlooked by historians. We can see from Blandford's evidence, that the Roundheads were receiving regular reports on the King's movements, and that the battle was not as unexpected as some contemporaries (most notably Edward Hyde) suggest. This is born out in the recent re-appraisal of field intelligence by historian John Ellis in his study *To Walk In The Dark*.

14   Sir William Balfour (abt 1600 - 1660) was a Scottish soldier who had fought on the Dutch side during the Thirty Years War. Initially a favourite of the King and Duke of Buckingham, he switched allegiance when Archbishop Laud's church reforms were introduced. He was a strict Presbyterian, rabidly anti-catholic, and a gifted cavalry commander. Whilst the Earl of Bedford was in nominal command of Parliament's Horse at Edgehill, Balfour assumed active control. Blandford calls his troops *Lobsters* which was not strictly correct. The Lobsters were Arthur Haslerig's London Regiment (not present at Edgehill), of heavily armoured cuirassiers, with an almost medieval level of protection. Balfour did have similar troops available at Edgehill, which he kept as a mobile reserve behind the infantry centre.

15   The Dutch Caracole, involved the cavalry acting as a mobile firing platform with pistols. The intent was not to engage in hand to hand combat with a sword, but to fire-retire-reload and then advance again.

16   Blandford's description of the deployment on the right flank at Edgehill agrees with the main sources, although he omits some details he must have known, and makes some other mistakes.

Two regiments of dragoons were actually sent out to the right flank under Wardlowe and Browne, and the position of the small brook mentioned has been a matter of scholarly debate. Blandford's account seems to match recent investigations into the battlefield, but he offers nothing conclusive. One new detail he adds, is the re-supply of powder and shot before the battle. Contemporary observers noted that the Roundhead musketeers were able to keep up a steady fire on the enemy ranks, whilst the cavaliers quickly ran out of ammunition, but offered no explanation. The Battle of Edgehill website provides a full interactive explanation of the different deployment theories, and an extensive explanation of recent archaeological research.

17   Blandford is not the only Parliamentary source to claim that the Royalists butchered innocents in Kineton. There was certainly fighting in the town, but afterwards cavalier writers vehemently denied any suggestion of a war crime. His use of the term *Tory* is typically eighteenth century, rather than from the civil war period. The term came initially from Ireland and meant brigand, but was used to denote the Royalist/Stuart party from the 1680s onwards.

18   Blandford could not have known about Damn-your-eyes Ballard and his cudgel from his position on the battlefield, and must have been told the detail afterwards.

19   Blandford seems to have taken one of the ensigns of Nicholas Byron's Brigade, which included the King's Lifeguard of Foot. 11 of 13 colours were lost from the King's Lifeguard. Under the combined pressures of Essex's and Lord Brooke's own Foot regiments to their front, Stapleton's cavalry (including Blandford) at their flank, and Balfour's curraisers to their rear, they collapsed and ran for the Edgehill, losing the Banner Royal in the process.

20   Cromwell's presence on the battlefield is disputed. Denzil Holles, who had every cause to hate Cromwell, claimed he spent the day avoiding the battle and climbing church steeples. There may be some truth in this, but it would seem Cromwell was looking

for the battle rather than avoiding it. The presence of another Oliver Cromwell on the battlefield also confuses things. Blandford, by no means an admirer of Cromwell, has no need to lie about the detail.

21   William Everard was baptised in St Giles, Reading in 1602, and apprenticed to the Merchant Tailors Guild in 1616. He next appears in the historical record in 1641 taking the Protestation Oath. Samuel Luke's journal testifies to his role as a scout in 1643, but there are gaps in the historical record before 1647.

22   Blunden's report explains the Roundhead view of the attack on Brentford. It was perceived as a treachery, and halted possible talks the next day at Turnham Green, where the two armies again faced off against each other. The King, heavily outnumbered, withdrew without attacking and the campaigning season was over. The explosion of news reporting during the Civil War was helped by the suspension of the licensing laws. The Reporting the Civil War Blog, produced by Tyger's Head Books, has a day-by-day modern transcription of some of the main pamphlets for 1642-43. Whilst Blandford gives us no personal description of Brentford, or the stand-off at Turnham Green, he was certainly present at the latter. Luke's Troop were involved in the aborted flanking movement by John Hampden and Bulstrode Whitelocke.

23   The Lines of Communication around London were pretty basic at the time of Turnham Green. Over the course of 1643, they would become much more extensive. The ring of ditch and rampart that Blandford describes would be strengthened and enlarged, and twenty-three redoubts, bastions, and forts were added. The defences probably played some part in deterring Charles I attack at Turnham Green, but were of no obstacle to the New Model Army in 1647 when it occupied the city. The defences were demolished in the same year. Nothing remains today above ground, although there is some archaeological evidence in Hyde Park, and Rotherhithe, and the gardens of the Imperial War Museum.

24   All Hallows at the Tower was badly damaged in 1650 when a gunpowder store exploded. It seems, from Blandford's evidence, that powder was stored there from the start of the war.

25   Stephen Darnelly was made Parliamentary Clerk of Deliveries of the Ordnance in March 1643, but little else is known about him. He was the beneficiary of a will by his cousin Richard Croshawe in London in 1631 of £20, and remittance of his debts. If Blandford is to be believed, his role was far more than official in the Board of Ordnance. Blandford gives us the only known description of Darnelly, who must have been in his forties by the start of the Civil War.

26   Samuel Luke was appointed Scoutmaster General of Parliament in December 1643. He quickly set about forming a Scout unit, and building up an intelligence network. Luke was finally voted funds to pay for twenty-four scouts by Parliament at the start of January 1643. Similar units were set up in the other Parliamentary Associations, and they provided the Roundheads with vital intelligence throughout the war.

27   Henry Carpenter was appointed Rector of St Michaels and All Angels, Hilperton, in 1638. A plaque on the wall of the church building, gives details of the rectors as far back as the thirteenth century. Nothing else is known of him, apart from Blandford's testimony. It seems, that he was replaced as rector by a Giles Thornborough but this was a short-lived appointment. Parliament abolished the post of Rector and appointed one Matthew Toogood as Parish Clerk. In 1662, after the restoration of the monarchy, Arthur Buckridge took up the re-established post of rector.

28   The church of St Mary-Le Bow on Cheapside, is famously one of the churches in the nursery rhyme *Orange and Lemons*. True cockneys must be born within earshot of its bells. The Thursday sermons took place at All-Hallows on Bread Street. All Hallows was destroyed in the Great Fire and rebuilt by Wren, but finally demolished in the nineteenth century, and merged with Mary-Le-

Bow. As the civil war progressed, London became the epicentre of new radicalism, and puritan ministers flocked to deliver sermons in the city. St Pauls Cross, in the churchyard of St Pauls Cathedral, was a regular meeting place for puritan firebrands, and Anglicans determined to rebut their claims. Jan Comenius describes Londoners taking notes at sermons to ponder later. Such open discussion would have been unthinkable before the war, but as theocratic control broke down, there was an explosion of radical thought.

29   A Droll was a short comic sketch, performed illegally in taverns, based on well known plays. They became popular when the theatres had been closed.

30   Christmas Day 1642 fell on a Thursday, according to the Julian Calendar, which was used during the seventeenth century. If Blandford is correct that it was the last Thursday before Christmas, it would put the date at the 18th December. The Julian Calendar was about ten days behind the Gregorian Calendar in the 1640s.

31   The Rose at Poultry was a well known inn, and the wording on the sign was as Blandford describes. It is, however, a surprising place for Roundhead soldiers to patronise. The innkeeper, John King, was famously a Royalist supporter. In 1660, when Charles II returned to London for the Restoration, the landlord's wife was on the point of labour. Charles II, ever mindful of good publicity, and with the common touch his father lacked, pulled up at the inn to salute her.

32   *We Wish You a Merry Christmas* originated in the West Country in the 16th century. It was, and is still, a popular standard at Christmas.

33   Anne Crosse (d 1655) is an example of a woman's (if only widows or spinsters) growing ability to own and manage businesses. The Apothecaries Guild was one that admitted women, although Widow Crosse seems not to have taken the exam. She was prosecuted by the Guild in 1642 for using an unregistered worker.

Crosse married her pockmarked suitor Thomas Cademan, which may also have earned the displeasure of the guild, as he was a founder of the Distillers Guild and a Roman Catholic. Blandford's memory must be at fault, however, as the records show Cademan and Crosse had already married by Christmas 1642. Cademan died in 1651 and Crosse then married the syphilitic poet Sir William D'Avenant, paying for his release from the Tower of London.

34   The first issue off the *Mercurius Aulicus* appeared in early January 1643. The editor John Birkenhead produced what amounts to the first tabloid newspaper, creating popular journalism in the process. The paper was filled with Royalist propaganda and smears against leading Parliamentarians. It is impact was immediate, and similar newsbooks soon flooded London and England. The bookseller George Thomason made a conscious effort to collect as many pamphlets as appeared in London during the war. From his base in St Pauls, he managed to accumulate over seven thousand different news journals. After the war, attempts were made to sell the collection, but they remained in private hands until the Eighteenth century, when the Earl of Bute bought them and presented them to the British Museum.

35   The ghosts of Edgehill were a widely reported phenomenon after the battle. The pamphlet, *A Great Wonder in Heaven*, gave details of the phantoms and was published in January 1643. King Charles sent a Royal Commission to investigate the apparitions, and they too claimed to have witnessed them. As a result, they are the only ghosts officially recognised by the Public Record Office.

36   Bestney Barker was admitted to the Inns of Court in 1602. He was only admitted on the insistence of his father (also a barrister) and an act of Parliament. Barker was called to the Bar in 1609. Like Elizabeth Candy, Barker was a radical in religion, despite his interest in the theatre. He married on Anne Timperly from Colchester, but fell foul of the religious authorities in the 1630s. He was charged with non attendance of church in 1632, and in the same year his nephew dedicated a translation of Peter

Ramus' Logic to him. In 1645, he was sequestered as a malignant by Parliament, marking him out as a radical independent. Barker must have been in his late fifties by the time Blandford met him in 1643.

37   £40 would be the equivalent of over £9000 in today's money. Pounds, shillings, and pence were the basic currency of Britain until 1971, having a value of 12 pence to the shilling, and 20 shillings to the pound. A straight comparison with the cost of living is difficult, since the relative prices of various commodities have changed. Blandford, as a Cornet, earned about £3 a week and drew extra as a scout, giving him an annual income of around £250, which was a sizeable amount in the seventeenth century. John Bunyan gives us a price of *four eggs a penny* in *The Life and Death of Mr. Badman.* An egg today will cost around 25p - four eggs to a pound. Therefore, at the level of basic foodstuffs, the factor of comparison with the modern cost of living is x 240. Items such as clothes and furnishings would be much more than that. For a fashionista like Blandford, keeping up with the current trends would be expensive. Drinking, whoring, and gambling cost money after all.

38   Blandford provides us with a rare description of the lost masterpiece Christ's Crucifixion by Peter Paul Rubens. The painting was destroyed by the iconoclasts in March 1643, and the remains thrown into the Thames. It was a very visible symbol of Catholicism in a puritan city. Parliament was more pragmatic about other treasures in the chapel, selling them off to raise funds. The Rubens painting was valued at £500 in 1643, almost £120,000 today. Were it still surviving it would presumably be worth considerably more.

39   The Aulicus is being particularly disingenuous with this report. Presumably, Blandford includes it because his brother Henry was serving with the Hoptonian cavalry in Cornwall. However, the actions around Topsham were not a clear victory for the Cavaliers. The attempt to capture Exeter failed dismally, and Hopton was forced to withdraw back into Cornwall, pursued by Roundhead forces. A successful stand at Bridestowe halted the

Roundheads, and fighting in the West ended for 1642.

40   Animal baiting was popular entertainment from medieval times right up until 1835, when it was outlawed by Parliament. In the sixteenth and seventeenth centuries, rings were popular in London, and contests brought in large crowds including royalty. Whilst baiting had become less popular by the eighteenth century, cockfights were still well attended by the lower classes. To modern morals, Blandford's enjoyment of animal cruelty seems obscene, but puritan opponents were very much in the minority in the 1640s. The banning of animal baiting in December 1642, following on from the closure of the theatres in September, was morally correct, but upset popular opinion which welcomed the return of such pleasures in 1660.

41   William Beeston (abt 1606 - 1682) had a long association with the Cockpit or Phoenix Theatre. Built by Inigo Jones, it was the first purpose-built enclosed venue in London, and first on Drury Lane, and capable of year round performances. Beeston's father Christopher (a famous child actor with Shakespeare's company) had established the theatre in 1616. It was damaged in 1617 by apprentices upset at the new exclusive venue, and renamed the Phoenix. Christopher Beeston was a successful impresario of the Jacobean theatre. He established the famous Beeston Boys troupe of boy actors, and was much sought after. His son proved less successful when he took over the concern, after Christopher's death in 1638. He was imprisoned in 1640, when his troupe performed a play that offended some of the Queen's favourites, including Sir William D'Avenant. Davenant was subsequently given control of the theatre, but was himself arrested in 1641 for involvement in the Army Plot. Beeston was restored as Governor in 1641 on release from Marshalsea Prison. His alias of Hutchinson is recorded, and he certainly had a reputation for shady business deals.

42   The Pelican, or Devil's Tavern, in Wapping was notorious for its clientele. Pepys mentioned its unsavoury reputation, and some of its patrons included Hanging Judge Jefferies, and Captain Kidd. Now known as the Prospect of Whitby, it lays claim to

313

being the oldest riverside pub in London. Whilst the building has changed little since the seventeenth century, the area around it has undergone a dramatic transformation. A number of images by the artist Rowland Hilder, show the Prospect before the modern construction work, and give us some idea of the river view in the seventeenth century that Blandford describes. The steps up to the street level remain, and are still known as the Pelican Steps.

43   The correspondence from this period was collected by Elizabeth Candy in Hilperton. However, James Candy expressly warns his brother against sending important information through Hilperton. Clearly, Elizabeth somehow obtained the letter, but how, and when, and whether it was delivered or not are uncertain. Henry Candy continued to send letters to his father in Hilperton regardless, but no reply to James Candy regarding this letter has been found in the archive.

44   John Pym (1584-1643) was a long time Presbyterian opponent of Charles I. In 1626, he had been a supporter of moves to impeach the King's favourite George Villiers Duke of Buckingham. He was a leader of resistance to the King in the crisis 1640-42, and led calls for the impeachment of Strafford, and his subsequent execution. However, Pym's role in forcing the Grand Remonstrance (A list of grievances presented to the King) in December 1641, alienated many of the less radical members. In January 1642, Pym, along with John Hampden, Denzil Holles, Arthur Haselrig, and William Strode had been the members that Charles I tried to arrest in Parliament. The King considered Pym his most deadly enemy in Parliament. When war broke out, Pym struggled to keep all the factions in Parliament unified, but was able in September 1643, to make an alliance with the Scottish Presbyterians. A move which changed the course of the war in the north. It was his last act of influence. Pym died of stomach cancer in December 1643.

45   *A Ramble in St James' Park* written by John Wilmot, Earl of Rochester, in the 1670's, can be shocking even today. It is a subversion of the pastoral ideal, playing on the Park's seedy nocturnal reputation. Blandford's self-identification as one of

the, *knights of the elbow and the slur - a Whitehall blade*, is surprising. Rochester satirises Blandford as a cheating gambler and insincere in love. Given it is unflattering depiction of our protagonist (who would have been about fifty when the poem was written), we can only assume the honesty of the character appraisal. Hampden's Mansion remained on the spot for another thirty years. On the death of his wife, it was torn down by Sir George Downing, who built a smart row of townhouses. Downing Street is now the heart of British Government and official home of the Prime Minister. In 2000, the John Hampden Society lobbied Parliament to change the name to Hampden Street, in honour of its illustrious former occupant.

46   Lucy Hay, the Countess of Carlisle (1599 - 1660), was the daughter Henry Percy, 9th Earl of Northumberland (The Wizard Earl). She was in her mid forties when Blandford first met her and was already famous. Hay was a favourite of Queen Henrietta Maria, and renowned for her scheming. Initially the Earl of Strafford's mistress in the crisis of the 1640s, she then seduced John Pym, despite his direct responsibility for Strafford's execution. She was subsequently rumoured to have warned the five members of their impending arrest in January 1642. Her infidelities were legendary. Dorothy Osborne wrote that Lucy's letters should act, *as models for wit and good breeding*, but added, *I am a little scandalised that she uses the word faithful - she never knew how to be so in her life.* Her brother, the Earl of Northumberland, despite initial opposition to the King, moved into the Peace Party after Edgehill.

47   The meal must have taken place in early February 1643, and the guest list is illustrious as Blandford says, although it is worth noting the Buckinghamshire influence of the group. Hampden, Luke, and Whitelocke all represented Buckinghamshire in Parliament. Bulstrode Whitelocke (1605 -1675) was Deputy Lord Lieutenant of Buckinghamshire, as well as an MP, and has left us with a detailed memoir of the period. Whitelocke was a radical neither in politics or religion, and seemed to stand against Charles I on grounds of good governance and Parliamentary privilege. In the 1650s, he urged Cromwell to take the crown to settle the country.

Despite his involvement in the Commonwealth, Whitelocke was not persecuted at the Restoration, and both sides recognised good humour and temperance. Robert Harley (1579 - 1656) was a leading Herefordshire puritan. It was his committee, that in 1643, passed a motion leading to the destruction of the Cheapside Eleanor Cross. He was also active in the field, seizing Hereford briefly for Parliament in 1642. After the War, he pushed for reconciliation with the King, and was excluded from Parliament at Prides Purge. He has left us a wonderful collection of his wife's letters, that give us an insight into both domestic life, but also the wider implications of the Civil War. Brilliana Harley withstood the siege of Brampton Bryan, and endeared herself to the local population with her leadership, whilst Robert was away in London. Their son, Edward (1624 - 1670), was the same age as Blandford, and would rise to the rank of colonel in the army. John Wallis (1616 -1703) was a cryptographer and England's most important mathematician after Newton. His parlour trick, as Whitelocke describes it, was first noted after a similar performance at a meal in December 1642. Wallis became vital to the intelligence effort, decoding Royalist correspondence. At the Restoration, his ability meant he remained on the government's payroll, and his cryptography remained an official secret until his death. Even the teaching of his theory was restricted.

48   Thomas Hobbes (1588 - 1679) is one of the most important philosophers in western history. His theories of the social contract have influenced centuries of philosophical thought, and his work *Leviathan* is regarded as one of the most important texts of the Enlightenment, directly influencing Voltaire amongst others. The book given to Blandford would have been, *De Cive*. Hobbes stayed in Paris for the duration of the first civil war, becoming Charles II tutor between 1647-48. *Leviathan* was published in 1651, leading to his alienation from the Royalist party and his return to England. His work left him open to accusations of atheism and republicanism, which meant he was in danger at the Restoration, but Charles II protected his former teacher. Hobbes died in 1679 from a stroke. His last words are said to be: *A great leap in the dark.* Blandford's choice of poem to start the chapter is interesting. John

Wallis had a long-term argument from the 1650s onwards with Hobbes, over Hobbes erroneous claim to have solved the problem of squaring the circle. The argument led to both men writing tracts against each other, and became quite bitter.

49   Mary Queen of Scots (1542 - 1587). Wallis would, I think, be pleased to hear the code Mary used in the Babington Plot, is now used in school history lessons, where twelve year olds are asked to break the cipher.

50   The Spotted Cow in Oxford was just outside the medieval wall. The innkeeper was a supporter of Parliament, and a tunnel in the cellars into the city dates from the time. It is now known as the Turf Tavern, and is the venue where former US President Bill Clinton famously did not inhale.

51   Edmund Waller (1606 - 1687) was a popular poet in the Caroline period and MP for Amersham. His verse was defined by the heroic couplet, and a move away from the intellectually heavy works of metaphysical poets like Donne and Johnson. Whilst his poems were certainly an influence on Dryden and Pope, his popularity and influence declined in the 18th century. The family seat was a great hall in Beaconsfield, and he was a first cousin to both John Hampden, and William Waller. Edmund initially supported Hampden and Pym in Parliament, but after the Grand Remonstrance gradually moved into the Peace Party. He was renowned as an orator. Clarendon describes him as speaking, *upon all occasions with great sharpness and freedom*. It was a skill that would save his life.

52   The ballad Blandford quotes is: *A warning to London from Antwerp*. Written about the sack of Antwerp in 1576, when Spanish troops had butchered Dutch protestants. Traditionally set to the tune of *Row Well Ye Mariners*.

53   The Great Hall of Christ Church, is now perhaps better known as the refectory of Hogwarts from the Harry Potter movie franchise. In the Civil War, it was the heart of Charles I court,

until Oxford finally fell in 1646. Inigo Jones (1573 - 1652) was the most important English architect of his age. He was responsible for designing the Queen's Chapel in Somerset House, restorations to St Pauls, and most famously, the Banqueting House that would be the site of Charles I execution in 1649. Interestingly, he also had a sideline designing theatre props and designs for royal masques. The Phoenix Theatre itself was probably designed by Jones. He was a prominent Royalist at court in Oxford, and was later present at the fall of Basing House. His career destroyed by the Civil War, Jones lived out his last years in Somerset House.

54   One of Charles I counterproposals to the Peace Commission, was that Parliament should decamp from London and sit in Oxford. Such an idea was laughable to the majority of the commons. As the War progressed, Charles set up an Oxford Parliament in opposition to London with his Royalist supporters, but it's authority was never widespread.

55   John Selden (1584 - 1654) was a moderate MP and renowned polymath. Milton called him, *the chief of learned men*. Selden is certainly one of the founders of modern historiography, moving it away from medieval concepts, at a time when divine justification was being used by both sides in the war. Despite his professed Anglican convictions, Selden sided with the mainly Presbyterian opposition to the King. Like Bulstrode Whitelocke, he was more concerned more with the good governance of England. Selden's extensive library and works were donated to the Bodleian Library on his death, and provide and extensive archive of the period.

56   The heads came from fleeing Cavaliers after the Battle of Turnham Green. Allegedly, Irish mercenaries and a small drummer boy. The ghost of the boy is said to haunt the pub today. Known as the Ship Inn during the Civil War; the name was changed to the Royal Standard of England after the Restoration. It is known by that name today, and is one of the oldest pubs in England still in use.

57   Venice Treacle or Theriac, was a panacea supposedly devised by King Mithradates of Pontus, who mixed known antidotes into a single recipe. By the seventeenth century, it was still regarded as a useful and effective medicine, although its real benefits are doubtful

58   There were contemporary rumours that Lucy Hay had stolen the Queen of France's diamond necklace. An anecdote by La Rochfoucauld (who was well known to both Lucy Hay and the Duke of Buckingham) implies that Lucy was responsible for the theft. Alexander Dumas based the plot of *The Three Musketeers* on La Rochfoucauld's revelations, and the character of *Milady De Winter* on the Countess of Carlisle.

59   Samuel Butler (abt 1613 - 1680) was born in Worcestershire and educated at the King's School Worcester. The son of a farmer, he was clerk to the Countess of Kent until 1643, when he was abruptly dismissed. He met John Selden whilst working for the Countess, and was certainly influenced by the older man. In 1643, he became Samuel Luke's clerk, and stayed at the family home in Cople when not on campaign. His attempt at painting is attested to, his editor claiming that: *his pictures served to stop windows and save the tax.* After the Restoration, Butler worked as a clerk to both the Earl of Carbery, and later the Duke of Buckingham. His satirical polemic *Hudibras* was fantastically popular, but Butler does not seem to have benefitted much financially. Today, he is chiefly remembered for the phrase, *spare the rod and spoil the child,* which rather than being an entreaty to beat children, is actually a snipe at the interruptus method of contraception. He was buried with full honours in Covent Garden in 1680, and a monument was erected to him there in 1732. Whilst his poetry lost popularity in the eighteenth century, his influence on writers such as Dryden and Pope is clear. Others were not so impressed: The diarist Samuel Pepys failed to find any humour in *Hudibras,* despite its obvious popularity.

60   Sir Edmund Sawyer (abt 1600 - 1676) was expelled from Parliament in 1628, after financial irregularities in gathering the king's taxes. He then attempted to deceive Parliament by pressuring witnesses to lie to a committee of the House. He was expelled from Parliament and declared unfit to ever return. Sawyer initially managed to get Charles I to indemnify him against prosecution over the widow's debt, although forced to repay her eventually. He did not take an active part in the Civil War, instead retiring to his estates in Berkshire, but was later accused of providing funds to both sides. His son Robert became Attorney General and Speaker of the House of Commons after the restoration, and he is the nine times great grandfather of British Prime Minister, the Rt. Hon David Cameron MP

61   The Percy family were descended from William Percy 1st Baron of Topscliffe who came to England at (or possibly even before) the Norman Conquest. By contrast, the Stuarts were descended from Walter Fitzalan, the itinerant third son of a Breton Knight, and took their name from their role as hereditary stewards of Scotland.

62   This would seem to be the son of Black Rod, also called James Maxwell. Maxwell Senior became disaffected with the Royalist cause after Edgehill, sold his office, and decamped to Scotland with a Son-in-law Lord Lanark. Jane Whorwood remained in Holton, Oxford, and did not see her stepfather again until 1647. He would eventually turn against the King and support the Covenanter cause in Scotland. As letters from James Candy and other sources suggest, Brome Whorwood left England for the continent to avoid the war. He was by this time estranged from his wife, and in a relationship with a Holton serving girl.

63   Lucius Carey, 2nd Viscount Falkland (1610 - 1643) was Charles I Secretary of State. It was not a position he held happily. Though a firm supporter of the King, he became increasingly disillusioned and melancholic at the war. Suffering perhaps from post traumatic stress disorder after the horrors he witnessed at Edgehill, Falkland needlessly exposed himself to danger during the

siege of Gloucester. A few weeks later, on the eve of the first battle of Newbury, he told his friends, *he was weary of the times and foresaw much misery to his own Country and did believe he should be out of it ere night.* He was killed the next day.

64   The Queen is referring to Henry Percy, younger brother of the Earl of Northumberland and Lucy Hay. Percy had been in disfavour with the King since 1641, and his alleged involvement in the Army Plot against Parliament. He fled to France initially, but became an agent for the Queen. Thanks to her patronage, he was made general of ordnance, and later created Baron of Alnswick. He was closely associated with the Queen's Party throughout the 1640s, remaining in contact with his brother and sister. He fled to Paris in 1645, rejoining the queen, and fought a duel against Prince Rupert in 1648. Percy died in exile in Paris in 1659. Letters between the Royal couple were constantly stolen and published in London. Press hacking royal correspondence for a good story, is not such a modern phenomenon after all.

65   Daniel Blagrave (1603 - 1668) was a Reading MP and prominent Parliamentarian. A supporter of Cromwell, he signed Charles I death warrant in 1649, and subsequently held office in the commonwealth. He grew fabulously wealthy during the 1650s, accumulating much of his income from sequestered Royalist estates. At the Restoration in 1660, Blagrave was a wanted man, like all the regicides. He fled to Germany and died there in 1668. The manor at Southcote was demolished in 1921, but photographs remain of the moat and medieval guardhouse that Blandford describe. It was much refurbished in the nineteenth century, with the addition of a large tower, but the photographs give a good idea of the seventeenth century building. Southcote was a small village in the 1640s, with open fields between it and Reading. Today, it is a built up suburb of the town.

66   William Lilly (1602 - 1681) was a famous English astrologer whose annual almanacs sold thousands of copies. Whilst he had many prominent supporters, to many others he was a, *juggling wizard and imposter.* After the Restoration, his support for

Parliament marked him out for scorn from the new regime. He appears in Samuel Butler's *Hudibras* as *Sidrophel*, a charlatan palm reader killed by the protagonist. Despite this, Lilly managed to accumulate a sizeable fortune from his writings, and retired to Hersham in Surrey, dying there in 1681.

67   From Blandford's description of the skirmish, the roundhead ambush would have been stationed on the north bank of the Thames, in the area that is now Caversham Lakes and the Redgrave-Pinsent Rowing Lake. In the Seventeenth century this would have been floodplain and farmland, but the lakes were created by later gravel extraction.

68   Both the Mercurius Aulicus and Samuel Luke's journal confirm the reinforcement of Reading by boats along the river, although they disagree about exact numbers. Blandford is the only source to mention the destruction of one of the boats. The Mercurius Aulicus made a point of claiming no boats were lost.

69   Whilst Blandford does not mention Strachan's first name, the details he gives would seem to match with Archibald Strachan (died 1652). There is no mention of Strachan at the siege of Reading in other sources, but he was active with Waller shortly afterwards, and is the only Captain Strachan of Dragoons listed in Waller's Western Association army. Strachan later returned to Scotland, and was involved in the campaigns against Montrose. When the political situation grew increasingly complex after Charles I execution, his support for Cromwell saw him excommunicated by the Presbyterian Kirk, and declared a traitor in 1651. Anecdotally, he was said to have been broken by the excommunication leading to his death.

70   The view from Caversham Park has changed considerably after three centuries of building work. St Giles spire no longer dominates the skyline as it did in 1643. The three church towers in Reading were targets for the Roundhead guns and St Lawrence's and St Mary's also suffered extensive damage.

71   The Fall of Reading was a significant blow to Charles I cause. The Parliamentarian success should have been the springboard for an advance on Oxford, but the army was ravaged by disease, and grumbles over the lack of pay were growing. Blandford's description of the battle on Caversham Bridge matches with other sources. The timing of the surrender, and hailstorm, gave succour to claims of divine intervention.

72   Seven Bridges spanned the several watercourses of the Kennet that cut through the middle of Reading in 1643, and is now part of Bridge Street. Blandford describes the area that ran behind Minster Street, alongside the Holy Brook in the seventeenth century. The brook was partially created by medieval monks to feed the Abbey Mill in the centre of Reading. By the civil war, breweries were a feature of the area, using the water from the brook to produce Reading's beer supply. Today, the brook runs through culverts in the centre of the town underneath the Oracle shopping centre and Reading Library.

73   Blandford gives us the only first-hand account of this incident, but it is documented and the depiction of the Roundhead indiscipline is accurate. Francis Plowden (brother of Edmund Plowden the governor of the New Albion colony in the Americas), his family and servants tried to escape back to their manor in Shiplake after the fall of Reading. They were looted of valuables and plate worth £500 (£120,000 today), and left with only the clothes on their backs. The family fled to Oxford for the remainder of the war.

74   Ezekiel Fenn (abt 1620 - 1643) was one of Christopher Beeston's boy actors in Queen Henrietta's Men, and was chiefly known for female parts, playing the lead in *Hannibal and Scipio*. He remained with the Phoenix as part of the Beeston Boys troupe, but was playing male roles in 1639. He would have been older than Blandford, but perhaps his slight size and feminine looks made him look younger. He was certainly still at the theatre in 1642, but until now nothing was known of him after the closures.

75   The Saracens Head in Carter Street was used as one of the central letter offices for the post. Mail would be delivered there to be picked up by the recipient. The Royal Mail had been established over a century before, but during the Civil War deliveries were sporadic and insecure. Private carriers only worked the most profitable routes, leaving some areas without any form of service. With such a large volume of mail being generated by the army, collection centres such as the Saracens Head were set up. The postal service would become far more efficient under the Commonwealth, and would be central to the republics counter-intelligence efforts. Interception and transcription of letters became a speciality of the Mail, uncovering numerous plots in the 1650s.

76   Blandford may simply be repeating Pym's propaganda. Laud was widely despised, and freeing him was not part of the plan as described by Waller to Parliament.

77   Lucius Brutus was the ancestor of Caesar's assassin. He was famous as one of the founders of the Republic, who expelled the last Etruscan King Tarquin the Proud. His example inspired Marcus Brutus to kill Caesar, to stop him assuming the crown.

78   A letter written by the Earl of Essex to the Speaker of the House, confirms Blandford's story. Essex describes Hampden going *abroad with Samuel Luke and onely one man*. Presumably, the one man was Blandford, but Essex felt no need to name him.

79   The great hedge that Blandford describes was a feature of the battlefield in 1643, and stretched from Cuxham to the battlefield at Chalgrove. Today, little remains, although it would have been much thicker and taller than modern hedgerows, and provided a real obstacle to the opposing forces.

80   Estimates of numbers are always problematic given the conflicting records, but the Cavalier force would have been around twelve hundred, whilst the Roundheads would have been little more than half that.

81   Blandford's description of the deployment agrees with the other sources. The manor at Warpsgrove is no longer standing, but the battlefield today is still accessible. Sadly, the building of a small airfield at its western edge, and the changes to the landscape over the last century, have obscured most of the seventeenth century topography.

82   There is a long held controversy surrounding Hampden's wound. Contemporaries describe Hampden being shot once or twice in the shoulder at the first clash. However, a story appeared in the Eighteenth Century claiming Hampden was wounded when his servant overloaded his pistols. It would seem that this was an invention designed by Robert Walpole.

83   A number of Parliamentary newsbooks carried the description of Luke's escape in the battle. The primary sources for Chalgrove are all based on two letters written by the Earl of Essex after the battle, and the Cavalier pamphlet, *His Highnesse Prince Rupert's Late Beating up the Rebels Quarters At Post-comb & Chinner in Oxford shire And his Victory in Chalgrove Field,* which described the battle from Prince Rupert's point of view. The Parliamentary *True Relation* was a clear attempt by Essex to deflect blame from the defeat, and is described by English Heritage as of little worth. However, it does provide some confirmation of Blandford's description of the build up to the skirmish.

84   The Earl of Essex moved to Aylesbury after the defeat at Chalgrove.

85   William Waller (1597 - 1668) was Parliaments General of the Western Association. A strict Presbyterian and MP for Andover, he was also the poet Edmund Waller's cousin. He won a string of victories at the end of 1642, and start of 1643, earning the nickname *William the Conqueror* from the Londoners who read of his exploits in the pamphlets. Waller was crushed by the Royalist forces, only a few days after the memoir ends, at the battle of Roundway Down. Waller's star began to fade and, despite victory at the Battle of Cheriton in 1644, he was increasingly eclipsed by

Cromwell. He was a staunch opponent of the independent faction, and was imprisoned a number of times during the Commonwealth. Waller was involved in the negotiations to restore the crown in 1660, but retired after Charles II return.

86   [85] It is unsure what is being implied here. Certainly Charles I did have *sexual relations* with Jane Whorwood, but this supposedly began much later. It is unlikely she had become Charles' mistress in 1643, and her closeness to the King may have simply been due to the vast amount of gold her contacts supplied his cause. Of course, we have no knowledge of Lucy Hay's spin on the situation to Henrietta Maria. The Queen finally met Charles I on July 14th at the battlefield of Edgehill. The return to Oxford was delayed until August, due to fears over the plague.

87   Caleb was one of the twelve spies sent by Moses into the land of Canaan. Only he and Joshua returned to give good report to the prophet. The story is contained in the Book of Numbers.

88   It is highly likely that the 'Cleland boy,' was John Cleland (1709 - 1789) or one of his brothers. Cleland's parents were close friends of Alexander Pope, and frequent visitors to Twickenham. Cleland was expelled from Westminster School in 1723, and joined the East India Company as a soldier. He returned to Britain in 1740, but was disowned by his mother. He was imprisoned in the Fleet as a debtor in 1748, and remained incarcerated for a year. Whilst in prison, Cleland wrote the infamous *Fanny Hill*, which was published and then withdrawn as obscene. It remained banned for over a century, and was not fully released until the 1970s. There was a rumour that Cleland had been paid a stipend by the government to stop him from writing any more pornographic material, but there is no evidence for that. None of his other works were successful, and he died embittered at the age of eighty.

Lightning Source UK Ltd.
Milton Keynes UK
UKOW04f0223250615

254096UK00002B/26/P

9 781909 374645